Office, Flat, Shop, Repeat

Sleep does not refresh. The room beyond the duvet is enemy territory, a hostile universe, cold and full of separate things. I will *never* be able to leave the bed—not ever—but in the middle of an everlasting no, I am surprised to find myself up.

Freezing in the kitchen, numb light picks out last night's squalid crumbs. Jacqui watches the toaster. She is two or three times bigger than usual, and more solid; her resistance to the world—and, as I am the most threatening part of it, to me—fills the room. I can't help myself though:

'I think Jonas is going to be pretty cheesed off with you.'

'Oh I know! Isn't it *marvellous?*' she says, brightening up instantly and swanning back upstairs.

She brought the most unlikely man back last night. He looked like everyone's angry uncle, a thin-nosed bald lawyer type called George, who combined strait-laced financial-district aggression and suspicion, with an inability to put his body where it should go. He stood in the doorway of the kitchen, and we all thought 'I don't *think* so,' and then he was gone to fuck Jacqui in Jonas' bedroom.

Jacqui no more felt at home in Jonas' sterile white German design-studio of a bedroom than he did in hers. Her room was forty-five years of gaudy; layered up like a gigantic surrealist cake—cracked bulbless Tiffany lamps, sequinned pillows, a large latex elk head mask, stolen Muslim prayer mats, broken accordions (×2), a cheese-grater in a mouldy fish-bowl, Victorian crates covered in photos, Norwegian postcards, tailor's busts, dolls with missing eyeballs, snapped mobiles and jam jars everywhere stuffed with unwashed paintbrushes, blunt pencils and clogged dipping pens—this the base layer, the sponge; on top of which lay perhaps ten or twelve wardrobes of clashing clothing—yellow and black dresses, huge white and scarlet plastic bangles, blazing pink mohair jumpers, bumblebee kitten heels—all expensive stuff, all extraordinarily tasteless—before, finally, a sprinkling of letters, bills, crockery, crisp-packets, CD covers, crumbs, loose tobacco and a tin of canned bear paw.

George had taken one look at this cathedral of bibelots and whim-whams and said 'I'm not fucking you in *there*,' and, without missing a beat, she'd said 'fine,' and taken him up to Jonas.'

I haven't eaten now for thirty-six hours and feel like someone has poured a bowl of bitter soup into my cranium. Jacqui's toast and sausages (fried in vegetarian Jonas' vegetable-only frying pan) aren't doing it for me though. Apparently, my body has given up asking for food. It's got the message now. I'm going through with this, but I'm going to take it easy, get the bus for a change.

Out in the street Igwe is resting on his broom facing two school kids, maybe eight years old, walking with their mother on the other side of the road, and he is calling out to them, 'Hello! You are good boys! You are gooood boys!'

Darren Allen is from old Whitstable, in the county of Kent. He writes non-fiction, novels, teleplays and graphic novels. His work addresses the nature of reality, the origin of civilisation and the horrors of work. Also death, gender, mental 'illness,' Miss Genius, unconditional love, and life outside the spectacle. He is not qualified to write about any of these things, thank God.

DROWNING IS FINE
by Darren Allen

ISBN: 978-1-838407-36-0 (paperback)

Published by Expressive Egg Books

ISBN: 978-1-8384073-6-0 (paperback)
ISBN: 978-1-8384073-7-7 (ePub)
Also available for Kindle.

10 9 8 7 6 5 4 3 2 1

Contents

For James and Bruce.

Mea culpa, mea culpa, de pullo mea culpa.

The mother looks back and smiles thinly, the children pay him no attention, but Igwe keeps calling out, long after they have gone, 'Bye! Bye! Byeeee!'

Then he sees me and walks over rapidly, his skinny arm outstretched. I don't want to talk, but Igwe is skilled in roping me in with his big pink gums theatrically mouthing words of great joy and earnest entreaty.

He triggers his elbow, going in for the black man hand-shake. I'm never really quite sure how to greet Igwe—or how to greet anyone; there's just no damn protocol! Usually I just wait to see what happens and do likewise, but the black man feels ridiculous, so as usual I go in fingers down with a whitey, and as usual we settle on a halfway palm-touch which is more ridiculous and awkward than either.

'I don't know why you are not on your bicycle anymore,' he says, confused, almost hurt.

'I've got lots to do Igwe, I don't have time...'

'No time? You are going to die!'

'Maybe.'

'Not maybe. Yeeesssss,' he hisses.

'Yes, okay, I am going to die, yes.'

'Daniel—listen to me. You look better on the bike: more alive, awake, you are *wiiiider.*' He spreads his arms. 'But today you are thin and like everyone else.'

'I *am* like everyone else.'

'No! You have conscience, and conscience is *God.*'

'Don't other people have conscience?'

'Do we live in this darkness if the people have conscience?'

'No, I suppose not.'

'Daniel,' he says, 'if you give me 420 pounds, God will give it back to you a hundred times.'

'Yes, I asked God if I should give you the money, and he said I shouldn't.'

Igwe's eyes widen like a 3-year-old's.

'What?' he says, 'You *have* the money?'

'Yes.'

'And you are *not* going to give?'

'Yes, strange isn't it?'

Igwe bursts into loud, unrestrained laughter. I smile. I don't want to, but I do.

'Look Igwe, I really must go.'

I slope away, Igwe calling after me down the street, 'Daniel I *like* you!'

It starts raining, thin, freezing, gusting. There is no room under the bus stop shelter so I have to take the brunt of it, clenched up, resisting it. The 484 is late, so everyone is *peering* down the road, straining for the bus to appear, trying, through force of want, to force it into existence.

Slowly passing headlights, thin rain, chug of waiting buses, suffocating acrid smell of diesel, cigarette smoke and dog-shit. The Mumbling Man shuffles past muttering to himself; enormous nose, no chin, spindle-thin, soft, smooth milky head, guilty look in his eyes. An overweight couple; the girl's folds of perfectly delineated fat spatulared into a tight red t-shirt proclaiming the legend 'pin up,' the man's hairy jewelled hand proprietorially splayed over her wide rubber arse. A push-chair, young boy, face puffy, red-eyed and wet with rain and tears, is screaming, his skinny mother behind, wearing earphones and smoking, pays no attention. Another couple of kids are fighting—a boy of five or so is smacking his sister over the head with a plastic sword. His distracted father hears her screams and tears into the boy as the bus roaringly arrives and I press myself in. The bus pulls away. The little boy outside is looking in at me, specifically at me, while his dad shouts at him. He theatrically draws the sword across his throat and then collapses into a puddle.

It is close inside, hot, cramped. Bodies bob and jostle. Greasy matter presses down, open pores, mass, fat, organs, bile, shifting around, getting near me. Not so bad in the morning though, because most people have washed. The woman next to me looks like she has steel bars for neck-tendons, but she smells nice and I comfort myself with that, although I feel a bit sordid smelling a stranger, even if it is for existential solace.

Two black girls are talking loudly, far too loudly. The nearest has scalp-stretchingly tight plaits.

"E knows not to call on me. I'm not silly.'

'Dat boy is *ignorant*.'

People who talk too loudly never say things worth over-hearing.

A life-crushed Chinese woman sits across from them, her toes squashed into her shoes, making four plump, red, little cleavages. Next to her a couple, he distractedly explaining something, she smiling falsely, not listening, not interested. Behind them a middle-aged man looks like he is about to cry, lips pouted and trembling, eyebrows pushed diagonally upwards in blubby despair.

All the facial features seem slightly too big, or too small, or too close together. I think of God on a conveyor belt of nice symmetrical faces, getting bored, and pulling them about, tongue out to rubbery stretching sounds. He intended this batch to be angels, but, in the end, he couldn't be bothered to do a decent job and I quite understand, because; neither can I.

I get off at Trafalgar Square, and walk north through Covent Garden to Seven Dials. People pass, and I endeavour to *see* them—I just can't help myself, even though I know that each look is like diving naked into an empty swimming pool.

It's one of the obvious facts of life, that everyone is thinking to themselves, but, like so many obvious facts of life, to really experience it is quite shocking, like the surprise you get when talking with someone and they say something which shows they haven't been listening to a word you've been saying, or when someone accuses you of something you can't possibly be guilty of. You know that life is like this, that people don't pay attention or that they nurse bizarre ideas about you, but when it happens it's as if it's the first time; *totally* out of the blue.

And so I walk in a state of out of the blue up to the plexiglass doors of Financial Objects and into the unnaturally hot reception. I have always thought that the worst thing about work is the smell of the carpets. The moment I walk in the *whole* experience of job suffuses into my core self, not this or that indignity or frustration, but the total bodily horror of it. My heart clenches and the walls slide in somewhat but, as usual, momentum carries me forward, overrules the animal instinct to run, *run*, and I mumble my hellos on the way to my desk which, for some reason (I mean Lord knows why they gave it to *me*) is the best on the floor, at least to my perspective, tucked in the corner with no way for anyone to see what I am doing.

I sit down. 8:45—poor timing! A whole fifteen minutes I've given away of my life, and an hour and a half until the first tea break. I look out the window across Monmouth Street into the offices over the road—an insurance company, or a fashionable publishing company, or something like that—and down over the last of the commuters, struggling to work, and the first of the tourists, struggling to fun; ghosts, immaterial dreamselves floating along, passing through walls and then doing what ghosts do, staring at strangers having sex, staring at other people's crimes, staring at famous places, secretly following old lovers around, getting pretend revenge on enemies, thrusting their bodiless heads through the insides of bodiless statues, or bodiless cows, flying their ghost eyes around neat 3D worlds or floating through empty space. That's what ghosts do. I turn back to the internet and do the same.

9:00 hits and it's time to pretend to work. I delay the inevitable for a few seconds by going to the stationery cupboard, past Don Broderick, a long-bodied, tall-browed, very much law-abiding American; past Geoff McCray, 'Mr Nice,' a tight-fisted, cynical, self loving Scot with no personality to speak of, who hides this from himself and others by being excessively helpful; past Ralph, a sad carp in tinted shades whose only topic of conversation is the house he's redecorating or, if anyone gets close enough, his reptile-minded ex-wife; past my boss, Tina Ween, a short, plump, frizzy, ever-fretting, ever-fussing woman of indeterminate age (late twenties? early forties?); past her boss, Graham, he of the ball-bearing head and immaculate beard, who does his best to make everyone feel *special* and *indispensable*, but he only ever leaves the impression not so much of being *special* and *indispensable*, more of being a small, plastic, very much dispensable, pellet.

Of my two bosses Tina is the more dangerous, despite her faffing, tutting treatment of everything and everyone as an unruly menial. Graham is glinting, wrapped and bound, with an unswerving commitment to his professional self, but like all men, at least all men in business, he can't really see me. He thinks—to my constant astonishment—that I am basically just like him (an anxious, driven, fundamentally untrustworthy spiritual bureaucrat) whereas Tina knows in her flesh that I am out of place here, an alien artefact from another dimension, protruding threateningly into this one.

I am most vulnerable when I am most myself. An unguarded moment of honesty, an expression of true delight or disgust and the internal censor pings on, running over what *they* will make of it, assessing where it rates on the Universal Scale of Non-cooperative Weirdness.

Already, walking back to my desk with my sad, futile pencil, I very much have the feeling that, you know, Christ, that I have come to this—that *we* have come to this—aren't we supposed to be riding wild horses through virgin valleys, chanting in warm wet forests, or writing long, loving poems on row-boats... and not converting RTFs to PDFs all week? Or something nobler, at least, than 'office, flat, shop, repeat'?

Such is my thinking at 9:08. I turn to my computer and, to calm myself, I look at some paintings by Edvard Munch and some drawings by John Bauer, but it doesn't help. It just makes my own work—I mean my real work—look all the more characterless, cold and inept.

I want to paint great things, I want to undo minds, I yearn to stretch into the abyss, to touch the living emptiness, to bring something radiantly new to the world—to bring life as it is back to existence as it merely seems to be... but when I draw all that comes out are cold lines and colourless disgust and human forms that look like mashed plastic and sausage meat. Something is wrong.

But is it? All art is ugly now. It just doesn't matter. Or does it? It does, yes it does. And *yet*. What do they want? What do they *actually* want?

Tina comes over. I drag what I am supposed to be doing over what I am not supposed to be doing.

'How's it going?' she asks, using a pleasant question about my general life in order to mask an unpleasant question about my specific task.

'Fine Tiny, *Tina*.'

Her checks jerk—a nervous twitch she has—'and the batch?' Graham comes over, because his management-antennae has detected that someone in the city is not working to full potential.

'Oh it's slow going, taking longer than I thought, there are so many of them.'

'Well, can you give us an approximate ETA?' she asks. Graham juts his head forward to offset the unmanagerly tone of her question—too pleady Teeny—and give me a bit of the old scrutinising Squint of Authority.

'Erm…' I calculate how long this sub-moron task will take, and add 50%. They're not happy with the answer, but have to accept it because, thanks to some earlier work-defying hex—I asked Tom the IT guy to slow my computer down—they're not *quite* sure of what is going on, and so have to accept my word.

They have to accept everything. They complain, or they put on the thin 'knowing irony' smile, or they pull the 'someone should do a TV show about this place' with the old *'isn't it awful!'* eyes-rolled-to-heaven. Yes, they complain, they all complain, but the complaint is built on a bedrock of acceptance. They often say to each other 'you're insane!' or 'you're mad!' and everyone smiles. When I say it, nobody smiles. When I say 'you're insane,' it's like I've taken a skull out of my rucksack and tried to photocopy it.

9:45. It is already another day of erecting barricades and sheltering from the poisonous arrows of many evils. 'Please, no need to explain'? or 'No need to pin me squirming in anguish to the walls of your empty heart for thirty minutes when you could just get to the point'? I often want to use the latter.

10:00. My empty stomach is having a strange effect on my attention. I am getting abnormally preoccupied with triangles of light and whassername's legs—I still don't know her name, the girl that works on the other side of my office, let's call her Tuesday—she's extremely attractive, wears short dresses and is usually barefoot. Everywhere she goes she trails the mournful, sexually-frustrated stares of the largely male workforce around with the pristine rotating orbs of her buttocks. Bristly, boozy Gavin next to me is, as usual, fretting into his phone (catchphrase: 'I worry about what day it is'). He's not overly concerned with Tuesday's bottom because he's worrying about the fact that it's Thursday, and also he regularly visits prostitutes during his lunch hour, as he explained to me, pissed off his face one evening. He calls himself a 'punter' and says that he is addicted to 'punting,' new words for me, as is 'retroactive,' which is the curious adjective he uses to describe the accumulation of sorrow in his life. I suppose he uses it because he's in the sales department, like Tom and Luke are always referring to their wives and girlfriends as 'human units, female class' and their relationships as 'non-compliant,' or 'buggy,' or 'legacy.' I try to use fancy words to describe my relationships, but can't think of anything other than 'shameful,' 'abortive' and... *'not'*.

10:15. Made it. Fifteen minutes of freedom. I say freedom, but the first thing I do is check my emails, as I do thirty or forty times a day. I break the spell of the inbox by walking over to Harold, big square Harold in his comfy cardie, with his comfy mind in his big square head. He's one of life's meek losers, afraid of small-talk and young people and answering the phone and all sentences that begin 'Harold...' make him expect the worst. He collects classical longplayers which he hides in his bag—why I'm not sure, perhaps he's been mocked for it in the past, or maybe he intuits that the Busch quartet are out of place in this thumping florescent realm—and then he furtively shows me the corner of the record, as if he's scored some uncut cocaine. He loves radios too, and pumps, and air-conditioning systems, and boilers. At his engineering school he was once forced to go to the National Gallery to balance his technical education with 'art appreciation,' and he and his friends had spent the whole trip trying to work out how the state-of-the-art air-conditioning system there worked, huddled between the Caravaggios studying a cooling duct. For Harold the death of culture is the death of engines and all things which you can no longer take apart and fix yourself.

He also likes wearing women's clothes. Again a public house provided the backdrop to a surprising confession of a colleague's sex life. I don't like the pub, actually, but if it weren't for alcohol I would never learn that Gavin is addicted to pros and Alexis is unloved and Harold here secretly raids his wife's wardrobe of a Sunday afternoon while she's at her mother's, prances around their flat for two hours exactly, returns everything as was and then steels himself for a weekly sexual encounter that more closely resembles a wrestling match.

'She's very competitive,' he told me. 'Even in bed. Especially in bed. It's not really sex, it's... it's hard work. She usually likes me to take a few whiskeys first, and she has some, and then she, you know, she wants me to *bang* her up against a wall, and her eyes are, they kind of, they're lolling around her head and her tongue darts in—and, it's very stressful, because she's barking instructions at me "harder, no, not *there*, okay now slowly and *don't look at me like that* Harold..." and, I never really know if she enjoys it, we don't talk about it, but I don't think so, I don't think we really like each other, but then who does? I don't know. Discuss!'

10:30. I return to my desk and gaze again out the window. The rain has stopped and Seven Dials is ablaze with frigid sunlight. Dave Cardwell, guitarist from The Spin Men, is on the roof of his flat over the road, wearing a leopard-skin dressing grown and neon green underpants. He smokes a cigarette, flicks it over the edge of the terrace and walks back in.

11:00. I'm starting to smell of carbolic acid and off bread. The purge seems to be working, at least if noxious bodily odours, foul smelling breath, feeling hungover and a sensation that my brain is swelling behind my eyeballs are good signs, which I believe they are. Something to do with that middle-class bogeyman, *toxins*. I go to the toilet and am delighted to see that I look god-awful.

I stagger over to Tina's desk and tell her I feel dreadful. I don't feel middle-class at all.

'You *look* dreadful Daniel.'

My inner saboteur, I mean the one that works *for* me, tenses up in expectation.

'I think I might need to go home, get some sleep.'

'Yes, you do that,' she says, 'you can continue with the conversions on Monday.'

I have to suppress a skip as the gates of heaven open up before me and a Soho-style flashing-bulb sign, pink and yellow, materialises above the stairwell, with an arrow pointing down to 'liberation.' My body slumps out, but my mind is on its knees, shaking skinny fists of glory to the sky.

Is work really this bad? Since leaving 'education' I have filled supermarket shelves, washed up restaurant plates, cleaned veterinary kennels, scraped congealed fat and excrement off the hides of recently skinned cows, 'guarded' a motorway being built, plucked turkeys, packed apples, picked tomatoes and French beans, sold executive hospitality packages for Royal Ascot and now—what am I doing? I honestly don't know, but it fits right alongside these other activities, and it fits right alongside the worklife of the world. The happy people, the worthy ones, fulfilled and driven, designing surgical instruments and teaching orphans to code and running gourmet peanut bars and teaching emotional management to Tibetans—are a cigarette paper thin meniscus floating on a vast stagnant lake of boredom (known officially as 'disengagement'), torment (known officially as 'active disengagement') and illusory duty (known officially as 'productivity'). Down here where things actually get done, I have never seen anyone joyous at work *because* of work. Joy is an embarrassment in the workplace; it's even more out of place than death.

And yet people willingly go. When they can't work, when they have to stay at home, they complain that they're bored. They can't think of anything better to do than admin.

I stumble out of the zone of evil and instantly feel better, in my heart at least. My body needs a quiet room, ideally on the moon.

•

I greet my bed thankful, apologetic even. Sleep is troubled though; I'm hiding in a cupboard because there's a burglar in the house and I think the best way to get rid of him is to try and convince him that the house is haunted. Next thing I know Toby is shaking me. He says he can hear me down the hall going '*wooo, wooo, wooooooo.*'

Toby says that Naeema is complaining that the vintage green wheelchair I'd pushed home last week is blocking up the living room, so we drag it up three flights of stairs to my attic room. It's incredibly heavy, made of iron I think, but also beautiful in an awful kind of way—'asylum chic' Toby calls it. It sits in my empty room, in a circle of grey London light which falls through the skylight like a chunk of masonry. As I say, I'm going through a period of self-denial; cold showers and fasting, more to see if I can do something like that, a test of will more than anything else—and I need the right ambience, a lonely room of stark empty grief.

I sit down and start work, start to draw, but it is hard, very painful, like rearranging concrete furniture. The back of my head and my forearms and my neck and the pit of my ribs all tell me to stop, they all resist like drugged dogs, but I push on, because I *must*, pulling teeth out of my head, but then I hear Stephen's wild cackle muffled through the door, and I feel like everyone—in fact every*thing*—in the world is having more fun than me, so I go down to Toby's room, which is so comfortable. No Bedlam-green iron-cage for Toby—he of the spine-shrouding leather armchair, which he perches in—nests in I'd say—rolling neat little joints with his neat little fingers and listening to experimental music and slowly going out of his mind.

Stephen explodes again as I walk in, and everyone laughs with him. It's funny how people enjoy other people really enjoying themselves. Maybe this self-denial thing won't get me a girlfriend after all, because Stephen never stops smoking, drinking gin and eating salty sludge, and he always seems to have beautiful girlfriends, although he also always seems to have problems getting girlfriends, but then, further, he always seems to be able to tell the stories of his problems so eloquently and cheerfully that somehow he ends up getting the attention of girls, beautiful ones.

'I dreamt last night that Van Gogh was throwing paper aeroplanes through big grass vaginas,' he says, wide-face, delicate, mobile, all beaming and… kind of *tearful*, I always think. He also exudes that vague 'debauched moisture' of inveterate dipsomaniacs, but again, girls don't seem to mind. The one next to him on Toby's bed—I don't know her, slim, dark skin, sharp teeth, attitude afro—is crying with laughter.

I hesitate. The only place to sit is next to her, but I immediately feel that if I do sit next to her it will look like I'm coming on to her; such a conspicuous move, they will all think, but then there really is nowhere else to sit, and that takes the pressure off and I sit down and nobody seems to think that strange.

Toby's room really is beautiful, all brown and orange and wood, his Dad's teak record player and hundreds of records colour-coded into a rainbow, fevered fractal drawings all over the walls, vague smell of cloves. Toby is wearing faded mustardy cords, and the kind of cardigan that Buck Rogers would relax in, ribbed and creamy and padded at the shoulders, and under that the CCCP t-shirt that I gave him and wished I hadn't because it looks cool now and not pretentious and impotent as it did on me.

I'm jealous of Toby—there, I said it—he's weirdly good-looking, a handsome, hairy, boney, electrified monkey, and everyone loves his art, and everyone loves his bright smile, and everyone even seems to love his animal panic and petrified horror of the world. I try to copy all these things, but that doesn't seem to work. Where Toby attracts, I tend to repel, anger, annoy—sometimes I repel, anger and annoy with such careless fascination for the event that I elicit applause and warmth and some kind of admiration, but it's not a very effective modus operandi. Luckily I am also deeply interested in what it is like to not be me, and that alone is enough to gain acceptance into humanity—at least on a one-to-one level—even if, unlike both Toby and Stephen, I cannot make groups feel relief when I arrive because, unlike them, I do not supply that peculiar social lubricant that more than three people need to operate together, that makes them unclench with relief when Stephen joins us. I just don't have it; I'm too selfish I suppose. Or maybe my oil is for a different kind of machine.

'Yes, it's nice in here,' says Stephen, looking around, voicing our thoughts, 'you've got the right balance between cleanliness and comfort, between, uh, this room matters and it doesn't matter. And you have your pictures up too. Yeah. I couldn't... lord no... my room definitely doesn't matter, it's a fucking pigsty truth-be-told, but I've got a date with Gallery Girl on Sunday so I'll tidy up tomorrow; it's the only time I *do* tidy up; which is—it's a win-win situation—either I come home with a girl or I come home to a clean flat, which provides nearly the same measure of self-esteem.' He pauses, then says to himself; 'Perhaps I should clean the girl and shag the house?'

How does Stephen speak this way? How does everything sound so natural and compelling, and how—here's the real mystery—how does he manage *to cue himself up*, as if the end of an utterance was planned. I know studying won't help much, but I can't help but pay attention to this kind of thing, which has the side-effect of making Stephen feel good, which is important because he's a fragile soul really. Underneath his witty show of existential anxiety and fear of life, really, in fact, he *is* existentially anxious and afraid of life.

The girl next to me, listening to Stephen, is trembling with silent, orgasmic laughter, but she collects herself to turn to me;

'How old are you?' she asks.

'Twenty five.'

'I only go with men over thirty four,' she says and turns back to Stephen.

He is talking about his art. Stephen is an art student. Everyone here is an artist of some stripe. I moved to London because I got an office job here and the monastery in the attic vacated at the same time, so I moved in to live with Toby, an old school friend (struggling artist), Jonas, an uptight German (designer), Naeema, a stuck-up ex-Iranian (art student at Goldsmiths), Jacqui a menopausal drug-addict (art student at Camberwell College; rents this house from an aunt and sublets to us) and Adam, an English guy who hates himself (photographer). I spend most of my free time going to private views, helping to organise shows, modelling sometimes and panicking with Toby and Stephen about the dreadful futility of all this.

'Sometimes,' says Stephen, 'I imagine everyone I ever knew in the art scene all talking together and laughing at me saying "have you seen what he's up to now? He's gone totally mad!" but,' he shrugs, 'I get over it. You shouldn't abandon your mission in life, even if it doesn't get you laid, because, eventually, it *might* get you laid...' he trails off. The girl gets up and walks out.

'Who is she?' asks Toby.

'I don't know,' I say, 'I thought she was with Stephen.'

'I've never seen her before in my life,' says he, 'She's not bad looking though is she?'

'She only goes with men over thirty four.'

'Really? I *am* thirty four, right on the cusp.'

'I think she's interested in you,' I say.

'That is the *surest* sign that she is no good for me,' he says. Toby nods, glumly. He too only attracts women uniquely designed to destroy him. He's with Sarah now, who looks like she's fourteen and has a false leg, which appeals not so much to Toby's para-paedophilic desire for young cripples, more because he loves the novelty of it, although it's 'getting old now' because she's pretty perverse, is Sarah, and her perversions all seem to revolve around putting Toby in danger. She wanted to dress up as a schoolgirl and have Toby pick her up from outside of a school, and for him to wear a long waxed-leather coat and brylcream and a moustache and flannel shirt tucked into his trousers, which he did. Then she wanted to visit Toby at his work and blow him in his work toilets, which he agreed to. And then she wanted Toby to break into her house and pretend to rape her, and he did that too. He's none too powerful in the arms and struggled to pull himself up onto the baywindow below hers, which was the bedroom of another flat below, which was woken by Toby's yelping and boot-scraping, which led to plod turning up to Sarah's ripe screams, which led to them almost knocking her door down—hammering, hammering POLICE! POLICE! which led to Toby, frozen in terror, hiding under her bed. P.C. Earnest Street bent down and shone his torch on Toby's naked body and said, wearily, 'are you coming out then son?'

'I can't keep it up,' said Toby, 'I'm shot to bits,' but she had some kind of hold over him, as all the women he went for did. He was into 'castrators' and often dreamed of metal tongues and toothed vaginas and so forth. His previous girlfriend, Vicky, was, in his words, 'a virago, a gorgon, a succubus.' He regularly dreamt that she had a cock—'and it was a turn on too; god I hope I'm not into ladyboys.' I never could quite understand, then, quite how, in what way, she tortured him, and he could never quite express it either. All I knew was that she sucked all the connected warmth out of a room just by being there. She was like Yoko Ono; perfectly passive, socially sterile, but *judging*, or no, maybe she wasn't even doing that, but she created that feeling, made everyone feel self-conscious; a vibic vacuum. She just operated on another, foreign, terrifying level of anti-life.

She also used to wind him up by wearing outrageously sexy outfits and then declare she was too tired tonight, or she'd secretly stroke him off under the dining room table while they visited his phenomenally straight parents (Dad a dusty account-ant, Mum a Castillian prude), or she'd enrage him by flattering his friends, teasing them, falling apart at their jokes… until, in the end, she went with Toby's [then] flatmate, the weedy, oily guy in the next room, where she made a point of screaming all night long, screaming and screaming; enough to keep the whole street awake.

'I don't understand it,' he said, 'she must be doing it to get to me.'

'Of course she is.'

'Is she?'

That unfortunate series of events led to him taking a massive dose of magic mushrooms and then taking the bus down to see me in Canterbury. He phoned me at 3 am from Maidstone saying 'I'll be with you in a couple of hours. I'm Jesus now.'

He said he was connected to a vast organism of pure, loving information that straddled all the dimensions in some impossi-ble-to-conceive way, although 'actually it's very simple,' he said, 'all you have to do is love and you're both there, *in* that thing. It even works over the phone.' He said he'd show me, and, strange to say, he did. Everyone I knew in Canterbury fell in love with Toby for those few weeks he was with me, yet all he did was chuckle and stumble around half-drunk on Bison Grass vodka.

There is huffing through the walls, then, other side of the door: 'That damn…' then in the room: '*woman.*'

Woman. It's the strongest word I've ever heard Jonas utter. He's out of breath, shaking, overwhelmed with anger. His tinybearded chin is all a-quiver.

'What? What's up?'

'Sheeee…'

'Who?'

'Jacqui, do you know anything about this?' Jonas looks accusingly at Toby, who panics a little, because he might.

'I don't think so, what?'

'Jacqui was in my room, used condoms everywhere; why?' I've never heard such disorder from Jonas' mind, 'didn't she, why? I don't get it, she *fucked* him in my room. What's wrong with her?'

Toby and I go up to look at Jonas' room, to offer some consolatory disgust, and when we return Stephen has gone. He doesn't usually say goodbye. You turn and he's no longer there — that, or he'll look you in the eye and give you the most generous, full, human goodbye you could possibly wish for in Peckham, a real gift of a goodbye, facing the enormity of it, the timeless animal truth of being in front of someone, chest to chest, maybe never seeing them again — but in this case he takes French leave because he's scored with the sharp mulatto, which Toby and I gnaw over for a while. We admit that, despite being paranoid and permanently half-plastered Stephen has charm and confidence which we so obviously lack and know no means of acquiring.

'But I have something Stephen doesn't,' says Toby, skinning up again.

'What?'

'What's the time?'

'Why?'

'Do you know it?'

'Not when I'm not working.'

'Come on, I'm busy.'

I get up and look in Adam's room.

'Half nine,' I say, returning with the ghost of tomorrow and work pressing on my chest.

'I'll show you in half an hour then.'

'What is it?'

'Something to keep dissatisfaction at bay for a few moments.'

'You're dissatisfied?'

'Yes, aren't you?'

'Yeah.'

'I don't know why. I'm just at a low ebb — I can't stop watching ASMR videos.'

'What's ASMR?'

'Autonomous sensory meridian response. It's a thing, relaxing euphoria, generated by soothing sounds. It's basically videos of women with nice voices doing the ironing or pretending to cut your hair. I spend hours watching them.'

'That doesn't sound so bad.'

'That and hardcore porn.'

Toby didn't really get off on porn, he just had to *look* at it. It was bizarre I thought; he seemed to have a fascination with the flesh of it; not really the sex, or the power-game, which I thought was the point, but the pure form of it. He loved vaginas, for example, their structure, their colour and variety and dark, alien nature. He looked at them as primal man would, I thought; as a literal doorway into the centre of the universe. Don't get me wrong, I love the vagina, but I'd prefer to *look* at a neck.

'Once you've — I mean it's the same routine,' he went on, 'blow-job, eat out, fuck in three positions, cum on face. Once you've seen that a thousand times, it... it becomes very odd. That's why I made the porn-ball.'

The porn-ball was Toby's submission for his end of course assessment at art college. At the bottom of a tidy wooden crate he'd secured, face up, a large television showing a looped porn film. On top of this he'd placed eight inwardly-facing tapering rectangular mirrors arranged together in a kind of octagonal funnel, cupping the screen in an area about the size of a salad plate. The result, looking in, was a huge sphere of kaleidoscopic flesh; duplicating and dividing portions of cocks, cunts, tits and arses seethed over the enormous illusory sphere, unrecognisable, inhuman, monstrous...

'When will I learn?' he said, tip-tapping at the joint, 'I know I'm not interested in porn, or drugs, or even coffee, but if they're there, I'll do them. I'll sit in front of the TV for half an hour or more, flicking through the channels in the shallow hope of coming across something worthwhile. I am—I am a product of my environment...'

'Perhaps you should shape your environment—for your better nature I mean.'

'Like a madman's wheelchair in a bare attic?'

'Yes!'

'But even when I know that nihilistic debauchery is a problem, I also know that somewhere underneath there is something even more wrong, some constant underlying dissatisfaction. Constantly slightly anxious, I am, constantly awkward, and I don't really know why. I can come up with reasons, but... but they're not very convincing.'

He passes me the joint.

'I think it's the grabber,' I say, 'the inner habit-maker, the thinking mind. It comes out of the top of your head, like this,' I mime a wanging probe emerging tentacle-like from my brain and lolling around, 'and then, it grabs some bit of what is happening, tightens up on something, isolates it.'

'Why does that make you dissatisfied?'

'Because it grabs at things for the wrong reason.'

'What is the right reason to grab?'

'The right reason to grab bits of the now is... erm... is when you want to get something done, isn't it? When you need to focus on something, name it or whatever...'

'...and then,' said Toby, 'when you've named it, you can put the grabber away. We're still getting up and having breakfast!'

'Yeah, uh, because a lot of stuff is already written in the programme. Most of life works fine without the grabber.'

'So when *does* it need to come out? Or does it need to come out at all?'

'It needs to come out when the programme isn't working, when you don't know what's going on, when you need to write a better bit of code...'

'But getting better implies...'

'More freedom is what it is—it's more capacity to deal with it all.'

'...but it implies... something partial, something that wasn't there, a process...'

'Only when you think about it. The actual experience of it is always... oh no, no...' The idea is slipping away from me, even as I speak, but then words come out of my mouth and they seem so meaningful; 'Yeah! Yeah, it is, it's only the *tool*, the grabber, the system that's been written, that gets better—the thing that's *making* it better is always the same.'

'It just gets closer to it.'

'Yes, but if the probe is stuck, you'll never actually experience what isn't code and... and... and *that* makes you dissatisfied,' I conclude, triumphantly, but also perplexed.

Toby stubs out the last of the joint. 'This explanation...' he says.

'Yes?'

'It's not very satisfying is it?'

I can't remember what we've been talking about.

'This, however,' says Toby standing up and turning off the lights, 'is.'

He motions me over to the edge of his bed, where I can look through the window, and then he pulls the curtains open. Just over the back garden a naked window reveals another bedroom. In it a girl is getting undressed.

'Isn't it marvellous?' he breathes.

She is athletic, perhaps voluptuous even, sturdy limbs, thick black hair. More Toby's type than mine, but I think in some ways I am more able to appreciate the beauty of women I don't go for. Not long ago I saw a curvy woman on a bicycle, wearing a tight black dress. She had stopped to use her phone and, one leg on the floor, one on a pedal, peered into the distance, speaking distractedly. My God, what a paragon of femininity! What power and softness and mystery... because I saw her clearly, with no desire, with no feeling that I *must* talk to her or forever regret the lost opportunity. And so it is I see this extraordinary woman, glimpsed across the dark suburban gulf of South London.

'Does she know you're watching?'

'I think so,' Toby whispers, 'I think so—it's always at exactly 10 pm, like we've... like she's meeting me, and,' his voice drops to a croak, '*behold*...'

She pulls her t-shirt over her head and then takes her bra off. Her breasts are superb.

Toby is clutching his head. 'It's as if the sun is exploding,' he moans.

She stands at the window, and then she starts softly dancing, swaying her hips from side to side with slow, slow, flowing gestures of her arms.

She slows down, looks at us for a few moments, and then draws the curtain. We are silent.

'She never shows her pussy,' says Toby, 'but I don't mind. Something spiritual is going on.'

I let it sink in for a bit. 'Why does it make me feel so sad?'

'Does it?'

I wonder, 'It's as if… as if Jah is telling me that I will *never* be allowed into paradise.'

'Or maybe He's giving you a taste of it? Giving you a taste of what lies ahead?'

'Jesus, I hope so.'

'It gets me through the night,' says Toby.

He does night-shifts at a company called The Registry, which sells information about adverts to media companies. His task is to sit in front of a TV all night, watching adverts from around the world, and then note, in a database, what he sees, so that—it's hard to imagine this happens, but it does—when a Russian newspaper or the government of Burundi or Chuck Norris phones up and asks to know everything about the world's shampoo adverts, they can package the work of Toby and his colleagues up and, for a very good price, hand over the data. They call it 'data warehousing.'

After doing this for three months bizarre things started to happen to Toby's mind. He began to have horrific 'nauseating architecture' dreams; collapsing buildings, furniture that crumbled on touch, shoddy cardboard palaces and a recurring nightmare of leaping five stories into the air, bounding high over the city, which sounds great, but was terrifying, awful, stomach-churning; propelling and plummeting.

The other consequence of The Registry was that Toby's doodles, which up till then had been the occasional crude, comic-like talking head, squid, mushroom cloud, vagina and whatnot, erupted into a quenchless outpouring of landscapes, bodyscapes and mindscapes fused into fantastic, strangely ordered, organic forms. While watching 'A Whole New Language of Meat, for Dogs' he would obsessively produce page after page of labyrinthine frenzy; lunatic, unworldy, designs—and yet not chaotic, but mysteriously ordered, mysteriously recognisable. They were, in truth, some of the most beautiful images I had ever seen. I knew they were immortal, great works of art, yet Toby just shrugged his shoulders and everyone else—well, they were gobsmacked too, but our friends were swept up in raptures over pubic hair scattered over a bucket of cooking oil, and mouldy bits of birthday cake studded with American flags and enormous oil paintings of dimmer switches, which kind of diluted what, I could see, was a rather different reaction to Toby's work, a different kind of 'wow'. He couldn't see it though. He found the idea that he was a genius, or handsome, or interesting, or even alive quaint, pointless, at best unlikely.

Where Toby produced beauty but couldn't see it, Jah had the opposite fate planned for me; one of his usual sadistic set-ups. I craved recognition and attention and produced *nothing* of value for the whole time I was friends with someone whose artistic judgement was practically infallible and who was the worst liar that ever walked the earth—and so was guaranteed to tell me the truth if I showed him anything—guaranteed, that is, to squirm, tighten up, do his pitiful best to say something charitable, but have the helpless rejection of the universe written on his face.

He gets up, looking around in confusion, patting his pockets. Then seems to remember I'm here.

'Are you coming then?'

'Coming? Where?'

There is a private view in a few hours, at the South London. I feel weak and caustic, like my veins are rotting, but Fear of Missing Out compels me to join him, to go a gallery in Camberwell to 'witness a happening.' An artist has locked himself in a big black box for ten days with just water, and the opening is to be a Work of Art which he has called 'The Void.' I have some sympathy with the idea, but this begins to evaporate when I get to the *space* and see the gallery-goers, chorging and yorging over white wine, and it vaporises completely when I read the little scraps of text around the room, which say things like 'interrogate the emptiness' and 'juxtapose yourself with yourself' in big tasteful Swiss fonts. Also the old classic: 'I explore themes of space and communication in my work. It's about text.' It's very often about text.

'I don't think I'm up for this,' I say to Toby.

'Oh come on, he'll be out in a few minutes.'

Stephen joins us. He's with Attitude Afro. She looks like she's being shown round an air-conditioning showroom.

'This place is full of one cloned woman,' says Stephen.

'I thought you liked the art world,' says Toby.

'Like? I wouldn't say that. I just feel slightly less weird in it.'

'Does the one cloned woman feel weird?'

'No, because she's got her artistic license,' says Stephen, 'which basically means you're *made*, like in the Mafia, you can do anything. You can literally exhibit your earwax and it will be snapped up by Charles Saatchi. When I get mine I'm going to submit 'Toothbrush in a Loaf' to the Arts Council or, I had another idea, it's called 'I Don't Actually Need This Job,' it's an in situ piece, a live installation, where I take a job that I hate but that I don't actually need, and then do what the fuck I want all day, like sit around reading comics, or shit in the sink.'

Stephen did actually make that one, 'Toothbrush in a Loaf.' It was part of his 'Thing in a Thing' series, comprising 'Porcini in a Test-Tube,' 'Memory stick in a Beer Can,' 'Luke Skywalker in a Packet of Revels' and 'Toenail in a Spigot.'

'How's your job?' Stephen asks Toby.

'It's there, and then it isn't.'

'Don't worry, you're a clever monkey, you'll get out one day, we all will.'

'I was on the bus coming home this morning,' says Toby, 'sitting on the bottom deck, in the corner at the back, and we're inching through Vauxhall and some homeless guy bangs on the window and starts shouting at me, "You! You're a stupid cunt! You're a stupid *cunt!*" over and over again as the bus pulled off, and I looked through the back window at him, standing in the middle of the street, still shouting at me, and I thought to myself; I *am* a stupid cunt.'

We all laugh, which is to say, we open our mouths and make strange noises at each other.

'You *are* a stupid cunt,' I say.

'We're all stupid cunts,' says Stephen. 'I am, I really am. Or, my brain is, the one I reluctantly live in. It just seems to want to go over and over all the painful things that happen to me. I don't think it likes living.'

'Uh, excuse me, esteemed guests!' an American woman's voice makes its way through the jibber-jabber. We turn towards the big black box in the middle of the room—which looks like it's been made with fruit pallets. A dumpy woman in thick glasses and alarmingly red lipstick tells us that the time has come for Tom Ashley to emerge. She turns to a fellow a few feet away and says 'I suppose...?' and he does a frown-shrug-eyes-raised-why-not? gesture and she turns to the big cube and says 'are you ready Tom?'

A muffled, 'yep!' comes back through.

She takes a lungful, holds it, looks around again—in her mind I think, to see if there's something to say, because there probably should be, but there isn't—so she releases her held breath, over-emphatically says 'okay then!,' and opens the door. We all peer inside.

A guy, who looks like an Eastern European children's show host, emerges sheepishly from the dark.

'Hello!' says the Tom.

Nobody says anything, nobody knows what to do, he doesn't know what to say, so we stand looking at him not knowing what to do. It's kind of tense, but then he starts talking to the American woman, and we all return to our conversations, feeling a bit let down.

I leave my fellows and walk through the gallery. Local artists each have a wall to present their work, which consists of a kitchen stool covered in spilled nail polish ('my work looks at identity and function'), a series of foamboards smeared in turmeric ('persistent concern with colour and light'), a plastic Jesus wearing a Manchester United shirt ('interrogating advertising, religion...') and so on. They really like the word 'interrogate.' Presumably they see themselves as Gestapo officers shining angle-poise lamps into the eyes of reality; 'Confess you rat! Confess! You're really a grid of laminated tiles held together with clothes pegs! Admit it!'

I think I may have underestimated the appeal of incompetent negativity. I stray through it all much as I stray through my converted PDFs. Who is all this stuff for? People who have had something very important subtracted from themselves. The cloned woman doesn't seem much more with it, although she's paying a bit more attention.

I hear a shriek from the next room and take a look, expecting a video installation of a doll's head on a spoon, but there's a little girl, a real little girl, in the middle of the room. She is flapping her arms and going 'weee! weee!' A group of adults are standing around her, smiling, and I smile too. It's very good.

'Oh hello.'

I turn. My housemate, Adam, is with Lauren; another old school friend. She's—oh, it's complex. The fact that even *I* know she is attracted to me is testament to how obvious she has had to be to make me know that, which is all wrong, because Lauren is subtle and sharp, and her advances are heavy and blunt. But I'm not attracted to her. She is beautiful—soft features, soft chestnut hair, lovely glidey posture (important that)—just not the Delphic nymph I've got my heart set on; yet I can't imagine ever getting on better with a woman. I'd take a potion to fancy her.

'I didn't know you two knew each other,' I say.

'We don't,' says Lauren, 'I just met this man. He led me from Toby to you.'

Adam has the most inexpressive face I've ever seen. His upper lip is stretched tight in a permanent half-grimace which he takes to be a genial smile. He looks like a sad, schizoid relative of the Lion in The Wizard of Oz. He's probably drunk, because he knocks back pure gin gimlets all day, but it's hard to tell.

'What do you think of the show?' I ask them.

'I like that piece!' says Lauren, pointing to the little girl, who is now kneeling next to a chair, with her top teeth clamped on the arm, looking at us. 'It makes me think about identity and function,' she says looking at me, eyes all hot with joy and conspiracy, mouth half open, expectant, ready to laugh with.

'The artist really understands the contemporary world,' says Adam, which, like most of his comments, seems like it has been calculated to pass for human. It's so hard to respond to him in the normal, accepting, joining-in way because it means inhabiting his distanced, ironic mode, which is dead painful.

Lauren is looking at the girl, wistfully. 'I wish I could do something that good though,' she says. 'I just don't know what they *want*. They never actually say.'

'Who?'

'My tutors.'

'Why do you care what they want?'

'I get to college all a shimmer with youth and exuberance, and then they talk about symbols and signifiers for twenty minutes and suddenly the carpet I want to weave seems... they have this way, you see, my tutors, of complimenting my ideas but actually saying, you know, actually—"it's terribly *gauche* you know." I feel like I'm going to *frrrreak out!*' She sings the last two words.

'What about you Adam?' I say, 'Going to *frrrreak out?*'

'What do you mean?' he says, coldly.

'Oh, erm, nothing.'

Adam grimaces. 'Shall we get a drink?'

We head to the gallery bar, which is packed, and squeeze up against a wall. Adam takes our orders. Water, I bellow, and he slips into the swallowing throng.

'Why are you drinking water?'

'I'm fasting. For three days.'

'Why?'

'Dunno. Seemed like a good idea. I'm feeling a lot better now though. I thought I was going to die this afternoon, but since I've got here my head has cleared up. Do I still smell?'

Lauren leans in and sniffs.

'Yeah, a bit,' she says.

The bar is full of artists, or possibly graphic designers, which in a way is worse. They gabber and guck, going through the motions, it always seems to me, of being a social creature.

I vent some spleen to Lauren about the basic joylessness of the modern social event, and the pain of the face in the street.

'Do you really think so?' she asks.

'Yes. Everyone is pretending to have fun.'

She looks around in wonder, blinking.

'But if everyone is pretending to have fun, what are they really feeling?'

'I think everyone feels the same way you do.'

Toby, Stephen and the new girl join us, and Adam returns with the drinks.

'Do you feel the same way I do?' Lauren asks Toby.

'I don't know, how do you feel?'

'I don't know. A *bit* anxious?'

'Then yes, I do. I feel like that.'

'I think everyone here feels like an artist,' she says.

'The one thing everyone in here has in common, is that they are not a fucking artist,' says Stephen. 'God knows how they keep the dread away though.'

'By locking themselves in a box,' I say.

'That's what this show should've been called,' says Stephen, "Attempt to Keep the Dread Away."'

'It's a nice title, but nowhere near ironic enough,' I say, 'people would laugh.'

'They would! Don't let the protective cloak of irony fall.' Stephen does spacey hypnotising hand gestures, 'Nothing is serious, nothing is real, all is shifting.' He stops and looks around, '*They're* shifting, look at them shifting! Gallery to gallery, studio to studio, show to show…'

'Where's Sarah?' Lauren asks Toby.

'She's going out with some guy from her college.'

'Oh I see.'

'We talked about it, and we decided we should try and have an open relationship.' Toby is happy to talk about his problems publicly. If you ask him 'how are you?' he tells you, which is quite unsettling and always received with astonishment.

'Was it mutual?' I ask.

'Almost mutual.'

'I think I might call my next album that,' says Stephen, laughing, 'Almost Mutual.'

'This is what I think,' says Toby, 'I think it's absurd to expect, through monogamy, that you should have exclusive rights to someone else's body. I mean you wouldn't complain about your partner going to see a film with someone else would you? Or going for a swim?'

'I think I might,' says Lauren.

'Seriously,' says Toby, 'all this energy that goes into seeking sex! I can see why some queer men believe they are a superior species. They don't have to conspire to fuck because they are handling prey that wants the same thing, all nice and simple. They can put all their energy into making furniture or playing tennis.'

'You're wrong there,' says Stephen, 'it's all about tennis.'

'What is the big deal about sex?' says Toby, not listening, 'I really want to know.'

'It's a social construction,' says Adam. 'It's entirely negative. It's based on fear.'

Lauren laughs. 'Ooh you charmer!'

Adam grimaces again—like I say, he thinks of it as a smile, but it's not; the little chaps operating his face muscles have all gone on strike, with just two bored lip operators tugging up at the corners when the boss tells them to.

'Adam is a glass-half-empty type,' I say.

He shrugs. 'I'm a glass-half-empty type when the glass is full of shit.'

Lauren laughs. Does she like him? I think she *does*. It seems incredible, but the body language is there. I go to the toilet and when I return it's even more obvious. Adam is talking about an abandoned asylum he'd broken into to take photographs for his magazine and Lauren is all gazey attention and hesitant wonder. I feel a kind of panic—she *can't*. I mean I do want her to be with someone else, but not with *Adam*. He'd tear her delicate heart to shreds.

I stand next to her, wedging my vibebody between them.

'I'm tired,' I say, 'I'm going to call it a night.'

'Okay,' she says, and this wounds me. She's supposed to protest.

'Let me walk you home,' I say, 'come on.'

'Um, o… kay.'

Outside the gallery are two mounted policemen—two hors-es, in the middle of Camberwell. Everywhere club pub London art design world, neon, beer, dope, smoke and fashionable shoes, and then two giant living horses, long heads restrained and jerking, soft ageless eyes flashing with mute confusion. They look like aliens. I want to apologise to them, or at least offer them some kind of explanation, 'we don't know what we're doing here either!'

We walk along Denmark Hill, chatting. Lauren is all bright and warm, but there's an undercurrent of hysteria. Her art course really is fracturing some integral part of her, or London is, or civilisation. She feels she wants to be free and to express how good that is, but the college atmosphere makes this feeling into something shameful, perverse, and it feels mad to think about it. She often says 'I'm going crazy,' and she wants me to know she means it, or she wants my help, but what can I do?

What I want to do is fuck her, or I do now. I want her to be mine, to be tied to me, but I don't put this insane desire into the light. It's too shameful, whereas frenzied, casual sex between friends is normal and healthy; happens all the time! That's what the newspaper says anyway, and the amusing American sitcoms, and who am I to argue with experts on the matter?

'What you said in the show,' she says, 'about everyone pre-tending to have fun. I don't think they are pretending. I think they really are happy.'

'Happy is unhappy's fuck-buddy.'

A white form, out of place, immaculately out of place. Adren-aline stabs me awake, Lauren seizes my elbow, while mind, far behind, grasps for what it is looking at; stark under a sodium streetlamp, all white but punctuated somehow, black eyes blankly taking us in, is a tall woman dressed in white, with a painted white face, masklike. She looks at me, looks darkly into me, for what seems like eternity, then moves off over the road, white dress tugged by the winter. She's wrapped in bandages, wearing a tit-pointy basque-thing, and, trailing behind her, a *tail*.

'Fuck my arse.'

The White Lady of Camberwell, one of several inmates from the Maudsley. Her name is Angel, or that's what everyone calls her. She'd been beaten and raped in Kennington park and now lives in a hospital flat in which she'd painted everything white, including herself, her whole black body—with white emulsion. Emulsion! God only knows what it's done to her face. She spends most of her time scaring the bejesus out of people by wandering around SE5 dressed as white death.

We gather our shattered bits. I feel on the verge of passing out, a cold, slick, livid sweat is hollowing out my neck.

'Maybe she was trying to tell us something?'

'Christ, I hope not.'

We head towards the bright main road, past the all-night Lebanese convenience shops and bawling pubs and Nigerian telephone card shops. An old man passes us, his trembling face etched in confusion, mouth open—terrified. A big black geezer buying plantains is wearing a donkey jacket with the words 'citizen of heaven' written on the back. A broom-thin man in a dirty grey windcheater is standing six inches in front of a gigantic Victoria's Secret bra advert—massive, rock-hard puffballs exploding from a malnourished rib-cage—supping from a 20 centilitre wine bottle. A woman is passed out in the doorway of the post office. She is covered in milk.

We get to Lauren's house, a maisonette set back above a Bangladeshi warehouse-reject clothes shop, and stop before the alleyway which leads upstairs to her flat. Some kind of momentum makes me say; 'Can I stay over?'

A moment's confusion crinkles her brow. She looks at me. Her clear green eyes, wide set, otherworldly, gently peer.

'Yes,' she says.

She shares a flat with Glen, a terrifying homosexual guy—barrel chested, tiny forehead, glittering hungry eyes—a small, skinny woman with long curly brown hair called Elaine who hates me, or possibly everyone ('dead vagina' is Lauren's diagnosis), and a neat Italian guy called Dino who, when we walk in, is in the living room with two of his friends. They nod greetings and get back to their conversation. Jonathan Ross is on TV behind them, talking about The Virgin Mary.

'Tavistock Street,' says Dino.

'That's easy, Covent Garden.'

'Try this. Marchmont Street.'

'Ooh, that's tough.'

'I know it, I know it, hold on...'

'Somewhere in Bloosmbury...?'

We go up to Lauren's room. She goes out to make tea and I sit on her bed, which is very soft, practically a cushion. She's got biscuit-red and desert pink Klee prints, lilac scarves, creamy yellow candles, big photography books and a theremin. It smells good, that's the important thing, soft and warm and human rather than, say, hard and cold and inhuman, which is becoming a bit of a theme.

She comes back with a tea for her and a hot water for me. I dearly want a bagel now, not out of hunger, more from a willingness to rejoin the normal run of things, but I'm going to go through with it. Not long to go now.

We talk for a while. I want to generate the feeling that it's 'us against the world,' so I pick on our problems. It creates a sharp space, but it's a space we're both in (this is half the reason, I think, why there's so much negativity amongst my friends; shared misery is better than solitary numbness). We talk about work and art and London, but what I really want to say is 'look, I want to have sex with you, but it doesn't really *mean* anything, it's just straightforward friendly sex.' I want something definite, written down if possible, cover my bases if it all goes Pete Tong, but I feel that if I start along these lines I'll fuck the mood. I've got a cement-mixer churning away in my belly, but if I have sex with Lauren everything will be o... *kay!*

We get undressed for bed. There's so much unspoken hanging in the air, there's hardly any room to move. She slips off her dress and turns away from me and I see that she is actually a *bit* chubby, little folds of flesh pushing over her bra-strap. I feel no attraction to her, just mounting desperation.

She gets in bed and we embrace. It is not nourishing. I need more, I need to kiss her, but that seems like a commitment so I kind of nuzzle against her cheek and hope that, even now, she'll make the decisive move, take responsibility for what is happening.

She turns her head towards me, her mouth is there, against mine. Her lips feel thin, like I'm still kissing her cheek. I push my tongue into her mouth and move it around a bit. It still doesn't feel like enough, so I pull at her t-shirt but it gets caught over her head. She disengages to do the job properly and I take off my boxers. My penis, painfully hard, seems like it doesn't belong on my skinny body. It all seems so ridiculous.

She turns to me; 'no condoms.'

'Hold on.'

I pull one from my wallet and put it on, sitting hunched over on the edge of the bed, then I get on top and try to enter her, but her vagina is tight and dry, so I think she probably needs some foreplay. I kiss her breasts. I am trying to remember how to operate this strange machine. A few kisses to the nipple, that's enough, move down, a few kisses to the belly, the inside thigh... I reach her vagina, but I don't know what I'm doing down here, so I give it a few pecks and come back up feeling like I've lost my travel card.

I try again to enter her, but it's still not working, brain saying 'come on, come *on*.' She helps me, and eventually I'm inside. Brain; *'made it.'* She looks confused but nods a little and raises her eyebrows, as if to say 'yes, go on, you were saying?' My penis feels distant, not so hard now, drained of sensation, voice in my head chattering away, 'touch that, no there, maybe roll her over? *nipple*.' All I can feel is the very tip of my cock, which, I don't want to, but I do, *I'm going to!* There, I've ejaculated.

I lie on top of her, head buried in her hair, nulled. Something dark is descending and I want to hold onto this moment of nothingness for just a few moments more before the hovering mass falls on us; before we have to communicate.

'I'm sorry,' I whisper.

'It's okay.'

I roll off—my penis has shrunk very rapidly. It's ashamed too. I reach for some tissues to clean up, workmanlike. Has this ever happened to Kirk Douglas?

She is staring at the ceiling. I am staring at the ceiling. The bed is so soft and hot, and foreign and now, somehow, so is the smell. I can't even bring myself to hold her hand. I'm already plotting how I can get out, how much time will seem polite.

We hug again, or our bodies do. I want to apologise again. I want to cry in fact, but I cling to her instead, planning what to say. Why do I have to go? What on earth could be a convincing reason?

'I think I'd better go,' I say.

'Why?'

'I just, don't feel right. I need to lie down.'

'You are lying down.'

'I mean in my own bed.'

Silence.

'Daniel why did you do this?'

'I didn't do this, *we* did.'

She sighs. 'You know I like you.'

'And I like you, but...'

'But what?'

'But I'm not ready for a relationship right now. Can't we just be...'

No, I can't say it. Lauren says nothing.

'Yes,' she says eventually, 'I expect this kind of thing—but not from you.'

An upsurge of rage runs through me. Well fuck you! I think, leaping to my feet and rapidly pulling my clothes on.

'And that's it, is it?' she says, quietly. She looks so ugly—like a sad, shaved baby monkey.

I can't find my right sock, but I don't want to linger so I pull my shoe on over my bare foot.

'*Look*,' I say, tense, 'we tried it. It didn't work. We'll talk about it later.'

'I don't want to talk about it later. I don't want to think about it now.'

'Fine!'

I leave. At the bottom of the narrow stairs is Glen. I'm desperate to escape, so I totter down (odd, my legs feel weak), expecting him to wait, but he comes up too. We squeeze past each other, Glen trying to catch my eye. It's just one more indignity to weather out.

'Where are *you* going in such a rush?' he purrs as I pull myself free.

'Back to the atom,' I say, wondering what that means.

I fall through the freezing dark to the Camberwell New Road and wait shivering for a night bus. The shelter is empty, but for an old guy asleep on the bench. Leaning against his knees is a sandwich board which reads 'The End is Nigh. Less Lust from Less Protein: Less Fish, Milk, Meat, Bird, Cheese, Egg and Sitting.'

The bus turns up and I fumble in my jacket pocket, which is empty. My wallet is on Lauren's floor but I can't possibly go back, so I start walking.

How could it have been so bad? I knew I was deficient in bed, but it had never been as horrible as that, as fleshly, and yet I *like* Lauren, at least more than any girl I've been with. It wasn't just that she didn't score a pneumatic ten, but something else. Something is missing, something is not here. I'm disintegrating.

Night workers hurry past, head down, and club-spill drunks stagger around sagging into each other or screaming Garys and Daves across the street. I pass the gallery, which is quiet and dark now. A small bald guy in a business suit and tutu is sitting on the gallery steps with a banjo, quietly singing. I stop to listen. He is singing the same line, over and over;

'It's hard and heavy, and cold to the touch, but if we hold each other, we won't feel it as much…'

His voice is cracked but high and, like the melody, sweet, and he means it. He doesn't notice me. He's not singing to anyone. I stand there, cast out with this bizarre little man, and my body is quietly sobbing. This is art, I think.

He hears me sniff and abruptly stops, shooting me an angry look. 'What the fuck do you mean?' he hisses.

'I don't mean anything.'

'Well fuck off then!'

Up the New Road and into Rye Lane. A pitter of rain drives into my face, through my clothes, wind booming in my ears. Dark concrete living units, blindingly bright petrol stations, mini-cabs and bricked up nail salons. It all seems so solid, so real, but in the cave of my belly I know that this, the dark city, is a fake, that the shifting night-crawlers haunting Rye Lane are not just victims of a bizarre dreamworld; we're all holding it up, bound by some mad collective agreement, a million years ago, to build this shoddy prototype, and then to forget we did it.

I reach Peckham Rye Common, grey-black, mauve-black, green-black. My freezing sockless foot is blistering, my guts hang round my throat like a dying man, but the blackness is a tremendous relief. I walk into it gladly, without my usual fear of *them*. Altogether there has been too much light today. It's intensely cold, cutting across my bones, and exposed, but there is something I need here.

I am next to a monumental lime tree, bare, craggy branches cracking a smudged moon. I lean my forehead against the trunk. It smells of piss. I pull myself up onto the first branch, and then another. The wind is still damp and freezing. I hold on to a branch as a squall rips into me.

'Aghhhhhhh!'

I want the wind to clean me out, I want to be just flesh and bone, but more than that I want to rage, I throttle the branch, wind roaring in my ears. Sodden, thrashing, blind beating on the limb of the tree which snaps, a long moment of confused hurtling, the brutal ground dull thunder in my head, and, for a shattering moment, nothing.

•

My first impression is pain, my second is the sky, purply grey, pre-dawn and my third is dog shit.

I get up — nothing broken, just throbbing bruises, and sickish shame. The branch I hated is on the floor next to me. I leave it there and am one exhausted dot on the vast common, creeping up towards Nunhead, where all is silent, just a lone sweeper.

'Daniel!'

It's Igwe. He drops his dustpan and walks up to me, all teeth and cheer, hand outstretched. I give him a desultory black man.

'How are you at this time of the morning?' he asks, 'you look disgraceful.'

'I feel disgrace Igwe,'

'The woman?' he asks solemnly.

'Well. Yes actually, amongst other things.'

'The woman is *cursed*, this is why she has to squat down when she eases herself.'

'Men too.'

'No, no, the man only squats to download.'

'Right, I see.' I don't think I need this, but as we walk together down Rye Lane, Igwe tugging his cleaning cart happily explaining to me how and why all women are damned, I realise that somewhere I am glad of the human company.

'But your Queen is not cursed,' he says with a reassuring air, sure that I must be fretting about that.

'Why is the Queen different?'

'When I was twenty,' he says squinting into the middle distance, 'Queen Elizabeth the Second visited Nigeria. I saw her and I loved her. I knew then I would serve her... as a very noble lady. That is why I am here, in the United Kingdom. That is why I clean her streets.'

'I hope she appreciates it.'

'Ha ha ha! Daniel you are my great friend. I like you!'

'Thanks Igwe, I like you too.'

'But you smell of excrement.'

'I know.'

'Do you have £420?'

'Not really.'

'Why don't you text me your bank details?'

'I don't have a phone.'

'Is it because of the colour?' he taps his wrist.

'No. Why do you need it?'

'I owe it to my fortune teller.'

Igwe explains to me a complicated story, which I only half listen to. He had a fight with a witch, it seems, in a sauna, and now he needs the money to lift a curse she has put on him ('fear catch me!' he hisses, 'I am in soup'). He says to me that because I do not give him the money, the curse extends to me too, which would explain a lot, but I'm not sufficiently convinced to hand over the money. I just want to lie down now, and inspect my wounds.

A group of black guys turn from a side road into ours. They are talking to each other, but when they see us, their volume drops. My body instantly cringes back. Igwe continues talking, but also quieter now. As we approach, the gang stop talking altogether, walking with intent, and the intent is probably us. I am tense and ready and nauseous with fear when Igwe whispers urgently to me, *'Walk tall my brother.'*

These words have an extraordinary effect on me. I feel like my chest is a balloon, being inflated with courage. I glance at Igwe, he is completely calm.

The group walk past us.

I deflate. 'I thought we were dead.'

'We are dead,' says Igwe with a gentle smile.

We reach Linden grove. The sun has come out—already warm. Igwe has to turn back, to serve the Queen. I walk down the quiet street, and just as I reach 28 I hear him shout, *'true to God Daniel you personal person!'*

Inside the lights are all on. I pass the living room and Jacqui calls my name. She comes in to the kitchen as I'm wrapping my shitty jacket into a bin bag.

'Daniel, where *have* you been?'

'I went to see the void.'

'How was it?'

'It was really awful, it still is.'

She's standing too close to me. I can smell her sickly perfume, and see all the open pores in her dry red skin. Her piercing blue eyes are manic.

'Why don't you come and have a pill?' she asks, 'Pistol Pete is here.'

'No thanks. I'm going to have a plate of beans.'

'Had enough of the monk life?'

'I've just had enough.'

'Oh yes, I *know*. Isn't it terrible?'

The beans start to bubble as Jacqui lights another cigarette. 'I have to sit down alone now,' I say, tipping the beans into a cup, 'I've had a bit of a rough night.'

'You must tell me *all* about it,' she says, winking, as she passes me, spilling white wine as she exits.

I go upstairs and sit in the cast-iron wheelchair. Grey London light pisses through the skylight. I was hoping the beans would taste like ambrosia, but it's like chewing packing foam.

On the wall and thrown over the floor are my drawings. They are excrement, they really are. I pull them down and pick them up, tearing them into strips as I go, slowly and passionlessly, and placing them in a neat little pile.

I come across an upturned newspaper, the remnants of a recent job search. Little rectangles proclaim; sales, dynamic, management, experienced, self-starter, secretary, executary, team-player, sales, competitive, development, excellent opportunity…

I'd rather die, as it stands.

I look at the problem, my mind oddly clear. I am a disgrace. I am willing to do anything to be free, that's also pretty clear to me.

But first I need a bath.

My Life is a Trombone

In order to claim housing and unemployment benefit I need to be fired, or made redundant. My plan is to appeal to Graham's humanity by pretending to be 'in need of help.' That's a bit of a long-shot, as I'm not sure Graham is human, so my back-up plan is to terrify him by pretending to be out-and-out psychotic. I'm not sure I have the front to pull that off though either.

I wait in the conference room at the end of the long walnut table, going over the speech, working up a bit of internal mania. I fix my face into a tense mask, straining away from the world, away from the threatening walls, all balled up inside I am, squeezing. It's not at all difficult—it's just a pumped-up and hectic version of the work mode, that tight sense of being imprisoned in an ersatz version of myself that cares about back-office functions and regulatory compliance.

Eventually Graham joins me, brisk, buoyant and slightly terrified of everything.

'What's new Daniel?'

'I have to leave,' I say trembling.

'Oh?' A clench of existential uncertainty in his eyes, before his smooth brows crinkle and his sitting down action slows to 'caring.'

'Why?'

'I'm losing my marbles. My family has a history of mental... *mental*... and I think I'm going that way too. I get intense periods of dread; sometimes, I feel like getting out of bed is—that I'm being forced into a hard aluminium mechanism designed specifically to ridicule and taunt me. I feel menaced... ashamed and... and... so incredibly alone.' I hang my head—this is easier than I'd thought! 'But worst of all,' I say into my chest, 'I'm convinced that everyone is a simulacrum, that nobody is really real, or, that they've all been programmed to execute this vast secret plan, which I can only guess at—I don't know, but...' I look up, desperation pasted over my face, 'I don't *recognise* anyone. Sometimes I sit at my workstation paralysed, sick, feeling... feeling that... being itself is to blame. Alone and in enemy territory and there's nothing even to take revenge on.

'I have to get out Graham, I *have* to get out. The only thing I'm afraid of is that it's *all* like this. Maybe there is nowhere to escape to? Maybe it goes on like this forever? a morning meeting to the end of time? an *infinite* spreadsheet? I don't know... I just know that I have no choice. I've got to get out. I...'

I break off, as if language itself has turned its back on me. Is he going to go for it? I watch his face, intently, ready to ramp up the weirdness, possibly rend my garment or take a dump on the biscuit tray. His neat head is an orb of superintent fear and concern. His dry red eyes blinklessly fix me from behind designer spectacles.

'So do I,' he says quietly.

'Sorry?'

'I have to get out too.'

'Do you?'

'Yes,' he sharply whispers, 'I *literally* have shit for brains.'

He looks around the room, teeth clenched. 'There's something *happening* in the world,' he says, 'it's the Rothschilds, or, I suspect, another organisation, one above them. First they replaced everyone on television with CGI, and now they're coming for us — it happens through the computer screens, they turn your brains to shit.'

I'm not sure what to say; he *does* have a point.

'Oh, what a relief,' says Graham, releasing the mechanical force that holds him together, 'I thought I was the only one here who knew.' He leans forward and looks at me, urgently, searchingly;

'Go.'

'Go?'

'Yes Daniel, get out.'

'Really?'

He nods. I nod back.

'I will Graham.'

'Is there anything I can do to help?'

'Could you sack me? Then I can sign on.'

'Don't worry about that. I'll sort that out.' He looks at me hard, earnest, then starts to crumble. 'Daniel,' he says quietly, 'my life is a trombone.'

'Oh Graham... don't... don't cry.'

He's not crying though, he's fighting it. 'Everything is cracking up,' he whispers. His face is contorted in suffering. The mask of management has fallen, revealing a jelly pond of pain and confusion.

'Graham, come on, they might be watching. Stay strong.'

'Yes, you're right. You... You get out. I'll... I don't know. I don't know what I do...' he begins to disintegrate again, but

gathers his bits together, 'I'll…' His voice tightens to an agonised whimper: 'I'll see you on *the beach*.'

I walk through the office one last time. I can't bring myself to
say goodbye to anyone—how can you say goodbye to someone
you never really greeted? I did share a bit of the old human
with Harold though, so I agree to meet him for lunch in Soho.

Outside it's hazy and warm. Men in striped t-shirts and
espadrilles drink Monmouth coffee on the seven dials monument. Taxis grumble past. Designers, Japs and Skateboarders
seem to predominate. I follow the stream down to Shaftesbury
Avenue. As usual anxiety is eating into me; from where? I
should be thrilled—work is over! But it's like the last day of
school—something I had looked forward to for so long, and
then, when it came, where was the rush of relief? Where the
liberating ecstasy? Just a normal day, after all. It must be the
same getting out of prison, or becoming a star.

I look for causes for the needling unease, and they are many.
I've fucked up with Lauren, I have precious little money and I
might not get a job. I think there's something I've forgotten to
do, something I've left behind somewhere, and it might be my
turn to have to clean the toilet. I've got a weird pain where I
think my pancreas is, I stained my new shirt yesterday, Green-
land is melting and I'm sure something is wrong with pop music.

But it's none of that. I've got this constant bunched-up ball
inside me of, what is it? of dread? of anxiety? of *what*? Mind
finds a hundred reasons but no problem solved brings relief.
The rock of fear remains and permanently blocks my path to
what is. I just want to see the snow, or the rain, or the roundabout and for it just be that. Snow. Rain. Roundabout. Just that,
without this other thing here. It wasn't always like this. There
was once just the thing.

I ask myself what is wrong, what I need, what will clear
my heart and purify me. And the answer comes. Sex. Sex will

definitely solve the problem; of this I am always uncritically sure. I feel it—constantly—just behind the sternum. A slight anger, a wispy grief, some restless watcher ever on the lookout, ever prowling, yet ever a moment too late, haunted by vague fertility in the street, the breasts-waist-buttocks shape; it will turn my head at the number 8, yet can never respond quickly enough to the presence of an actual woman. The fuck-probe is always there, lying in wait, looking for an opportunity, a way in, assessing her strengths and weaknesses, but when it comes to actually *doing* something, *saying* something, it instantly shrivels up and dies, like a leaf in lava.

Occasionally I see a girl who is so perfectly, perfectly beautiful that it seems to me—I mean it seems in the frenzy of trembling despair that washes over me when she pops out of nowhere—that no woman could *ever* outdo her, that I therefore *must* accost her, now, or for the rest of my life have to settle for second best. That's how stalkers feel I suppose. I am a spontaneous, serial, stalker, leaping from one target to another like Frogger. Look, there's one. I'll watch her go into Cath Kidston, wait outside, eating my liver, planning what to say when she emerges and then either bottle or freak her out with a sweaty *excuuuse me*; in both cases slinking away like a severed lizard, sticking imagined up needles into my head.

There's always the feeling, seeing or being with a girl I desire, that I must fuck her now, it must be *now*... the fuck instinct is like a chained-up dog; it has no conception of time. The fury is eternal. Like all men, I suppress it, but like all things suppressed, it stagnates, festers and then leaps out with the weirdest fucking comments.

Just one orgasm—one majestic, obliterating orgasm, possessed and possessing. That will free me, that will dissolve my perennial corrosive funk, and enlighten me forever. Please, just one.

I shamble around Soho—just the place to be if you're suffering from the rage. I've never been in a sex-shop, but obviously
that will ease my omni-lust, or kill a few minutes.

I'm dead nervous though. I must look such a bloody perv;
but the shop is empty—midday is not peak creep. The central
counter, strewn with straw, displays the apparatus that a horse
wears; the bit and all the reins, with a rosette for the 'winner.'
Next to that is a stuffed crow with a golden beak and advanced
looking dildos, and leather gimp masks, and books of complex
knotting systems for bondage—very serious and technical—
and pubic toupees and 'Noble Ecstasy Love Ducks' and Soft
Demand 'Emotion Type' Sod Lotion.

'Sexy show sir?'

The woman behind the counter is middle aged, kind of
friendly and kind of sad. She looks like a bereaved aunt.

'Pardon?'

'Sexy show sir?'

'No thanks, maybe some other time.'

'Anything else, sir?'

I point towards the crow and rabbit.

'How are these employed in the sex act?'

'Decoration for a lavish bed scene sir,' she says rapidly.

'I have a stuffed crow with golden beak fetish—very precise
isn't it?'

'We've a range of young girls sir,' she says, 'and there's a
discount if you're clean.'

'How do you determine that?'

'A woman can tell, sir.'

'I suppose so.'

'A woman can tell most things,' she adds, ominously.

Mmm. Unless power is involved, then their psycho-spiritual
Geiger-counters go out of window. Men are very discerning
too—unless they think they might get a blow job out of it.

'Sexy show sir?'

Oh, I don't know. Shall I go and watch a young girl? The boy I am wants to—maybe even should—but the man I want to be surely wouldn't slither into a cum-stained booth and wank over a bored pro humping a chair. Also, I'm scared. Also, it's time to meet Harold.

I wait in the Saggezza Italian cheap-eat surrounded by booths of oxblood vinyl, Lapidus beanpoles, cooper black signage and a wall-length mural of a taffeta goddess. In the booth opposite a very nervous and sensibly dressed chubby Dutchman with a pony tail squats over paperwork talking rapidly into a mobile phone to I think his boss, or all people are to him his boss perhaps. Painful-irresistible watching him shift his notepad around, pick up his pen, flick dust off his laptop, widen eyes, take sharp breaths, go to say something too soon, change his mind at the last moment, put his pen down, break into the first moment of big laughter, freeze, justify himself, and on, and on. On the other side of the aisle is a nicely dressed girl; black slacks, cream trainers with wine-red trim, beige cream army coat, dark-red neckerchief thing, red plastic sports holdall. I assess her for long and short-term mating prospects. Nice smooth skin, good straight nose, but the pouty way she checks her phone messages, along with the fact that she's waiting for her change and about to leave, places her into the category of 'unboyfriendable.' I split up with her; sad, of course, but knowing it has to be this way.

Harold enters all ahhs and eyebrows. He sits down, rucksack beside him and pulls out a vinyl record 'Dino Lupatti: Chopin, Ravel, Lizst,' makes a kind of saucy 'ooh' face and slips it back into his bag, which he taps in a cute 'that's mine, that is' way.

'Very nice,' I say, more at his gestures than at the record.

We order our pasta and I explain my final encounter with the Graham. Harold chuckles—he is a chuckler—and hands over a titbit of Graham-related gossip. Apparently he had phoned his estranged wife—who, I've not met her, but who Harold describes as a 'hefty Canadian prude'—a little while back and said to her 'I fucking miss you,' which she had heard as 'I miss fucking you,' and that was that. She doesn't take his calls anymore.

'How do you know this?'

He shrugs slightly. 'People tell me things.'

I get it. I tell Harold things. He's... What is it? What is that weird quality that makes me want to talk to him? I think it might be that he's actually interested.

'What you been up to, then?' I ask as our food arrives. The place is filling now, with chatter and cutlery scrapes and urgent voices from the extravagantly gesticulating pizza chefs.

'I've been going to car boot sales, looking for a biscuit tin to make a doodle-bass amp chamber. I got one in the end, but by golly carpentry is hard. Have you ever tried it?'

'No.'

'You should. You should do something practical.'

'Art is practical.'

'But I never see you drawing.'

'I'm working up to it.'

'A great artist does not wait to feel inspired,' he says.

'I'm working up to it.'

'It's not good for you, having nothing to do.'

'I'm free now. Loads of time to not wait to be inspired.'

Harold carefully winds spaghetti round his fork. 'Although, I say that,' he says, 'but I never really know if I'm just filling a hole, collecting rare vinyl, distilling potato juice and building instruments out of confectionery vessels.'

'What's in the hole?'

'Nothing. It's a hole.'

'Right. Right.'

'I'm proud of my hobbies—but I don't want to be proud of my hobbies. I want to be proud of my life.'

'What should be in the hole then?'

'Love, Daniel, love.'

'Oh yes, of course.'

Harold puts his spaghetti-scarfed fork down. 'My wife doesn't see me you see, not really, and I suppose I not her. She doesn't notice that my kisses are 75%.'

His big mild head looks at me. 'That they are 75% is sad,' he says, 'but that she fails to notice is worse.'

'What percentage are her kisses?'

'That's hard to say. In one sense 140%, but in another 27.5%'

I bet she doesn't think of their relationship in terms of misaligned kiss-percentages.

'I don't know why I'm telling you all this—I'm so sorry—I really should call my mum.' He laughs to himself and returns to his food, 'what about you? How's your love life?'

'Also a hole.'

'Oh dear me.'

'I have no idea what to say or do with women.'

'They are mysterious. At least the ones worth knowing are.'

'But you're what? Fifty?'

'Fifty five.'

'You must have learnt a thing or two. Can't you give me some advice?'

He stops and thinks to himself, taking the question very seriously, and then speaks, slowly, as if channelling truth from some other, better place; 'She likes it when she doesn't have to tell you how to be… when you just know. And she likes that you take a chance, yes? So if you don't know… it can be better to not blurt out that you don't know and just try something. She can like it more if you keep some things to yourself. She can like it if you trick her, but only as long as you love her.'

I am writing all this down. Harold realises he's reached the end of his wisdom and snaps to.

'No absolutes or apply-alls though eh?' he says cheerily.

We finish our lunch and part on the narrow pavement. I shake Harold's goofy hand with a warm conscious grip and watch him amble splay-footedly back to work. What a nice guy—strange that his wife is a rapacious monster—except, not strange. Nice guys always seem to be with harpies, don't they? Harold doesn't seem to play the victim though, like Toby does.

I float back through central London, directing my urban drift beyond the perimeter of the lunch zone and into Oxford Circus, which seems to be the unhappiest place on earth—rivers of people, grim-bent on getting; hard-set and fixed—until I cross Regent Street and enter Mayfair, which *is* the unhappiest place on earth.

Why does everyone look so tense? dark? watchful? It's not the gloomy frost of rain, it's not the audible hiss of the vanishing sands of time, it's not even the weight of the unworld. It's sex. It's all sex! Either they're not getting any, or they're not getting enough or what they are getting is nowhere near as good as it should be. 'Dead Vagina' says Lauren of her tight-necked flatmate Elaine. What if all of tight-necked London had a stupendous sexual encounter this morning? a complete, resurrecting blending, an eyes wide open mind-melting rapture? I don't think they'd be queuing up outside the Apple Store. What if the scraggy panhandlers of the underpasses slept with their filthy but devoted lovers in St James' Park? Alright, they'd still need houses to be happy; but what if the Prime Minister, glowing with sexual confidence and satisfaction strolled out of number 10 with his wife, mind unmade, cheek-radiant, deep with the wisdom of adoration? What would he say to them? Fuck it! Take one! Take ten! Here—we've got thousands!

Oh God, them. *Them*—look at them. Confusion and desperation are never really far from rage, rage and hatred for this grim lizard world of endless misery. Look at them—look at the world. We don't stand a chance. We're hurtling towards the abyss and *these* people are in the cabin.

'*You're all fucked!*' I shout, at the top of my voice.

A ripple of fear passes outwards. Eyes tighten, fingers tense around phones, shoppers and tourists arc around me and danger, exposure, grips me. *I* have become the threat—me, which is ridiculous. I dart into a back-road, shame sweating through my pores, and into a coffee shop. I wait in the long queue—and feel reassured. Queues are so reassuring, out of the optional, until the gruff cook asks me what I want, and I say nothing and return to the back of the queue for another calming round of waiting. When I get to the cook again he smiles and says 'still nothing?' and I say, 'still nothing,' and leave.

I catch the number 12 and press my cold hot forehead against the dry glass. London shop-goers fight their way to menswear and home furnishings, lunch-breakers cram what life they can extract from an hour down their clenched necks.

Yes, there is some justice in the End of All Things. Nowadays, when I watch superhero films I nearly always support the evil genius. Please, Dr. Darkness, wipe us all out, you'd be doing us a favour.

As the bus crawls south my spirits lift again. Partly because there aren't any good-looking women on the top deck, but mostly because in the centre of London I am all vinegar and despair, all grave and peering, all pinched and skewered and given to visions; but as we cross the river, rumble our way through Vauxhall and pull into Camberwell, something in me senses that, although nothing has changed—not really—here at least, there are a few more people with less to lose.

The rage slips away revealing what is. I am jobless and free and lifted. Yes, there is ease, there in uncertainty, intimations of eternity in not-knowing. A few quid in my pocket, all doors open and everything seems to say so; the chill clarity of the air and the yellow-white sunshine heavenly and beckoning at the living source of universe, which seems to be down the A3.

The only problem, and there is a problem, sort of nagging away in the background, is that I'm a complete fucking mess.

·

Back home everyone is watching retro porn, the Pamela Anderson and Tommy Lee sex tape. Jacqui has a new fella over, Eddie, a recklessly self-destructive cripple who has a tendency to obliterate rooms, collapse in the corner and scream 'I am the Expressive Egg!' Jacqui sits next to him, her red rubbery head yanking back and forth, looking at a chocolate bar in her hand and mouthing words to herself. She seems to have a constant monologue going on in her mind—*'ooh, I love Kit-Kats! I like biting the top off first then going in for the wafer, I fancy one right now actually, although I have to phone Ben because he might have scored by now...'* which never *quite* reaches zero volume. When an opportunity to converse presents itself she turns the dial up to eighty and lets her braintape out. Except it's more like a radio than a tape, permanently tuned to 'Compulsive Irrelevance FM.'

Adam's here too, stiff and assessing, Stephen, gentle and wry, Gurt, a bubble-headed Flem with an impossibly deep voice, always stoned always cynical, Gurt's Italian girlfriend, Piscina, tall, willowy, blonde, kind of tragic, and my housemate Naeema, cute but angry; always unhappy about feminist issues. They're all crammed on to the sofa. I join them—not having had enough of sex for one day, evidently.

The two pneumatic D-list ex-megastars are on a boat. Pammy says 'where are we?' then Pammy and Tommy are in a 4×4 driving somewhere and Tommy gets his cock out, which Pammy blows, and Tommy says 'Oh my God.' Then we cut to Pammy swimming naked in the water next to the boat.

'Does silicone float?' asks Gurt.

'Maybe that's why she had them done,' says Stephen, 'as a floatation device.'

We then see Pammy naked on the prow. 'Where are we?' she asks and Tommy closes in on her vagina and says 'Oh my God.'

'Fake,' says Jacqui.

'What, her *vagina* is fake?'

'Definitely. She's had it neatened up.'

'It does seem very organised.'

Tommy dives in the water and Pammy says 'I love you,' with a note of desperation and Tommy says 'I love you,' but he's holding something back I think. More oral sex and more 'Oh my God.'

'He's a very religious man,' says Stephen.

Finally some hard pumping. Jacqui cackles.

'Ugh,' says Piscina, 'do people actually enjoy that? Boom boom boom.'

'I fucking *love* it!' cries Eddie from behind the sofa.

The video ends with a 'where are we?' from Pammy.

'Do you think they're happy?' I ask.

'I think they're *stupid*,' says Naeema.

'That's a kind of happiness,' says Adam.

'Do you think they feel happiness though, in their bodies?'

'No way,' says Naeema, 'They're too fake.'

I like to think I'm not fake, but I recognise their awkwardness. And I too constantly wonder where I am.

'Would The Righteous Da approve?' I ask Gurt. He gives me a cold look.

'Dershan is a sacred experience,' he says quietly.

Gurt and Piscina are devotees of Shami-Da, aka Da Free Roy, aka Roy Franklin Foster III; an American acid casualty turned guru who ran a commune in the 1980s on 'The Carpet of Attention.' His thing back then was 'crazy wisdom' which involved Foster ingesting large quantities of alcohol, amyl and cocaine, soliciting lavish donations from 'people of wealth and influence' and taking nine wives, including a playboy centrefold and a friend of Gurt's, who once told him 'I'll never forget the first time I went down on the Lord.' Toby calls Shami-Da a 'baby-headed paedophile.'

That's a point; 'where *is* Toby? Not like him to miss flesh.'

'He's upstairs having a threesome,' says Gurt.

'Oh. Right.'

I am a bit gutted at this.

'Who with?'

'Sarah and Vicky.'

Everyone exchanges knowing smirks. Jacqui stands, pulling Eddie to his feet, and regally gusts out. 'Oh come on, who hasn't had a threesome these days?'

We all look at each other, ducking Eddie's helicopter limbs as he exits, and shake our heads. I haven't—have you? No.

'I wouldn't know what to do,' I say, 'I mean you only have one penis, don't you?'

'Speak for yourself,' says Stephen.

Silence falls on the room. I'm thinking about Toby. Gurt, Stephen and Adam are looking inward too, doubtless coveting the same morbid tableau. Piscina looks at Gurt and he at her; he knows she knows and she knows he knows. They'll have an argument later.

I quite fancy Piscina actually. She's got something smouldering under that sad, languid, lazy, look; something that Gurt cannot possibly know how to activate. When you say 'how are you Gurt?' he usually replies 'decaying.'

Rapid, stair-descending thumps boom through the walls. We turn as one towards the living-room door through to the hallway as Sarah—one legged, prosthesis dangling under her right arm—hops to the bottom of the stairs, propped up by

Vicky, and towards the front door. Vicky opens the door and Toby's two girlfriends hobble off, arm in arm.

We exchange fucking-hell glances. Naeema, who knows Sarah—almost as well as she knows an opportunity to disparage men—runs out after them. I go upstairs and knock on Toby's door.

'Go away,' he says, so I come back down.

'I suppose it didn't go very well then,' says Gurt.

'Maybe they didn't even have sex?' Piscina suggests.

'Maybe they played cards?' says Stephen.

'There aren't any good card games for three people.'

'What do you do after orgasm?' says Adam, bitterly. Nobody is quite sure what to say to that. 'I don't even care about orgasm,' he says after a pause and the way he says 'orgasm' without a determining 'an' makes me think he is talking about a religion or a television show.

'I don't care about anything,' he says, 'I get up because I have to go to work, but if I died on the tube I'd be okay with that. Death is better than boredom.'

'The collapse of the world,' says Gurt in his deep monotone, 'is not a tornado that lifts up cities, it is not a deluge of flame, but an endlessly proliferating nowhere, in which we do nothing, over and over again, forever.'

Awful, bleak silence.

'I've decided I'm famous now,' says Stephen, 'which cures all problems.'

Silence reigns still, but its power has been adequately challenged.

'You guys should try it! It's a responsibility, I admit, but life is about feeling good about yourself first and foremost, and you can't feel good about yourself if you haven't achieved a status and lifestyle recognised as desirable by the mass media—it's as simple as that.'

We laugh, not because it's that funny, but because we need relief from Adam and Gurt.

Yeah, I like Stephen. I don't even mind him having all those tasty girlfriends. But then I wonder; perhaps we should be addressing Gurt's misery and Adam's alienation directly?

Adam leaves and we watch after him anxiously.

'Who's on suicide watch tonight?' asks Gurt.

'I'll do it,' I say.

'I thought Adam liked his job,' says Piscina.

'Evidently not.'

Adam works for a company called *:Rising* in Brixton; he's a photographer for their hip magazine *Rebl*, which calls itself 'the voice of the postmodern revolution.' Their first revolutionary target is the letter 'e'. After that, realism, the 'right' and religion. Adam's revolutionary task is to take photographs of skinny models in Pretty Polly stockings standing next to burning vagrants or blowing bored kisses at riot police. They're allowed to get drunk in the *Rebl* office, wear gorilla suits and stick it to the man, but Adam, it seems, is not finding all that so very liberating.

'You should see the girls he photographs,' I say, 'but he never manages to pull any.'

'He lacks game,' says Stephen.

'What's game?' asks Piscina.

'Well, it's a post-game world now,' he says. 'There was a ten-year window of game, where everyone—not everyone, men—were learning to be pickup artists. Projecting confidence, establishing hook, noting indicators of interest, overcoming resistance, negging, kino…'

'What's negging kino?'

'Negging is putting girls down in a friendly way and kino is non-sexual touching; there's a whole body of thought about that, when to do it, how much…'

Piscina is fascinated. 'It sounds like cultural theory.'

'Yeah, it is. They're both about naked power. And they're both mainstream now. The new thing though is post-game, where you don't do any of that.'

'Just be yourself,' says Piscina.

'God no! Who would want to be themselves?'

'So who are you?'

'The post-game answer is; I don't know. I don't know who I am, I don't know who she is, I don't know what a damn thing actually is and I certainly don't know what I'm supposed to do; but that's all alright. We'll find out together. Now get your frock off.'

'You make it sound easy,' I say.

'It takes practice,' he says, 'or age.' He throws up his hands, 'I don't know do I!'

One thing I've noticed about Stephen is, for all his charm and chatter, he doesn't like to be the centre of attention, on the spot. It makes him paranoid. He'd prefer to chuck little bits of food into the collective pot, from a distance. If you turn to him and say 'what are we cooking anyway?' he'll say 'I thought you knew!'

'Somehow you have to wear down the desperation though,' he says, 'Desperation is repellent at the cellular level.'

'So is awkwardness,' I say.

'Yeah, that too. Jesus, yes, the awkwardness. I wouldn't be ten years younger for anything. I couldn't confidently buy a book in my twenties. Although I still have problems with that actually. They *know*, don't they, people in bookshops?'

While Stephen has been talking, Piscina has been making 'shall we be getting a move on?' signals to Gurt, but he pretends not to understand, and now that Stephen has stopped she sucks in a lungful, eyes widening, and says, 'well, I have to be on my way.'

She leaves to get her coat, Gurt pulls his body onto its feet.

'What you doing tonight?' asks Stephen.

Gurt shrugs, bored, mimes a slow wank and slouches out.

'Does anyone, *anywhere* have an unfucked-up relationship?' asks Stephen after they've left. I move over to the sagging leather armchair and Stephen stretches his legs out on the now vacated sofa, looking up at the ugly Mondrian print we've got on the wall.

'I've not seen one.'

'I'm ready to hang up my dreams and just go with the best option, the best team player.'

'Really? Are you?'

'No.'

'You've got to hope though, haven't you?'

'Hope leads to desperate hope.'

'I joined a dating site a few days ago.'

'Oh yeah? Seen anyone nice?'

'Well, of all the girls on there who've faved me the prettiest ones write least and write the sharpest. It's a depressing fact. I mean it's understandable, but that's why it's depressing.'

'They have a lot of mails to write.'

'They do, they do.'

'Us sperms, in our masses; most of us perish.'

'It is our fate to end up in the teat of a condom.'

'They do write to someone though,' says Stephen. 'There will be one lucky winner.'

'I don't think it will be me.'

'Why not?'

'Well, I'm not good looking for one thing.'

'Yes you are. You're just not your type.'

'I'm skinny, bony, prematurely balding…'

'You've got more hair on your balls than you'll ever have on your head.'

'What does that mean?'

'You'd be surprised how far character will get you.'

Perhaps I haven't given this enough thought.

'Last night,' I say, 'I was chatting with a girl on there, and I was feeling saggy and mouldy from all the work I'd done and I listed these things, saggee, mouldee, deadlee and I said 'what ee are you tonight?' and she writes back saying 'I am feeling cluckee. I just saw the movie 'Knocked Up.' Wanna knock me up?'

'Blimey.'

'Which is different to all the polite playful lines I usually get on there.'

'Too right.'

'It was like playing chess. Hmmm, now I wasn't expecting *that* move, what to do next?

Stephen sits up. 'What did you say?'

'She's a redhead, so, well, I wish I'd simply said: "red beaver", that would have been perfect.'

'Would it?'

'She would have enjoyed the surprise. I mean "red beaver". It breaks the rules right?'

Stephen is shaking his head rapidly. 'Does it? How?'

'Well would you expect a description of your genitals so soon?'

Stephen leans back, pondering up at the ceiling, 'Question: Do you want to have sex with me? Answer: Your twat is red.'

'Yes!' I say excitedly, 'Exactly! Exactly!'

'Erm... okay... but go on, what did you say?'

'I said, I put, "I already have—did you really not feel a thing—a smooth operator me".'

Stephen's wild laughter fills the room. 'Hahahahaha! What? That's fucking awful!'

'You mean you disagree with the move, knight takes c4?'

He sighs, 'For me the moves are not chess, but some other

game I have never played, perhaps which doesn't exist in this dimension. For all I know the correct response is a beachball down the toilet or a series of whooping sounds.'

'No, the answer is red beaver, I assure you.'

'I'll take your word for it.'

We sit in silence for a bit. I feel annoyed, put on, failed and resentfully young.

'So what would you have said then?' I ask with a touch of sulk.

'Oh, erm, I dunno. Let's see. Ask me.'

'Alright, wanna knock me up?'

'As in make you pregnant, or whack up over your tits?'

'Love the universe together, bodily.'

'Yep, I'll be round in 5.'

•

I spend an hour zimming through pictures of girls. It's a miracle of human judgement, walking into a room in which there are twenty thousand members of the opposite sex, and instantly assessing each one of them for mating potential.

No. No. No. No. No. No. No. Err, no. No. No. No. No. Hold on—(check other photos)—no. No. Definitely *not*. No. No. No. Oh dear, no. Hold on, hmm, mmayyyybe...

I send off a few jaunty emails to my 'E-ros matches.' Not desperate, not awkward, that's theme of the hour, although I do have my doubts about worldbrain dating. There is something tragically literal about it. I know, for example, there are a lot of girls here, online, who will instantly reject me; girls that, in the real world would be interested, listen, be curiously attracted, consent to a date and spend a couple of hours chatting, before rejecting me.

JesusfuckingchristthoughIwanttofucksomeone.

I'm considering looking at dirty pictures when there's a knock on the door. Toby comes in. I've got a seat for guests now—another wheelchair. They are very comfortable.

'What you up to?' he asks, not really caring.

'Shopping.'

I swing my wheelchair around to face his, two able-bodied men in cripple's chairs, on a bare floor, like an avant-garde play. 'What happened?'

'It started off okay...' he mumbles into his belly.

'First off, how did it happen?'

'Sarah suggested it. I didn't think Vicky would go for it, but she was interested, she wanted to. Bored I suppose. We ate first. Sarah made us Thai chicken...'

'What to?'

'Hm?'

'Nothing, go on.'

'We ate, and it was alright, and then we went to bed.'

I feel tight, images of Vicky's superb carriage fogging up the old brain box.

'...but then it got weird. The atmosphere wasn't right at all—not all loving and decadent and frolicky, not like I'd imagined, but hesitant and distracted. They were sizing each other up, I think, or maybe nobody was quite sure what to do. I got off with Vicky for a bit, then Sarah, then they kind of fiddled with each other, and I took Sarah, because she happened to be closest, or I tried to—the problem was I watched an anatomy documentary last night, The Autopsy it was called; where this guy cut out the sex organs of a male and a female, put 'em on a table and then systematically took them apart, all the... all the... My God, just... a plate of meat. Cock meat, Cunt meat... and that... it was still on my mind. All I could see was the meat, the anatomy...'

'"Flesh puppets" Gurt calls us.'

Toby is staring at his hands. 'Right! It's just MEAT! Meat, meat, *meat*. That's all, big deal. Anyway, no, Gurt's right, not very arousing. Took a while to get it up, and then all I could think was *"don't come, don't come, don't come."* It was a real effort, hard to enjoy, but she got there, I think, so I went over to Vicky and I thought "oh the pressure's off now" and came immediately, which made me burst out laughing.'

'Why?'

'Well I do, when I ejaculate, laugh.'

'But why?'

'I don't know. I just do.'

His voice is all tight and pleady.

'I have to explain this to girls,' he says morosely, 'but for some reason Vicky burst into tears, and that set off Sarah who started having a go at me for upsetting Vicky and for manipulating them both into it.'

'Did you?'

'No! I didn't manipulate anyone—it was her idea!'

Yep, always the victim, Toby. I'm kind of glad it went badly. Part of me wants to see my friends fail; and when I say 'part of me' I mean 'all of me' when they fail with girls I fancy.

'It got ugly after that, Vicky started bringing up old stuff, Sarah said I had no loyalty, and then before I knew it she was hitting me over the head with her false leg, which broke—the heel bit pinged off, Vicky said I was pathetic and then the both of them left.'

'Yeah, I saw them.'

Toby looks at me, all pleady, 'at least they've made friends.'

I feel a well of rage. He *is* pathetic.

'I can't shake the feeling that all this relationship business is just not right… that it's a compromise and a lie. But I don't understand what exactly is being compromised, or what the lie is.'

'You!' I cry, *'you're* the lie. What's *wrong* with you?'

I want to beat him up—the thought actually crosses my mind. Give him a good kicking. Some part of me distantly wonders 'why?' but the hatred is overwhelming, rushing through me; it's making my eyeballs quiver.

'Don't you *want* to be happy?' I say.

He's a skewered worm, a wriggling little homunculus on an almighty fork, and I'm force-feeding him peanuts. He wants to suffer, and I'm fulfilling that role.

'You're the reason for all this,' I say, 'it's *you*.'

'What? What's got into you? I don't need this!'

'Fuck off!'

He gets up, shakily, and fumbles in his pocket. He pulls out my wallet and says 'I saw Lauren today, she said to give this to *you*.'

He tosses it on the floor and leaves. Then he comes back and says 'and this,' and throws my sock on the floor too.

My tendons feel like catgut. I pick up the wallet and open it—maybe she's left a cute little note? But no.

Fuck her! Fuck 'em all! Fuck everyone! Either, they're either beady little birdmen, all watchful and blinking, or bland pap-people, or, or you know, all these self-proclaimed realists who are actually abrasive and depressing hardcore cynics? Or just absolute nutcases? Everyone is into shutdown of flow, that's the thing, stifling the space, the inner freedom. *Them*. It's all really a weird menacing power-play, like some life-draining demiurge is watching through their eyes, waiting to pounce, waiting to show you that, oh, you know the friendly thing we had going? Well, actually, yes, it was all about me after all.

Shivering still with a nauseous tension I sit back in the wheelchair and arch my back until my neck is against the outer curve of the handle. I push the muscles of my neck against the chrome tube, but it's not enough…

There's a knock at my door. It's Jonas.

'Daniel, do you have the wi-fi password?'

'Christ all right,' I bitterly pull a post-it off my computer and give it to him.

'Thank you,' he goes to leave, but I stop him.

'Jonas, erm, actually, could you do me a favour?' I ask.

'Perhaps.' Very precise is Jonas. Checked shirts immaculately ironed, his jeans turned up precisely four centimetres, 'flow and comb' looks machine-made and his room, which Jacqui soiled, is a wonder of perfectly white, perfectly clean order, like a vector graphic. He's designing the perfect kettle at the moment—rapid heating, cool to the touch, multi-temperature and a soft sighing 'ping.' I suppose we all live in the rooms we need to live in to do what we need to do—in Jonas' case, design a perfect kettle, in my case, nothing.

'Could you push your thumbs here and here, really hard?' I point to the very top of the back of my neck, the little cave where the muscles disappear behind the skull.

'Daniel, I'm not sure about this.'

Jonas is not at all comfortable with physical contact, and, also, he's a bit afraid of me.

'Just for two seconds.'

He carefully puts the post-it in his pocket and I sit down in wheelchair #2 with my head bent forward. He presses his thumbs against the muscle.

'Up a bit, up a bit, in the divot, right, now *push*. Harder. *Harder!*'

Jonas' thumbs dig savagely into my cords. Something is bending, straining, reaching a limit. *'Push!'*

A final jab and it snaps, an oily crunch in the back of my head. Relief echoes across my shoulder-blades and some kind of amber liquid leaks down my spine. I collapse forward with an 'uff!'

'Okay?'

'Yeah, thanks,' I mumble.

'Can I go now?'

'Yeah.'

He leaves, returning to Age of Empires, and I weep. Weird empty weeping—not crying, not sorrow, not anything.

Toby *is* a fool, but there was no need for that was there? I was in a good mood. It's been a good day. Goodish. Something black slipped through the back door at some point, something poisonous, and now I want to push it away.

I turn back to my computer and launch 'Second Me,' a virtual world simulator that's been sitting on my desktop for a while. The first thing to do is build and dress my avatar. I create a man with short legs, big belly, skinny arms, oversized hands and a huge bulbous head with squirts of wispy hair and big sad eyes. I name him—Halfman— put him in a nappy and send him sliding off into the digital universe.

I walk Halfman around the Las Vegas-style streets and smooth grass gardens and eerie, flat beaches. Stark, frozen faces zoom up to me and skid rapidly away. Millions on here, apparently, and millions more gaming—why don't people notice the nightmarish quality of CGI faces? Fixed eyes, frictionless faces, bizarre, unnatural jerk of mouth and white of teeth. It's getting better, I know that, more 'lifelike,' but most of the 'lifelike' people I meet in the real world freak me out for the same reason.

Oh yes, that reminds me. Adam. I turn off Second Me, return to First Me, go downstairs and knock on his door.

No answer.

'Adam?'

Pause. 'What?'

'Can I come in?'

'Yes,' he says, with an 'if you must' subtone.

Adam's room is dark—always dark—but for red lights which reach up behind tall shelving units neatly stacked with videos,

CDs, DVDs, comics and hard drives. He is sitting in his 'starship captain' gaming chair in front of three 55-inch TV screens playing Grand Theft Auto. He pauses—a spray of smoke and gunfire bursting from a black Mercedes—and looks at me with set black slits.

'You alright?'

'Sixth tier: facilitator.'

'What? No, I mean, here, in the real world.'

'Real world?'

'Yes, you know, where your body is.'

He looks at me for a long time.

'Fine,' he says, eventually.

'I thought you were going to kill yourself.'

'I'm too bored to kill myself.'

'Right you are. Well let me know if you're going to do it, I'd like to say goodbye.'

He turns back to the screen, and I leave.

I pause in the hallway. Outrageous screams of sexual abandon, and deep laboured grunts, are coming from behind Jacqui's door. The screams are Eddie's, the grunts Jacqui's.

I'm ready to crawl into a hole, but some irresistible inner urge is still sniffing out society, looking for human warmth, someone to say 'hello,' which means 'you exist,' so I head downstairs, towards voices.

Naeema is sitting in the kitchen with a friend of hers, Christie; a flushed, inflated Australian. I say hello in a 'you exist' way and they say hello back in an 'oh dear, I'd forgotten that you exist' way, and so I make myself a pretext tea, as in; tea is why I'm down here, not love, because that would be weird!

'It all comes down to our bodies,' says Naeema in her tense, throaty voice.

'It's voyeuristic,' says Christie, in hers.

'Men are judged on who they are, not what they look like,

so he can get away with that kind of statement.'

I dip in; 'What are you talking about?'

Naeema's having a bit of a hard time of it at the moment. She goes for effeminate doe-eyed men with ambiguous sexuality and 'beautiful hearts,' and she made a bit of a mistake by finding herself with one who pretty much fit the template, but who was a strict Christian and, hence, celibate. 'On paper I'm fine with it,' she'd told Jacqui (who then told all of us), but had discovered, as we all do, that while in theory 'in theory' and 'in fact' are the same, in fact, they're different. Apparently, she used to flog him off to just before climax and then he'd have to go for a run, which is why he always brought his tracksuit and trainers round. In the end she'd had enough, but I sometimes see Hugo tearing round the Rye at 2am, so I suppose he's found someone else.

Anyway, Naeema tells me that one of the Goldsmith students is submitting for his degree show a painting of himself raping a prostitute.

'A real prostitute,' she says, her dark little eyes triumphant.

'Was the rape real?'

'All sex is a form of rape,' says Christie, 'at least potentially.'

'Maybe he was being ironic?' I suggest, tentatively.

'That's what he's claiming of course, but if he was a woman he'd never get away with ironic rape.'

I think he might, but I don't want to prod further. They'll only get upset. Most people know just enough to have an opinion—if you probe beyond that, they'll hate you. Naeema already hates me, but not yet very obviously. Won't be long though.

She's rich, upper middle. She went to a twenty-grand-a-year boarding school, became anorexic, made a half-hearted attempt at suicide, went to a mental home for a few months—just long enough to get a 'troubled past' and a nice little mental illness—discovered feminism, and hasn't looked back.

I make my excuses and climb back to my godless monastery.

I'm afraid of Naeema, and her feminist, gay-rights, anti-racism, anti-plastic, pro-muesli friends. A few years ago I thought, alright, yes, women and gays need rights, good on 'em. But now they seem scary to me. They're just so sure that they're the goodies, and when you ask for details, they tell you to read a book.

I look again in the wallet. Maybe I missed something? Lauren's mysterious. Maybe she hid a message in there somehow.

But no; just a five pound note and a library card.

I log into Sprak. Her little button is green, online.

'Hello,' I write.

Long pause.

'Hello.'

'How are you?' I ask.

'Shit.'

'Why?'

'You really are an idiot, Daniel. You think you're clever, but you don't have a clue.'

'Tell me, what's wrong?'

Pause.

'I was fine with my own problems,' she writes, 'and now I have yours.'

'You don't have my problems. Don't be so melodramatic.'

'Why don't you like me?'

'I do like you.'

'Strange way you have of showing it.'

'I just want to see other girls.'

'What? Why?'

I think about this. Careful Daniel! You might be walking into a trap here. 'You like cheesecake,' I write, 'it would be horrible to only ever eat cheesecake for the rest of your life wouldn't it?'

Long pause.

'I'm not a cheesecake.'

Laurenonthemoon is offline.

I sit back and look around my empty room. A crumpled up pair of jeans lies over the back of my spare wheelchair. I should do my washing, but for some reason the thought of doing this, of having to do it, fills me with a sense of hopelessness, of terrible apathy. So I wash my clothes; and then what? They'll get dirty again. Doing my laundry will not lead to joy. Only a girlfriend will, *she*—but where is she? Why is she not here? I'm a good guy, funny, sensitive, I can make sorbet...

I might as well have a wank. The thought makes my heart beat a little faster, a pleasant-yet-unpleasant demanding momentum.

'I won't actually masturbate,' I think, 'I'll just take a little look. One quick look. Just to see what it's like.'

I turn my browser to private—I don't know why; no doubt the FBI right this moment are getting ready to watch me beat myself off—type in the dreadwords 'fleshtube' and plunge myself into a horn of lecherous plenty, a million different women—all expressions the same.

In fact that is what I look for in porn, by far the most erotic element, is a face, a living expression, which looks human; a soft, steady, connected eye with a glistening, living point of light, instead of that weird, flat, workmanlike drone-state. 'The lights are on but nobody's home'—but you *are* the light. That's what makes eyes flexible and aqueous, that gives them the gleam. That's what makes me think that these girls have dropped their torches down a drain.

I open up one tab after another, edging between them, but none quite do it for me, none of these girls seem quite into it enough, into *me* enough, so I close my eyes and think of Sophie, Sarah, Rachel, Lisa, Tuesday, Vicky, that girl in Boots the chemist; every girl I have ever known long enough to enjoy the idea of flashes over the fleshtube of my mind's eye—a porn ball of liquid female forms, relentless.

I feel myself coming, and want it to be over the right image, an ecstatic Ravenous-Nympho, or that girl in the HSBC adverts, or Piscina on a trapeze, but as the rush rises the Pope pops into my mind, get out! think of anything, planet earth, corn flakes, the Italian flag… I ejaculate to a stuffed gold-beaked crow; but I don't care what I am looking at, or thinking about, and as the pleasure—if you can call it that—subsides, don't care remains. Void of wanting, my charred body is a hollow meat silo. I know it's not fashionable to be ashamed but, as I bundle my semen up into a tissue, I can't avoid the feeling; stretched tight over the surface of myself, thin, so thin, over the poisonous scooped-out husk where I used to be. An astronaut who has masturbated out of a porthole, sadly watching pearls of sperm float into the cold infinite vastnesses of space, and the space is me.

The screen is still heaving and humping with raw meat, pop-up pneumatics with stretched anuses screaming and a blinking advert, 'Feeling shit? Phone now and we'll credibly insult you—cunt,' which is not the normal thing. The reasonable part of me, on the surface with the pain says 'why would anybody want that?' while a deeper element feels drawn in, in need of a good telling off. God, I'm not a masochist am I?

I turn on Sprak and, mechanically, before voice of reason can interrupt, I punch up the number. Yes, why not?

'Hello?' comes a jaded woman's voice, digitally warped a little by our overloaded bandwidth.

'Yes, I'm… er…'

'You want to be insulted?'

'Do you mind?'

'No, just jerked off have you?'

'Yeah. How did you know?'

'Fucked yourself. That's what you've done.'

'Yes.'

'Why don't you get yourself a girlfriend?'

'I can't, I don't have...'

'The balls.'

'Perhaps not.'

'You're not man enough to get a girl, or stay with one, that's the problem isn't it?'

'Yes, you're right. How do you know this?'

'You're pathetic. Pathetic.'

'I am, but is there any hope?'

'If you grow a pair, but right now I'd wallow in self-pity if I were you. That's what you normally do isn't it?'

'It is actually.'

'Go on then, sod off.'

'Okay, thanks.'

'You're welcome.'

Bit weird. I do feel a bit better though. Clearly Catholicism was on to something. Perhaps they should try bitter women priests sarcastically putting sinners down for their lack of manly integrity.

But the tightness and bleakness is still here, and the shame too, if somewhat softened now.

Force of habit alone compels me to load up Halfman, who is standing on a glassy beach, next to a glassy sea, waiting for orders.

There's a luxury beach condo up the bluff, with lots of people enjoying a poolside party. I toddle up the driveway and float under the luxury arches into a vast Californian beachside property. Boom-chakka-boom music is playing and tall, slender, symmetrical avatars chat over Champagne. I walk up to a pair, looming over me, and type 'you two look real,' but they don't reply. I go for a simpler 'hello' with the next little group, but nobody replies. Neither does anyone else; some groups turning away before I reach them, others pretending I'm not there. After half an hour of this I walk out, to the back of the condo, where there is some kind of little river, or possibly sewage outlet. I look around—anyone here? No. I walk into the water, up to my head. The little bald brow bobs about for a bit, and the huge hands do a bit of digital thrashing, and then nothing. It's 'dead.' The freakish little body bobs up to the surface, floats downstream and washes up on the cardboard shore, face down in virtual mud.

Frankensheila

I can't seem to enter rooms, or leave them. Something inter-
venes, trying to work out what will happen on the other side. I
fear all the happy laughter I can hear will cease when they see
me, or that I'll be punished for rejecting the mass-mind when I
chinlessly snake out. Ringing phones and filling inboxes give me
the same anxiety. Interview rooms rise up before my projecting
mind like the castle of Otranto.

I am outside Job Centre Plus, walking up and down the
street, blocked, somehow, from just strolling in, paralysed by the
reluctant beast in the throat that never seems to quite go away.

Eventually a moment comes where I just get fed up with
the fear—a moment I seize on to throw myself through the
portal. On the other side a huge bald black guy dressed in a
badly fitting suit is waiting. He says 'Welcome to Jobcentre Plus
Peckham, how can I help you today?' with a curiously unreal
smile, like it's drawn on.

He's one of three bouncers, all with curly phone wires drap-
ing up to an earpiece, receiving commands from the adminis-
trative mothership.

'I've come to sign on,' I say shakily, showing him my crumpled application pack.

'Certainly sir...'

With a gesture of mostly welcome he directs me to the ap-
propriate zone. I sit down on an extremely soft chair between a
tattooed peroxide guy in a wife-beater and a thin, slope-headed
man with a ruined face. Nobody in here is beautiful (except
the people on the Department of Work and Pensions leaflets
of course). Perhaps they have been sanctioned? Wife-beater is
on his mobile,

'I got some bruv, I *got* some. I'll meet you down Luke's, but
listen, oy, Den, I have never had shit like this. Den, it is gonna
fucking *blast* you. It is *Off*.'

Jesus, it's so *hot* in here. Is this to pacify us?

Ahead of me, before the life-giving desk of fair judgement,
an existence-exhausted mixed-race woman is cradling her head
in her worn hands.

'But I *applied* for three,' she says.

'The working week starts on a *Tuesday*,' says the obese,
black jobcentre advisor with a 'patiently explaining for the
hundredth time' tone; 'and you applied for *three* last week and
three on Monday, which means only two this week. The rules
clearly stipulate that failure to meet the quota that you agreed
must result in a thirteen week sanction.'

'What am I going to do for thirteen weeks without money?'
says the woman.

'There's a form you can fill in.'

'I want to speak to your manager.'

The fat woman shrugs and turns around, 'Graham,' she
says, wearily.

Are all managers called Graham?

A stumpy bald man with a beautiful little red mouth appears beside her, they talk quietly for a while and he *calmly* explains the rules to the woman, who begins to emotionally escalate. The *lovely* security guard is called over and the woman is *gently* escorted out.

Next up is Wife-beater.

'Have you done any work in the past fourteen days?' asks the advisor, very slowly.

'Nah, bin *sick*.'

'You don't look sick, you're wearing hair gel.'

The stoic to my right turns to me.

'You in first time?' he asks in a Russian accent, nodding to my forms.

'Yes.'

'I give advice.' He hardly moves as he talks. Eyebrows, cheeks, shoulders, hands—immobile. The bottom lip alone quivers as his straightforward words emerge from the pit of his stomach.

'Alright.'

'First you do not give them your cv. They will ask it, but you do not have to give—it is personal data. Show, but do not give. Hold hard or they strike.' He blinks. 'Second, your jobmatch profile—you filled this?'

'No.'

'Good. Do not tick DWP box, or they will send many evil emails. It is hard to find, little box, but find it because DWP will fuck you in arse through little box.'

'Okay, I should write this down,' I take out my sketch pad.

'Third, tell them you kill advisor, or wife.' I reflexively check his cheeks for irony, but they are clock-like literal. He nods slightly towards his advisor, a huffy, beaverish man at the next desk down. Then he looks at me, very carefully, up and down. 'You are not violent man. Blackmail also good. Hire private detective.'

'Sounds a bit much.'

'This is time for a bit much,' he says.

A shouty explosion. Wife-beater has lunged across the desk at his advisor, hands round her throat, tightening her scream to flapping gurgles. Security pour in from all directions, shouts of calamity and fuck-you-fuck-you and phones held up. He's skinny, Wife-beater, but it takes three huge men to pin him against the tottering desks, arm-lock and drag him through the office. *'How's that fer fuckin' aspiration!'* he shouts. The advisor is huffing and warbling, a swarm of Grahams emerge from trapdoors.

While order is restored my Russian mentor—Andrey his name is—explains that London is entering the first stage of collapse, which involves wiping out 'superfluous to requirement.'

'They have quota,' he says, 'Advisors must sanction five people in week or they lose pay, or must retrain, or get red mark of death.'

'What happens to the five sanctioned people?'

He shrugs. 'Free world. Work or die.'

'And this is the first stage of collapse is it?'

Andrey nods to a poster. A joyous young woman beams radiantly at us. Underneath it says 'I'm really pleased they cut my benefits, because it encouraged me to redraft my cv. It's going to help me when I'm ready to go back to work. Poppy.' The slogan at the bottom of the poster reads *'Change your mindset. Unemployment is a lifestyle choice.'*

'You see?' he says.

'Sir?' The desks are back to order and my advisor is more or less composed. I sit down—another very comfy chair—and Latonqua (for it is she) looks at me with naked, dehumanising contempt. Her lip, the corner of which cradles a bead of saliva, actually curls.

'Now then…' she begins, with a 'must we go over this *again*' sigh, and tells me that I must apply for twelve jobs a week and record my 'positive actions' in my ES4JP 'job hunting log,' I must be continually available for work, I must attend advisor meetings—which I'll be notified of through text or phone…

'I don't have a phone.'

'You don't have a phone?' The confused heap of her face collapses around a solid, superdense polyp of fear.

'No.'

Latonqua gathers her composure and shrugs, 'Well you'll have to get one.'

'Are you going to buy me one?'

Sighing heavily, 'no, but you're going to find it very difficult to get a job without one.'

'I don't want a phone.'

She strains her neck one degree to the right, calls Graham over and explains the problem to him.

'*Why?*' he says, wearily, clearly expecting me to put a colander on my head.

Well, for a start I look at a screen enough as it is, and I happen to quite like, you know, the *world*. They make you stressed those things, and stupid. And I also think you'd be fucking stupid to carry a tracking device, a microphone and camera around with you… but I don't say any of this. I just go with; 'I can't afford it.'

He leads forward onto the table, getting serious now. Around his starey little eyes muscles tense—I don't think they are used very much. 'We notify you of your advisor meetings through the phone,' he says, 'If you don't answer, you'll be sanctioned.'

'But I'm not going to answer am I?'

'Then you'll be sanctioned.'

'Can't you just *tell* me when my next advisor meeting will be?'

'No, the times come from the decision makers.'

The decision makers: the beautiful people, sitting around on Eames chairs, in enormous exposed-brick kitchens of unbleached cotton, planning minimalist salad strategies before turning to their laptops, checking my profile, and hitting the 'sanction' button. I think Poppy might secretly be a decision maker.

'So what are we going to do then?'

Graham stands up, hands on hips. 'Can you give us the number of someone you live with?'

I give them Jonas' number.

He exits, glumly appeased, and Latonqua returns to the script. I'll get my rent paid (or rather my landlord will; more forms, and a different office), be allocated 12 pence a week for living expenses and given access to DWP computer terminals. She nods to one of the 'pooters around the room, and says I should start looking today.

I have no intention of working, of course, at least not legally, but for the sake of the form, and in order to put a bit of planet between my nose and Latonqua's stress-sweat, I take a look. Commercial Control Agent, Executive Kitchen Steward, Industrial Cleansing Officer, Sanitary Enhancement Operative… It takes me a while to decode these into security guard, washer-upper, street cleaner, toilet cleaner and other tasks I would prefer not to do, but it is the experience and qualifications required to do them that closes portals I'm glad I don't even have to pretend I want to enter. I don't have a masters in 'evacuation management' and that's that.

I can feel the ceiling descending, the walls closing in; but the humiliating event is just about over so I can escape. On my way out I hear one of the advisors, behind a partition say; 'the third turd over there needs a DLA 1A.'

The outside is a clean, chrome trumpet proclaiming freedom from work, from office, from *that*. Andrey is rolling a cigarette. Next to him is a boy of about eight; buzz-cut, silver necklace, t-shirt, more muscles than me and the same hard, inscrutable, assessing, indomitable face as Andrey. I make a half-step of should-I-thanks-goodbye? and Andrey lifts his eyes down Rye Lane to say 'we walk,' which we do, in silence for a weird little while, before I ask him what he does for a living.

'Windows,' he says. I wait for more. Selling them? Fitting them? Gazing through them, waiting for Natushka to return? I don't ask, and he doesn't tell me, but I'm sure he'd do all three with the same implacable focus, even if he were on fire.

'What is your job?' he asks.

'Artist.'

'Why?'

'It's what I want to do with my life.'

'You rich?'

'Do you think I would be signing on if I was rich?'

'But why do this if no money?'

'I don't care about money.'

'You enjoy being artist this much?'

'I don't enjoy it at all.'

'So why you do it?'

He smiles, I think. His smooth face striates into a lattice of deep wrinkles, somewhere between amusement, confusion and pain. For a moment he looks twenty years older, and then they vanish.

'I have no choice, I must. I... I want more than anything to... to be free... and to make something free, and beautiful. I want to channel beauty into the world. I just don't see why else to be alive.'

He takes a contemplative wincy drag on the last half centimetre of his cigarette. 'I have friend he work sometimes as driver in London,' he says, 'One day he get call, go to such address. It is The Bishop Row, you know this road?'

'Yes.'

'Yes, very rich. He arrive late, one am. Driveway have Ferrari 599xx, Porsche Panamera, Jaguar F-Type Coupe, Lexus LFA, Aston Martin Vanquish; perhaps Bentley Continental, I forget. Four girls come out—four—and they are perfect. They are perfect—you know what this means in Russia? Perfect girl?'

'Yes. Well, yes, I suppose.'

'So he drive to airport, ask 'why you here?' They say they are girlfriends of oligarch. They say he has seven girlfriends. Seven luxury car and seven of God's girlfriends.'

He looks at me with, it seems to me, paternal simplicity, '*This* is why else to be alive.'

'If I had one of God's girlfriends I'd spend seven years in bed, just looking at her.'

'Ahhh. I see. You don't fuck.'

'Not much, no.'

'I give you gift,' he says, 'to help you.'

We have stopped on the corner of Rye Lane. Andrey starts to speak, but, hold on,

'Where is your son?'

Andrey looks around, without concern, 'I don't know,' he says blankly.

'He was here.'

'I know.' He looks at me; why am I talking about this? There are more important matters.

'First thing, simple trick,' he goes on, brushing aside my bizarre interest in the whereabouts of the boy, 'Asda superstore on Old Kent Road; you know?'

'Yes.'

'There is also Halfords, and PC World.'

'Yeah?'

'You go to these places. Also Ikea in Bromley—large superstore—and choose expensive item you want. Write down barcode. Take very cheap item you don't want. Write down barcode. Go home, download barcode generator, print out barcode for cheap item and print on sticker. Go to shop again, stick cheap barcode on expensive item, over barcode. Go to till with most bored person. Pay cheap price.'

'Will this help me get a woman?'

'No. *This* is for woman.'

He hands me a thin plasticky business card which, next to an image of a snake in a heart shape, eating its own tail, the words, in a surprisingly tasteful typeface, 'Original Sin Escorts.'

'These best girls in London, believe me. Not best, but good for you. Reasonable price, clean and friendly; not place of evil.'

•

Raw electric light, bright red modular shelving and chip-pine dividers; PC World is jostle-full of leggings and tracksuits. 70% of the customers are overweight. While I'm standing at the printers a young boy, three or four, toddles over. I smile at him. His mother—pretty but crushed, holding a boxed web-cam— sees me smiling at her son and calls for her Robbie, who wilfully totters off. She, creases on her forehead, voice flutter-ing, mouth-only smile to show ha-ha! she's not *that* frustrated, picks him up and he starts screaming and writhing in her hands, knocking over a stack of promotional leaflets for body monitors ('for you or your staff').

I turn back to the task at hand. The choice here is over-whelming. If only there was just one good thing, and I could have that. I do actually feel intimidated by consumer choice. No, more than intimidated, actively persecuted.

'Can I help you?'

I turn. Even before I've taken her in am hovering with adrenaline. She is tall—as tall as me—and slim with thick hazely hair and serene blue eyes. Characterful mouth—one too many teeth—excellent bearing—nice and straight—with a big nose—the nose of a girl who does dangerous things, who probably wants me to doodle over her long back and fuck her in chocolate.

Yes! This is the One! The witchy-pixie She-for-Me, who will save me, and I—less importantly—her. She dances madly to classic beats, bends over warm rocks in remote forests and shares anecdotal information about the nature of the universe.

My eyes try to convey epochal recognition while my mouth asks if, erm, this comes with a guarantee? She—Ruth declares the name tag—says yes, she thinks so and takes the labelling machine, furrowing over the small print. My brain is repeating the same message, over and over again; 'say something *funny*.' I'm trying to think of what, but can only think I can't think of anything. She hands the box back to me and says, 'two years I think.'

'Two years is a long time—in show business.'

She smiles cautiously and says 'anything else?'

'No,' I say, swallowing reflexively.

Show business? Why? Oh Lord the number of times I have fallen foul of just trying to find something interesting or funny to say. The woman wondering why I said it.

The situation is slipping away from me, my hand is drifting up to my chin.

'Actually,' I blurt, 'a frightening Russian man I just met just told me how to get loads of cheap gear for nothing by printing out false bar-codes. He said this wouldn't help me get a girl-friend, but fuck it, right? you never know.'

The effect of this dose of honesty is magical. The strain in her posture leaks away and she looks at me… perhaps even *impressed?*

'I'm not sure I can help you with either of those things,' she says.

Now what do I say? A second honest thing? It's another game of chess, but this one on a galloping horse at midnight. Her posture now has, it seems to me, a *slight* taste of 'let's see what you've got' to it. Or perhaps I'm panicking that up.

'You're not impressed with men who own a great many electronic devices?'

'Not really.'

'And yet here you are working in PC World.'

I want this to sound sympathetic, perhaps 'ah the irony of life!' but somehow it comes out as patronising and competitive. Wrong move! Wrong move!

She sighs, 'well, if there's nothing else,' and moves away, to Tibet, and I curse my inept brain in the office supplies department as my soul mate, the only woman I could ever really care for, dies in my arms.

I should leave now; she might be on her way to rat on me to the police. Or maybe not. Maybe she'll just look at me, which would be worse. I watch her walk away, blood draining from my face, I should pursue, this is my last chance, ever, she will *never* be mine. I walk fast, waddling, sweating, until I am behind her.

'Excuse me.'

She turns, a shade of irritation, or fear, flashes across her.

'Erm, would you like to ha...' I gulp, reflexively, mid-word, '...ave a drink with me some time?'

'I have a boyfriend,' she says with instant, reflexive finality.

Maybe she smiles, maybe she's nice about it, I don't know. 'Oh, okay, lucky guy,' I blurt and turn, run almost, from the store.

Outside, shaken, but still manically plotting, I consider dribbling back to have another shot, or maybe running in and giving her a piece of paper asking her out in some superior poetic manner, or I could wait for her to finish work and casually bump into her?

I walk round to the tradesman's entrance to assess this option, but the rear approach road is lined with bins and somehow that seems unromantic. The day is grey and the sky hopeless. There is nobody and nothing here, just warehouses and tarmac, the high, bleak wind of the Old Kent Road and true love lost for eternity. I stand next to a double-wheelie overflowing with display boxes and consider my state of affairs.

I pick up one of the empty boxes, for a digital drawing pad, and read through the specs, not really taking any of it in. I am dreadful with women. That's the fact. With Lauren I sometimes felt perceptive, charming even, but that's because she was so into me. Or, no, it's because I didn't *care* with Lauren. I wasn't trying to fuck her—and when I was; well, look where that got me!

My brain seems to think that this is the perfect time and place, in the wasted, howling, anus of a south London business park, to review my sexual prowess, my charm, my 'game' and my romantic life generally. Under a sign which reads 'these waste containers are for commercial use only' a montage of ghosts of girlfriends past plays the main themes of my love story; missed cues, missed chances, stupid comments, frantic, frustrating set backs, will she write back tonight? tomorrow? ludicrous posturing and put-downs, confusion before alien logic, blind, utterly overwhelming excitement, mysterious vaginas, premature ejaculation, instant boredom, captious bile, consoling wanks and need, always need. I see Lauren and Sophie and Sarah and Rachel and Ruth, the demiurge, the dark one, peering out at me from their mocking eyes, laughing at me with the scorn of all woman. I taste poisonous alkali on their skin, I smell rancid apples... but, oh no, that's the wheelie bin.

I *did* have one moment of success back there though, when I said what was really on my mind. Jesus though, what a risk; how can I possibly say what is really on my mind to a woman?

But then, how can I not?

Cheque and Pawn, WHSmiths, Peckham Afro Foods and *Many Items*, Big Girl, BetFred, Sabrina Beauty, the Fishcoteque, Curl up and Dry, and Chinese Herbal where, Jacqui tells me, you can get a hand-job for £40 (seems a bit pricey?). A heavy-set bearded and masculine Turk, standing at the doorway of his hairdressing establishment sighs a surprisingly high-pitched sigh. I pass a kid, too old for his pushchair, who looks mildly up at me, while his mother's eyes suspicion from under her burka. I pass a squad of black schoolgirls, impeccably dressed, and a massive Nigerian woman in a billowy white taffeta gown and turban, and a pockmarked Caribbean casino owner? priest? wearing all black with red braces and a bright red pork-pie hat. Concert and rave posters, forty layers thick, hang from the bricked and boarded walls and the smell of old leather and dried foodstuffs wafts from the neon-lit shops which are all dirty yellow, because I suppose yellow looks good in Ghana, but not in Peckham. Not in Peckham.

The general atmosphere is tight, stressed, screwed-up, aggressive and black, as is the hateful music that fires out from slowly cruising bass-cannons. It seems impossible to believe that these people once listened to gentle reggae, moogy highlife and silly funk. Nowadays it's hipsters who listen to that stuff, the little 'community' of hyperbland designers and artists that I spend my weekends avoiding, who, even now, are huddled in the poshed up containers behind Rye Lane, listening to Johnny Nash and William Onyeabor, while a wrathful black universe, largely comprised of Johnny and William's children, encircles them, waiting for their moment.

The Mumbling Man approaches, polished, peanut-headed and clearly brain-damaged. As he passes me I turn on my heels and quick step to his shoulder, craning forwards—he smells of armpits and glove compartments—to catch the sense of his sotto voce stream of consciousness.

'Twenty five degrees, possibly warmer, high pollen, areas of low cloud and fog towards evening, temperature dropping to an unseasonable fourteen degrees overnight, low chance of rain…'

I turn, back into the deep-fried river of despair, pushing myself past the hard, dark, Bakelite bodies. The evil is descending, the sickening sense, again, that I am living in a two-dimensional topological film, spread over a plummeting void, the very substance of death, seeping into the flesh of the world. I say 'living,' but I don't mean that.

I pass into the murderously overheated 'Everything Too Cheap!' where I buy ten kilos of flour, five kilos of salt, a tin of wallpaper paste, a huge bucket and a surprisingly middle-class wrapping paper. Then over into Ozzie's Coffee Shop and Sandwich Bar to take a rest from Out There.

It's soviet-basement dark; cracked tiles, peeling lino and aluminium chairs cold to the kidneys. There's just me and a plucked couple. He—pale, plump and fidgety— faces she— toothy, curly and bored—across the laminated table. She's watching something on her phone and he cranes over to take a look, 'ah,' he says, cheerily, 'watching the soaps?'

She pulls her earbuds out 'Yes' she says tetchily, 'I can watch a soap-opera if I want can't I?'

He says nothing. The waitress—Spanish I think—comes with my coffee. She slaps it on my table with jobcentre warmth. I fiddle with my box and wrapping paper.

'What shall we have for dinner?' says the guy.

'Well,' says she, with exasperation, 'what do you *want?*'

'When I say the same thing to you, you always say (he adopts an exaggeratedly mopey voice) "what are you asking *me* for?"'

'Well, I don't know!'

'You decide.'

'Why can't you think for yourself for once—like a man?'

'Like a man?'

'Crab!' she yells, and breaks into tears.

The Spanish girl watches them with heavy-lidded detachment.

'There there, there there,' he says, in an exaggerated tone of consolation 'it's all going to be okay.'

'No, it's *not*.'

I finish my coffee and exit. The low grey featureless ceiling that calls itself 'sky,' has gradually turned into a milky, sour, home-store pink. The rush-hour stream is all around, all of us pouring through the streets, in trains and buses, towards our pods and barracks. We're just one big happy family! I am about to cross over onto Rye common when a screech of brakes and shouts of horror detonate to my right. A bus has hit someone on Copeland Road. Folk peer and crowd, taking phone-photos.

I feel a manic urge to run over, 'stand back, I'm an artist!'—but then I spy the crooked leg of the crushed man, and his trousers… and, I know that man.

I shoulder through. 'Igwe…'

'Don't move him!'

'You know this guy?'

'Yes, Igwe, it's me.'

But his head is in an unnatural position. His neck is broken. He is dead, and it is immediately obvious he is dead. Panic and photos all around. The bus driver, a little Asian fellow, is stricken, leaning against his bus, 'he just walked in front of me.'

Some people slip away, everyone else stands hopeless. I look at Igwe, but he's gone. There is no life there. He's all gone, all of him, and the absence is like, like, nothing.

The police turn up and start securing the scene and making notes. I tell one of them—a small, tight woman who speaks from the back of her tight neck—that I knew him.

'Igwe, I don't know his second name. He's a street cleaner.'

'Okay sir, that's useful. We'll follow that up.'

I tell her what happened, what I saw, although that wasn't very much. 'Can I come with you?' I ask her.

'No sir, there's no need, we can trace his family easily.'

'But… I'd like to help.'

'We'll tell his family, sir,' she says with a touch of menace, as if I might leap into the ambulance and throw myself on him.

The death is declared non-suspicious. They take my statement and my details, and I drift away feeling exceptionally narrow.

That's it. Igwe's gone. He was here, and now he isn't. I didn't know him, but I can still feel connections and pathways abruptly severed, a cluster of dead-ends over a black hole which I cannot enter, cannot even look at, because there's no me to look.

What has gone though? And what has come? Something so massive the universe sits in its hands, yet so small you could weigh it on a dealer's scales.

Back home Adam is in the kitchen, staring at the wall.

'Hello,' I say.

No answer.

I put the kettle on and stand at right angles to him, looking out the window at the wall of the neighbour's house. It's an ominous, unright scene, but people should stand unusually in their rooms more often.

'It's not anything,' says Adam, quietly and with strained determination.

'Eh?'

He's silent again. There is something radically different about his face. It's not just a change of mood or more stiffness. The skull is altered in some kind of fundamental way.

'Adam?'

He slowly turns to look at me.

'Adam? Is everything okay?'

'Everything?' he squints.

'You, are you okay?'

'I'm not everything.'

'No, I know, but, I mean, what's wrong mate?'

He smirks, humourlessly. 'You can't get me that way.'

'I'm not trying to get you.'

He nods, slowly and returns to the wall.

'I'll come up in a bit. We can, er, play Mortal Kombat?'

No answer.

I take my tea upstairs. Toby's room is open. I look in. Stephen's there, leaning back on a new beanbag, and Jonas, on Toby's bed.

'How's you?' asks Stephen. He's wearing quite a fancy shirt, cream with little porcelain green flowers.

I sit next to Jonas. Suicidally sombre East-European folk music is playing. I tell them about Igwe, who is absolutely non-existant now.

'I wanted to go with him, but they wouldn't let me.'

'Death must be removed from sight,' says Toby, handing me a joint, 'It's a matter for the Authorities.'

'He said he was cursed, and that I should pay him £420 to lift the curse or I'd be damned too.'

'He said the same to me, I thought it was a scam.'

'I could never work out if he was a con-artist or the Buddha.'

'So you're both cursed now,' says Stephen quite seriously. He's superstitious, Stephen, a 'magic-thinker,' pays a lot of attention to his dreams and is always second-guessing God and saying things like 'If she texts me back in the next hour, it's meant to be.'

'I don't think it will make a whole lot of difference,' I say.

'You could have your leg bitten off,' says Jonas, without irony.

'Alright it can get worse. I just mean it's bad enough now.'

Stephen shrugs, 'we're all cursed.'

'Yes, we are; but what with?'

'Cursed to feel the same thing, every day, over and over again, forever and ever. No new feelings, just microscopic variations of boredom.'

'You're right,' says Toby, 'I need a new feeling. I haven't had one in a long time.'

'It began in 1996,' says Stephen, 'that's when time stopped. It started slowing down in the eighties, but it stopped completely in 1996. Nothing has changed since then, no new culture; just more of it. More of the known.'

'What is wrong with the known?' says Jonas.

'The known is boring,' says Toby, 'what is nice is the surprise, isn't it? the not-known.'

'The known lives,' I say. The joint's with me again.

'But if you are full of the known,' says Stephen, 'then you miss the unknown.'

'Yes, but I mean the known lives. It's made of concrete jelly.'

'But it doesn't have to be your business,' says Toby.

'I just mean,' I say, 'it's all well and good saying the unknown is aces, but it doesn't necessarily stop the known getting its teeth into you, does it? Burning your toast.'

'But we are making the unknown known again.'

'What, right now? Are we?' asks Stephen, all pretend panic.

'By complaining you mean?' I ask.

'No, I mean "oh yeah, the unknown... I know about that".'

'Right; although, for me, it's less that I'm saying "oh right, the unknown, I know about that" and more that I know the known will come back and shit all over me.'

Stephen laughs, 'you know that do you? Doing a bit of knowing, are ya?'

Jonas is sore perplexed. Such talk is painful to him, so he listens politely, thinking that we're idiots, or stoned, or English.

'I don't know,' says Toby, quietly.

'I'm shot away,' said Stephen.

'Have you seen Adam?' I ask.

'Adam needs *a* feeling,' says Stephen.

'He's been down there all day,' says Toby.

'What's wrong with him?'

'I dunno. He said to me 'it's like there's never been anything before.'

'He's losing the plot,' says Stephen,

The minor-key wails from the wasteland behind us.

'Although I do wonder about the plot. Would you go and watch You the Movie?'

'Would I fuck.'

'Brad Pitt stars as you, or…'

'Jimmy Stewart.'

'Okay, Jimmy Stewart. He goes to a school and he doesn't know why, and he moves into a house, and he doesn't know why, and he raises kids and he doesn't know why. And then he dies. The end.'

'Maybe Adam's just left the cinema?' I offer.

'I've lived with him for a year now,' says Toby, 'and I know as much about him as I know about Pac Man.'

'Constantly consuming. Needs power pills to combat ghosts.'

'I think he's just had enough of trying to be normal,' says Stephen, 'I know I have. But then I have a break—I get home from work or talk to someone or have a walk in the park, and I don't have to try anymore. But for Adam there is no break.'

I see. Christ, imagine that; imagine your *whole life* was work. I think of Tiny Whine. Whenever I let a comment out at work, unfiltered, I would actually receive my thoughts as she did; I'd think 'God that guy's weird,' or 'what's he telling me this for?' or 'I'm like, whatever!' These were Tina's thoughts—but I was thinking them, feeling them. Imagine that, but all the time. Imagine *everyone* was your line manager. What would you do? You'd resign. That's what you'd do.

Talk of work has bruised the mood-belly.

'Here,' I say to Toby, 'I got you something. A present.'

I hand over the box. He unwraps it: it's the box for a digital drawing tablet.

'It's empty.'

I explain Andrey's plan to him, and that I'm going to sell electronic goods, and to get him the pad. Jonas is aghast.

'But this is *stealing*,' he says.

'Better than working.'

'I just do not understand this.'

I've tried to explain to Jonas that work is literally hell (painful, meaningless and eternal) and that we're living in virtual prison and all that, but he's having none of it.

'If nobody worked, society would shut down!' he says.

'It's already shutting down.'

'I do not understand why this makes you happy,' he says glumly.

I'm getting excited now. 'It's not happiness, it's relief. Everyone will feel it soon. You know at the end of the Roman Empire they *begged* the Barbarians to come in—and then life got better for ordinary people.'

'The empire never ended,' says Toby.

Naeema puts her head around the door.

'Could one of you come down while I make my dinner? Adam is freaking me out.'

'I will come,' says Jonas, glad to be free of this conversation.

Stephen leaves too. He's meeting an old flame, he says, although he's terrified because she wants to get involved with him; 'it's one thing to abandon a girl who finds you funny, or handsome, or interesting, but it's something completely other to stamp on the heart of someone who actually likes you.'

'I don't think any girl has actually liked me,' says Toby after Stephen has left.

'No result with Vicky and Sarah then?'

He wilts a bit. 'They're moving in together.'

'That's a kind of result.'

'To be fair, I'm not sure I really liked them either.

Toby gets up, changes the record to Kimio Eto, then sits back again. 'Last night,' he says, 'I reviewed all my previous darlings and assembled them, Frankenstein-like, into the woman I'd live and die for. It's quite simple really; she accepts me, doesn't force guilt-trips, envelops me completely in her love but let's me be free, and is a foaming beast-woman in the sack.'

'She's out there. She has to be.'

'Yes, but I have to get myself up to snuff or I'll end up treating her like I did all the others. Very shoddy.'

We sit in silence on that.

'God I'm sorry girls,' he says.

'Me too.'

'But very grateful.'

'Meanwhile you've got the goddess in the garden,' I say.

'No, she's left me too.'

'Has she? No! Where's she gone?'

'She hasn't gone anywhere. I just don't see her anymore. Her window is empty. Look.'

He opens his curtains. The window of glory is naked, but no body is there. Instead a light is shining stage right from within her room.

'Oh dear Christ,' Toby says.

'Oh fuck....'

The light, which must be from a bedside lamp of a thousand watts, is beaming from the window, projecting two silhouettes onto the neighbours' house on the other side. It is a large shadow man roughly fucking a woman, bent over in front of him—their distinct shadows, three floors high, filling our window.

It is the most sadly erotic thing I've ever seen.

On my way up to my room I pass Adam's room. I can hear him talking through the door, muffled, but clear. On the phone is he?

'I have a good soul though don't I?'

No, he's not on the phone. He's talking to himself. Next door Jacqui and Eddie are at it, moaning and grunting and thumping the wall.

'Then I'm evil?' Pause. Thump, thump, moan. 'And people die because of me?' Grunt, grunt. 'Surely there's a way out?' Thump, thump. 'Then I must kill myself?'

Jesus Christ Adam: I knock on the door.

'Adam?'

Nothing.

'Adam mate are you alright?'

Long pause. 'Fine,' comes his voice, stretched.

'You sure? Do you... can I come in?'

'No!'

'Alright, I'm, er, I'm upstairs if you need me.'

'Thanks.'

●

I pour a kilo of flour into the bucket, then half a kilo of salt and slowly pour in water, mixing and kneading. When it starts to get elastic I mix in a cup of wallpaper paste.

The plan is to make doughcraft figurines and sell them at the markets—Camden or Columbia Road, something like that—catch the Christmas crowds; clean up! I've done a bit of research and found that people like really horrible stuff—cats, cute little men with funny hats, tacky little cottages and shiny flowers—so I'm going to focus my energies on doing things I hate. The other half of my stock is going to be whatever I want to do, not sure what this is yet, but it will be edgy, arresting, dazzling, daring, joyous...

Toby joins me and makes some hideous old men's heads. I have a go and find the medium, dough, does lend itself to small geriatric busts, so we spend most of the evening making aged, bald, wizened little heads until my floor is filled with several hundred tiny, scornful life-scarred faces looking at us.

'You think this is going to work?' asks Toby.

'It has to. It's this *or* work.'

'I don't think watching adverts for nine hours a day is for me.'

'I'm starting to think that no work is for anyone,' I say, 'I'm starting to think that Christ Himself would have pulled sickies, bunked off, signed on...'

'I think my mind is trying to push me to breaking point, until the steady diet of porn and dope and video games and television and despair breaks.'

'Breaks what?'

'The vice-like grip they have on my feeble mind.' As he speaks he's shaping a woman's body, sadly forming her little putty breasts. 'But it doesn't seem to be working. I just don't seem to be able to stop. The porn is getting out of hand—nothing does it for me, so I'm having to go to some really weird places.'

He focuses on rolling his doughy nipples.

'Alright, what?' I ask.

'What what?'

'What are you watching now?'

'Obese women mostly.'

'Why?'

'I dunno. Just something mesmerising about all that flesh. But I also look at other stuff. You'd be surprised at the range of fetishes out there, or maybe you wouldn't.'

'Like what?'

'Er bollock stamping, fursuits, probe-porn, farming equipment, elbows and ears...'

'Ears sounds alright.'

'You're an ears man?'

'Yes, no. I dunno. I'm more missionary and a firm handshake.'

'The worst thing about pornography is catching a glimpse of your reflection in the computer monitor. That fixed, retarded, drooly stare—regressed. I'm regressing. Actually, not even regressing. Children and animals are more awake. I don't know what it is. I can *feel* something collapsing, something essential. Inside me. Nothing is quite real.'

'That's what Adam kept saying. "It's not anything."'

'Adam's losing it.'

'We're all losing it.'

'But what are we losing?'

'I don't... know. I...' something in me is reaching out into some other place, what *is* it that I have lost? It's not just happiness, it's not that, because the happy people have lost it too.

We work in silence for a bit.

'How are your dreams?' I ask.

'Sickening. Last night I was on some kind of fuck production line, a huge factory and, er, I was hanging over a conveyor belt of gigantic naked women upturned, presenting their arses and I was on a kind of hydraulic arm, like a human stamp, which, as each woman passes under me, my punch-body was rammed into their bottoms, stamping them, *branding them*, with me, with my form.'

'I wonder what you're subconscious is trying to tell you.'

'You know when you play computer games for hours, and you go to bed and all you can see is the game?'

'Yeah. The Tetris effect it's called.'

'I have that with adverts and porn, but all the time. A permanent hyper-rapid flashcut montage of porn and adverts whenever I close my eyes.' He sighs; 'I'm finding it hard to look people in the eye.'

'Maybe you should, you know, knock it on the head?'

'Should, should, should. I hate that word. I should leave work, start work, be celibate, be promiscuous…'

'Oh yes, I have that. I should leave the room, I should enter the room…'

He sighs. 'I should ask my Dad for help.'

'For money?'

'Lord no. No chance. He's got contacts in the City, he can get me a job. I was thinking of leaving The Registry and, I dunno, getting out.'

I can more easily imagine a giraffe working in the City than Toby, but why not—dart in, get some money, dart out—I'd do it if I could.

Are we all too sensitive for the office? Are we all too brilliant for the factory? Are we all NSFW? We are, aren't we? And yet I can't claim heart-raw welfare, or get signed off for impractical yearning.

Toby's naked dough-woman is looking ever so good, but he's struggling with the head. He tries one after the other, but they all look terrifying, bird-like, satanic. Eventually he shows me a mighty Amazonian female form, the perfect body… topped with a miserly old man's head.

'Let me try.'

'Maybe one day I will have it figured out…' he says handing me the figure.

I pull off the old man's head and start to shape a woman's.

'I'm beginning to think that my Canterbury epiphany was just the drug-addled confusions of a fevered mind,' he says, 'I remember, at the time, I was alternately both terrified and resigned to my fate, that I wouldn't feel that way again, until my death bed, but I knew that feeling it, back then, that it guaranteed to me that I will eventually come into that blissful state once more, even if it is with the death of the Toby event.' He stares at the carpet, 'But now that's all just a distant idea, a myth. It's the weary, shoddy, base, ordinary worldview that is the real one.'

'There.'

I hand over the woman. Somehow, I don't know how, I have created a beautiful head. I'm trying to act cool, but I'm excited—this woman's head, with her full lips, high cheekbones, enigmatic eyes, carefully layered strips of dough hair and, anchoring it all together, a perfect nose, is truly a thing of loveliness. It is.

Toby looks at it, really looks, and then looks at me. 'That's good.'

The Wizard Priest of Kume

It's hard work being unemployed. It used to be okay being a nobody, but by the official definition, I am not now a somebody, a *job seeker*, prowling around jobland, sniffing the air for jobs, ready to pounce the moment a job scuttles across my tracks. It is an endless pointless quest, and millions of us are on it, afraid that we won't reach the top, that we'll return home without a kill, less than human, haunted by *positive actions* but at least free to play computer games until four am. I find I look forward to weekends more than I did when I was at work. At least it gives me a break from being unemployed.

And so I am applying only for jobs that I have no chance of getting—hyperbaric welder, dice inspector, professional bridesmaid—but the DWP is forcing interviews on me, and these I have to discreetly bugger up: Look eager, carefully manage my idealised market-self, but, at the same time, subtly sabotage my chances.

I did do a day's work, last Friday but, thank the Jobless Gods, they had no need of me after that. It was in a catering company, out in the ghastly unworld of Bermondsey. Street upon street of secure desolation. Supply-centres, mostly, depots and distribution-nodes. My job, in a freezing, windy warehouse, was 'on fish,' assembling pickled whitebait canapés, slicing open the tiny creatures and delicately arranging them in little frosted glass ramekins with eight blobs of salmon roe, three sprigs of dill and *no more* than twenty-five toasted sesame seeds.

I stood at a long table upon which the ingredients slid down in slotted canteen trays, working at a psychotic pace, fingers throbbingly numb. Opposite me were two old South Asian guys, on feta and cucumber, their hands a blur as they arranged the slender side-dishes.

Every now and then the taller one, with yellow eyes, would stop and say,

'Why did you do that?'

And the shorter one, with hairy ears, would stop and say,

'I did not do that!'

And then they'd get back to the rush. They did this perhaps forty times during my shift. Maybe more.

During lunch the workers huddled around in the eating area—a covered bay that backed onto a bus garage. It was bitterly cold and the air stank of burnt petrol; but it was home! At least it was when a Scouse guy bonded the table by asking what was the worst job we'd ever done.

Portuguese woman; 'Fruit salad factory: placing two grapes at a time in passing tins.'

Old English fellow, a Geordie; 'Inseminating bulls.'

Chinese guy. Simple and devastating; 'car factory.'

A Sudanese man, who was sitting next to his wife, worked in a factory that made fridges, and when the time came for their answer they replied in unison 'turned screws.'

And so it went on, until we got to the Indian sewer cleaner; he won.

I spoke later with this guy, Priyank, a squat and genial man who smelt of sweaty cumin. He started life as a runner in an H&M sweatshop, then found better work crawling around in the excrement of Delhi (better!), then took another step up, getting work in the UAE laying breezeblocks in fifty degrees, and finally came to London on a spurious student visa (issued through a spurious Whitechapel 'business college'), where now he makes sensational canapés. I concluded, from talking with him, that I live six levels away from rock bottom; assuming that military prisons are below Asian sweatshops and concentration camps below those.

Of course they are, but you'd be surprised what you can learn about zero-hour temping from death camp testimonies (Dostoevsky, Levi, Shalanov, those guys). Take this comment, from Dachau survivor Viktor Frankl—'on average, only those prisoners could keep alive who, after years of trekking from camp to camp, had lost all scruples in their fight for existence'—replace 'prisoners' with 'employees,' and 'camp' with 'ring-road business park' and you've got yourself some top-level employment mentoring.

•

Meaningless, meaningless, meaningless. Unfruitful, matter-of-fact, clever and terrifying. Humanity, I mean, a vast naked mountainous pyramid, stretching from horizon to horizon. At the bottom emaciated Asians and Africans, crushed by the weight and compacted by the filth of the millennial mass above them. Next, the fat white working classes, then cleaner and leaner types, and so on up. All thrashing around, grabbing and kicking at each other, fighting to claw their way up, and up, tearing each other's faces, crawling over each other to get to the summit where a few slim, bronzed, beautiful people sit, comfortable but terribly *concerned*, saying 'isn't it tragic?'

I wake, as usual, tense, tight, irritable and restless, like there's something terrible I should be worrying about, some dreadful *thing* that is going to happen, some great shame temporarily obscured, ready any moment to reveal itself to me, sarcastically laughing… yet what it is, I know not. The facts will not reveal to me the dread loss they are concealing.

Today I'm going for an interview for a 'personal assistant' to a paraplegic author. I'm in Clapham, slouching up one of the tidy professional streets, looking for number 59, which turns out to be a dark closed pub, muggy with stale hops and sweat. I sit at an oval ashwood table, opposite me in a wheelchair a little guy, all broken up, with a big rubbery head, wearing punky leather, and behind him a huge guy with curly hair and a beard, looks like a bouncer or Britain's Strongest Man.

I yibber on about having had a disabled grandmother and always wanting to care for people and looking after rabbits and Lawd knows what else, when he interrupts me to ask — in a back-of-the-nose kind of twang — what I would do if he brought a woman back.

'Well, erm, I'd say… hello?'
'Would you help me in bed?'
'Oh yeah. Yes I would, yes.'
'With her?'
'Yeah!'
'How?'
'Erm…'
'I can't move my body, so I would need you to do all the actions for me. Would that be okay? Could you do that?'
'No problem; fine.'
(Thinking: Bit weird though).

'Would you take my arse in your hands and push my loins into her gusset?'

'Yes,' I say, from somewhere in the pit of my neck.

'Could you keep up a nice rhythm?' asks the bouncer in a deep Welsh voice.

'I think so, yes.'

'That's excellent. Thanks. I'll be in touch.'

As I leave, and the door closes, I hear them laughing.

No time to savour that experience. Another interview in twenty minutes, Wandsworth, in some kind of cram school for coaching GCSEs. I am interviewed in a small shabby office by a heavy-jowled Pakistani reeking of aftershave who tells me that I'll have to teach mathematics and business studies.

'But I applied to teach art.'

'That doesn't matter. This is an opportunity for you.'

He starts laying down a load of rules—I must prepare lesson plans a week in advance which he'll vet, I must wear a suit at all times, I must be ready to cover other teachers, I'll be on half-pay for three months.

I'm finding it hard to sit still. I can feel spasms of pre-fury shooting up my thorax.

'How would you feel being an ambassador for the company?'

'I'm sorry...?'

'I want to know what you feel about representing the company in business meetings, business lunches, after a conference, that kind of thing; being the face of the business.'

Something in me snaps, or, rather slumps, like I've just walked into a swamp.

'Are you okay?'

'Oh God... Look. Sorry, I just can't do this. I've had enough of... that world... I can't... And I feel quite sure that working for you would be something approaching hell and I'm already in danger of vomiting into my eyeballs.'

I stand up and walk out, and as I hit the lower landing he bolts from the room and calls down over the banister, *'you should be more rational about your career!'*

I wait in Wandsworth Town station. He'll tell the job centre. Goodbye free money—at least the dole. Maybe I can keep housing benefit? I'll be alright with that, but I'll still need some kind of job, one a little less chancy than selling the stolen consumer goods piling up in my room.

It's turning out to be unpleasant though that, the barcode scam. Fear of getting caught has been a large part of my mornings of late—and that *is* work. I might as well be afraid of getting caught in a more settled environment. Or—surely there's some other way of earning my sad leaves?

A train arrives. As it slows I watch my reflection bouncing off the shuttling windows and doors. I don't like my posture. I look defeated. But I am defeated. It is an ongoing state of defeat. Perhaps I should just end it all here and now? But I can't be bothered to wait for the next train, and besides, I might get laid tonight.

People pour out. I stand back as they stream past me, then haul my way through to a seat. Relief! No matter how bad your life is, or how dull, you can put the whole show on pause when you step on to a train. I look through the window, dirty gold in the winter sunset, miserable but partially protected from it. The commuters waiting to get on are vague and hazy, but their shadows, passing over the window, are dark and distinct. I am wide awake but my face is knackered, my eyes hot with fatigue.

The train starts moving. The entire carriage is a whole, moving through space. The red sun moves round as the track curves, flickering behind trees and strobing from the windowed grids of Zenbu Holdings and Farzone Systems and Themis Unlimited.

In front of me sit a couple, vulturous, underclass, long loving looks at each other. Opposite them a beady-eyed, shiny-lipped, tiny-moustached little man, head shaped like a rugby ball on its side. Two people get on, one a geeky chubby Japanese guy, who sits diagonally opposite, and another a wild looking little old woman with a half-demented flaming look in her eyes, who sits next to me, opposite the man, their knees touching. The woman gets out a radio, no headphones, a normal radio-with-speaker, and turns it on. No sound comes out. She puts it to her ear and listens to it, intently.

The Jap guy takes out a handheld computer game and starts playing. After a couple of minutes the woman starts leaning forwards to try and look at his screen, to see what he's doing. She cranes her body forward, he looks up, and she quickly sits back bringing the radio swiftly back to her ear, looking blithely around, as if to say, 'who? me?' After a few minutes she again starts stealthily bending forward until peering over his lap, he again looks up, she again sits back and pretends to be listening to the radio. After ten minutes or so of this, the guy gets up, comes over and sits next to her so she can get a better view. They spend the rest of the journey this way, he playing, she watching intently.

We pull into Elephant and Castle. A little boy behind me says 'There's loads of castles daddy. There's *loads*.'

'Yes, London is full of castles,' says Dad.

'There are no elephants in South London,' says the boy.

He's absolutely right. I can't see one elephant.

The train inches forward, out of the station, then stops next to the back gardens of a row of grimy council flats, old Victorian tenements divided up into microscopic 'studios' at the very lowest end of the 'shared metropolitan living-space' market. A woman emerges into a small grey garden, wincing on a fag. She stands under the air-conditioner unit of the kebab-shop next door, one arm hugging her cheap faded-blue dressing gown, thinking of work I suppose, or of Lucy who only ever thinks of herself, or of *Dylan* whose surety and bone-structure are hot but who has other options and keeps her guessing… back inside, smell of aging rugs, unused chicken seasoning and yesterday's grim fucking; stains on frayed hallway carpet and lino peeling at the skirting board, thin walls broadcasting muffled sounds of self-loathing, cold shared kitchen of furtively delivered pre-work utterances, fridge is a tomb, corpse of chorizo, sense of futility dripping off the walls of the dark bathroom where she runs a bath through rattling pipes, chlorinated steam fogs up the little box and she sighs about Haley who never cleans her section of the bathroom cabinet overflowing with clogged eye-liner.

The train creaks away. We pass backs upon backs of terraced houses, empty because everyone's at work, paying for the houses that they can't live in, because they're at work. We trundle through the scrubby backlands of Battersea and Victoria; clumps of ragwort, nettle, rank spring grass and lilac buddleia push through the crumbling sleepers. Brick bridge walls, stained soot-grey, covered in scrawls amidst which, in tall square letters, 'Work is fucking shit.'

I don't need to imagine a gargantuan fist smashing London to bits, I can feel it, the reality of it. What hurts is—I know it's game over, I know that 'late-stage capitalism' actually means 'late-stage world.' The edge of the cliff is one commute away; and yet here I am looking for *work*. Why am I not painting naked women on Mexican mountains? Why am I not living in a field and stealing eggs from Cotswold cottages? Why am I not sinking my teeth into the sun-fringed peach of life, golden nectar, chin dribbly, laughing, madly laughing…? *Why?*

I get off at Kensington and get the number 10. It's dark now, spittling cold and I'm really not in much of a mood for a blind date at this point, but that is what's next. Jacqui has set me up with a girl 'I'll be *perrrfect* for,' whose name, I'm rather afraid to fully consider, is Melissa.

Actually I had a date the other day, with an internet 'match.' Not with Red Beaver... God I'm glad I didn't end up writing that. What a nob. Stephen was right—but why, I wonder, must it take weeks to see it? the stupidity of a comment I think is clever? or the crapness of a picture I think is a masterpiece? If only there were some way to see now from a greater height, from further away than now.

No, Red Beaver—I never did find out her name—she turned me down, as have most others on there, but I got a date with an Albanian girl called Blerta, who looked like a Blerta, poor thing; not because she was ugly—I mean she was a *bit* gawky and had poor skin and a dreadful posture, but she could have been pretty—she looked fine online dammit. The main problem was the superdense mass of unhappiness sucking all her features downward, sucking everything down, reality entire funnelling into the mulch, and making me think, as soon as I spied her in the Royal Festival Hall, 'I want to get this over with as fast as I can.'

She was gabbling from the get go, lots of little grimaces and winces punctuated with a high-pitched humourless ra-ta-tat laugh. All copied stuff, but also the instinctive nervous need to over-emphasise everything. Too much facial punctuation—facial italics really. She talked and talked, in a tense throaty voice, about her two jobs (dental nurse and lab assistant for one of those drug-testing places) and some stupid fucking boxset and where she wants to go on holiday... and I thought 'this is work. *Again.* I seem to spend my life sitting with someone that I'd like to be escaping from and I can't, and here I am sitting with someone I'd like to be escaping from... and I can. So I'm going to.'

She blethered on about food and weather and television and how interesting London is as our heads bobbled on the sea of theatre and gallery goers while I thought 'Right, how can I do this gently? Sweetly? After all, no need to be a cunt is there?'

So I asked her whether she trusted her first impressions, and she said, cautiously, 'sometimes' and I said 'My first impressions are generally trustworthy, and I don't think… I don't get the feeling that it's worth going on really. I just have, you know, a feeling inside that we won't get on.'

Her eyes and tone of voice dropped, and she became nervous in a down way, rather than nervous in an up way. She wasn't stupid. She knew I didn't like her and she asked me to be honest, which generally achieves the desired effect, of shaming me into delivering the blunt, merciless, *fact*, and so I said she seemed sad, at which point she burst into tears and told me about her sick mother and the boyfriend that had just dumped her, and that she lives alone in a city she hates with nobody that she likes.

It was better after that. More honest. Little hug. I felt sorry for her. In fact I felt like I was dumping her; almost like we'd had a relationship. So I said 'okay, let's have lunch shall we?' She looked quite pretty now, covered in tears.

'Do you really want to have lunch or are you just being polite?'

'I'm just being polite.'

So that was that.

Today I'm meeting a girl I've never met before. I don't have very high hopes, given the odds and given that she was chosen by Jacqui who I wouldn't trust to select a t-shirt for me, let alone a life-partner. The idea is that we'll have cocktails in the London Hilton Windows Bar and then kebabs on Edgware Road, sample two ends of the central London social spectrum.

I wait at Marble Arch. Commuters stream past, head down against the petrochemical spittle driving down dark Park Lane. I'm early and I can hear violent sermonising from the blustering darkness of Hyde Park, so I go in to take a listen.

Speaker's Corner is empty but for one tall, bony man, standing on a stool, violently declaiming to an audience of one, a small fuzzy, ratty little guy clutching a can of special brew. The tall guy passionately cries out;

'More women in power! More women in managerial positions! More equality! Let's shatter the glass ceiling! Let's blow away gender stereotypes.'

'Bullshit' snides the little guy in a dry, almost nerdy, tone, 'why don't you look at the world? It's never going to happen, women will never take control from men...'

The speaker doesn't listen. 'Let's see women at the very top of huge corporations!' he shouts, 'Let's see these totalitarian, centralised, dictatorial systems, which demand complete subservience, run by *women* for a change! Because...'

'Blah, blah, blah, tell it to the Guardian...'

'...because the only women who can reach positions of authority in institutions which punish honesty, freedom, radical generosity, wild spontaneity, and organic, embodied, context-embracing physicality, are, ipso facto, predictable, safe, aggressive, tight, unnatural, focused, abstract and basically dishonest. Such women are therefore *much* easier to have casual superficially satisfying but loveless sex with, much easier to get pissed with, much easier to talk about sport and news with...'

'Hold on a minute...'

'...soon, yes my brothers, one day soon, all genuine femininity will be *eradicated* from the planet, and then, finally, I'll never have to worry about my lack of soul... because there'll be no-one left alive who cares.'

He throws his arms up into the air and bawls triumphantly into the stormy night;

'And then, finally, *I'll get laid!*'

The strange radar that tells me someone is coming detects a feminine figure out in the street. I leave the park, pre-consciously aware that she is my date and that she is pretty.

'Melissa?'

'Yes,' she says, 'hello.' We kiss each other's cheeks (too much perfume) she says 'shall we?' turns on her heels and strides up Park Lane ahead of me; fast. What am I to do? Lose-lose. Trot after her like a leaky-penis? Don't think so. Tell her to slow down and immediately get into a battle of wills? I opt for a dishonest and weird half-measure—I limp a bit and say 'sorry, I can't keep up. Could you slow down a bit?'

'I'll try,' she says, 'I don't like walking slow though.'

The rain, which had paused, starts again; a fine, driving marrow-freezing mist. Melissa has an umbrella, but it's useless and keeps getting hooked sidewise and blown inside out. I thought the Hilton would be closer but actually it's right down the other end of Park Lane and so I do want to walk fast now but I'm supposed to be a bit of a raspberry ripple so we lurch on in grim silence until we almost fall into the bright gold lobby and I can finally get a good look at her. Her blonde hair is straggling around her face, her make-up is a bit blurred and her cheeks are red and moist. She doesn't look happy. She is also much better dressed than me. I feel well out of place in my ill-fitting cords.

We stand in the lift with a huge-jawed bronze guy with a thin pink cashmere jumper folded across his shoulders and an incredibly pissed-off looking middle-aged Latin woman dressed entirely in red—red dress, red cardigan, red shoes, red purse; all precisely the same shade. Melissa is wearing tight jeans, brogues and a loose black and gold blouse. She's quite rattly. Not quite sure where the beads are, but she clinks and clatters a lot as she jiggles her leg and fiddles with her watch strap.

'Everything okay?' I ask, trying to be chipper.

'Oh it's alright, I just had a bad day at work.'

'Why's that?'

She rolls her eyes, 'Oh *God*, usual stuff. Hold-up with the suppliers, incompetent temps…'

'What do you do?'

'Event management. We had a banquet today for property developers, and it was a total nightmare. *Nobody* knew what they were doing, but this is what happens when you hire from agencies. Do you watch Mad Men?'

I have a feeling that I've made another terrible mistake, but the instant we walk in to the clean, softly-lit, vaguely seventies, bar I know I have. It's not so much the barking vaudevillian HA HA HAs of laughter, the clean steely tone of the chatter, the gold and white dresses and faux fur gilets and smooth wide faces, but, rather, the penetrating sense of being thrown into an alien dimension where nothing makes sense, nothing hangs together.

We deposit our coats in the cloakroom and sit at a long, thin poseur table in the middle of the room, a cramped row of eight people all facing more comfortable window-side bars which we covet.

A waiter brings a drinks menu and places some finger food between us — whitebait and caviar.

'Oh, I made these the other day.'

'Do you cook?'

'No, well, yes, beans mostly. But, I mean I actually made *these*, in a warehouse off the Old Kent Road.'

She looks confused. 'Jacqui told me you're an artist.'

'I am.'

'So what were you doing in a warehouse…?'

'Working.'

'Getting inspiration?'

'No, getting money.'

Her face briefly registers an emotion somewhere between revulsion and fascination.

'Are you ready to order?' asks the waiter, a man so beautiful and assured I feel I should be serving him.

'1934 cosmopolitan,' says Melissa.

We're here to have cocktails but I can't bring myself to con-front one of these joyous confections, so I order a whiskey, a nice one. Melissa starts to protest, but is interrupted by her phone.

'Did you get my text?... Exactly... Tell me something I *don't* know... You better be joking... Oh my God *no*... No darlin' you're the bestest... You know what? *he* can do it...'

As she 'speaks' I turn my attention to the couple who have just settled into the stools to our right—both groomed and meticulous, he smug and pudgy, she pretty and scowly. They have hardly settled in their seats when she asks;

'How much do you earn?'

'58 before tax.'

'Are you fertile?'

'As far as I know.'

'I want three kids.'

'I could take a test.'

'Good. How often do you ejaculate?'

'Depends. Once a day usually.'

'Do you take hot baths?'

'No, I shower.'

'What bad habits do you have?'

'I pick my nose and eat it.'

'In public?'

'No.'

'Okay, that's fine.'

Melissa hangs up and we return to our conversation which is less matter-of-fact, but has essentially the same aim. We begin with socio-economic priorities. I ask her about her job, and she complains some more about the bloody temps.

'I'm a temp,' I say.

'But not permanently,' she says.

'That's right, temporary.'

'It's a scandal how graduates can end up in such jobs.'

'I'm not a graduate.'

'Oh!'

Her fascination ebbing, leaving the flinty shores of revulsion. I try to rescue the vibe by changing the subject.

'Do you go on many blind dates?'

'Oh some. Usual stuff, internet-dating mostly. Too busy to do the groundwork IRL.'

I offer my theory that women are more disadvantaged e-dating because they're less interested in explicit communication, and she grabs an invisible pair of testicles and says '*balls.*' She says I'm gender stereotyping. She's not really interested in conventional relationships—in fact she's not really interested in relationships at all.

'Either I don't like him as much as he likes me, or he doesn't like me as much as I like him,' she says, shrugging 'This is just how sex, romance, and life generally works. Living in society means slowly acquiring facts about other people until you discover you don't like them.'

'So what's the point?'

'Of what? Of dating? The same point as everything; fighting, fucking and feeding.'

'Is that it? Is that the point?'

'Yep.'

'I dunno. Maybe, you're right. I suppose I've just had enough of all that.'

'All what?'

'The soul-tearing cannibal solitude of sex without love.'

'What?'

'The dread-horror lovelessness of the world.'

'What are you *talking* about?'

'You're the one who brought it up!'

She looks at me, eyes scalding. 'I'm just going to the toilet.'

I watch her leave. My heart is beating. This is horrible.

Fuck this. I fiddle fifteen precious quid out of my pocket and tuck it under my glass. The men in front of me start laughing again, their eyes wide and staring, desperate, shouting into each other's heads. Pretty and scowly says to smug and pudgy; 'I'll do anal once a fortnight, that's my final offer.' I dart over to the cloakroom watching the indicator light on the lift. The damned thing is touching ground floor.

'Are there stairs here?'

'Just down there sir, but it'll be quicker to wait for the elevator.'

I throw myself down the stairs, four at a time, for twenty eight floors, powered by the adrenaline of sexual combat. In the lobby I'm sweating and out of breath—I must look like I've burgled the king executive—best slide out the back, take the rear exit through the car park.

It's pouring outside, tides of rain plashing thick in puddles, machine-gunning my jacket, instantly papping my trousers tight over my thighs. The back streets, slick, black, drumming with rain reflecting halogen pink, are mostly empty, which is a relief, because I can't bear to look at another hard probing human face. I can't bear to be with another human being—and yet I can't bear to be alone. I can't go home, I can't stay here. I don't want to do anything, but I don't want to do nothing.

What I want is to be with someone; someone who loves me, or—if that's too much to ask—at least with someone who I love. She could just sit there and I'd love her. I think that would be alright.

I slop through the streets. I couldn't feel more alone, more out of place, more futile if I were on the moon—at least I'd be dry there. The dark rain pounds my self-pity, which tries to keep me dry with moaning, the melodramatic voice of the morbid one, narrating my sad state to nobody. No girl, no job, no family, no talent, nothing I can possibly expect by way of help from the society collapsing around me and nothing but pain, noise and meaningless unnature in every direction. If an elephant appeared now, on Piccadilly, it would chew its trunk off.

The pain is interesting though; I mean the emotion. In some way it's hardly anything, a very slight sickness across the chest, a weight in the neck. You couldn't even call it painful, not really—and yet it is the pit of horror. People who commit suicide feel like this, I'm sure. I know my reasons are not so convincing; in some ways I wish I had a better reason to be miserable—a more solid reason, like a brain tumour or a history of child abuse—something that was as bad as this—but the reasons don't actually mean anything. That's why friends and family of suicides always say 'it wasn't *that* bad.' Of course it wasn't—the evidence never is.

So where is the pain coming from? It's so very hard to see; like when you burn your retina by looking at the sun then close your eyes and try and look at the afterburn... it drifts away always beyond your foveal grasp. So it is with this emotional pain. I try to inspect it, understand it, but it never *quite* comes clearly into view. I am both the self which is looking for the wound, and the wound itself.

But even this distant understanding provides no relief. Such thoughts are like raindrops on the sun, past and future evaporating into an eternal now of self-disgust and exclusion. Yes, suicide seems perfectly reasonable, but then so does returning to the forest—not so much a bad idea, more a far distant one.

Much closer is a phone box. Just outside of it, standing in the rain, is—I suppose you could say he's halfway between a busker and a tramp; straggly white beard, skin so dirty it's black, four coats, playing a guitar with one string. He's just playing the same note, over and over again.

I pull myself into the cubicle, search through my wallet for Lauren's number—but I can't find the scrap of paper I keep my numbers on. All I have is the business card for Original Sin Escorts.

She could just sit there and I'd love her.

I look out at the busker-tramp, playing his one note. I can just hear it through the sarcastic applause of the rain. Tong, tong, tong, tong, tong…I look at the card. An hour of love, of warmth. But then she might be a bitter, corrupted immigrant, a pitiful sex-slave who begs me to free her, or a snaggle-toothed hag. I'll just call and see. A phone call won't cost my soul. Just take a peek, as it were.

'Hello?' the voice on the other end of the line sounds normal enough. Late thirties? Eastern European?

'Hello, is that, uh, Original sin?' Through sheer terror, I whisper the last word.

'It is. Who would you like to see?' Is this the voice of a woman who will steal one of my kidneys? It doesn't sound like it. And that guy, Andrey, he was scary, but I don't *think* he was evil—he really did want to help me.

'I don't know.'

'And when's it for?'

'Do you have anyone now?'

'We have Annabel, Cherie, Lulu and Daphne. What kind of girl do you like?'

'Do you have any friendly girls?'

'They're all *friendly* dear.'

'I mean really friendly. Erm, nice, sweet, caring?'

'A mother? An older woman?'

'Not… really. I just… Do you have anyone with a good heart, that's… what I mean.'

'I know just the girl sir. Daphne. When can you be here?'

'Where are you?'

'King's Cross.'

'And how much?'

'£200 ninety minutes. Authentic girlfriend experience.'

My consciousness reviews, at light speed, all the pros and cons of prostitution and then zips through my entire social-sexual-moral matrix, then considers my rent situation, then staggers up to the doors of my mouth and sicks up a squeezed 'Alright then.'

It takes a while to find the flat. I have to duck into a newsagent's to consult an A-to-Z, twice, and then I keep stopping to have life-or-death street corner arguments with myself. It's not right, is it, paying for sex? But then, it's not right, I think, paying for milk. But then, 'I am not a cheesecake.' But then, by Christ I'm desperate. But then, I might catch something, or she'll be horrible and £200 is a *lot* of money to me—just about all of it. But then, by Christ I'm desperate.

The flat is quite nice, at least from the outside. Doesn't look like a volcanic citadel of evil. If only I could just go in, take a look, get a feel for the thing and make my mind up then—but that's surely bad form in the punting game.

Christ yes, punting. I'm now part of the same demographic as beery, bristling Gavin from Financial Objects, sweating over sad, sunken Asian girls during his lunch hour. I have this grotesque self-image-vandalising thought as I am buzzing Daphne's flat. It's enough to make me bolt, but her human voice—'hello, come on up!'—sounds completely undemonic, Polish I'd say and they're always nice, aren't they?

A grievous sense of unquestionable momentum sucks me on, in, up the too bright stairs, towards the door of her flat, slightly ajar, and in.

•

She is human and beautiful. Moony face, long dark hair, patterned cream dress, size 8 I think they call that body, quite the hips, kind blue Pole-eyes (sort of slightly upward looking), mid-thirties perhaps. She puts her arms around me and gives me a kiss, and it's soft and giving, and then she leads me into her bedroom. I follow her in like a dog and pull out the money—a bit too hastily I think with panic, but she takes it with a little accepting smile, and tells me to sit down, she'll be back in a minute.

The room has four items of furniture—Malm, Billy, Ektorp and Lack—a green and orange rug, a few candles, lots of knick-knacks and a small lamp. No photos or anything particularly intimate-looking, but then there wouldn't be.

Must have been a lot of men who have sat where I am now. I shouldn't think that, but I do. I wonder how many were as nervous as me. I wonder how many spilt semen on the Ektorp. I wonder if the ghosts of their ecstasy and shame have accumulated in the plasma of the walls. I do believe that—emotions lodge in walls and make rooms feel the way they do... But this one doesn't feel of much; all I can feel is my heart rattling round the tumble-dryer of my guts like a plimsoll.

Plimsoll is a funny word. Sounds like a nerd's surname—Gavin Plimsoll—or a type of acne, or a sanitising spray or a town in Norway. Plimsoll, plimsoll... Ah! The door opens, she comes in, closes the door very carefully and sits next to me. We kiss some more. On her side, she's warm and soft and friendly and on my side I'm just so damned grateful. I can feel gratitude pouring through my body, like I've been given a precious gift from on high, like I've found a hot bowl of soup in the Arctic.

We stop. 'You kiss good,' she says, a bit surprised.

'Thank you.'

'What do you want to do with me?' she asks.

Under any normal circumstance this question would explode into a mental polyptych of gyrating, begging, stretching, moaning and porn-eager pneumatic yielding. I would want her to enjoy it, to yelp and moo, but the essence of the composition would be a desire to please *me*, to submit and writhe. Maybe even say the word 'baby.'

But now I want something so bizarre and perverted I can hardly bring myself to say it, even here. She sees me swallow and hesitate and says quietly, 'it's okay, say anything, we do anything.'

'I want...'

Why is it so hard to say it? It's hard because I know, in the pit of my bellymind, that there's a good chance even a prostitute hasn't heard this one.

'Yes?' She's doubting now, probably expecting something that involves a roll of kitchen towels.

'I want... to love you.'

She blinks thickly and, for the first time, looks at me. I want so much to say something, to qualify this lunatic confession, to shift around apologetically but I am here now, in mid-air, and land can only be reached by holding onto the rope. She blinks again. I feel like she is aiming a gun at a tiny apple on my head. Hold on! She smiles — and, dear God, I hold on — before she bursts into superb laughter.

'Okay,' she says.

'Is that strange?'

'Yes. Strange.'

The way she says this 'yes, strange,' eyes twinkling a kind of 'why not?' vibe makes me sag with relief, like she has accepted some part of me that I have been ashamed of for a long time.

She tilts her head, gently 'You know how to love?'

'I...' I clear my throat, 'I don't think so. Um. No. I don't.'

Yes, I don't know what I'm doing. There. It feels as if it could be the last time I'm with a woman; it could be the last person I ever see. I have no idea what I'm doing. Why pretend? I've nothing to lose I didn't lose a long time ago.

'Okay.' She's smirking, but it's fine, 'Okay,' she says, pulling herself together somewhat, 'is not this.' She grips my wrist, tight.

'Right, yes.'

She lets go 'Is release,' she says, 'everything release, but not...' she slumps forward a bit, miming a crumpling puppet, 'not this, not weak.'

'How come you're so nice?' I blurt.

She laughs, 'you are lucky boy, is why.'

'I've never been with, erm...'

'Prostitute,' she says.

Yes, prostitute. That is the word. They call it 'sex worker' now. Sex *work*. As if that makes it more dignified than prostitution.

'I've never met a prostitute, but I didn't think they would be so nice.'

'Paid to be nice is not nice. But you are a good boy, so I am gonna help you.'

'Thank you.'

'And is my last night.'

'Oh really? Why?'

'I have money now. Tomorrow I return Poland, marry, start family.'

'You're getting married?'

'Yes, after two weeks.'

'Does your fella know you're a pro?'

'Sure he does.'

'What does he think?'

'He don't like it, but he have to accept. I don't give my heart another man.'

Well, it makes sense. A job's a job. I suppose there's not much difference between working in Financial Objects and being sodomised by an Arab—but then I think of Gavin looming over me, which *is* worse than picking tomatoes, plucking turkeys and scraping tiles off walls. But then, what would happen if there were no prostitutes in the world into which mankind could fuck its hatred away? We'd tear ourselves apart.

'I don't give my heart to you,' she says, 'but I show you how to give, if you want.'

'I want that.'

'Okay, you relax. Take deep breath. Nothing to worry.'

(She says 'Take a deep bref' and 'nuffin' to worry.')

'Can't give with head,' she says, 'only body.'

'I see. Yes.'

'Head and cock same thing.'

'Is it?'

'Yes, no love. You go to body. Love.'

'Okay.'

'Now we kiss again.'

We do. It's fantastic, but I start to feel the urge to claw, the old hungry panic. I clutch her head and she pulls away.

She's patient though, friendly, taking care of my ego, even a bit clinical—I feel like I'm at the dentist. 'Is okay. Animal is good,' she says, 'but first you stay in the body. Later animal. First you give, but not like little man.'

Like a great man, Daniel.

'You enjoy,' she says quietly. 'Enjoy scent.'

I take a good snort.

'No! I am not piece of meat! *Scent*.'

She is right, all this is *in the body*. It's not an emotion, or some mystic voodoo, and it's not in the imagination; it's just the body feeling good. The enjoying, under the wanting. The body, under the thinking. The scent, under the smell. It feels like I've never been in my body before.

But I'm not sure what to do now. Should I go for the neck? Undress her? Or is that a bit previous?

She pulls away, 'You think again.'

'Yes, I wasn't sure what to do next. I was wondering if I should kiss your neck or lie down or…'

'This how child thinks,' she says. 'Man does what he enjoys, just enjoys and then does something else he enjoys. Doesn't ask. You kiss my lips, kiss my neck, take my clothes off… just do. If feels good, just do. Women like men who care, but they also like men who don't care. You see?'

'Erm, I think so.'

I take a deep breath and we start again. There's a lot to this. Why didn't anybody explain it before? Surrender, but not feebly; strong, not sadistic; kind, but not weedy. Enjoy it! But not grippy…

But underneath the confusion, desperation, fear, imagination and slathering, humping fuckbeast, which is *there* (feel it?), underneath that, it's not complex at all, there's just the body which…

'Ahhhh.' I moan—sounded a bit sissy that though, bit whimpery, but… *judgement!* I'm thinking again. Back to the body, back down to the black cave.

'You like this?' she asks.

'Honestly, it's so good.'

'Yes, is good.'

I want to kiss her all over now so I stand up and take her over to the bed. Pull her clothes off or tell her to undress? Feels a bit of a risk that last thing, but the big man just does, apparently.

'Take your clothes off,' I say, swallowing back my shyness. She pulls her dress off and, Gentle Jesus, I can't quite believe that I can be allowed to see something so beautiful. I have a feeling, like I am being allowed into completely different world, a terrifying Other Place—where everything is stripped away, naked of matter itself.

'Come,' she says, patting the bed.

I lie down next to her and kiss her some more.

'I...'

'Mmm?'

'You're...'

'Say it,' she whispers, 'talk is friendly.'

'You're so beautiful.'

'Thank you.' (Fank you).

Actually I've always liked the idea of talking during sex; not dirtywhore viper talk, but really boring daily stuff, like humping during the washing up and chatting about what to have for lunch, or oral sex on the phone to Tesco, that kind of thing. I was put off vocalising with Kate, the second girl I slept with, who I practically bribed into sleeping with me, pleading and wheedling my way back to my room one night after the pub, culminating in the usual detached and cackhanded congress which was punctuated, in the middle, by her asking, in an eerily clear voice, if I wanted to watch David Attenborough.

I struggle at Daphne's bra and she helps me—I'm starting to not feel so ridiculous now, by which I mean this whole thing is ridiculous—sex is, Toby is right, utterly bizarre and clumsy, not at all like the films—but I don't care so much, because she doesn't.

I pull my trousers off and shirt. She smiles because I am wearing a white vest which is two sizes too big. I look like George Orwell's gym instructor.

She nods to my feet, 'Socks.'

Oh yes, take those off.

I pull her knickers off and her body looks odd. Not quite human. Not quite what I imagine: not the sexy mindform of the comics. Her waist is *slightly* thicker than it should be, her pubic hair *slightly* more disorganised and her nipples *slightly* flatter and darker. Also her breasts do not erupt from her body like two honeydew melons. In short she is a real, living, actual woman of human matter, and I'm just not prepared for that. I can feel the lift withdrawing from my penis and panic. I leap on her, trying to get the horn back, but it's wilting away.

'I'm sorry,' I say, swallowing back my shame, 'I don't...'

'Is okay. Cock hard for sex or love, not both.'

I must say I am unaccustomed to beautiful women casually uttering profound truths about existence. The thought occurs to me that perhaps I've been looking for the universe in all the wrong places. I lie back on the bed, then glance over at the clock on her bedside table.

'Don't think about time,' she says, 'let's get in bed.'

She pulls back the duvet and squirms into the bed and I do the same. Once again I feel gratitude; not, as usual, the sense that I owe someone something, but an actual experience, in my stomach... of what? It's almost nothing to my brain, but it's warm and, for once in my pitiful life, merely unafraid.

She pushes herself against me, looking up, eyes all 'yes, fine.'

'Why you here?' she asks.

'I'm lonely.'

'But you are nice guy. Bit handsome. What your job?'

'Bit?'

'Gentle eyes, good shape mouth. Is enough.'

'Thanks.'

'What your job?'

'Artist.'

'You have family?'

'No.'

'Why not?'

'They're not around any more.'

'What happened?'

'My mum died a few years ago.'

'Oh, sorry 'bout that. Dad?'

'He's dead too.'

'Sorry about that.'

I tell her a little of my life and she tells me a little of hers, back in Poland, also parentless, although her Mum and Dad were just absent through work. Her grandparents raised her, in the Białowieża Forest.

'Sound like a folk myth.'

'I like walking in forest,' she says, 'never alone in forest.'

'I have some friends, but I think loneliness is... I don't think it depends on what is happening. It's a kind of sickness. A feeling that you don't belong.'

'Belong?'

'Yes, belong.'

'Nobody belong anymore,' she says.

'That's true.'

'You are artist to help people belong.'

'I love you Daphne.'

'Oh yes.'

'No I really do. I mean I feel love. I can actually *feel* love.'

'Cock hard now,' she says and turns round for a condom, which she places on my penis in a single gesture, one handed.

'Now you enter, very slowly.'

I get on top of her. The desperate need to fuck her and fuck her and fuck her is here, kind of hovering around the divot in my neck, but I, me, am under that, entering her.

'Slower,' she says.

I slow down, as much as I can, and as I do—in violation of all the laws of porn—the pleasure increases.

'Tell me again you love me,' she whispers.

'I love you.'

How slow can you move? There gets a point where there is no difference between movement and the will to move. Then, when you slow down even more, it becomes just will, or just consciousness, or just... God only knows what it is. It's so good, but not what is happening; it's what this is happening *to*, what is in or operating the body. Me, or I. The I is changing. I am something else.

Her scent, the feel and taste of her, the sound of her moans, the words she speaks and the fluttery way she says them, the look in her eyes, all lips and surrender—there is more pleasure than I ever could have imagined, but the strange beauty of it, of this, is that which is enjoying it; who it is happening to. I feel more me than I have ever felt, and yet there doesn't seem to be anybody here, just pleasure and beauty and love and gratitude; words I would never before have been able to utter without a sense of embarrassment and fraudulence, but what else possibly to call this sensation?

The body moves, with excruciating slowness. The body holds her, moves her... then a voice in the back of my head says 'you're doing it! you're having sex with a girl!' She sees I'm getting lost, getting a bit fucky, and she whispers, 'come back, tell me you love me.'

Time elongates, like a blob of oil in space, each moment longer and longer. She winces, her breath is short, a slow, far away sun of pleasure is growing, something awesome, enormous. Neither of us are moving now. Totally still.

'Breathe,' she says, 'make noise.'

Oh yes, I've been holding my breath, trying to control it. Why? God knows, although a voice tells me that the sounds I am making now are absurd. Ignore that voice though—it is the enemy.

The sun, the shattering sun of pleasure. It's absurd, ababa-ba... just...

'Can you feel that?'

'Yes,' she said, oddly clear.

And then the world is full of blazing light, for a long, incredibly strange, timeless moment.

For the first time in my life I lay unanxious, undrowsy, unsad. No peeved need to get away, no shame, no moral sickness, no spikiness, no torpor, no horrible strange hyper-clarity.

'Thank you.'

'Is okay. Very good. At the end, very good.'

A fly lands on my thigh, which, I dimly perceive, is odd for two reasons. Firstly it's December. Secondly, I don't care. I am immune to all irritation. I could probably even phone the bank now.

'I should leave,' I say.

'No, you stay. I leave also tomorrow.'

'Do you have to go?'

'Yes, of course.'

'But...'

She presses herself against me again, 'you want pickled fish?'

'Alright.'

She skips up, puts on her pyjamas and goes out. I hear another girl's voice. Can't hear the words, might not be English, but the tone says; question... funny... surprise... funny... details...

I look around the room, at the be-gemmed boxes and harlequins sculpted from pipe-cleaners and guitar-shaped cushions, a tea-caddy, a little wooden mouse... and feel a profound sense of belonging, like my heart belongs here. It is cheap this room, made by Ikea, yet, on top of that, how pretty it is! and that prettiness is Daphne. Strange that I didn't notice it before. All these trinkets, which Jacqui's room, and many like them, have taught me are the fungal outgrowths of a disordered mind, now, here, they don't seem useless at all. They, like her, are the stuff of life.

Daphne comes back with a tray containing rollmops, herring, sauerkraut, two small glasses of vodka and some water. We eat on the bed.

'How long have you been here?' I ask.

'Two years.'

'You've been a prostitute all that time?'

'No, first year I work in hotel. Then I work in warehouse, then I became ice. Second year I fuck strange men.'

'How did you become ice?'

She puts down her drink and lies against me.

'I tell you?'

'Yes, tell me.'

'I work in packing warehouse, lifting totes, very difficult, very heavy, I become very strong, but too heavy and, you know packing warehouse, is like prison, prison walls, prison food, prison guards, horrible, horrible. I work twelve hours six days every week, lifting, pushing, running, no water—you know you cannot even piss, they don't allow to piss—so I was almost dead. And then, it was my period and I was working and I was lifting and I feel blood, so I went to toilet and I was bleeding, bleeding... And I didn't stop bleeding. I go home, I'm worried, of course, and I go to bed, but bleeding, oh my God, it was, what is the word?'

'Haemorrhage?'

'Yes, I have haemorrhage, and it doesn't, did not stop. So my landlady, she become very worried and I go to hospital, she drive me in her car. And, oh my God, I was in hospital, alone, I don't know anybody, alone in this place and weak and the doctors and nurses, God *bless* those people, they care for me, they really care, and they come and give me drug and put me on, er, profusion, the liquid bag one...'

'Drip?'

'I don't know. Profusion, but I don't stop bleeding, and now my pulse is slower and slower, and they are worried, and one night a doctor comes into my room and a nurse and they're talking. I can hear them, they don't know I could hear them, but they say, "we are going to lose her, she will die." And I think, "so I am going to die. Okay." I was so sad, but I thought, "okay." A few hours later they take me to surgery, but it didn't work. I am still bleeding and my heart now is beating so slowly, until they say okay we give the blood, we find donator and give her the blood, not profusion...'

'Oh, transfusion.'

'Yes, for blood. They bring the blood, two bags, and I watch it, I watch the new blood enter me, and it was *so* cold. It was *so* cold. And so slow, this cold, cold blood creep through me.' She stops and sniffs. She's crying. 'I became cold then. I became ice. That was when I became ice cold person. I stopped bleeding, I got better, they gave me depression pills, but I was ice. I am still ice.'

I don't know what to say. 'It sounds awful.'

'Yeah, mostly awful.' She picks up a cracker and nibbles gently. 'That's when I thought, I'll be whore. Already ice, so why not? I don't care. I'll fuck, don't care, suck cock, don't care. And I start this life. At first, difficult, strange, first men, but also just like normal fucking, somehow, like normal fuck-fucking, so it becomes normal quickly. Everything becomes normal quickly.'

She's right. 'I see every kind of man,' she says, 'Man who treat orgasm like taking a shit—disgusted after, polite man full of anger, man who don't want to be seen, man can't get hard-on who want to be punished, sadists—lots of sadists,' she shrugs, 'most men hundred per cent fucked up.'

'Yeah.'

'Is getting worse too. Men don't treat old ones so good.' she turns and plunges her face into my sides, 'I'm old fish now.'

'You're not old.'

'Ha! But I am fish!'

'Well I don't know about that. You're not old though.'

'Thas true. But I don't feel so much in heart now, or in pussy.

But I will again, when I get home. I think God send me you to say I can go home now, time to go.'

'You believe in God?'

'Course. Don't you?'

'Yes, but...'

'But?'

'I think he's a bellend.'

'What's a bellend?'

'An, erm, a fool.'

'Oh yes, God is a fool, of course.'

'He seems to have made your life tough.'

'Can't love God with *easy* life,' she says, as if it's the most obvious thing in the world.

'My life's hard, but I don't love Him.'

'Her.'

'Alright, Her.'

'Not hard enough then,' she says, reaching for the butter, 'Must get more hard.'

'What a horrible idea.'

'Is okay. But why you don't have girlfriend?'

'I'm afraid of women.'

'Men always afraid.'

'I'm afraid of talking to them, making a move on them, living with them, having sex with them, committing to them, splitting up with them. I'd be gay if I could.'

'Gay is easy way.'

This again. 'You think? I don't think gay people would agree. They seem to think they have a hard time of it.'

She tilts her head. 'Pfff!'

'I think I have it all wrong with women. I thought I had to feel good, be confident, then women would like me.'

'No, don't matter how you feel. Just love.'

'But love is a feeling.'

'Love is not a feeling. This is sensation for me. But... I dunno. Masło maślane.' She smiles, swallowing, 'like always I have some doubt. That charm of me.'

'Your husband is a lucky guy.'

'Yeah, he lucky. Bit stupid too.'

'Why don't you stay here, with me?'

She laughs again, 'Of course I don't!'

I find I don't mind too much, not really. I don't really mind about anything. I could be taken right now, by the ministry of truth, and that would be fine. Maybe that was Winston's problem—sex with Julia just turned out to be a bit ordinary.

'What are you going to do then, in Poland?'

'I'm gonna take long rest. In Poland I'm gonna be rich, so I take long rest. Read books, buy shoes, pick mushrooms, pretend to be bird, learn chess.'

'I thought everyone in Eastern Europe played chess.'

'No. I can't.'

'I'll teach you.'

'Now?'

'Yeah, why not.'

'I don't have board.'

'We'll make one. Won't take long.'

She pads off to find some paper and scissors. We cut out bits of paper, draw chess pieces, colour in a board, I explain the rules, and play chess cross-legged on her bed. She puts the radio on; *He Ain't Heavy He's My Brother* is playing.

'Who teach you chess?' she asks.

'Erm... I can't remember.'

'I kill your king,' she leaps her knight over eight squares.

'No, you can't move there. Like this...'

'Okay.' She thinks about the board, then cranes her head, listening to the song.

'He ain't heavy?' she asks.

'No, that's right, he's my brother.'

'And that makes him lighter?'

'Yes, I'm strong enough to carry him, you see, because he's not heavy, because he's my brother.'

'What happened to him?'

'I suppose he had some kind of accident.'

'Poor him.'

'They're singing about a long, long road, so I guess it's some kind of traffic accident.'

'That the theme of the song?'

'Yes, drive safe.'

'Unless you've got a brother.'

'Right, then it doesn't matter. Drive as fast as you like.'

And so we gabble, and drink, and play chess very badly.

Imagine living this way, every day, making wonderful love, playing strip-chess, easy flow. I could paint her, or she me. Pop each other's knuckles, bit of animal humping even. I dunno do I? I've only been granted one night. The second might have been tougher.

•

I am in a huge train station, and I'm flustered. I left my bag under a chair, but it's gone now, someone has taken it, and I don't have anything, no money, no tickets. I'm stuck in this place.

I go up the stairs to the platforms. It's Paddington, but different, bigger and somehow 'higher.' A train is arriving, but I don't have a ticket for it, which means I can't get on it. I'm frustrated, because the train is getting nearer; but then I think, 'it's alright though, it's just a dream. I'll just start the story again.'

It's just a dream. But if it is just a dream, then none of this matters. I can do what I want. I can stands in front of the oncoming train. Why not?

I get down onto the tracks. The train is coming—it's huge, a big old steam train with chimney and buffer and that pointy grill thing, charging towards me, and I think well no point in half-measures; I'll *run* towards it, so I sprint up the track, and the train hurtles towards me, huge, and it hits me and *booooiiing* up, up into the rafters of Paddington station, floating up towards the ceiling and out into the blue blue sky… and I think, 'I've won. I've won reality.'

'You're dreaming.'

'Hmm?'

'You said "woah, woah, WOAH… *Jesus*."'

'Did I?'

Daphne is leaning over me, her cool hair in my face.

'What you dream?' she asks.

'I dreamt I was flying round Paddington. It was sublime.'

'Sublime?'

'Very great.'

She lies back revealing sunlight striking the corner of her open window, filtered through my eyelash it sprays a luminous fern across my vision.

'I don't dream no more,' she says, 'When I get home I'm gonna dream again. Too painful dreaming here.'

A pigeon coos outside, wooo-wooo-oo, woo-woo-oo. I copy its call, surprising both Daphne and myself with the accuracy of my mimic. Surprising the pigeon too I think—its call changes to a tenser, more questioning tone.

'I love making love then confusing pigeons.'

I shower and then breakfast on cucumber and mystery-meat in Daphne's little blue and yellow kitchen. She orders me an Uber and I give her some money for it. Her flatmate comes in to the kitchen—nice looking girl too—looks Greek to me, amazingly straight nose, like she should be on the side of a vase, seems tired though, and matter-of-fact.

'Do you have an email address?' I ask Daphne.

'Course.'

There's a wrong pause. She continues eating her yoghurt.

'I thought we could keep in touch?'

'Don't fink so.'

I feel The Clench.

'But, you know, just email, chat.'

'Bad idea.'

'Why don't you want to? I thought we had a connection?'

She looks up at me.

'Daniel, most men they have always-wanking face. You had good face. Now, not so much.'

She too looks a bit lumpy now, boyish and blotchy.

'Don't you want to then?'

'No.' She returns to her yoghurt.

I feel like I've been kicked by a horse.

'But why?'

'Doesn't matter why.'

'Yes it does. Come on.'

It's so strange. How can she *change* like this?

'Daphne, come on,' I say, pleady.

The bell rings, the taxi is here for me.

'Come Daniel, let's say goodbye in nice way.'

'No, I don't want to say goodbye. This is stupid.'

'Don't be child.'

'I'm not being a child, I'm being grown up!'

We've moved to the hallway now, but I'm not leaving until I've got something. I can't leave without *something*.

'Daniel, open hand.'

'Easy for you to say, you're a whore.'

I see pain and confusion cross her face. Part of me is glad—she deserves it, obviously. Another part feels sorry for her. I often feel pity for girls I hurt. It makes me feel better.

'Daniel *leave*.'

Rage erupts in me. 'Fuck you! No!'

She changes instantly. 'Get *out!*' she screams. I step towards her, she shrinks back. From me? Her flatmate appears, holding a sword.

'A fucking *sword!?*'

'I can use this,' she says coldly.

The moment hangs forever, like eternity has tipped itself into the cramped little stark-lit green hallway. Me, here, Daphne, furious and disappointed and ashamed, Greek girl, long thin steel blade in her hands. The whole scene does wonders for my sense of fairness.

I back out, 'look, Daphne, I'm... I... Uh...'

'Go away,' she says.

'But we *had* something...' I mew.

As soon as I'm far enough out of the door they both run against it. I hear bolts and chains.

I go downstairs, out into bright, warm, white sunlight, shaking, sick with adrenaline and strange meat, and get in the taxi.

Unreal. How did that happen? How did it escalate so quickly, so weirdly? I was in paradise ten minutes ago. Five minutes later and Medusa herself was ready to run me through with a sabre. Is the good thing so fragile? Is the fiendess ever so close?

The Uber 'driver-partner,' a bald, stubbly Spanish guy with a prominent forehead and a voice like a lorry exhaust *immediately* starts complaining about his job—interspersed with violent but evocative volleys of swearing at the cars around us. We're hardly in Bloomsbury and he's laid out how Uber is exactly synonymous with the Whore of Babylon.

'I earn shit, shit, I give 20% to Uber and they make me wait in popular area for guarantee system where I can't refuse ping but I am obligated to do three trips in hour, *I shit in your fucking milk!* and why? Ask me why!'

'Why?' I ask, not caring. She could at least have given me a false email address. Why did she have to argue like that?

'So Uber can map most popular routes and, after ten years, replace with self-driving car, and then I work in Sainsbury, but Sainsbury also self fucking checkout, *Fuck on you and fuck all over your whore mother!* so, look at this bastard, where does he go? No more jobs here, yes, but try live in Spain! Impossible!'

He glances at me, and then seems to collect himself.

'So, what, you a teacher?'

'No.'

'You look like a teacher.'

'No, I'm an artist.'

'My niece is artist. She draws her pussy.'

'Me too.'

'You draw my niece pussy?'

'That's all I draw.'

'Hope that you draw it better than she. She can't draw finger.'

I look out the window, self-righteousness leaking away, leaving the ordinary residue of shame. Seems like I've been here so many times before, looking out of a window whispering 'you fool' over and over again, leaving behind another woman who I am praying will one day forgive me or forget me.

As I pick over scabs of my self-inflicted emotional wounds the driver's ragged voice, far away, recounts a life I couldn't possibly care less about because whoever is driving also gets to drive the conversation, that's the big pull for these mind-torturing prattlers. He was a patissier in Extramadura, working in a cafe, then he got addicted to cocaine and freaked out one morning and started throwing chocolate éclairs at the customers. He had to detox in Belgium where he lost his savings in a Casino but learnt English and came here in his car, which he parks each evening somewhere in Hertfordshire and sleeps on the back seat.

'That sounds difficult,' my mouth says. Amazing how mechanical the small-talk function is, or in this case the medium-sized talk. Even wracked with self-disgust my social mechanism gives the required displays of interest.

Does everyone feel the same way I do?

'I go back to Spain soon. Fuck England, fuck English people, fuck English food, fuck English weather.'

'Mm, perhaps you *should* fuck off?'

The pressure in the taxi doubles.

'I fuck off? *I* fuck off? *You* fuck off! *Everyone* fuck off! *Everyone go to the shit!*' he yells.

I have the distinct feeling that my despair and anger at life has actually created this aggressive bald taxi driver. That before now, he didn't actually exist.

I see his fingers grip the wheel, knuckle white. The side of his head seems full of dense ignorance. I want to knock it through with a brick, or defecate in his glove compartment, but fear holds me. He could ram us into Greggs or pull out a rapier.

We sit in emotionally-raised silence. By the time we reach Peckham I'm pretty sure he won't kill us, but the atmosphere is thick and soiled. Eventually he pulls into Linden Grove.

'You'll rate me?' he says between gritted teeth.

'What?'

'Uber system. Driver rating.'

I am still simmering with guilt and contempt, yet some kind of genetic courtesy makes my mouth say 'Oh, okay.'

There's some commotion outside our house. Ambulance, police, door open, the vibe of Public Problem.

Problem; everywhere problem… but I'm beginning to feel that the problem is not the problem.

I go in. A couple are in the hallway, *very* straight looking; they look like they've just been to the opera.

'Hello.' I say. No response.

'What's up?' I ask, directing my question at the woman, as she's closer and facing me, but she turns away to her judge-like husband, gesturing towards me, as if to say '*you* talk to him.'

'*Our* son is ill,' he says. I wonder why he stressed 'our.'

'Adam?' (for it can only be).

'Yes,' he hisses.

'What's wrong with him?'

'We should be asking *you* that,' he says with Voice of Authority.

'Why?'

'He was fine when he moved here.'

'Was he?'

'Of course he was!'

Adam appears at the top of the stairs. There are two men with him, doctors perhaps. I briefly spy Toby behind them, who shoots me a glance of panicked erk then slips into his room.

Adam is led downstairs. He looks exactly as he always does, only more so; hard fixed and grim. And, dreadful shitty smell. Father awkwardly comforts mother, mother looks rather evil, like an angry featherless bird, father turns to me; 'we'll be back for his things this afternoon.'

They leave. As I close the door I hear Adam's mother;

'I just could never discipline him!'

'Don't worry darling, that's what the *professionals* are for.'

I go up to Toby's room.

'What happened?' I ask, accusingly. Toby is probably to blame.

He tells me a funny smell started coming out of Adam's room last night. They'd knocked and knocked—only he and Jacqui were in—but no answer. Eventually they'd gone in and Adam was inside a box.

'He'd pooed himself.'

'Eh? Why? What happened to him?'

'Go and see for yourself.'

Jacqui is outside her room. 'Have they gone?' she whispers.

'Yeah, I just saw him leave.'

'It's his parents I'm worried about.'

'They're all gone now.'

'Have you *seen* his room?' she points to the door, as if he might still be in there, or something else, something worse.

The room is as it was—high tech, ordered—but with all the furniture piled up against the walls; tipped up bed, Star Trek chair on the table, everything unplugged, cleared away from the centre of the room which is empty but for a large cardboard box. Next to the box are three tins of black paint and everything— walls, bed, table, windows, floor and the outside of the box—is covered in ordered scrawl; a single symbol repeated over and over again, covering every square centimetre of the room.

'What is it?'

The symbol comprises six thick horizontal lines, arranged in a square, with the second and fifth lines broken.

'It's an I-ching symbol,' says Toby.

'What's that?' asks Jacqui, 'like I-phone?'

'Kind of.'

'What does it mean?'

'I looked it up,' says Toby, 'It means fire.'

'Fire?' whispers Jacqui *'Why?'*

'No idea.'

'We should clean it up,' I say.

'Yes,' says Jacqui, with urgency. I've never heard her so eager to clean, but then she's right next door. Can't be nice. We get mops and buckets. I feel hot resentment, like I shouldn't be do- ing this, it's not my business—but it doesn't take too long—the piss and excrement are only in the box, where Adam has been living, so we gaffer tape about a hundred bin bags to it, take it outside, crush it, put that in another half-dozen sanitary layers and stuff it in the wheelie. Before I can find anyone to really blame, the job is done.

We convene in the kitchen, sunlight bright, disordered with the smell of old onions.

'If I had parents like that, I'd look to the box,' I say, shielding my eyes from the morning glare, 'typical emotionally over-involved high-class fuckers.'

Jacqui knows his parents. She's the type who knows everyone.

'He can't function in the real world,' she says, 'at least that's what his sister reckons. He's a brat with his mother.'

'So it's their fault?'

'Oh nobody blames parents these days; I think he had a broken heart,' she says, busying around making tea. She tells us he was after a girl at work, a Japanese model and, a few weeks ago, he'd asked her out.

'I was with him when he got a text from her, two symbols, you know, Japanese symbols. He looked them up on his phone—I'd never *seen* him so animated—flick, flick, flick—until he found the meaning. Impossible, it said.'

One word; impossible.

'Not enough to send you into the box though,' says Toby.

'No, sad though,' says Jacqui, 'Oh, Daniel, I'm so sorry about last night.'

'What do you mean?'

'Melissa, it's awful what she did to you.'

'You what?'

'She said,' says Jacqui, trying to look serious, 'she said that she couldn't take it anymore. She'll pay you for the drinks.'

'*She* did a runner?'

'Isn't it *awful?*'

'Yeah, it's awful.'

So there you have it. A date so bad we *both* ran away.

Jonas comes in.

'Didn't know you were in Jonas.'

'Phone call for you' he says handing me his mobile with exaggerated rigidity and a tight sigh.

'Thanks. Hello?'

'Hello? Hello?'

'Yes, hello?'

'How are you I'm fine how are you?'

'Fine thank you.'

'Good! How are you?'

'I'm fine thanks.'

'Friend of Igwe?'

'Me?' I say, 'Yes, sort of, I knew him.'

'Can you send money?'

'Who is this?'

'Nnimmo.'

'Who?'

'Igwe brother.'

'Oh, hello. I'm sorry about…'

'We no have enough bring Igwe home. You help?'

'How much do you need?'

'Four hundred pound sterling. I give you transfer detail.'

'Hold on, hold on, let me get a pen.'

I write down the numbers and tell him I'll see what I can do. He doesn't hang around for pleasantries; seems to assume that I'll send the money and that's that.

I give the phone back to Jonas.

'I'd prefer if you didn't give my number to everyone,' he says.

'It's not everyone, just the police and the government. And credit agencies. Toby deals with male friends, Jacqui with female friends—it's all carefully shared out. You've got the official stuff because you're the only person I know who never breaks the law.'

'Can't you get a phone?' he asks, wearily.

'If I got a phone people would be able to easily get hold of me, and I'd be able to easily get hold of them. It's a two-way street Jonas.'

'This is the point! Don't you want an easy life?'

'Hmm… You know, I'm really not sure I do.'

He huffs out.

'That was Igwe's brother. He's asking for four hundred quid to help get the body out to Nigeria.'

'Four hundred?' says Toby.

'Yeah, creepy isn't it? We should pay.'

'We?'

'Yeah. Can't you chip in?'

'Erm,' he says doubtfully.

'It's not that much, but I'm hitting rock bottom. I've had an expensive couple of days.'

'I think not; I'm not sending money to Nigeria.'

'But come on, poor old Igwe. Besides,' I say, *'four hundred quid.'*

'It's just a coincidence.'

'It's juju!'

'I don't dig the juju.'

'The juju digs you.'

'That is just not true. Juju has completely abandoned me.'

There's tension in the room. Once again two people are trying to communicate across the mood-divide. It's a far more imposing obstacle than the language barrier. Not only is it a mile-wide gulf, but it's almost impossible to believe that anybody is *really* on the other side of it.

'For fuck's sake Toby, the guy's dead.' My two-tone emotional pendulum has swung back from self-disgust to anger.

'So what? We're all dead.'

•

Gravity sucks me towards porn. Again. I've read Essays in Idleness, sent some futile flirty emails into the inboxes of the sexual elect, made my three positive actions, painted a few doughcraft serpents and now there's the computer screen in front of me. Wifey drilled in library, horny teenager craves cum, ass-shaped asteroid strikes bristling forest of cocks…

The Wizard priest of Kume is said to have lost his supernatural powers when he spied the white legs of a woman as she squatted washing clothes. I can believe it; I feel my own eternal yang draining away as the fixed living-dead pornstare takes over my system. *It's just meat.* It's like I've never really seen porn before… except when I first took magic mushrooms. I was camping with some friends in the New Forest and I went off for a piss, next to a river, became superaware that my self was a construct and that 'everything is true' and, when I came back, the two guys who hadn't taken any mushies were frying bacon over a camping stove, and I looked at the bacon, sitting in the pan, and I tell you, I have never seen anything more charnel, more repulsively unliving, undead. And that cadaverous viscera is humping and grinding on the plasma screen now. *It's just meat.* Flesh puppets. Bags of muscle, lymph, bone, bile and fat; one rank above corpse. The cocks look so aggressive too.

I consider a bit of self-abuse, but somehow, with hundreds of tiny little old men's heads dotted around the room, all staring at me, I can't get into it. Or maybe I'm just a meat puppet too? Or maybe, *maybe*, I just have better things to do. Like video games! That's what real men do; play Cities. I turn on my carefully built world and start working on my transport system, get my suburbs on the metro, upgrade the roads through my financial district—ah, but I see my civilians near the oil refinery are complaining about pollution and the new office district doesn't have enough educated workers, so I have to invest in some high schools…

Anxiety, a sick feeling of restless futility, an edgy empty need to *get*. It never goes away. As the city grows the game unlocks assets— unique buildings, monuments, advanced zoning, different kinds of civic decoration—which dangle before me like a phone number, a touch, a kiss, a hug, a naked body, penetration, orgasm… and then total disinterest.

The games I play—Civilisation™, and Cities™ and Ordinary Daily Life™—they imprint themselves on my mind with the same aggressive intensity as porn. Like the ever-flicking mental fapbook of cocks and cunts these virtual worlds are continually beamed from my pineal projector, zooming and panning over the screen of my eyelids; digi-terrains that follow me unto dream, restlessly populating my memory with the same insatiable momentum as the towns I plan on my CGI landscapes. I'm going to have to send this the same way as Cumshot Compilation #171. I spend weeks building my city, until it has reached the limits of the play area, until it has covered every piece of green, until there is nowhere else to go, and now what?

Armageddon! The creators of the game realise that once you have spent a hundred and fifty hours creating a city that nobody in their right mind would want to live in, all there is left to do is rain fire down from the sky and send in Godzilla; after which I feel exactly as I do after I've ejaculated into a tissue.

No, I can't face the porn funnel, or the simulated city, or another joint even. I turn on Sprak and call up dial-a-bile.

'You again?' comes the sarcastic drawl.

'Yeah…'

'What is it? Jerked off, blown out or just giving up?'

'Er, blown out, possibly giving up too.'

'What happened?'

'I fell in love with a tart and then she drew a sword on me, or no, her friend did.'

'Hahaha—you got rejected by a prostitute?'

'Yeah.'

'Hahaha—can you get any lower?'

'Um, I *think* so.'

'I think so too.'

I hang up. She's right, but it's not helping so much.

What is happening to me? I don't want to be a Taoist renunciant. I *like* people—or, you know, I like joining in. Apart from anything else my mammalian brain is fairly anxious about being cast out of the tribe. Yet phones, porn, work, video games, club-going, ritualised consumption of socially approved narcotics, ritualised validation of centrally-organised spectacle, social media and abusive telephone confession services fill me with profound existential dread, and the self-disgust of the vanquished.

We're all dead. It's just meat. I can't be bothered to kill myself. My life is a trombone. Back to the atom. How could I have turned on Daphne—the grabber. The stuck grabber. I have projected my heart out onto the screen of my mind, where I look back on a once living theatre now as flat and unreal as I am.

The gathering matter of my room doesn't help. I have stacked boxes of illegally acquired flat-pack furniture, electronica, sports equipment and God knows what else ranged around the walls, unsold, unused, shoddy, plastic, plasterboard. It disgusts me, yet I want more of it, I want more albums, I want Daphne, I want travel, I want fame... all boxed-up things on shelves lining the same exitless labyrinth of silent compromise that Adam scooted up and down in, until he retreated into his box and painted his walls with runes.

My So-Called Self

'Dear Jobseeker. You are currently participating in the work programme. You are expected to work, voluntarily, for twenty hours a week for *Saturn Cleaning* at *The Meadows Community Carehome* (address follows). If you refuse this assignment you will incur Jobseeker's Allowance sanctions for up to twenty five weeks, and you will lose National Insurance credits. We wish you every success in your new endeavour.'

Yes, the Pakistani guy ratted on me, but for some reason they didn't stop my benefits straight off. Instead they've put me on a compulsory voluntary work programme. After buying £100 worth of flour, salt, paint and glaze, then purchasing an evening of erotic satori with Daphne for £200, then paying £400 to exorcise Igwe's posthumous juju, I'm skint. I'm even looking for real jobs now; but in the meantime I have to go on this poxy thing; which, what is it? It's not work, because I'm not getting paid for it, but it's not not-work, because the whole point is that I'm supposed to be working. So I'm not a worker at work, or a non-worker at non-work. I'm a 'participant in a work-related activity.'

So far I've avoided those vile training programmes they put us on. *Crawling out of Entrenched Unemployability Through Self-Esteem Enhancement.* I heard of one old geezer who had to do a 'Cleanliness Exercise' where they taught him how to wash his face and adopt an 'Employable Hair-Parting.' And that's before you get to thirty hours a week of free classes at the 'University of Sainsbury's.'

The Meadows is a dark, two-storey warren of hospital green griefholes, smelling of Glade, disinfectant, talcum powder and dissolution of the flesh. I am introduced to my agency supervisor, a woman called Magda, a stiff-lipped Pole who instantly hates me. She explains my duties in a tone of boredom, impatience and contempt. I can detect a little condescension in there too. No point in asking questions of course—*never* ask questions at work. Just listen and nod. Sign in here, pick up hoover from there, right, trolley from the store room, these rooms first, then those ones, got it?

Yes, yes, off you go Magda. She leaves me on the bottom landing next to the lift, which I take up to start my four-hour shift. The doors open. An old woman—hundred and fifty?—is standing there, staring at something invisible to mortal man. As I pull my trolley out she turns to me, shaking and gumming— her face carved with many, many years of confusion and misery and abandonment—and says something in a tiny hoarse voice.

'Sorry dear?' I say, craning down to her.

'Please kill me,' she whimpers, 'please.'

'I can't.'

'Oh… (long pause)… nevermind then.'

'Can I maybe help you in some other way?'

'No.'

'Alright.'

I set to work. The first door I go to is half open. I tap it, 'Cleaner? Can I come in?'

'Come in! Come in! Quickly!'

The room is dark and smells of excrement and sweat. A woman is leaning against a wall facing away from me. Between us is a commode. Her pyjama trousers are partially pulled down and I can see wide arse-cheeks hanging down in thick pale pachydermal folds. A slight smear of shit.

'Quick,' she gasps with terrible urgency, *'toilet.'*

I go in, 'what do you want me to do?'

'Trousers you fool!'

I hook one arm under hers, yank down flannel trousers with the other, and then lower her as slowly as I can—she is very heavy— onto her commode. The second she touches down a farting cascade of shit gushes from her.

She glances round and vaguely sees me gagging and wincing.

She wipes her arse and then pulls herself onto the bed, yanking at her pyjama trousers. I retreat to the door.

'I'll come back later.'

Nat King Cole's 'When I fall in love' is playing on her radio. I gently turn off the ceedee player as I leave and pull the door to.

'Do you mind?' she says quite distinctly.

I put it back on.

In the next room is a big old fella in a chair, staring out the window.

'Cleaner. Can I come in?'

'Aye, come on.'

'Thanks.'

He turns. A good man—so easy to tell with old people; their whole lives are written on their huge faces. This guy has the biggest nose and ears I've ever seen. He could have been sculpted by me and Toby.

'Where's Donna?' he asks, accent thick and northern.

'Not sure. I suppose she does another shift now, or maybe she's left.'

'Hope so. What's your name then?'

'Daniel.'

'Derek.'

'I'm not sure what I'm supposed to be doing actually Derek. I'm a bit scared of my boss.'

Derek chuckles, his front teeth are missing, 'she's a cow. Just sit down and have a chat. I'll cover for ya.'

'Right you are!'

I sit in Derek's guest chair.

'So how's… erm… life?' I ask.

'Life? Life ain't no problem, it's the *living* that's grim.'

'You're retired now though.'

'I'm not talking about *work!*'

'What did you do?'

'I was a miner.'

'Blimey.'

'Aye.'

'What was that like then?'

'Oh, hard. Every day, crawl up t'gate, used t' have to shove yer shovel in front o' ya. Used t' have ta get off, strap yerself into a hole, fill the belt wi' coal, pitch black, cutting and shovelling, ten hours, fourteen. Hard, awful… but that was being alive; you know, it were a *purpose*.'

'Right, I see.'

'When you done a day's work, all cleaned up, finished, when you, when you pull up a bass, tugging away at the line, when you, *uppercut*' he hisses, shadow boxing a knockout blow—that's life. All this,' he gestures around the room, vaguely, 'just *living*.'

'Were you a boxer then too?'

'Used to like a scrap.'

'Maybe you could give me some advice. If I'm in a dangerous situation. Let's say, I've never had a fight, and I know this
evening I'm going to have to, you know, engage. What would
you suggest? How should I go about it?'

He thinks for a moment.

''Ave him.'

Oh, right. I see.

'What you do then?' he asks, 'You en't a cleaner are ya?'

'I want to be an artist.'

'That's alright, but you gotta live first. Nothing to say otherwise is there? You look at all this stuff now, on the telly, it's
all nonsense. None of 'em have *lived*.'

'You think so?'

'They're not living. How *can* they be? You gotta *live*.'

'It's quite hard I find, that.'

'Just throw yourself out into world.'

'Is that all there is to it?'

'Well you gotta train too. That's true for everything you do
in't it? If you want to be a man you have to master your tools.
But don't make no difference if you ain't got heart, courage.
In't that right Mam?'

He looks over at a small photograph on his sideboard.

'That's me Mam,' says Derek.

I get up to look at the photo. It is ancient, slightly out of
focus, yellowing at the edges, black and white with a slight
sepia mask. A woman stands on a beach, in a cloche hat and
long coat. Although blurred, the shape of her face, the dark
blobs of her eyes, the shadows under her cheeks, the way she is
standing, slightly off-centre, slightly, gently, smiling, somehow
with her whole body—it all says integrity and resilience, but
also womanliness. There is something impossibly noble *and*
sweetly feminine about her; impossible, I mean, today—I've
never seen a woman look like that.

'This woman looks amazing, Derek.'

'People looked different back then,' he says.

We both look at the picture.

'Whassat?' says Derek.

'I didn't say anything.'

'Not you, *Mam*.'

He listens.

'She says you'll be alright. Just keep going.'

'Okay, I will.'

In less than three minutes, without saying anything particularly deep, or even sane, it feels like this old guy has answered all my confusion about art and soothed my anxieties about life. Or his long-dead mother has. Live, master tools, open your heart and keep going. How simple! I'll get right on it. First of all though I have some waged work to do.

It's early, but everyone seems to be up, bodily at any rate. Most are out to lunch, but they're friendly enough. I ask them what they want done, try and have a chat, if they're compos mentis, bit of hoovering, empty commodes. It's quite literally shit, but there's an actual purpose and actual human beings are involved so it's okay. Shame I'm not getting paid.

The old folk have an unusual way of expressing themselves I find. The old women, in particular, very often say things like; 'My niece got married last week, lovely it was, her brother-in-law died of cancer, he loved fishing…' or 'So much raping going on these days—would you like a biscuit? I can't move my thumbs any more…' Initially I was confused, but, from watching them talk to each other, I find the way to do it is match your response to the rapidly changing cues as fast as you can—wince, ahh lovely, *ooh!* ugh! realllly? oh *no*—like a game of emotional face-snap.

Tea break comes around, and it's also a draining affair. The atmosphere in the staff kitchen is tense and cackling. Working class which, under optimum conditions, makes me feel at home, but not here. I sit quietly in the corner, instinctively intuiting from the petulant slouch of the young girls and the hag-like yacking of the older women that a single word will immediately banish me to an alienated state of self-loathing. Better to be 'the quiet guy' while they loudly share names and refer to stories I do not know, conspicuously chuckling, trying to make me feel ignorant I suppose, letting me know that I am an outsider here.

There's a very tired looking care-assistant at the table to my right. I want to talk to her, but feel hesitant about puncturing her exhausted inwardness. A professional enters, blond and beady, with no such scruples. She walks straight up to the nurse and starts talking in the cutting colourless semi-nasal tone of the graduate.

'Ah, Dalia. I was thinking, would you like to know what a drama therapist does... so that we can better co-ordinate?'

'Okay then,' says Dalia with a gentle smile. She's got a tough life, Dalia, very obviously, and it's one thing to have a hard life, but it's another to have a sweet smile like that, trying to struggle up for air.

The professional sits down and takes out some cards. All precise and important. I wonder where the girl is, underneath all this.

'Do you want the postcards or the emotion cards?' she asks.

'The emotion cards,' says Dalia.

'Okay, good,' she says, very much enjoying the important performance or the performance of importance, 'take a look through those, and I want you to pick two or three and tell me why you've picked them.'

Dalia picks a couple and says, 'well I like the smiling face on this man, and, er, this house looks quite pretty.'

'So you see?' says the girl, beaming, 'This is how I establish a rapport between myself and the patient.'

'Mmm, I see. Yes, thank you Zoe.'

Zoe smiles, happy to have explained this complicated business, and then leaves. If only Dalia had some cards to establish a rapport like that, instead of having to spend months and years with patients, accepting their company, slowly building up a human relationship with them. A pack of cards like that would be really useful.

•

I've only got an hour to go—just enough time to do the public areas, mostly the main recreation area. Around the mint green walls, separated by plastic flowers, Glade freshmatics and scant tinsel efforts, are about fifty chairs pointing towards a massive TV and in the chairs are bodies in various states of decomposition and collapse. On the television is a huge pair of breasts advertising shampoo. This is followed by an advert for deodorant featuring a tank. Then the show starts—a cop show. Nobody watches, nobody cares.

Christmas cards are stuck to the walls. I gather the 'guests' are encouraged to contribute their cards to the common cause. All pretty boring to read of course, 'best for the new year, love Natalie and the family.' But one says 'I hope you have a reasonable Christmas.' Realistic?

I'm on my way out, changed out of my formaldehyde-yellow overalls, but stop on the stairs because an old gent is stepping down backwards, very, very slowly. He looks up at me.

'Sorry love,' he's got a broad Lancs accent.

'Don't apologise. Take as long as you like.'

'Where ya from?'

'Kent.'

'Oh! I was there. In the war. Maidstone. My cousin's from... er... uh...' he stops to think, 'it's not coming... I'm eighty-eight.'

He looks it. Liver-spotted bald head, long nose all of bones.

'Yes,' he says, 'and you're twenty five.'

'Yes!'

'Aye, I'm a good estimator... six foot one are ya?'

'Yes, right again.'

'Aye.'

'Where are you going, sir?'

'I'm going to die.'

He slowly, slowly creeps down the stairs, walks across the lobby and out the front door where an ambulance is waiting for him. He sits down on a wheelchair which is winched up to the interior. I stand watching him. Just as the orderly wheels him back into the jaws of death he waves to me.

'Ta-ta then!' he says.

•

It is a world of death. Life is a drumskin stretched over a bottomless well of unbeing. It's another one of those things that 'everybody knows,' that we're all going to die, but they don't know it—how can they? If they did they wouldn't be shocked when people died—amazing! he died! The collapse of the world will be the same I'm sure, everyone walking around saying, 'I can't believe it.'

Nobody talks about death, nobody thinks about death, nobody looks at death. Dead bodies are whisked off the street before you have a chance to confront the void. It's as Toby says; there's this vast conspiracy to keep death out of view. We're *ashamed*. We know that we should be confronting nothingness, not all goth-morbid; but frankly, simply, to look; to look into the almighty what-is-not.

God only knows what survives death, but one thing I am stone cold certain of, whatever I can describe, imagine, remember, want, hope, plan, touch, think about, worry about, measure, assess, decide, fear, hold, get or win—my so-called self—is not going to make it. So why do I care so much about myself? I know, it's obvious why—I've got to get up and make breakfast and I fancy Audrey Tautou in Dirty Pretty Things—but it's also obvious that, in the end, in the end, my ordinary me cannot possibly matter; because it isn't matter.

Such is my thinking as I arrive at Adam's old Graphic Design company in Brixton :*Rising*. It's in the ground floor of what used to be the Brixton Tate Library, and seems to be made entirely of zinc, plexiglass and polypropylene. They've also replaced the segmented Georgian windows with crystal clear panels to complete the vivarium vibe. It's a modern space, alright. They don't use 'place' anymore. It's a *space*. The walls are merely conventions!

I enter, carrying my doughcraft box, and tell a muscular woman with no eyebrows that I'm here for an interview with Noah Zeeman, then sit down to wait in the lobby quadrant, reading brochures which say things like 'The Thought Factory' and 'Land of Node' and 'Beast of Freedom.' :*Rising eschews trends or corporate cash cows, we have taste, but we might not be tasteful, we don't think in terms of 'disciplines' rather of 'realities.'*

I flick through an issue of Rebl. Articles about sex workers, Mafia fixers, Rio trash-pickers and other things hipsters like to read about. Lots of pictures of meat, and bricks. Huge glossy pages of stick-thin girls looking dead in a city of flies.

Earlier peoples worshipped the goddess in two forms. One was the large round life-woman, with 'shelf effect' buttocks and enormous breasts; which represented the universe in its creative sense. And the other was a straight skinny woman; the tomb goddess.

This means, perhaps, I think, looking at the adverts in Rebl that the world today worships the angel of death. I know I do!

'Daniel; hi, had a good day?' Noah, a tall, toothy, bearded man with long curly hair, wearing tight blue trousers and calf-brown brogues, greets with a clammy handshake and leads me into an interview node, a plexiglass cubicle which hums with soft blue light when we materialise.

'Depends what you call good I suppose,' I say, sliding onto a plastic panton chair and placing my box on the floor.

'Well, that's what we're here to talk about,' he says, pulling out my portfolio, which comprises a single photograph of a tiny little planet, in a kind of smooth, fleshy cup: looks a bit like an eyeball. Underneath, written in Unica77—the most fashionable and expensive Swiss font I could illegally download—is written the legend 'The Ignoble Path.'

'Now,' Noah says, 'we don't usually agree to see referrals from the Jobcentre, and your portfolio, I must say, lacks a little in terms of existence, but I'm a big believer in instinct and we don't look for qualifications here, or even experience. Just talent, no matter how raw, and I thought to myself,' he taps my resume, 'there *might* be something here for us.'

He nods slowly and significantly.

'So, I tell you what,' he says, 'why don't we start by you explaining your image here?'

'Alright. What you see here is a close up photograph of a marble inserted into my anus. I've called it 'The Ignoble Path' because that's what I believe all paid work to be, no matter how prestigious. The work space is nothing more than a warped, attenuated, comfortable concentration camp. A mirror, a microcosm of a world full of idiotic, miserable people—idiotic *because* they're miserable. We're all asleep, living in the past or the future or in some minute fabricated identity. Fear rules. This is how it is, and keeping all this together is, ultimately, the purpose of work—keeping us unhappy, addicted, separated from each other, identifying with teams or clubs or beliefs, continually consuming, continually wanting, never at rest, never at peace—unless you happen to be far enough up the mountain of excrement to be cut off from your own human heart. And people say "oh well that's human nature, it won't change, the masses will never change." I say fuck that. What about *you*? Are you saying *you* want to be alone, bored, frustrated, helpless, unloved your whole life; and then die? Are you happy with this lot? I'm not, and, you know, you only live once. Or maybe you don't, maybe you live a thousand times—who knows—but you only live *this* life once, that I do know; this life, in this body; and I'll be buggered if I'm going to live it arranging luxury canapés, or boxing up phone chargers, or panhandling for a wage in a graphic design node. I am not a hard, cold glass bead, rammed by economic necessity into the anus of the world. Fuck that, and fuck you.'

Ringing silence.

Noah takes a deep breath. Holds it. Slaps his hands onto his knees and exhales.

'That's an interesting take Daniel.'

'Thanks,' I hiss, politely. I'm pretty fuelled up now. I can hear my heart booming in my chest.

'Erm, I don't think there's much more to say really is there?' he says.

'No, not really.'

'Okay, well, thanks for coming in, feel free to grab some muesli on your way out.'

I shake his hand, quite amicably under the circumstances, open the top of my cardboard box, where twenty or so glazed old men's heads are lying on bubble wrap, and give one to Noah

'There you go Noah,' I say, 'it's an old man's head.'

'Thanks.'

I pass through the play space, the muesli node and the lobby quadrant, back out into a freezing grey Christmas in Brixton.

Beautiful Brixton, of top-ranking sound-systems and Studio One, home generators, Farah slacks, Wing Chun and meat patties, ackee and saltfish and violent uprisings; all long gone, hit the bucket. Now pop-up entrepreneurs, professionals and the glorious precariat; now H&M, Specsavers, Santander, and gourmet coffee shops full of designers browsing for gigs and very many, very clean, pink men.

'Yeah, yeah, went to Wilderness last summer. The heyday is over though mate. It was great, but it's already getting too commercial, you know what I mean? Yeah, yeah. Got any of that Rwandan coffee? Off camping for a week in Norway and I need the fuel, hahahaha! Cool, cool, let us know what you're up to before I go, because I'm doing a digital detox...'

Yet something rises in me, something uncalled for, unconditional; some swelling, itching, shuddering enormity. The clouds make a room of the dreary world, but that room is luminous and alive—and I am that life. I am that muted mood. I am that big room. I inhale the whole world and the whole world breathes me out. I'm set free, and the freedom is a *thing*, a liquid, surging up my spine like a river of light, bursting its banks and flooding into my limpid limbs. Oh the causeless glory!

I stroll into deeper Brixton, a part of it, a part of everyone and everything. I feel *them*, their blank fixed quality, shutting out the unshaded glare, shutting out each other, all doors closed. We're like a funnel of marbles in a darkening mall, but I can *feel* it. It's so vivid, for a moment it's all so real, the bricks, the clouds, the actual horror. Yes, the horror, but, for a moment, I let it in, unresisting, and, for a long, long moment, something else is breathing.

I wait in packed Pope's Road for Toby, who's bringing the other doughcraft box. The youth freckle in and out of Pop Brixton, intermingling with the denizens of Station Road; the Pakistani small businessman (which, as far as I can tell, is a tautology because all Pakistanis are small businessmen) the Sudanese, the Brazilians, the Nigerians and the Vietnamese. People shuffle around roadside market stalls of mobile phones, underwear and unknowable root vegetables, which are marshalled by huddling leg-jiggling young men of preposterously neat goatees—bored and ever on the lookout for an opportunity. Everyone looks like they're sucking on a burnt match; haunted, vengeful, tight and yellowish.

Behind me is a shop called 'Internet / Carpets' from which chikachikachikaBABOOMBOOM ragga plays at world-hating volume. A minute old black woman is sitting just inside, next to an inactive TV set. She leans forward and switches the TV on, then sits back in her seat where she cannot see the fucking thing anyway, and continues looking out the window and gumming her lips.

But where is Toby? He's usually late, being as, before he leaves the house, he has to check his backpack and 14 pockets, come outside, realise he's forgotten his Rizlas or portable saw, go back inside, skin up again, answer the phone, rush back into the kitchen, stuff a biscuit in his mouth, stop, wonder what he's come in here for, and so on; and in addition to that, he can't say no to a conversation, and, in addition to that, like many people who are always late, he just doesn't experience the passing of dead time, or the passing of other people's dead time, as pain.

Forty minutes after our 2 pm meet, he appears, and he is wearing a fez; not his usual choice. His monkeyish face is wild and pleading which, like many of his expressions, has the frank intensity of a child.

'I've,' his eyes dart around, 'we need to go inside,' he fixes on a greasy spoon and I follow him as he pro-walks over the road into the dark café. When we are installed in the furthest cubicle, he violently relaxes—if such a thing is possible—and I ask him what?

'I've just had a terrible, terrible...' he says, swallowing back agitation.

'What?'

He'd parked in Angell Road, and was walking up here, when he saw, in the concrete basketball court on the corner of St James' Crescent, a dozen kids, fifteen years old, who had cornered a young woman and were pushing her into the five-a-side nets. Toby watched the scene through the diamond mesh, hoping that someone else would step in, or she would escape, or something would happen; until one of the boys grabbed the woman's hair and she shrieked. Pointless to call the police, pointless to ask for help, thinks he. The woman tried to escape, but the boys pushed her back. *Okay, you have to do something...* and sick with fear, Toby pushed the iron gate and started walking towards the problem.

'Excuse me!' he said, shaky, voice all back-of-the-nose. The boys turned towards him. 'Is that really necessary?' he asked, at quavering volume.

The mobmind instantly assessed Toby—his voice, bearing and dress—and began walking towards him with purpose. One kid picked up a piece of gravel, then others did the same; and Toby turned on his heels and ran.

'Fuck him!' shouted a boy at the front, and they began throwing very small pieces of stone.

Toby dropped the doughcraft box and, frantic with adrenaline, sprinted out of the court and down Gresham Road, heart sick panic. He glanced back—turned into Brixton Road—stumbled into 'March Hare, Novelty Partywear' and asked the girl if he could sit down behind the till because he was having a palpitation.

Toby, explaining this to me, was calming down now.

'She was very nice,' he said, 'she made me a cup of tea.'

'And sold you a fez?'

'Oh yes,' he takes it off and looks at it sadly, 'no, I asked to buy this. I thought it was the least I could do.'

'How long were you in there for?'

'About half an hour, I think.'

'And the boys had gone when you came out?'

'Yeah. I dunno what happened to your stuff. I'm really sorry.'

'It's alright.'

'Maybe I should learn some martial art.'

'Maybe you should learn some balls?'

Toby nods, 'Sarah said the same thing.'

I leave Toby in the cafe to see what's happened to half my work and, yes, it has been destroyed. Fragments of heads and flowers and little birds and big feet and nipples and shiny mushrooms lie in bits all over the road, including the Goddess, which has been dismembered and scattered over the five-a-side court. The head I almost wept over for wanting has been ground into the gravel.

Toby is all apologies back at the cafe, but no point in moaning, I say, let's just try and sell the half we have left. We take our wares over to the Arts and Craft Market and lay out our picnic rug.

'Sorry, what are you doing?' A market official—a sarcastic looking woman with dreads—appears before we've unpacked half the box and tells us we need a permit.

'Oh come on, we've only got a few bits.'

'Sorry, no.'

'I didn't think we'd get collared quite so quickly.'

'Do you know where we can go?' asks Toby.

'We were thinking of Windrush square,' I say.

'You'll get busted anywhere,' she says, 'you can't just lay down a blanket and start peddling.'

'Oh.'

'What you can do though,' she says, 'if you can find a closed down shop, or a derelict building, is you can sell stuff in the doorway, because it's not technically in the street.'

So we yomp around Brixton looking for a failed business. Eventually we find a closed down bookshop on Ferndale Road and spread our display out in the doorway

It's quite diverse, the product. In the end everyone got involved. Toby did a few more old men's busts, Jonas contributed some startlingly realistic Roman weapons (he's into ancient warfare), Jacqui made a big gay pope with bee's eyes, Naeema did a triangle, but that got stomped and, all told, I spent quite a happy week mixing flour and salt, shaping little balls, wetting them together, baking them hard, painting and glazing. Stephen, Gurt, Piscina and Eddie all stopped by too, did a bit of bread-art, bought a barcode-discount iron or mousemat, chatted about sex, politics and TV. All very civilised you see.

And so here we are huddled under a derelict awning as customers of the Post Office and the Chocolate Museum turn their weary way back to the main road, ignoring us. Nobody, but nobody, stops to look at the kaleidoscope of creative weirdness on sale here, each item less than a tenner.

I try a bit of barrow-boy sales patter, out in street—'ladies and gentlemen, one day only, beautiful hand-crafted figurines'—all of that; but I sound like a pillock, a man too young for his intent, so we just stand there in silence looking at the doughcraft like a dog laid it.

'I logged in to Sarah's email account last night,' says Toby, 'and read all her emails. One that she'd written to a friend of hers, about me, ended with her recounting something I'd said. I'd said to her "Is love the truth and all the pain an illusion, or the pain the truth and the love a lie?' and she wrote after this, to her friend, "I'm like, yeah, *whatever*, you weirdo."'

'Some would say it serves you right, snooping around like that.'

'I just don't think those kind of rules apply in a relationship.'

'What rules do apply?'

'It's hard to see how any do. The only person I know who is happy with women, is Andy.'

Andy Augusta, author of 'Myself Fucking a Whore,' was Jacqui's choice to replace Adam. Naeema, author of 'All Men are Clients,' was none too pleased.

'Yeah, but you can't take Andy Augusta as a model,' I say.

'Why not? He's happy.'

'He's a wanker. A dickhead.'

'Well which one? A wanker or a dickhead?'

'What do you mean?'

'Is he a wanker or a dickhead? Or an arsehole?'

'Erm.'

'Because each of those words have different shades of meaning.'

'You can find a bit of everything, I think.'

'But it's all subjective, innit?'

That's the thing with Toby. He just has no, I dunno, no standards somehow. Or, what is it? I've felt, all my life, that, he and I, we *have* something, you know 'our thing,' and then he moans about me to Jacqui, or he says Andy is alright, or he hangs out with ludicrous fools, with no talent, and takes their advice on his works of genius, or... Can it be *loyalty* I'm missing here? Is that it? It seems such an old-fashioned word—who cares about loyalty in this day and age? Me, apparently.

'I just, I think I'd like to be a moron,' says Toby, 'then I wouldn't have any problems. Look at them—they're okay.'

I take in the river of scorn flowing around us. The overall aesthetic is 'grim determination.' A woman passes who's removed her face and painted on a whole other one. A young girl in standard tiny-t-shirt and leggings, struts past chest-out in a bruising 'I've got places to go!' hyper-exaggerated swagger. Just behind her a Bangladeshi guy, shamelessly, morbidly, staring at her admittedly wonderful arse.

'I don't think they are okay Toby. And I think these people go to pieces if their iPhones don't charge properly or if the World Cup gets cancelled.'

'I used to think,' he says, 'that all I needed was to find a beautiful girl and then everything would be okay. We'd be happy. But relationships aren't like that, are they?'

'What? Happy? They should be.'

'Should is the devil's favourite modal verb. Frankensheila is all dressed in should. I don't actually need the 36-24-38 body, young Kathleen Turner's face, familiarity with cultural theory, nice record collection, blah, blah, blah, blah, *blah*...'

The art theory bit is interesting. I mentioned something intellectual to Daphne. I said to her something like I couldn't work out if it felt good with her subjectively or objectively, because the feeling didn't seem to be either in me or in the world, and she just shrugged and said 'I don't care about those things,' and I tried to explain but she was having none of it. And; I always thought I wanted a girl who was my intellectual equal; but for an instant I realised that my intellect is no more important, really, than a bicycle repair manual. Of course bike repair is useful, but you don't need it to love someone, to share yourself with them, to touch the world behind the world, or even to ride the thing. Do you?

I don't tell any of this to Toby. I haven't told anyone about Daphne, but I wouldn't tell Toby anyway as he's an inveterate blurter.

Just a bit down from us, next to 'Game,' the council has put up a 'Christmas Wish Tree,' a piece of plastic street furniture that you can attach little postcard wishes to. I leave Toby—head down, hands in his pockets—at our 'stall' and wander over to read a few:

I wish Burger King were cheaper.

I wish Ben would go out (is Ben a dog?).

I wish a broken heart wasn't so time-consuming.

I wish everything was as easy as getting fat.

(Childish writing) I wish granddad was a frog or bison.

I wish Tim was here.

I wish reality had an undo button.

(Child again) I wish I was 300 metres tall.

I wish everything were different.

I go to write one myself, but the pen has run out of ink, so I slump back to my pitiful bid to live as an independent artist, shivering under a dead bookshop, itself one of the most depressing things. A failed business I mean, or a failing one— empty shop, bored man behind the counter who has risked everything for his dream must now sit there, day in day out, as it slowly dies around and within him. Not so long ago there was a shop in Peckham specifically for running shoes. I went in once—Running Wild it was called—to buy a pair of laces and the owner, a meepy little guy with no chin, looked at the laces and said, with intense bitterness, '*is that all?*'

Toby looks at me, 'shall we call it a day?'

'Give it half an hour more.'

'I really should go. I've got to study for my interview. Get a haircut.'

'Just wear the fez.'

He looks at it. 'Nah... do you want it?'

He's accepted his Dad's help; a telephonist job at financial data giant Apollo Incorporated: 'Entry-Level Global Customer Support Representative—Spanish speaker.' The interview was something of a formality, given that his Dad pretty much ran the department, but he had to look the part and read up about the company and work himself up into a lather of contrived enthusiasm about the opportunity

'Yeah, alright.' I take the stupid hat from him, and put it on.

'I'm sorry about what happened Daniel.'

'It's alright.'

He walks off, as people do on freezing cold days in Brixton; pushing through a hostile substance. I hope he's going to be alright. He's turned a corner, I feel, but somehow I'm more worried for his spirit now. Number one suicide profession is artists don't you know? I imagine many of those topped themselves when they *got* a job.

I wait another hour, squalid and desperate, all the weird aliveness of the morning has trickled away. This stuff on the floor, tucked in a doorway, and me too young and nervous and self-conscious of my feeble display to either make a show or even comfortably stand here. I look dodgy and desperate and so everyone avoids me, particularly women.

This thing of leading a concentrated meta-life of God-thundering freedom; it isn't going very well. Lauren should be here. Sod it—enough! With the parachuting relief of giving up I put everything back in my big box and walk down to catch a bus.

As I am going down Gresham Road I pass an old woman struggling to get into her flat with some boxes of her own, so I stop and give her a hand. After I've helped her I reach into the box and pull out a statue, a jaunty sailor with pudgy antlers made by Piscina.

'Here, take this,'

'Oh!' she says, surprised and pleased with the thing, 'how much do you want dear?'

'Nothing—it's free.'

'I'll give you five pounds, but I can't afford more than that.'

'No, no, take it, it's free—a Christmas present.'

'Oh!' She looks at the shiny little man warmly, 'thank you!'

This box: obviously I should give it all away. What other purpose can it possibly serve?

I return to busy Brixton High Street, taking stuff out at random and handing it out at random.

There are three kinds of reaction; some people swiftly walk away, registering, *'stranger offering'* which immediately hits the *'trying to get something out of me, therefore avoid'* button (one man throws his hand into the air and bellows 'NO! NO! NOT TODAY!'); some people just take the thing and walk off not saying anything, looking at it confused; and then a third group of people have the reaction of the old lady, surprise and pleasure.

It's quite the marvellous thing, spending an afternoon giving away things you've put your heart into. After I'm twenty or so items down I start to get a bit more of a sensor to who to give to; more of an awareness of who might be a category three receiver.

A charged rush envelops me, a returning swell of delight and glow, the rich sense that I am made for some extraordinary contribution, to pour something eternally new into the body of the world, a world simmering in anticipation, supervivid with readiness to receive everything I can give, and give again.

I am *not* on a pointless quest. This crumbling world is my amphitheatre, and the collapsed marionettes in the proscenium are waiting for my song, yearning to be blasted free of their strings, aching, trembling in readiness, for artistic truth, for songs of ludicrous freedom, for unbound howls of recognition and laughter.

Okay, so now its just dumpy little doughcraft nudes I'm giving away in Brixton, but I know there is something as beautiful as the roaring void I felt—that I *was*—with Daphne. Yes, as beautiful as that. I can give that experience to the crowd, with silver trumpets, I can tear the oily meniscus that is stretched over eternity, and pour my loving essence into the crucible of mankind. I'm *huge!*

A guy—a pleasant looking gay—tries to invite me for a drink, a drunk woman tells me I'm like Jesus, and another woman gives me an Oasis CD. I do my best to refuse it—fucking Oasis—but she's adamant, so, alright, thank you.

I'm down to a few apples, Toby's fat ladies, a moon on a stick and a minotaur in a pink nightie.

'Here have this,' I say to a pair of shocking eyes which are just there, in front of me. Slim-limbed, cool smile, sandy bob and snow-blue eyes compelling, defiant, expensive. She is wearing a greyish overcoat, black leggings and snakeskinlike ballet-flats, which aren't quite right somehow, but nevermind.

'I like your hat.'

'Thanks.'

'Why are you giving these things away?' she asks.

'It was my grandfather's dying wish,' I say, wondering from whence this aimless lie.

We stand in front of each other. I feel I have The Great Secret in my mouth. I glance at the determined stream of people rushing past us, then back to her. She seems to be more intensely a woman than any I have ever seen. Something horrifying. She knows.

'Nobody else is making friends,' she says, archly, flicking glances up at me.

'Well, they've got work to do.'

'Have you got work to do?'

'Yes.'

'What do you do?'

'I'm in the business of inciting the right kind of feeling.'

'And how do you do that?'

'Giving everything away.'

'Everything?'

'Yes, nothing.'

'And what happens when you've got nothing left to give?'

'Well, that's the beauty of it, I never actually *had* anything in the first place.'

She looks at me briefly with a 'Yes? Well?' and then says, 'It's been nice meeting you, but I have to go.'

'Where are you going?' I ask.

'Into the centre, I have to do some last minute…'

When you get a chance, you get *one* chance—miss that and it's gone forever. Usually I miss it because I'm trying to get something, or sort something out. I miss it because I'm trying to *get*, and today I'm giving, giving everything no less, so there is nothing between me and the moment of truth.

'How about I come with you?'

She looks at me for three seconds and then her mouth smiles, 'No.'

'Let's go.'

●

I am prepared to descend into hell—I mean central London at Christmas—in order to spend time with this woman. Her name is Evgenia.

On the Victoria line to Green Park she asks me about my life and I am surprised to discover that I know something about it. It is pleasant, when in the middle of speaking, to discover for the first time how I feel; usually, I find, I'm the last to know.

'I am prepared to do anything to be free,' I say.

'Free of what?'

'Free of work, and free *to* work; to really work; to contribute to the human library, to serve mankind, to master the tuba, pretend to be Spiderman, wrestle my friends, erm, grow peas on the mountain… to do what I feel that I need to do.'

'I see.'

'I am not on a pointless quest.'

'But you *are* unemployed?'

'Technically, yes.'

'So where are you going to get the money from?'

'From wherever it is at the moment.'

'I admire your optimism,' she says.

She admires my amble too. Green Park station is heaving but, as I tell Evgenia, I have a powerful egg, emanating from my fez, which is shielding us from the stress and mania and, although it's a joke, it seems true. I feel a hum of invincibility in my viscera, a peculiar feeling that the world cannot touch me, that I don't care what it does, or is.

At Piccadilly Circus we follow a mother and her little boy. He is stepping only on the black slabs. Then he stands on the escalator; a moment of intense concentration looking down. Mother moves his foot, because it's on the pre-steprise crack. They ride up and he places his hand on the moving rubber handrail in such a peculiarly conscious way—just places, to see how it feels.

We get off and reach the doors, very heavy, and they squash the little boy a little and he looks up at me and I smile.

We stroll up Regent Street, oblivious to the tuts of the charging hordes streaming round us. The sun has come out, and it's quite fierce. Evgenia takes off her coat and folds it over her shoulder bag.

We're shopping for her five-year-old son, Barney. First stop, Hamleys, which is the red hot centre of a fascist dictatorship, but the glove puppets are objects of beauty. I persuade her to get a couple so I can entertain Barney.

'He's a bit old for puppets.'

'Is he? I'm not.'

'I think he'd prefer a computer game.'

'He plays video games?'

'Of course. All kids his age do.'

I gently suggest to Evgenia that she get young Barney something a bit more actual, but she says video games are harmless and I don't want to argue with a woman I'm planning on spending the rest of my life with, so she gets Mario Party and I buy the stripy purple glove puppet.

We duck out of the Regent Street death parade into the sparser back streets of Soho. She's not very talkative, but I gradually extract a few fragments about her life. She's 28, from Poole, has a kid and lives in Dulwich in the house her parents left her (Russian Mum vanished when she was six, English Dad died of cancer five years later).

'So what are we going to do then?' she says. 'I don't have much time so it had better be entertaining.'

'What do you want to do?' I ask, rather lamely.

'Something I've never done before.'

'Have you ever done a stupid dance in a shop before?'

'Nope.'

'How about that then?'

'Nope.'

'Come on. It will be beautiful.'

'For you.'

'Alright then. I'll do something for you first.'

She thinks. 'I'll do a stupid dance if you pinch the bum of a human statue in Covent Garden.'

'Alright.'

It's a weirdly mild day now, alternating cloud and white sunshine, spring almost. The plane trees are budding and speed of tourist amble has subliminally slackened. There are a few human statues in Leicester Square. We inspect them—I used to think it an odd thing to do with your life that, stand still for money, but now it strikes me as the acme of sanity.

One old guy is dressed as a classic tramp, or as a statue of a tramp—black face, black bowler hat, sprayed on cobwebs, Chaplin shoes, etc—and, as we watch, a pigeon lands on his head, which delights the small crowd. A kid with a screwed-up face starts shouting 'Dad! Dad! Look at this!' and runs up behind the statue just as a pock-marked Japanese guy bends forward and tosses a pound into the statue's hat, which—standard human-statue practice—causes a change of position. While the kid continues to bawl and holler, the statue does a slow, mournful dance, thrusts his leg out behind him and kicks the boy in the head. The kid screams, the pigeon flies off, the human statue slowly bends over, looks down at the ground, and freezes in this new position, hiding his face in his hands.

The boy's dad, a very middle-class moderate, comes over. He stands in front of the statue and says, shakily, trying to be composed, 'did you just kick my son?'

The statue doesn't move. More people gather round.

'Did you kick my son?'

No movement; the kid, by his mum, is still making a right racket—a kind of outragey shout, demanding revenge.

The statue is still hunched over. 'Look, you *really* should apologise to him,' says Dad. No movement. The man stands in front of the statue, not sure what to say or do. He shifts his weight from foot to foot. He puts his hands on his hips. Then he sighs, as if to say, 'well, I give up! It's just not worth it!' and walks off. As the family walk away the mother says 'don't worry darling, we'll give you five happy points for this.'

We all stand watching the hunched over statue for another two minutes, until he straightens up, does exactly the same morbid dance as last time and freezes in the position he was originally in, this time with a soft smile on his face. The pigeon then flies back and lands on his head.

Evgenia applauds. She *understands*.

Not long ago I asked the women I know about how important is that moment between you and your partner of big-eyed, electric belly connection, of 'yes, yes, *yes,* I know *just* what you mean… that happens to me too… *yes,* Exactly!' And the results in the main I found rather odd. Most of them didn't rate it as being very important at all! Why? How can you live together without *this?*

She is standing *slightly* closer to me than I believe she would if she didn't fancy me, and glances up at me, her blue, wry eyes saying something like 'that was good—and therefore I like you a bit more.'

There's the usual struggle: do I show her how interested I am (the truth) or do I feign a little disinterest (not the truth)? Which would she prefer? Me? The truth? That's what everyone says they want, but it does seem very unlikely.

Anyway, I have a job to do. I walk up behind a guy dressed as the devil, painted red, head to toe, and frozen in infernal fury, and give his arse a good pinch. He whirls round.

'What's the game, you fuck?' he hisses.

I back away as he swipes at me with his pitchfork. He seems reluctant to get down from his pedestal though.

'Sorry, I thought you were someone else.'

He raises his arms in fury and freezes. I toss him a pound coin and find Evgenia.

'Very good!'

'Your turn,' I say.

We cross over into Long Acre. I'm on the lookout for a shop to dance in. The impossibly cool, fashionably empty garment shops of Floral Street seem an ideal target, but Evgenia doesn't want to now. I cajole, but she's icily firm.

'You do it,' she says. I protest, but in the end I think sod it, I will do it, I'm free! I strut into Ted Baker, but the stylish atmosphere immediately wilts my élan. I pretend to look at the distressed legwear, anxiety beating in my guts—perhaps, no, I think, but then I see Evgenia through the window, all 'come on then if you've got the balls,' and it occurs to me that I'll fluff my chances with her if I chicken out. It's a bit the cold showers I was having during monk-week; I looked at the taps—lovely, warm, *safe* water rivering over my shoulders—and I kept looking, while my mind said 'no, don't do this, don't do this, it's madness' until I realised I was stuck and the only way out was for my *body* to turn off the hot and turn up the cold and then, there, bang! It's done. It's agony, but it's just the body writhing around.

The cretinous techno fades into Let's All Chant by the Michael Zager Band and I turn the cold tap on, shoulders curled, palms back, pelving and yanging—working my body, no point in half-measures now. The assistants are nonplussed, seen it all before, but, as I strut outside to the beat, Evgenia is smiling and I wonder what I would do for that smile. Terrible things.

I'm two-nil up now and, as we reach Covent Garden, unwilling to back down. There's a clump of balloons bobbing above a courtyard café. I ask a waitress if I can have one for my little girl, and she gives it to me.

'Alright, fill your lungs with helium, go into the Disney Store and ask—no, *demand*—to see Mickey.'

'Nope.'

'What? Come off it!'

'No, I'm not. No.'

'For fuck's sake.'

She looks at the shop, 'no,' she says, tense to herself.

'Do it! Let go!'

'*No!*'

I push the balloon into her hands. She pushes it back into mine. I push it into hers. She pulls off the knot, inhales the whole balloon—eyes fixed on me—chucks the spent flap on the floor, marches in, and in a mad, ultra high-pitched voice shouts at the man at the counter, '*I want to see the fucking mouse!*'

She's so wound up, so coldly furious, nobody laughs, least of all the poor sop at the till, who wears a contorted, anxious smile of polite confusion.

'Mickey's not here,' he says, with effort.

Evgenia slaps her hand on the counter and villainously squeaks, 'tell him his days are numbered.' She storms towards the exit, stops at the huge plastic Mickey at the door, makes a two-fingered eyes to eyes 'I'm watching you' gesture, and then strides out.

Why haven't I done this before? Surely—alright it's childish—but surely this is what cities are for?

She's heaving with the stress of it.

'I didn't enjoy that,' she says, still with squeak.

'I did!'

'I'm not doing any more,' she says.

Shame, because I wanted her to go up to the poor little Asian guy trapped in the cigarette booth and sincerely tell him she loves him. But, alright, no more.

We have a coffee in the square as a wash of spring rain strafes the cassette awnings. We have to shout sometimes because there's a mic'd-up juggler booming inane pre-show patter.

'Why doesn't he start?' Evgenia says.

'He will eventually. Ninety-nine per cent of street performing is getting an audience, then whipping up anticipation, then there's a quick wow and that's it.'

'Sounds like sex.'

'You're not impressed? with sexual intercourse?'

'It depends on the wow. Men are all patter.'

A sharp, cold wind whips up the rain across our table. Am I all patter? I might be.

'What do you mean?' I ask, but I know what she means.

'My ex tried to legally change his name to "Beef Supreme." Twice. I dated that man for five years.'

'So it's men you're not impressed with.'

'It doesn't take long to figure them out.'

'Have you figured me out?'

'Not yet.'

She looks at me and I at her. Her jaw and slim neck are as if sculpted, her dark eyebrows, the tiny creases around her mouth and her piercing blue eyes are mortally beautiful. I have a sudden thrashing sensation of entering a reality with rules I am not familiar with.

She squints at the rain, 'I should leave,' she says, and stands up.

I take a nervous sperm of a movement towards her for a peck and she seals the deal with the egg of yes.

She takes her phone out, 'what's your number?'

'0793 554455—that's the number of my housemate, Jacqui.'

'Your housemate? I'm not phoning her.'

'But I don't have a phone.'

She takes a pen out of her bag

'Got any paper?'

The only paper I have is the sleeve notes of the Oasis CD.

'Oasis? Oh I *love* Oasis.'

'Yeah? Me too.'

She takes the card and writes her number on it. 'You'd better get a phone,' she says, and walks off.

•

Wintry sunset, sky dying-ember crimson. I get off the bus at the Rye and walk with romantic completeness past naked fractal cracks, black black against the evening mist.

Trees. In theory drawing a leafless tree should be easy, but on paper there's always something wrong with the rate of tapering, degree of fill, and points of departure of the branches, so I study the forms, just as I occasionally study the outline of countries, in case I have to suddenly draw one, or practice handcupped owl whistling for ninja night missions, or write a perfect cursive r backwards for last-minute messages written on the windows of a lover's departing train, or twirl a baton for those master of ceremony moments, or learn how to say 'that's the biggest egg I've ever seen' in Catalan.

Ah yes, Evgenia. What a beautiful name—what a beautiful future. It's going to be oh, like *this* and like *that*. After all this trouble and pain it seems only fair enough, that I should be rewarded for my struggles, and my good taste, and my heart-rending honesty. It's all going to be alright now.

A moment of panic. Do I really have the number she gave me? I take the CD out of my pocket. Yes, yes, I do; but I could lose it. Better keep it in my hand, or commit the number to memory, or both.

•

Andy is arguing with Naeema. She has had daily arguments with him since he moved in ten days ago. It started with his most recent painting, 'Baby Orgy,' which she somehow managed to construe as an attack on motherhood.

'You have no idea what it's like to be a woman,' she says as I walk into the kitchen.

'Hi guys!' I say, sure, as usual, that everyone feels the same way I do.

They both chuck me a cursory before returning to the fray.

Andy Augusta is well built, a Brummie, heavy sarcastic eyes in a square head, friendly energy and disarming courtesy ('may I use your butter?') combined with brutal sexuality ('see if I can get me a foreign chick tonight, bash her rear end in') and an insatiable thirst for violence; loves boxing, and realistic 'mow 'em down' PlayStation games. From his bedroom comes constant sound of gunfire, screams, etc. Eats only meat, drinks constantly, pallor strange mix of healthy (semi-professional boxer, works out for hours) and unhealthy (greyish-yellow bags under bloodshot eyes, sick acne). Occasionally gets in a savage, dark mood. Says he's a Buddhist and prays to his burger before slapping it in the pan. Smells a bit of goat.

'We are forced to participate in a never-ending beauty contest,' says Naeema, 'the only thing we are allowed to own is erotic capital.'

Andy shrugs, 'Thatcher, Clinton, Merkel...'

'But they're not feminists. They're right wing.'

'So the problem is that left-wing *feminists* aren't allowed to be powerful? Is that right?'

'Let me be clear; powerful women are stigmatised.'

'Powerful women are a pain in the neck.'

'There, you see!'

I sit down and eat the flapjack I bought in Covent Garden. Watch a bit of intellectual carnage.

'See what?'

'Typical patriarchal reaction to empowered women.'

'Which is?'

'Oppression. Men instinctively oppress women.'

'It's only natural. Women want to be oppressed.'

'What?!'

Andy, sitting the other side of the kitchen table stretches his legs and clasps his hands behind his head, 'Women love being told what to do,' he says with a slight, feral smile.

'Make no mistake,' says Naeema, standing at the sink hips set to confrontation, 'women do *not* love to be told what to do.'

'Make no mistake? Let me be clear? You sound like a politician. I bet you go for little boys too.'

'What do you mean?'

'Pale, whelpy little bisexuals with big brown eyes; probably called Oliver or Edmund?'

'Now you're just being *offensive*.'

The doorbell rings and I answer. It's Stephen.

'Wotcha,' he says. He's got a nice suit on, tweedy.

'Andy and Naeema are having a gender contender.'

'Great!'

We lope back into the kitchen. Andy is alphering all over his chair, legs splayed, slow, languid nod-greetings to Stephen. Naeema is all wound up, irregular breathing, knuckles white.

Andy turns back to her. 'Have you ever had an orgasm that lasts half an hour?'

'Typical, it always comes down to attacks on sexuality. You'll be calling me ugly next, or fat. I *bet* you troll feminists.'

'I don't think you're either fat or ugly. You just need to be tied up and driven through the gates of ecstasy.'

'I don't have to listen to this,' she storms out as I finish off my flapjack.

'She'll soon be back for more,' says Andy to me.

'You've really got a way with women' says Stephen.

'Women are straightforward. Tell the intelligent ones they're beautiful, tell the beautiful ones they're intelligent. Feminists *are* tricky—but their standing up to power is all theoretical. They go running to the boss if someone disagrees with them. And confronted with *actual* power, the power of a real man, they go weak at the knees like any other woman.'

'They do go for other things,' says Stephen.

'Like what?'

'Ooh, I dunno, creativity, sense of humour, kindness...'

'They're all power plays.'

'Some go for feminist men...'

'Feminist men are feminist men to get into feminist women's knickers.'

Andy makes my skin crawl. I can almost see him rotting. Yet he gets all the girls—it's extraordinary but I can't deny, there *is* something fascinating about him. I suppose that's what they call charisma—which I always thought was a kind of beauty or social skill or something like that, but now it seems more like dark sorcery, or a personality magnet, dreamt up by an evil genius, inserted in big—I mean literally big—heads.

Jacqui *adores* him, because he's such a *rascal*. He's a 'networking genius' she says. For his degree show he sent two hundred taxi drivers to bigwigs in the London art world to present them with miniatures in his 'Anus and Child' series and a free ride to the horror-show he'd set up in New Cross Gate. A few turned up and now he's on the borders of greatness.

A networking genius—and rich, which helps. He developed a reasonably successful phone app called *'serf the net,'* an Uber type thing, which enables you to hire someone (or rent yourself) to be obsequious for half an hour to a stranger; fawningly appear out of nowhere, be a half-hour slave on the streets, allow yourself to be insulted, beaten; you choose your 'degradation parameters.' He said he wanted to do a version for prostitution; 'we hire our houses with airbnb, no reason we can't do the same with our bodies,' he said, 'or our beds. This place would be a great weeknight brothel.'

He leaves me and Stephen at the kitchen table because he's got work to do, he says, which means making plaster casts of his erect penis, which means bringing one of his women back to keep his creative member in 'artistic readiness.'

'I've done some art,' says Stephen and rummages in his rucksack. He pulls out a clear perspex butter dish. Inside is a blob of soft butter and two die-cast legs sticking out of it.

'It's called Saruman in Butter.'

'That's Saruman is it?'

'Actually no, it's Gandalf. They didn't have any Sarumans. But nobody will know the difference.'

'Why don't you call it Gandalf in Butter?'

'That's a good idea! I didn't think of that.'

He puts it on the table. I want to tell him it looks pathetic, but it's pretty obvious to both of us. Although maybe that's the point, the message. We are magicians stuck in butter.

'I don't think it will do as well as Andy's cock,' he says.

'No, unlikely.'

'He's on his way up I hear,' says Stephen, 'one of his videos went viral last week.'

'What do you expect of a virus?'

'It's amazing that he not only functions in the world as it is now, but actually *thrives.*'

'That's not amazing at all. There's a constant stream of women through here now,' I say, priming the kettle.

'How are the men taking it?'

'Toby couldn't care less, Jonas is horrified, but I think he is asexual and it doesn't bother me—at least it doesn't yet. He has a very generous entry policy though I must say—big ones, small ones, brown ones, white ones, all kinds...'

'I'm settling down,' says Stephen.

'Really?'

'Charlotte is moving in with me.'

Charlotte, the old flame, is the least spectacular-looking lass I've seen Stephen with; pretty, small, rotund, short-sighted, cute, shy, friendly, French. It seems a surprising choice.

'So you really are going for a team player?' I say.

'I don't feel like I'm in a relationship. I mean there's me doing what I always do and there's someone who's in love with me, knocking about in the background.'

'Doesn't sound very promising.'

'I really have no idea how it's happening,' he says, 'It's almost as if I have nothing better to do.'

'That's very poetic.'

'I don't understand her,' he says, picking at crumbs on our long unwiped eating surface, 'she knows I'll break her heart, but she keeps turning up anyway. But it's okay,' he says, looking up and smiling, 'I can offer her the emotional support she'll need from getting involved with me.'

'Maybe you're just ready to settle down?'

'Well I've definitely had enough of running round like a cock with its chicken cut off; the old brain box assessing every word and every gesture of every woman; "Was that awkward expression a 'No?'" "Am I staring into your eyes too long? too much?" "Am I demanding too much intimacy too soon?" "Am I working too hard?" "Not working hard enough?" "Should I call?" "Is she going to write tonight?" I'd rather just be miserable with one woman than spend so much energy being miserable with twenty... but it's... it's ever so hard living with someone. I've done it before—after a bit the pressure of intense coupledom starts to build up, the feeling that you have to escape, be on your own... you know? "*ahhh*...just the one of us".'

'The cult of two.'

'Right!'

'I've got the "is she going to write tonight" blues myself.'

'Oh yeah?'

I tell him about Evgenia.

'What do you suggest?' I ask.

'About what?'

'About when should I call her?'

'Three days is the usual isn't it? But then if you wait three days you're signalling your conventionality. I dunno.'

'Better to wait.'

'Fan the flames of desire with the bellows of indifference. Don't turn into a ridiculous little puppy.'

'No, you're right.'

'Daniel! Phone!' Jacqui's muffled yawk radiates down.

I leap up. Maybe she has called? Ooh! Ooh! Upstairs Jacqui is standing in her doorway holding out her arm with a long-suffering look of disdain. The whole of creation rushes in on the moment as I take the phone from her in slow motion knowing that the universe has not yet decided who will be on the other end until they speak…

It's a man's voice. I make rapid, stabbing, two finger signs to the speaker.

'Hello? Is this Daniel?'

I'd forgotten Jacqui's number was on my cv.

'Yes.'

'Daniel. Noah from *:Rising* here. Sorry to call you so late, just wanted to tell you that you've got the job, if you want it. I just *loved* your energy, your passion, your unorthodox 'fuck you' attitude—it's just what we need here at Brixton *:Rising*; that kind of revolutionary spirit is… yeah, *just* what we need. I've emailed you what we're offering, it's a *pretty* attractive package—but don't decide now Daniel. Think about it—take a look and let me know when you're ready, okay?'

'Jesus, alright, I'll think about it.'

'Yeah. Death to the world!'

Knocked Conscious

'Wednesday today, soon be end of week, and that'll be February finished.' Derek is in the habit of dispensing of time in this way, 'winter almost over, then it will be summer, another year gone, soon be dead,' he says, immobile in his chair like a sack of potatoes.

Sunday afternoon, boiled cabbage, Songs of Praise, damp outside, and dark—the uniform grey non-thing of the South London sky—chipped paint on the bathroom plumbing, steam, sour bodily odours, slightly faecal, overcoated with disinfectant, but never *quite* completely. Such is The Meadows in Derek's little room, overlooking the cold car-park and the service alley to the Chinese, and a plume of smoke rising from a burning box of Meccano.

'That drama therapist just been in with her bloody cards. Therapists, teachers, doctors, priests, I've had enough of 'em,' he says wearily, 'They grow up in a professional house, go to a professional school, then to a professional university, then they get a nice professional job, and they don't know a bloody thing about life, not a thing—cowards they are, mostly.'

Derek leans forward and whispers, 'you got any tobacco son?'

'Sorry, no.'

He shrugs and settles back. 'In the mine the vicar, they brought him down once, he wanted to see it all, he stepped off cage like, got to the mothergate, "aye," he said "thas enough." They said "you haven't seen the men working." He said "don't want to". He was frightened. They're all frightened, *priests*, and then they go around telling us how t' live! And it's not like you can just forget about 'em, you need a priest, I mean a professional, for everything, or at least every bit of bloody paper. Didn't use to be like that.'

I can hardly imagine a world without professionals. It seems so… unprofessional.

'Anyroad, can't see it lasting much longer.'

'What d'ya mean?'

'I mean, I think, it seems to me that everything is just… crumbling. There's new stuff all the time, but it's—it's paper-thin, underneath everything is crumbling.'

Like a loaf in the rain.

'"There'll be another war before long,' he says, 'and it'll all come crashing down!'

'You think so?'

'I do. All rich countries trying to keep the poor ones out—there en't wall *high* enough.'

'You've been in trouble though, had hard times, seen death.'

'Death? Oh yeah. We was on face one night and we were building the pack for the roof. Group working on one side, we were on t'other. And I could just see—I thought, "that bastard's sitting down" Their lights were pointing down. I said "eee!"—about thirteen foot from us. Went round, they were *flattened*.

Gone. Four men; gone. Happened all the time. Wives'd never let us go to work on an argument. Worked well though, *that* did.'

We sit in silence, listening to the pipes. I feel the tension of freedom. Magda will be along soon, poking her long nose into my tea break. She has the hyper-observant mania of the lower manager, constantly on the lookout for a calorie of wasted workforce energy.

Yes, my tide of defiance washed away, revealing the black, flinty fact of penury. I turned down the job at :*Rising*, which turned out to mean registering for their 'mind-milkery' which would periodically send me 'micro-projects'—like designing a GIF or laying out a worksheet—which I would then have to drop everything to turn in, or lactate out, and which paid peanuts, so sod that. Instead here I am cleaning for Saturn, tending society's superfluous humans at The Meadows, playing Super Cleanerman™, turning rooms over at breakneck speed and try-ing to avoid the Magdatron who throws open the doors, trying to catch me in an unguarded moment of non-digital reverie. To be fair, she herself is under enormous pressure to check every room in an anaemic sliver of untime, but she blames me for that, me or one of the other cleaners.

We are Eastern Europeans or Africans mostly, or the frag-mented and broken working class. This is not a job for the edu-cated, or for someone who can speak English, or God help us, a laggard, and so I am an anomaly, but I am beginning to think I might be an anomaly everywhere. When I go to Private Views and photo shoots I feel like an epsilon minus semi-moron, and when I turn up at The Meadows the staff look at me like the Mekon just floated in. And, actually, at home, I'm starting to feel like a bit of a cunt too. I'm not sure why, but the groupmind seems to be turning against me somehow.

At the The Meadows I gravitate towards the kind-eyed crinkles of friendly, dark, little Lithuanian Dalia who tells me we'll one day have 'holy peace' and the 'absolutely no bullshit whatsoever' heft of Big Mother Babs, a cross between a grand-mother and a Panzer who seems to treat the inmates like lug-gage, but whose innate dignity mollifies even Magda, and they tell me their horror stories of working the luxury hotels, and Poles attacked by night, and 'fucking hate this place and dread coming here,' and torture-machine trolleys 'but the all-round rubber buffer cushions the blows,' and 'the rich don't care about the poor, simple as that.' And we all dream of taps.

'Better than cleaning houses though,' said Babs, who did a couple of years in rich folk's homes in Berkshire. 'Meanest, tightest, most suspicious people in this world or the next,' she said, 'one place I did had locks on the *fridge*. Who puts locks on a fridge!?'

And I sit with the old dears, listen to their blether, strangely comforting I find it, particularly the ones that have had some contact with actual—I mean *actual*—reality. After a life of office-people and desk-monkeys and 'sales-ninjas,' talking to these oldies is like getting a one-on-one with Zork from the gamma quadrant.

Actually, I was thinking about aliens. If I saw a UFO landing in a field, I'd run like scaddle. Not because I'd be scared to con-tact people from another planet—alright, that too—but think about it! What would it actually take to reach a level of tech-nology where a race could build spacecraft capable of travelling light years across the galaxy, to get all that scientific knowledge together, all the materials, build this impossibly complex piece of tech... they'd be as fucked up as we are, worse! Who'd come down that ramp? It would an alien version of Richard fucking Branson. Sod that!

Anyway, back to Derek. 'We were right on the coast,' he says, going back to *his* planet, 'High tide used to come in front door. We never had carpets. We had rugs that me mam could

roll up when the bloody sea came in. Put on settee. Water used
to be in house about that deep.'

This is why I sit with Derek when a space opens up in the
juggernaut of the day and I can shelter under the wall. I'd prefer
to sit in this crumbling world, with crumbling Derek, than talk
about the TV and the news, which is just more work. It really
is all work now.

I even spent Christmas day here. Didn't have to come, but far
better here than up in my lonely room. The Meadows Christmas
celebrations comprised a troupe of local homosexuals giving
amazingly camp performances to the hundred or so assembled
residents, cramped up on tables in the big recreation room,
decay papered over with balloons, watched on by three huge
Russian bodyguards (why were they there? None spoke English).
The extravaganza began with a failed actor gay-guy fabulous
sweetie doing an item where his head sat upon a little lacy dress
puppet's body in a Punch and Judy box-theatre singing Kate
Bush's Cloudbusting with utmost soprano campness, eyes like
golfballs forming strained yay-ay-yay-ay-yay-ay-ohs. No idea
what the Russian granites made of this. Or any of the audience
for that matter, nobody reacted at all. This was followed by four
guys dressed tidily, but all in black, doing a heartfelt barbershop
version of 'Rhythm of Life' from the musical Sweet Charity
which everyone joined in on, turning the TV room into a tightly
choreographed headwaggling and rumpy-pumpy barrel-rolling
down the aisles extravaganza, the old guys and gals a-waltzin,'
the bored families leaping through the windows, the Russians
throwing the pretty care-assistants around... Well, it should
have, the energy those tidy little men put into it. Maybe everyone was imagining the same thing as me, but the applause was
yeah, so? The old girls around the edge of the room gabbed
and tattled, craned their heads to look here and there, nodded
meaningfully at various staff members while conspicuously

gossiping about them, not paying attention to *anything* that was going on. The old boys slept, or stared with outraged contempt.

I met a couple of new inmates; an old cripple, Dave, who didn't show signs of being mentally ill, although he said he was insane and had been sectioned many times. He'd been sleeping rough for several years before the authorities decided he qualified for The Meadows. He had everything stolen, he said, and felt freer than ever, just creaking round libraries and sitting on park benches watching people. He talked in a congenial wheeze—missing back teeth making his rs sound like gs—about how blinkered working people were, with no time to really see anything or even realise what they were doing. I took notes; up until the point he said to me, urgently, between clenched teeth; *'I'm not even here. I'm not supposed to be here. This isn't happening. Nothing is happening.'*

Then there was Crow, who sat in the TV room with his bag, a scary amount of uncontrollable head and spine movement. It seemed to calm down enough for him to drink and scoop in xmas pudding. Long beaky nose, one tooth I think, long black coat and socialist's cap. Seventy? His chest rested just about on his lap as he sat. When he'd finished eating he asked if the bedrooms were open. I found out and they weren't yet—twenty minutes they would be. An hour later he was still sitting there.

'They're open now,' I said with that feeling you get when you forget to feed the hedgehogs.

'Only problem is,' he wheezed, 'I need someone to carry this bag up for me.'

So I followed him up with his bag, which was so pitifully light it sort of choked me up to hold it. He seized the banister, body just as bent standing as sitting, and put the same kind of effort and concentration into each upward step as I might do carrying a priceless cello. I say cello because his whole life seemed to be accompanied by a tragic, lonely sonata. I wondered that he had survived for so long, his life seemed so purposeless, but what do I know? Maybe he had agitated for anarcho-syndicalism in 50s Whitechapel, or maybe his ex-wife was a spy and he shot her Ukrainian husband, or maybe he invented the yo-yo? I wanted to ask him about these things, but I had to help out downstairs and when I came back he'd gone and nobody knew where. Probably just sitting next to Victoria Park lake like a duck.

I fell briefly in love with one of the volunteers, Diana, who had a big bright smile and healthy, freckly cheeks and had grace, or it might have just been basic sex appeal, but she made everyone's hearts lighter, with a quick back-rub or asked if their leg was better or if they liked the gravy, which nobody did because it was like engine oil, but they all looked at her with eyes glittering in gratitude, not generally how they looked at me, even though I'd wiped most of their arses or perhaps because of that. I wished I was one of these burnt-out husks just so Diana would squeeze my shoulder and say 'you'll sleep well tonight Daniel.'

I sat with Derek at the back of the room, drinking Mackeson Milk Stout. He was more cheerful than usual, although he never laughed, chuckled rather. He told me about his wife, Ellen, and how he missed her, although they used to argue all the time and he was 'fed up with her for about fifteen years,' but then when she started to die he realised how much he loved her. Again I had the sense that I was talking to an alien creature who lives on a planet with two suns where people live for a thousand years. *Forty* years they were married. How is this possible? How?

Derek shrugged, 'you just get on with it.'

'I just don't think I'll ever be able to.'

'Well you're young.'

'My friend Stephen, he's just got back together with a girl he lived with for four years. I can't even understand how four *months* is possible.'

'Well you can't fathom it, it's impossible. You meet a girl, and suddenly she's… there. A beautiful thing, just there.'

'But Stephen's new girl is ugly.'

Derek coughed on his stout and his face darkened.

'*No* woman is ugly!' he said, aggressively.

'I just mean…'

'You just don't love her you fool. If you don't love her, sooner or later, she'll become hideous to you.'

This was new information to me.

'No woman is ugly,' said Derek again, quietly to himself. 'There are just levels of beauty.'

'Yeah, and she's on the lowest level.'

He chuckled.

I spent Christmas at The Meadows, came home, and then woke up on Boxing Day morning to an email from the job centre telling me that I'd been sanctioned. I didn't fill out my online job-search evidence form to show that I'd looked through all the new jobs advertised on Christmas Day. You are sanctioned. Merry Christmas!

I heard the other day of a guy who had a heart attack in the middle of his assessment interview and they sanctioned him there and then.

So I had a rough couple of weeks. It's not easy to find a job just after Christmas. In the end, miraculously, Saturn offered me a few part-time hours—making me one of the only people in the country, I think, to be upgraded from a 'work-related activity' to 'actual work.' I also got a couple of quid looking after some boats on Dulwich Pond for Derek's nephew; a shabby, wan, mumbling little man called Bob who owns one of the piers there. He normally closed for winter, but with it being so warm recently he'd opened up at weekends and needed someone to row over to the little island they were chained up on, unlock them, row them back over to the pier and hire them out.

On Saturday Bob shambles down around three, takes the money from the kids and lovers, and then shambles off to the bookies or the pub, leaving me with anything I can make after that, which usually comes to about forty quid.

This morning it was raining, so I phoned Bob to see if it was worth coming in, thinking he'd surely call it off, but he didn't, the greedy twat, so I cycled down to Dulwich in the dark and driving drizzle, slipped around on the boats, hands numb, pulling them along the shore, cursing the gods, until Bob showed up, like a medieval peasant in the mist and we stood in the fine rain for about an hour, hunched up, small talk between gritted teeth.

'Why don't you do the boats then Bob? By yourself?'

'What, you don't want the money?'

'Course I do. Just wondered why you don't just sit here yourself. It's quite nice.'

'Oh very funny.'

'Well?'

'Don't like to be here by myself. I get spasms.'

'Spasms?'

'Epilepsy, I'm alright when I'm with someone. But I can't do it alone. Dangerous.'

'What about your wife?'

'Wife?'

'Aren't you married?'

His straggly sandy moustache twitched as he sucked on his tiny little fag.

'Nah. I'm seeing a girl in Birchington,' he said, 'been seeing her for about fourteen years. It's not very serious though, I just go and see her when I need a leg over.'

'That's beautiful.'

He shrugged, 'Easier alone.'

'But what about the spasms, if you're at home?'

'I pull me emergency cord, get social services over.'

We stood in the dreary January spittle for another hour before Bob called time and I lugged the boats back. Three hours to suck the freedom from before work began again. Peckham's dark grey turned to temporary light as I read The Moomins in my freezing room, then into my Saturn overalls, bombed down to The Meadows, inhaled the odour of infinite despond, up the stairs and the race was on, get the hoover and the buggered trolley which are tucked stupidly in the linen cupboard (the nice trolley in the larger store cupboard is only for battle-grade cleaners), stacked up with towels and sheets and the motherfucking top shelf collapsed and so I had to pick up all the handtowels, bathroom slip mats and soap boxes, and then the dirty linen sack wouldn't attach properly to the trolley, so I pushed a hole in the top and bound it on with gaffer tape from Ronny the caretaker, then out into a maelstrom of dusting, changing, smoothing, hello Rita, no I'm not your dead husband, tight smile to Fran who's not talking to me, don't know why, Hector threw up on his breakfast, twenty-three rooms to go, swift warm smile to Dalia, no thanks don't drink tea, no I didn't see Britain's Got Talent... or the news... or Celebrity Mastermind... until my break, which Magda makes it very clear I'm selfishly taking because the whole team will be held back.

Derek, aside from the battle tales, and reporting messages from beyond the grave, tells me that 'the Nazis had team spirit.' He also tells me that Bob was once the bassist in Tommy James and the Shondells.

·

I leave Derek in his four bloody walls—and walk down to the bus stop, taking in nothing of planet Peckham for my mind is permanently working away at *she*, at the problem of woman.

Well? Does Evgenia like me? I go over every last detail of our meeting, assessing each one for definiteness of sex. It turns out that most of the things she said and did actually meant 'the next time we meet I'll take off all my clothes.' At the time I took it all at face-value, but now that I pick over it all, it's all quite obvious. The evidence is all there, and *yet*, where is she? Could I be wrong? She doesn't seem to be quite operating in the safe realms of Definite Fact. I want *proof*, yet all is plausible deniability. She's not one to follow the three-day rule. I think very, very carefully about my emails and texts to her (yeah, I bought a phone). I go over each word, arranging them to look casual, off-the-cuff, attempting to find the precise point before friendly becomes needy, and non-desperate becomes aloof, and kind of sexy becomes kind of creepy. I put myself in her shoes; what will delight her with boldnesss, but doesn't go too far? I put myself in my own future shoes; what is going to cause me pain later? I put myself in Mifune's shoes; what would Mifune do?

After this I stare at the send button, willing it to press itself, to take responsibility from me. But no, I have to do it and *thenitsdone* and I feel all sweaty, but with a glow of manly achievement and I can put this silly seduction business all behind me now. Three days pass, but nothing. Why doesn't she write? Why doesn't she text? What could be wrong? What should I do?

Get a grip Daniel! What would the Wizard Priest of Kume do? I consult my notebook, where I write down various bits of advice about women that I've discovered, or read, or heard from the likes of Harold and Stephen, or song lyrics:

- If you plan what to say to her, it will come out creepy.
- Don't worry about her being slightly cool, or about her not giving up totally to you. She doesn't give it all at once.
- How do you expect to be able to handle her emotions if you can't handle your own?
- Why should *you* know? *She* doesn't know!

- Loving a woman is basically hypnotising her. If she left you and you bumped into her ten years later, she'll have absorbed the next guy and you'll be thinking 'who *is* this?'
- Now you're the only one here who can tell me if it's true / That you love me, and I love me.
- A woman can fake an orgasm, but a man can fake a whole relationship. Sharon Stone said that.
- Forget your dreams, forget your plans, stroke your chin with cowboy hands.
- Sex will crucify you.

No. No use, none of it. I start to get that needling feeling I've said something stupid to someone recently, that there's something I should be worrying about—I was worrying about it earlier, something, but then it slipped my mind, leaving clench, dis-ease. And then a phrase from the mail hits me—strikes me in the guts.

'I want to feed you to my horse.' I wrote that to her—*why?* Why did I say that? How seedy and weird, trying so hard to be surreal and clever, but actually just coming across like a nob.

I tear at my face, stab at my stomach and—I do this whenever I recall something shameful that I've said or done—I do a gigantic pelvic thrust into space, to try and 'fuck the problem away.' Everyone does that though, right?

I skulk back to what I wrote and reread it, sadly. How could I have written all this? She's going to see what a fraud you are now Daniel—but then someone had to, you loser.

I go to bed and dream of carnivorous horses.

This goes on for a few days. I am desperate to write to her, to explain everything, to apologise, but a fine, fabric-thin, gossamer strand of hope keeps me from doing so. She may yet see it in her heart to accept me, despite my awful failings.

I slowly forget about Evgenia and the marvellous life we could have lived together, and how I was to paint her blue and roll her around my floor, and what we'd call our kids, and tight-harmony humping in Sardinia; when... she writes! Nothing in it of horses at all. All she says is: Free Sunday. Where?

And that's it. Off we go!

•

The monotone morning, chill and gummy, gives way to mottled bulbs of white light which break up the dome of the sky into luminous lumps of mashed potato. As the number 12 chudders over the Westminster Bridge and round Trafalgar I prepare to submerge my individuality into the massmind of Piccadilly, but London, like the clouds, seems also somewhat busted, empty even.

Yes, it is all curiously clear here. As I stroll past Fortnum and Mason, past the Royal Academy and the Ritz hotel a sweet sense of alrightness settles on my chest. I can feel the first warm breaths wafting down from Hyde Park, the rustling of the London plane trees seems to say 'we have awoken.' It is mildly, delicately, gently, miraculously spring, in the air, in the trees, in the women, all so enthralling. But especially the women.

Women, women, women. I look at men and think— no, I feel, 'ah, yes, there is the known. I know.' But women call up the void in me, not an otherworldly experience, but the compelling, mindless *what* of this life. Look at them! They're so *mysterious*. Derek's right; no woman is ugly—this irresistible, fascinating, unfathomable what-what-*what-is* thing, there, in all of them. All of them! *Most* of them.

Pricking with expectation I am, in Green Park, but with some kind of power in me, something primaeval and right is shaking the dust from its mighty muscles. This is it, isn't it? No more problems now, not really. As far as life is concerned, I've *arrived*.

I'm early, so I go to the coffee hut at the edge of the park. As I wait for my latte to be prepared, there seems to be, amongst the three girls working there, busying themselves around the paper cups and espresso machines, some kind of tension. One, dressed in a white frilly frock and DMs is saying, with a not very convincing air of unconcern, 'well, it took me a long time to get ready,' while the faces of the other two are set with scowls. I immediately feel, after the sublime outside, this unpleasant boxed up atmosphere seeping into me, clogging my mojo.

'It's going to be the most spectacular spring any of us have ever seen,' I blurt, to all three.

The girl in front of me who has been unhappily concentrating on steaming the milk looks up at me.

'Why do you say that?'

'It happens to be true.'

The older of the three—thin hair, jowly, big forehead but lovely yellow-flecked blue eyes—says, with mechanical politeness, 'yes, the weather is very nice.'

'No! not just nice,' I go on, charging past her attempt to be done with me, 'This spring the whole world is going to go up in a frothing conflagration of flowers.'

Silence.

'Also, everyone is going to fall in love.'

The girl in white laughs, 'everyone?'

I feel exuberant, flashing, Hindu somehow. 'Yes, everyone, and all problems that already couples have will be sorted out. Everyone is going to be in love. How about that?'

'That is good news,' says the girl serving me, smiling.

'Bye then,' I say, taking the coffee.

'Bye!' they say, all three together.

Fucking yes! See?

I wait on one of the Green Park deckchairs and take in the workforce making their monoway to Mayfair. No lumpen proletariat here, unless they're going to artex the Japanese embassy ceiling or have come down to wave their little flags around on The Mall.

I sense Evgenia before I pick her out, walking towards me across the park. She has a big bag over her right shoulder and slouches somewhat. Something in me twinges at what seems to be a pose of insouciance and skinny jeans, but it's just a momentary thing, the stiff Mayfair vibe edging my perceptions. When she spots me her eyebrows arch. I stand, hold out my elbow, which she takes, and we walk slowly south through the sparse park.

'Do you like this day I have arranged?' I ask.

'Very much.'

'I've been up at the crack of dawn, hanging blossom on the trees, pumping up clouds, coming up with just the right shades of blue for the sky, organising the people of London, giving them their scripts and rehearsing their cues. Very busy.'

We cross Pall Mall, into St James' gardens and walk through cold shade alternating with brilliant frigid sunshine, spring wind concealing and revealing.

A small tubby man with a red face and a large white moustache comes huffing up the path.

'That, for example, is the second grand duke of Saxony.'

'Oh?'

'Yes, I've decided to put only royal personages in St James' today.'

She looks around, marvellingly.

'Who's that?' she asks, nodding to a stick-thin woman sitting on a bench reading Bleak House.

'That's Lady Harrrrr(my inventing mind stutters)pole.'

'Harrrrrpole?'

'Yeah The man you see behind her is Sir Leicester Harrrrrpole, Baronet.'

'He looks like a paedo.'

'He is.'

'Mm, I see.'

'Everyone in here is a paedo. It's a park for royal paedos.'

And so on. Nonsense chatter, but through it I discover she can't be offended, which is one of *my* Franksheila check-boxes ticked off.

We stop and I pull a blanket from my rucksack. We sit down, and I set up the camping stove to make tea, bring blue flame, light roar, to the camping kettle, while Geni leans back on her hands, her ankles crossed in front of her.

I take out my biscuits which catch her leaning attention.

'Did you make those?' she asks.

'No I laid them.'

'Laid them?'

'I have an ovipositor…

'…that lays biscuits?'

It is good to make complicated tea for a girl who looks so sexy. I want an old school-friend to pass and come up and chat, and we'll breezily catch up while he burns inside with jealousy and amazement. How could *she* being going with *Danny?*

But I am now stuck in stage four of the ascending gateways to paradise. 1. How to talk to girl. 2. How to get her number. 3. How to get from virtual exchanges to an actual date. 4. How, how while on date, to touch her. 5. How to get a kiss. 6. How to get her clothes off. 7a. How to get penis into vagina. 7b. How to ask for a blow job. (Then there's usually 8. How to get out of the hell that paradise has inexplicably turned into.)

It's all supposed to happen naturally. Let the flow float you both to where you are fated to go. Even atheist girls believe that. But I have will, I can make decisions, or so it seems—but all I want to use this will for is to simulate fate, make it look like it was meant to be.

As we stroll with knowing irony over the invented landscapes I spread before us, I sense, somehow, that underneath the surface there is some kind of dinosaur battle going on, some kind of epic quest, some kind of challenge from a force so enormous I dare not let it fully into my awareness, lest it burn my eyeballs out. All I can focus on is the moment, the surroundings, let go of the grabber, the part of me that wants to seize that *neck*, those *wrists*...

We stroll through the horse guards into Whitehall. Tourists everywhere, a few politicians, police with their hands tucked across their chests. Evgenia admires the Houses of Parliament.

'Really? I find them oppressive.'

'That's just because of what goes on inside.'

'No, it's fake. Compare this to a real Gothic masterpiece, like Canterbury Cathedral and it's like comparing, I dunno, Angkor Watt to Minecraft. Real Gothic is saying, "the universe is the face of Jah", this is saying, the "British Empire will..." er...'

'Sit on your face?'

'Yes.'

'I know a few of them.'

'Who?'

'Politicians.'

'Do you? How?'

'Work.'

We squeeze through crowds of schoolchildren photographing Big Ben, past *I love London* souvenir stalls and hot-dog stands.

'What do you do exactly?' I ask.

'I'm a photographer.'

'For a newspaper?'

'Sometimes, yes.'

'So who else do you know?'

She mentions a few people who I haven't heard of.

'I'm not really into politics.'

'No me neither,' she says, 'Politicians are horrible people. Sexual deviants.'

'How do you know that?'

'I just know. It's my superpower. I can look at a man and tell what he's like in bed, how he kisses.'

'That's... really?'

'Mm hm.'

I have the thought *'this must mean...'* but there's no time to pursue it.

'What's *your* super-power?' she asks.

'Err...' I look around Westminster bridge, and as I do a woman drops a can of Gatoraid.

Evgenia laughs, 'that's it is it?'

'Yes, I can make people drop Gatoraid.'

Maybe that *is* my superpower?

'So what about him? What kind of kisser is he?' I ask, indicating a guy coming towards us. She squints as he passes. I too take him in. I have a half-formed theory that you can tell a lot about people as they walk, because, really, they're all walking into the unknown, and some clearly resist that, some puff their spiny bodies up, some imperceptibly shrink back...

'He's all in himself,' she says, 'no real connection with any woman, treats their bodies like fruit-machines, stick a coin in, perhaps hit a jackpot.'

This seems to fit.

I test Evgenia on a couple next. We're at the top of the stairs which lead down to the South Bank. I pick out two people quite far away. They've just been looking over the river, and have now turned towards us. Again we assess as they approach and pass. He is hairy, small, chubby, with quite a characterful mouth—big gap between his teeth—and cheery-squinty behind not-very fashionable glasses. She is taller than him, big bum, splayed feet, long-fingers and a serene chipmunky face.

'You know what,' says Geni, 'I think it's going to work out.'

'I think you're right.'

Other couples drift over the concrete heaps of the South Bank. They talk, listlessly, or cling to each other, or warily watch their kids, or eagerly sell themselves over coffee, but mostly they float in a standard mix of suffocating separateness and Stephen's 'intense coupledom'.

'I dunno though, does it ever work out?'

'Sometimes it does,' she says.

'I've not seen much evidence of it.'

'Me either.'

'So how do you know it's possible?'

She shrugs. 'Most men just want themselves in female form.'

That's an interesting one. Do they? Do I?

'What do you want?' I ask.

'I want to find a man I can die with,' she says. This seems to be a moment to connect, but she never looks at me, just shoots sideways glances. She seems to want to make a connection, but, I dunno, is she shy? It seems unlikely, self-conscious maybe—but that must be a good sign? Is it? I feel I should stop hovering over every sign and signal, reading them like tea-leaves.

We get some hot weak tea and take a bench overlooking the brown river which drifts past, bored and inevitable.

'How do you want to die then?' I ask.

'How do I want to die?'

'Yes.'

'Drowning.'

'Ugh! Drowning? Oh no.'

'It has a bad reputation.'

'Good Lord, anything but drowning.'

'There's the panic, the intense feeling of being trapped, and the desperate struggle... That's not pleasant,' she says. 'But as soon as you realise, this is it, I'm dying: when that moment comes, and the water floods into your lungs, and there's nowhere to go but down, and you have to give up, then you give up more completely than you'd ever imagined. Then...' All hunched up, she relaxes, limbs falling to her sides; 'then drowning has got to be alright. Just floating there, painlessly dying.'

'Hmm. When you put it like that...'

'How would you like to go then?'

'I suppose morphine isn't allowed?'

'Why would you want *morphine!?* You'd miss the most amazing experience of your life.'

'Then, erm, falling off a tall building I think,' I say, 'or blowing up. Or a plane crash, a plane crash would be nice.'

'I always think I'd enjoy being quite calm as everyone else was screaming in torment.'

'Asking the hostess for a warm towel.'

'No, I'd be with my partner,' she says, 'We'd just be holding hands.'

Which makes me want to hold Evgenia's hand. But then that seems too cheesy at this moment. At the back of my mind is a fat kid's voice on a loop 'is it right now? what about now? are we there yet? but *why?*' with a parent's voice in front of that saying 'no, no, nope, just because.'

'I dunno,' I say, 'I like the idea, dying together, but something in me says you do that alone.'

'No, you can die together.'

'Surely it's like being ill. You do that alone. Or going to sleep. Can you do that together?'

'Yes, you can.'

I want to argue, but I want more to not fuck this up, so I accept she might be right. It's a nice idea after all.

We amble further, past the Festival Hall, the National Theatre, that skateboarding bit. It's sunny now, raw but heatless. Bleached and windy. Slight pressure.

We arrive at the Tate Modern, the castle cubed of death.

'Shall we go up and throw ourselves off then?' she suggests.

'Yeah, alright.'

Inside are the usual collection of large rubber inflatables, photo-realistic prints, lozenges of colour, everyday objects suspended from wire, piles of lego, out of focus videos, burnt polaroids and the kinds of faces, figures and trees you'd expect the unhappiest of your uncles to draw. All of which is ironic; not that irony is to blame, any more than even temperament is to blame for chillwave and dream pop.

'What do you make of it?' I ask Geni, tensing up somewhat. We are looking at a two metre tall kitchen chair with a dustbin-lid sized latex fried egg dribbling over the edge of it.

She shrugs, 'it's a big chair.'

I relax. Thank God! If she'd said she'd *loved* it, my heart might have sunk to somewhere difficult to fish out. Although, then again, it might not have, I'm feeling pretty forgiving.

She's right you know. It *is* a big chair. On this floor are strange-shaped cheap-looking mass-produced things. On the next floor up are bleak things (black and white photos of walls in Dagenham). Then there's irrelevant things (lists of places the artist hasn't been to written on a postcard or grains of rice stuck to a pigeon-feeder). Then titillating things (big nipples, real brains, warm gusts of air smelling of corn flakes). Then the ironic floor, which displays cut-outs of Madonna and little plastic dead babies floating in a cup. Before, finally, the floor full of pictures made out of fingernails or crisps. You'd almost think, this being one of the pre-eminent art galleries in the world, that bleak, titillating, purposeless and meaningless futility was what the world is all about.

'I quite like that though,' she says, stopping at a few random splashes of paint over a photo negative.

'Really?'

'Yes, don't you?'

'Not… much.'

'It's passionate, I think.'

'Mmm.' (it's not passionate; it is definitely not passionate).

'I know the artist actually,' she says, 'we exhibited together at Cabinet.'

'Have you ever exhibited here?'

'No, they don't do photography much.'

'You'd like to though?'

'What, exhibit in the Tate? Of course I would.'

We have a difference of opinion here. It seems like I care about this, and am pretending I don't; while she doesn't care and is pretending she does.

Up we go, to the seventh-floor bar. There is a good view over the river, but the room is packed and hot with commentary, anecdote and variable-reinforcement back-channelling. There is very little room to move our actual bodies, while our psychic bodies are genuinely suffocating, so Mifune the Buddha tells me to take Geni's hand (cool and clammy I note) and lead her along the narrow room, looking for some breathing space.

Ahead of us there is a door which says 'no entry.' I lead her through into a corridor of crisp alpine relief, empty and overlooking the entire city. We walk on, alert for employees. A waiter passes, and then some kind of administrator, but we show no guilt at being where we shouldn't, and so are allowed to pass through the doors at the end of the corridor, which read, 'East Lounge. No Entry.'

Inside, seems like outside; a large room, surrounded with windows; a glass box hanging from the darkening clouds. It is empty but for a couple of leather couches in the centre and a few trolleys around the edge, and, after a regal tour of our domain and decisions about where our alien friends will live, and how we will coax the wilderness into growing The Royal

Institute, and which coral and jellyfish we will model our cathedral-complexes on and what Blackfriars will look like with herds of wild elephant bathing in the mud, we sit.

'So how's the unemployed life?' asks Evgenia.

Now it's me who can't quite make eye-contact. I turn unseeing to the purpling Thames, 'I'm kind of employed now.'

'What are you doing?'

'Anything. Anything shit. If it's shit I'll do it.'

'Oh?' oddly, she seems quite interested, 'what have you done?'

'Erm, loads of stuff, data entry, delivering semen to hospitals, sorting packages for Parcelforce, killing moles, go-kart track attendant… Now I'm cleaning toilets, hiring boats and selling knocked-off electronic gear.'

'Sounds interesting.'

'You think? It might be interesting to look back on, in twenty years. Doesn't feel that way now.'

Work is marginally better than doing dreary futile battle with the Department of Work and Pensions, sanctioned for writing the wrong number down or for clearing my throat mid-beg; but I'd still prefer the dignity of being without a job.

I squint up the vanishing Thames, prickling now with window-lights, and I feel somewhat emasculated. I have the sense, based on a great deal of circumstantial evidence, that a girl like this can never, ever, be interested in a flake, and I have it on very good authority that beautiful young women are on permanent alert for good-for-nothings that will attach themselves leechlike and suck their youth and beauty away. And yet I also have the feeling that this woman is not looking for some kind of bearded patriarch who will masterfully take her waist in one hand and her anxiety about the future in the other and lead her away to a gleaming paradise of car-job-house-holiday-kids. Perhaps she's simply wealthy enough not to care.

I face her. 'Employee means "used". "I'm used now", "I work for a new user now", "My users are going to use fifty more people in their new office".'

She smiles.

'I'm just not into being used,' I say, feeling manlier now.

'You prefer to use do you?'

'Not really.'

'That's a shame, I like being used.'

My heart expands in my chest, squeezes itself through my neck and begins slapping the back of my face. Did she say that?

I look at her, and she looks, fully, into me. A hurricane-wave of pale fire, smashing and raining down. I forget to breathe. Now is the moment!

I take it, and kiss her.

She is abandoned, passive, lazily responding and for a moment, kissing and kissing, I am on the peak of life's hill, with nowhere to go. We move to embrace and I position myself for maximal body contact and leave the wanter behind to enjoy just that.

It's all relief and ease, a volcanic bath, but the warmth, the more I go into it, seems to be more of an atmosphere, a cloud-covering to a weird radiance that is *not* warm, a cold light, beating, massive, slightly terrifying…

'Can you feel that?' I whisper.

'What *is* that?'

'I don't know.'

No, but what *is* that? We kiss and kiss, and something weird is building up, some kind of life unknown, a completely new kind of feeling, building up, chattering, *chattering?*

The doors burst open and a crowdstream floods in talking, yakking, clinking, laughing. There's a man with a swan's head crowning round the back of his ears, a couple of beautiful young gays wearing angel wings, a woman with what looks like metal hair wearing jesus creepers and a padded pin-stripe, harsh-harsh American voice 'exCUSE me can you READ?' shrill, piercing ugly laughter, seven-foot tall women with eyes on the side of their heads and haughty pouts, lascivious little Svengalis with three chins, a blue Michael Jackson in a Tudor frock coat, a man with tits wearing a space helmet and a guy wearing a big latex vulva and 'I'm a cunt' written across his back. Nobody pays us any attention, they just wash around us, as if taking up positions. I think I recognise a couple of them—that Indian guy's here, the one that does the cast-iron bats. A rain of chatter, like electrified ball bearings, sprays around us.

'She makes history repeatedly. *That's* her metier.'

'Homophobia? I find rain is more of an enemy to drag.'

'He specialises in lawns.'

'Isaac Asimov died of AIDS?'

'Xavier! Xavier! *Xavier! Xavier!*'

'Imagine speed dating, naked, on ecstasy, wearing VR.'

'She used to be sexy. Now she's just one more skinny peroxide *nothing.*'

'Ev-*gen*-ia! What are *you* doing here?'

A tall, pale, frazzled-looking woman in a crinkly black dress looms over us. A top-selling artist I discover as introductions lead into status updates and short-term plans, although I don't really need to be told what she does as she has *I Am Culture* written all over her, they all do. Another joins us—a shrivelled Rhesus monkey in a straw hat, also vaguely familiar—and sails straight in with a pointed 'what do *you* do?'

I tell him I'm a masseur at Crystal Palace and leave it at that.

I can't tell if Evgenia is annoyed by the cream of the London art-world interrupting our unprecedented merging.

'He's joking,' she says of me, 'he's an artist. Pen and ink.'

'Anything I might have seen?' he asks me, one eyebrow raised.

'I doubt it.'

'Have you exhibited?'

This guy is actually, and immediately, trying to drive Evgenia and I apart with his successful artistic Rhesus-monkey cock.

'No, exhibiting gives me existential nausea.'

'Ha! *Marvellous*. I used to think that when I was at college.'

'I'm not at college.'

And now here I am justifying my fucking self.

'Look,' I say to Geni, 'I've got to be somewhere.' Meaning—let's go eh? Get back to that world behind the world, yes?

'Okay,' she says, with outrageous unconcern, 'we'll catch up later.'

Fool! You *fool* Daniel. I go for a power-gambit and lose, blown-out, and the girl is now in the hands of this *tradesman*.

'Okay, bye.'

She hardly looks at me as I walk out, pushing past the harlequins and the columnists.

It could be Weimar Germany, or the salon of Mme Geoffrin, or the 'wine and meat pool' of King Zhou, or some swanky Pyramid do in the Middle Kingdom. This party has been going on since the dawn of civilisation, and when the world is a charred husk these screaming, bellowing, bored swans will still be floating over the darkness in their gaudy bubble, talking about Miami Art Basel, tilapia and yurts.

Hatred burns in me, a scalding magma in the pit of my chest. These people are the gatekeepers of artistic truth. *These* people, who know no joy, just prestige, and the giddy satisfaction of being in the know. If there is one good thing about the coming cataclysm it's that they will suffer so much more than the rest of us, fall so much further. Although it's a shame, I think, as I descend through the ziggurat of meaninglessness, that I won't be there for it. Perhaps I should just take a piss now on Louis Fangos' 'autobiographical' stuffed rucksack with legs. I'm close to doing it too, looking around for the inevitable CCTV and mapping the coming and going of the gallery guard, but then it occurs to me that the reek of stale urea will probably enhance the value of these 'philosophical masterpieces' anyway.

I slope away, feeling impotent, feeling defeated, feeling fifteen years old. I can't bring down the artistic establishment with my piss, I can't make anything beautiful enough to take its place, I can't rebel—my hatred just serves that which I am desperate to refuse—and I can't bag the Woman of my Dreams, when she's right there in my hand, *asking* me to take her. You child!

On the first floor I find myself in a room of 'eclectic wonderment.' There's a Tardis, a stuffed bull, a plastic moon, a testicle cast in bronze, a knitted spider, a tennis racket, an eyeball, the obligatory Unusually Big Thing; but then also, four heads. Something odd there though.

I approach miserably, the heads calling to me, as dolmens do.

Four plaster-cast moulds, 'life-masks' they're called, of Coleridge, Wordsworth, Shelley and Blake, sit in a display cabinet, perfect replicas of long-dead artists. I look, and keep looking. They are works of art. Blake's especially is a masterpiece. A dome of continental endurance, a phrenological manifestation of mountainous will, sculpted by a master.

I look, and keep looking. I begin to feel that I want a head like this. And; this is something which I can have. I know it and the choice is clear. I can have fame, sex, money, power and fun—or I can have a head like that; and I want a head like that. I want the shape of my head to tell the truth. I want my brow to be a work of art, an expression of the immeasurable.

I leave the room and, just as staring at a blue card for half an hour makes all the blues of the world pop, so my meeting with Blake has turned the outside of the Tate into nothing but an exhibition of modern craniums—botch jobs. More botch jobs. A mudslide of despondency sucks me into myself. Why should I be surprised that there is no difference between the pedomorphic puppyish busts around me and what they produce? Of course there isn't. The world is a botch-job and so are the botched heads that make it.

I *must* put it on show

•

'Yeah that was stupid,' says Toby. We are in the kitchen, dark outside. He is tinkering with some kind of pilaf and I am sadly staring at my peanut-butter on toast.

'I just got angry.'

'Well there you go. She was already yours, you didn't need to win a pissing contest with, who was it again?'

I tell him.

'Right, you had the higher ground and you just strolled off, back into the dark cave.'

I'm too sad to reply.

'But I think it's okay,' he says, 'she'll call.'

'You think?'

'Yes. I think you are going to go through hell. I think you've got pockets and walls undiscovered, and *she* will locate them.'

'God I hope so. You're right though. I have never known such power from a woman; there is something enormous in her, too much for me even maybe.'

'It will interest me to see what you do when you are under the watchful eye of someone who can *really* get to you.'

'I'll die a thousand deaths—if she'll let me.'

'And what is her life made of? work? friends?'

'No; independently wealthy.'

'What?'

'She's loaded; kid, house in smart Dulwich.'

'Fuckety fuck, what a weird combo.'

'I want to be the breadloser of the family.'

Toby stands at the hob, stirring and tasting.

'She'll call back.'

'When? How soon?'

'How soon is a piece of string?'

'Er, the boiling point of… caesium?'

'A connection like that? Of course she will. I don't think it's gonna stick though; I give it months.'

'I'll take that right now.'

'If you mind me saying that?'

'No, yes—why just months?'

'I just have a sense of what your partnership in life will be like, and it's not like that.'

'Evgenia doesn't fit me?'

'Well, I can't see you travelling around the world as an add-on with them; her setup doesn't fit with you, her money.'

'Why is the setup wrong?

'You've been clear in the past that folks operate differently with money and without it and your preference is to live without; and the trappings of a kid and the family groove may not give you freedom, *your* kind of stability.'

'What? But she's… I am aghast, to be honest, how you have reacted; you of all people.'

Toby holds his wooden spoon aloft; 'Then I declare you as foolish!'

'I tell you of the most passionate, romantic womanly experience of mine or anyone else's lives and you declare me as foolish.'

'You react as if you've never been declared foolish before.'

'But you're giving it a month!'

'Mm. Four tops, but I am also tight about something. Jealous I think.'

'Are you?'

'Oh yes.'

'Great!'

'It's like you've hit the jackpot.'

'But I've just lost the jackpot.'

'She'll call.'

'Well anyway, that's better. I don't mind four months, as long as you're jealous.'

'Yes, yes, but you've got it coming sunshine.'

I feel more hopeful now.

Thumps on the stairs declare Naeema's imminent presence. She is a heavy treader, not an attractive quality in a woman, but she's certainly not into winning guys like me. But then she comes in wearing more makeup than usual, nice it is too.

'Hi guys!' she says, breezily, 'ooh, let me try a bit,' she swipes a piece of my mournful toast and takes a bite. Mouth full and all twinkly she says, 'I've got a toast-shaped hole in mah fuckin' belly.'

While I am wondering what Naeema-shaped entity has taken over my stroppy housemate, in walks Andy, dressed like Lou Reed, slaps Naeema's bum and says 'come on.' He winks at us and leaves. She smiles, does a little eyebrows-raised 'laters' wave and leaves with him.

I look at Toby.

'Yeah,' he says without turning from the pot, 'he fucked her last night.'

'You *what!?*'

'She was all over him.'

'Can this be true?'

'It is.'

'But Andy is feminist anti-matter.'

'Apparently not.'

'He uses women.'

'I suppose she wants to be used. Or wants to think she's using him, or... oh I don't fucking know do I?'

Toby was seeing a married woman who he'd met at the swimming pool. She pounced on him, he says, and he thought why not? And then wavered, because maybe it is immoral to sleep with a married woman? Stephen put him straight a few evenings back at a party we'd given up trying to get laid at;

'We are socially conditioned to be monogamous, manifested as being possessive and jealous. This is "ok," the norm, a social construct, a paradigm, an almost universal subscription to an inherited code of ethics... but without questioning it, its motives, its base...'

'Alright, yes, I think *that* is pretty watertight,' said Toby. We were semi-stoned in the garden at this point, sitting on a damp discarded sofa, 'I mean, there are other social constructs, just take polygamy as the most obvious.'

'This has always appealed to me,' I said, 'I really don't know why.'

Toby went on, 'Probably a nightmare in practice, but *I don't know.*'

'But you do know,' said Stephen, 'it was a nightmare.'

'Yes, but I need more evidence.'

'You're monogamous,' I said to Stephen.

'Now I am. No problem.'

It was a naff party; one of those empty house affairs, with about fifteen people standing around the edges of rooms, cleared earlier that day in the expectation of a debauched LA teen movie, rather than the middle-class dinner party it ended up merely wanting to be. No good-looking girls either, so what's the point? The music was good though. Can's Halleluhwah undercurrented our manly talk of emotions.

'Stephen,' I said, 'I don't... I don't understand how it's working. Charlotte seems so different to the girls you're normally with.'

'Less beautiful you mean?'

'No, no! Of course not. Yes, *kind* of. Less classically beautiful.'

'I now believe it is impossible to find a beautiful woman worth living with,' he said.

'This cannot be true.'

'Oh it can. Beauty is power. If you're a woman born with it, it gets into you, into everything you say and do, it shields you from reality, makes everything just that *bit* too easy—even the nice ones, the intelligent ones, the dangerous ones, uh, the quirky ones—good grief, the quirky ones are worst of all; underneath the crazy hats, a kind of predictable, frantic, blandness is going on. Beautiful women know there's nothing there, and so they scrabble around to bolt something deep and meaningful on. People born into money are the same; they never really have to let go.'

'What about girls who grow up ugly and then become beautiful?'

'They're the ones to get. But they're like famous people—you have to get them as they turn or they'll go off.'

'Like an apricot,' said Toby.

'Another one,' I said, not really listening, 'is a beautiful peasant girl, raised away from civilisation, whose parents die, tragically, and, she has to walk bare-foot into the modern world, where, erm, where I pick her up by the side of the road, and take her home, and feed her soup.'

'Yeah, you'd like that,' said Toby.

'You're better off with a normal girl, with genuine aliveness,' said Stephen, 'healthy kidneys, bright eyes, nice hips—that should be enough for any man.'

It sounded to me like Stephen had given up on the good, but he had also given up drinking and was taking on a more human pallor, and he seemed more restful, so perhaps it was working for him. But then he hadn't had a bizarre psycho-spiritual experience with a Russian goddess, now had he?

Anyway, it wasn't going well with Toby's married woman, an Italian called Laura. The first time they'd had sex he had tried to be all macho and say '*strip,*' like in that shit Milan Kundera book, and she did it, far too rapidly, stood in front of him naked and said 'there, I look like a frog, happy?'

'Erm.'

'Now let's fuck.'

'It seemed inauspicious,' said Toby, skinning up.

'Was it?'

'Well after that, she being 'an older woman' I thought perhaps I'd try out one of my fantasies, "the dominant woman", you know, *do what I say, lick me here, on your knees worm*". Jeeeesus— but she said it was humiliating. I said "I don't mind!!!" but no...'

He held out his hands in a 'but-why.'

'It's all a bit of fun,' he said, 'it's just a *game*. Please, I am *not* a pervert.'

'You're a frustrated pervert,' said Stephen.

'That's right. It's completely different.'

They'd had a 'perfunctory coupling' and for Toby that was it. He said that she smelt a little bit of decay, so he didn't return her somewhat desperate texts and turned back in shame to porn, which he'd begun to justify by trying to have something of an academic interest in. He was going through the porn of the world detailing how they deviated from The Standard Routine (no cunny in Spain, anal big in the US) and what variations there were (UK comedy porn, Japanese tentacle porn, etc). I ask him about Russian porn and he just shrugs and says 'brutal.'

'Come and look at this,' he says, covering his Pilaf. We go upstairs and he pushes open Andy's door.

His room—Adam's old room—is bright and layered with half-used canvasses and prints. On the walls are his own paintings; mostly of himself naked, a few of naked women holding antlers, a goat. Art it is, that's for sure. The bed is in the middle of the room, not the most practical position but necessary for the set-up around it—a high-end digital camera, couple of stage lights and a huge plasma-screen television where the headboard should be.

'He makes porn?' I ask.

'No, he just likes to watch himself on TV.'

'Fucking?'

'Yeah, while he's fucking.'

'*While* he's fucking?'

'Yeah.'

'How very modern.'

'I'm not so sure,' says Toby, 'I'm starting to think that it goes back a long way, getting off on the *image* of what you're doing.'

'Is that what you do?'

'Isn't that what you do?'

I think about this. Do I? Somehow perhaps, yes, I do. The *idea* that my godhard porncock is sawing into a writhing sloppy shebody—the act does tend to come second to that. I wonder though...

'What's that smell?'

'It's enemy bull,' says Toby backing out, 'let's get back to our own territory.'

He goes to bed with a bottle of whiskey and I retreat to my boring cloister. There is much to consider in the wheelchair of solitary doom. Do I want a man in female form, for example? A half-peasant sex-kitten, big-giving eyes, but underneath really just the same kind of thing as me? Goes fishing, doesn't wake up with an inexplicable moody, understands the off-side rule? Is that what I want? I don't think so. I *do* want something very strange—and that's why I'm so sick of porn. Even at its most surreal and specialist, something about it is grabbable, graspable, the known, again. It's just more stuff on the screen of my mind. Like modern art.

I look at my most recent attempts to art—sketches mostly, a po-faced self-portrait and a collage thing I did when I was bored, cutting up the TV guide and replacing the eyes of the breakfast presenters with moon craters—and it too looks knowable. I know how I did it; and that's just not what I love. When I see a work of art that I love I *don't* know how it was done. I have the feeling—awe mixed with envy—that no matter how much I practice I will never be able to do that. I want to feel like that looking at my own stuff. How did you do it Daniel!?

My phone buzzes. Message from Geni. 'I'll be in the King's Head until midnight. I should be so grateful if you were to, you know. A woman, Caucasian, late twenties / early thirties.'

I check the time—11:30. Toby is drunk. Won't get a taxi fast enough. *Can* make it on my bike though. Thoughts racing. Is this some kind of test? Gotta leave *now*. Wait—check the map, check the internet. King's Head, 14 mins by bike. East Dulwich Road, Lordship Lane, second right, memorise…

I bomb south, propelled by frustrated sexual energy, and reach Dulwich park in 10 minutes, but then take a wrong turn. I hurtle down to the lights and ask a non-threatening tidyman where the King's Head is—and somehow it's where I've just come from, back up College Road. Check time, curse.

By the time I work out where I am, and where the King's Head is, I am hot with desperation sweat. I stop on the approach to the pub and try to pull myself together but see Evgenia coming out, so I scoot up, sweating but casual like.

'Fancy a lift?' I ask. She doesn't really seem like the type to ride backies, but she sidesaddles on my back rack, left arm around my waist, pointing the way.

'I didn't think you'd make it.'

'Can't have you walking back alone,' I say, thanking God we're going downhill, letting momentum carry us back towards the park thinking, 'I'm definitely going to have sex now!'

'How was the party?' I ask, pointlessly.

'Awful, but I had business to do.'

'Art business?' I call back with the wind rustling around us.

'That too.'

'Sorry I had to leave.'

'I understand.'

'I just, I find a lot of parties, don't meet my standards.'

'Keep going!'

'What?'

'Don't put your brakes on!'

We are gathering speed, heading down towards an intersection which the South Circular crosses: usually empty at this time, but far from a carless road.

'What?'

'Keep going! Don't brake!'

Faster and faster, the tick of the chain becomes a wild rattle.

'Geni, we'll *die!*'

'If you squeeze those brakes you're not coming back to mine,' she whispers quietly.

'Ack,' I croak. I want to brake, so very much, but sex with this woman is actually more valuable to me than my life. We are now hurtling towards death. My 'ah' elongates into a long terrified 'ahhhhhHHHHH!' Evgenia cries out joyously 'Woooooooo!' The main road swings into view, an out of service bus, windowless, black, is rolling up towards us. My brain calculates braking is more likely to kill us. We hit the South Circular, my cry throat-strangled, Evgenia screaming, sweep past the front of the bus—close enough for me to see the surprised 'oh!' of the bus driver—and into the other half of College Road, alive.

'Fuck *me.*'

'That was fun,' she says into my ear with eerie calm.

•

Her flat is sparse, wooden, black and white photos and full-blown lilies all over the place, but I notice very little on the way to the bedroom, pulling my trousers off, pulling her shirt off, grab that bit, avoid the millennium falcon, onto the bed, oh Lord what a rack...

Slow and in the body, slow and in the body, but, but, how reckless it all is now, carried along by some avalanching, grinding, river of want, roaring in my ears. It works though; the slower I move, the more painfully good it feels, and the better I feel, the less I care about clawing at her, clamping her.

Then comes the voice, at the back of the head;

'Well done, look, you're fucking a beautiful woman. You did it.'

Shush! Back to the senses, back to the senses.

In every sense there is pleasure—her sound, taste, feel, smell, shoulder, nobbly bit on the shoulder—and relief from the cursed voice, relief from the river of rocks. And again a feeling of being so damn lucky leads to the inner body, where there is nothing but the good, the good, and something beyond myself which is taking over the body and rattling through it, empty waves of colossal energy crashing down my nerves, into her, pulsing through us.

Slower and slower, stiller and stiller, until there is no physical movement, but all is silent, white fire, hurtling. I'm getting it. I really am getting it. It's going really well! Oh, *please* shut up.

She cries out—quite hoarsely, I distantly think, not very feminine, intense, pleasure and confusion in her eyes, but there is some holding on, some confusion, 'what *is* that?' she whispers.

Yes, what *is* it?

It relaxes, sufficient to breathe, and then it comes again, like the centre of the universe whum-whumming detonations so powerful I feel sure I am going to pass out. It subsides,

subsides—but then more intense, and more, until there is no more me to know it, or describe it. I'm coming apart.

It's nothing.

I have no idea how long it is nothing for, before it is over.

We lay in the darkness, life returning. Yes life—there was death in that. Something beyond human experience. The room forms, a film of moonlight settles on the breathing bed.

'Jesus Christ,' I whisper.

'Yeah.'

'I channelled the spirit of Jesus.'

'Yeah,' she says, not apparently caring.

'That's a bit gay,' I say.

'No it isn't. Jesus is Jesus.'

'Well I do feel like Jesus.'

She looks at me. 'You look like Jesus.'

'I could easily die for humanity's sins right now.'

'Do you want to move in with me?'

'Yes.'

'Why?'

'Why? I love you.' These words form themselves and while I watch on, amazed, they emerge from my mouth.

'I love you too,' she says, and I feel a twinge of fear, but sleep is coming down and we lie limbs knitted as it settles.

•

Knocked conscious. We lie in charged silent ease, thoughts roll like golden honey through my mind, all poetry now. Everything is slow and quiet and the world could do anything, I could lose everything, and it would be a lazy, laughable nothing.

I close my eyes; a vast underground cave, warm, lit from within a million honeycombed cubbyholes, breathes before me. Lambent, paper-lantern walls seem made from sunlight. I open my eyes; and I am again swimming in blazing, liquid freedom, flowing into a friendly universe.

I wonder if I will ever get out of bed—there seems no reason to. But as I wonder this and that, I find we are coming apart slowly, unfolding. Evgenia swings her legs out of bed, looks around the floor and takes a towel. As she stands, with the towel held against her, I glimpse a tattoo next to her pubis—a scorpion.

'Why are you covering yourself?'

'I don't want you to see me.'

'Right, but why?'

'Does it matter?'

'Erm, I just don't see why. It's odd.'

She smiles, 'so it's odd.'

'Leave the towel.'

'No,' she says with simple finality, and pads off for a shower.

I wander around the flat. It's minimal, scando-style, chilly, almost empty, bits of fluff and dust in the corners. Lilies and trailing plants straggle over empty shelves and large bleak photographs cover the walls. It's hard to tell what the photographs are of, which is probably the point, as they look nice enough, big blobs of fuzzy black and grey which eventually resolve into organic curls of fabric, perhaps, lying on stone pillars is it? or some kind of plinth.

Geni joins me, scruffling her wet hair.

'What are they?' I ask.

'Does it matter?'

'Erm. I don't know, maybe.'

'Wanting to know what something is, doesn't help you to see it,' she says.

'I suppose, but then I could draw anything. I could exhibit a thousand squares, or a snapped lollipop stick.'

'You can.'

'Alright. I still prefer drawing real things though.'

'But what *is* real?'

'Erm. This. Weird thing.' I gesture from her to me, 'This us thing, isn't it?.'

'How can you draw this?'

'That, I would like to know.'

She shrugs. 'I don't have to pick Barney up till lunch. What shall we do?'

'How about Nunhead Cemetery?'

'Sure.'

•

As we step out into the sunshine, Geni's next door neighbour steps out alongside us. He's a pale little guy, with a head shaped like a light-bulb and a hesitant darting demeanour.

'Ah, ah, ah, Geni. D-d-d-d-*did*-the radiator start working?'

'Yes, thank you Brian.'

He fiddles manically with his key ring, face very mobile. 'I, heh, laughing, mustn't laugh, thought you could be, could be, under wwwwwww... *water* by now!'

'No, I'm fine. This is Daniel.'

'Oh, hello; Brian.'

'We're just going to Nunhead Cemetery now Brian.'

'Oh that's lovely, a lovely place, of parrots and d-d-d-*death*.'

He gets his keys out and goes back indoors. Why? I don't know. Maybe he forgot something. Or maybe, like me, he'll go to any length to avoid small talk.

'Most people are nutters here,' says Geni as we idle towards the bus stop. 'The old woman, the other side, she never comes out, never seen her. Just twitches her net curtains. I met her son, he said she just sits all day listening to Elvis Presley.'

'Yeah, our neighbour is mad too. God-intoxicated. She

regularly reminds us that the creator of the universe doesn't like us one bit.'

'One in four people are mentally ill apparently,' she says.

'It's more than that though, it has to be.'

'What, two in four? three?'

'Four in four, I believe.'

'As many as that?'

'I don't think it will be long,' I say, 'before everyone, everywhere is rocking back and forth in the corner, counting their footsteps, violently arguing with Jesus Christ, wrapping themselves in cellophane…'

'Are you mentally ill then?'

She's still not looking at me, full on. Just arch flashes. Can't say I mind too much today either, although I do get a sting with this question. It seems to me that the point comes in a relationship, quite early on, where a woman tries to work out what *my problem* is. It's not like they're suspicious—or are they? I don't know; it seems to be some kind of instinct. Probably not a stupid one though.

'I have my problems,' I say.

'And what are they?'

We get onto the 37, find seats and start rumbling down Dulwich Village road, enough time for me to compose an answer.

'There is an entity in here that calls itself Daniel, but it is not me.'

'Who is it?'

'I don't know. It's a voice.'

'A voice in your head?'

'Yeah.'

'Not you?'

'Oh it's me. It's my voice. I don't have any other characters in here.'

'Well that's normal isn't it?'

'Yeah. That's the problem.'

'Do you obey it?'

'Er, yeah, sometimes. Not a good idea though. It's a complete moron.'

'So why don't you deal with it?'

'I don't know. I once thought it needed to die, or be drugged, or meditated into oblivion, but I reckon I need it. And anyway, I don't think it can die. It just needs to get out of the fucking way. I need to get out of the way of myself.'

'That's the kind of talk that gets people sectioned,' says Geni, smiling.

'Does it?'

'Yep. You better not play up or I'll have the men in white coats round.'

We reach Ivydale Road, next to the mighty Victorian necropolis. I have always wanted to bring a girl here. It is one of the most beautiful places in London. A massive graveyard left to the wild, creepers running across graves sinking ever deeper into the black mud of old London. Yew, Hornbeam, shrubby ash, cypress funeral and Balm of Gilead twine through mausoleums and monuments.

We crunch up the main gravel path, and into the dark woods, tuk-tukking with woodpeckers and chattering with thrush, finch and escaped parrot. The air is nonchalant; close, hazy, summery and silent.

Geni bends over a gravestone, deep green with moss. 'William Lawson closed his eyes on 28th April, 1874 and went to sleep.'

'They never say *die*,' she says, standing up.

'Nobody does.'

She moves to another grave. 'Why, what would yours read?' I ask, 'Evgenia fell to the floor, screaming in pain, vomiting black blood, and *died*. She *died* and now she's *dead*.'

She shoots me an approving squint and turns back to the inscription.

'Was everyone called William?' she asks.

We wander past more of the broken headstones, picking out the inscriptions, talking of death, and madness.

'Death brings out the best in people,' she says, almost wistfully, then turns to look at me, full on, and says 'there should be more of it.'

This comment unnerves me a bit. It's the kind of weirdness I had always hoped to hear from a staggeringly beautiful woman, but I find myself with the quavering feeling that I might be getting into something a bit on the big side.

We emerge into one of the open areas and lie down on the grass, underneath a magnificent chestnut oak. Huge it is, but perfectly proportioned, and alive.

'Some people are afraid of cemeteries,' I say.

'Strange isn't it?'

'I never feel less alone than when I am sitting here.'

'Now we're both not alone, sitting here.'

We kiss, and hold each other, lying on the warm grass. Daniel, the entity I have now identified as the spoiler, just falls into the unknown pleasure of it; and again here is the *thing*, the experience—how to describe it? It's like the feeling of love *before* it reaches the body. The rays of the sun, before they hit matter, are cold, nothing… it's that. All we can say is 'are you feeling that? Is it just me?'

She murmurs 'yes,' far-away amazed yet also dreamy, as if she knows the thing, recognises it as a friend. I'm not so sure. I feel I am stumbling into the truth of existence, the hidden human reality behind the entire universe.

It is not completely pleasant.

Hell is Fun

Eight ducklings in a bucket, a high-striker, larger-than-average bouncy-castle, gourmet ice cream stall, hot-air balloon going up and llamas stand around chewing the cud. Three hundred employees of Apollo Inc. financial software, data, and media company drift, with their partners and children, from one stall to another. They smile a bit and do their best not to talk shop. There is a stifling, bleached, motionless paste over the world which I could almost believe was harmless, were it not for the floor show.

'I've entered a whole new world of Absolute Work,' says Toby, 'Flexible I am now, you see—I can work at home, work on the bus, work in the park—and soon they'll find a way to get my laptop into my sleep so that my dreamself can work through spreadsheets on Neptune.' He is, he tells me, beginning to inhabit The Blank State. 'I'm never done with work now, and I'm never not done with it.'

We are sitting on wooden foldout chairs in front of an empty stage erected against the side of award-winning events venue Halhurst Place. I am Toby's plus one at the annual company fun day which I half accepted in order to see what happens at such a thing, and half because I never see Toby any more, although the Toby I once did see, with the shocked hair and splattered rusty trousers has been replaced by a neater shirted version, hair-brushed and narrow, like everyone else.

'I don't live at home anymore,' he says, 'I'm *based* there.'

'At least you've got some money.'

'I just spend it on saving the time I used to have.'

'Yeah, but not having to worry…'

'I just worry about different things.'

'So why work?'

He shrugs.

A gamelan gong dongs and six or seven barefoot Indonesian girls dressed in silky pink and yellow robes walk out all elbows and wrists, shaking their chimey bracelets and tiaras to the clashing boing-boings of the little orchestra behind them. They are wearing faces of frozen serenity, like this is the day job, which it is. Once upon a time they danced for what? a means to entice the god of thunder to fire-crack the marital bed? to celebrate eating the infinite onion-rings of the universe? gratitude for figs? Just for the hell of it?

Do not cultivate rare birds or strange beasts in your own land.

I turn to Toby, 'this is horrible.'

'Yeah, sod this, shall we go and look at the ducks again?'

We float like flotsam towards the mini farm, stopping en route at Toby's boss, a thin, joyless Scottish woman who, because she is a sadist, immediately asks me what I do.

'I clean toilets.'

'Ooh, that reminds me, sorry to talk shop Toby, but did you think of a better title for that report?'

'Well yes, but it's a difficult one Fiona because there's no way to translate the pun. I can either be accurate and lose the joke or express the joke but say something slightly different.'

'No need to mansplain Toby,' she says tightly, 'I translate too.'

'I'm just saying…' he drifts off.

'Alright,' she smiles thinly, 'we'll talk about it next week. Let's have some fun shall we?'

'Yeah, see you on Tuesday,' says Toby mournfully.

'Fucking mansplaining,' he says with quiet hatred, as she walks off, 'She uses it to mean "a man explaining."'

'Why don't you leave?' I say.

'It *can* just be a fucking explanation.'

'Toby, look at this place—this isn't you. This is savage Omar the manager and Hector the Lindy-hop eccentric and Ron Bone the programmer.' I feel guilty that I was ever jealous of him, the old Toby I mean. I want him back.

'No, I can't,' he says, 'I've got things to do with my life. I need the money.'

'Fiona probably said the same thing ten years ago.'

'I'm not going to end up like *Fiona*.'

We stand around the ducklings, a couple of toddlers jostling us for a fumble. I wouldn't mind giving a duck a bit of love myself, but feel a bit awkward about asking the guy, so I just kneel down and gently prod one. They are lovely, but terrified.

'I think I'm going to go Toby,' I say, standing up, 'this place is bringing on the fear.'

I sense constant low-lying agitation and digital check-pressure in the minds around me, looking around for something to fill the space where scrolling should go.

'I'll walk you back to your bike.'

When we're out of sight of the workforce I roll a cigarette.

'You're smoking now?'

'Yeah. Geni smokes, so I thought I'd join her.'

'Mm hm,' says Toby, with a touch of irritation, or so it seems.

'Do you know the worst thing about being in love? I mean really being in love?'

'Yes please?' says Toby, still none too enthusiastic.

'You can't get excited about it with anyone. Nobody interested. Always "the wrong time".'

'I suppose no one else is in love?'

'No.'

'Like me.'

'That would seem to be the case.'

'I split up with Laura for good,' he said, 'I got stoned and fucked her in the arse, then we had an argument and then she left.'

'How do you feel about that?'

'Nothing. Nothing. Nothing.'

We walk in silence down a long tree-lined lane, towards the car park. London smoulders on the wan, white skyline.

'I feel like I'm insulting people when I tell them I'm in love. In some small way.'

Toby kicks a pebble down the lane. 'Like who?'

'Who what?'

'Who have you told?'

'A few people. Friends, but I've given up now. I have learnt.'

'Apparently not. Why do you need to anyway?'

'What, tell people?'

'Yeah. It's a bit like someone enthusing about their LSD trip or talking about a dream. Who gives a fuck?'

'I dunno. I suppose I wanted to share my good news. Perhaps spread the cheer, even if you don't feel like it.'

'I see. I think in your case it is a bit like the boy who cried wolf.'

'What? I've never described love like this.'

'Then why don't I get it?'

'Because you're miserable.'

'I get it, but I don't get it. Not long ago you told me you re-alised you were going to be a world-famous genius. Do you see?'

'That's still true. It's even more true now.'

Toby sighs. 'Yes, but do you see?'

'No I don't.'

'This isn't in contrast to you generally.'

'What? This is totally different.'

'It doesn't seem that way.'

'Maybe I haven't explained it well enough.'

'Or it could still be *you*. Not the world's fault.'

'I'm not blaming anyone,' I protest, but somehow I fear.

'But you know what I mean.'

'Yes, but this is true love. I have never been in so much love. When I stop doing something, anything, I think "oh great, I can be in love again." I sit down and am in love, I wake up in love, I go to sleep in love.'

'Ugh.'

I struggle against anger, rising. 'Don't you remember being Jesus and sharing love over the phone?'

'Yes, but...' Toby looks down on me as I unlock my bike. My hands are shaking a bit, I can't get the key in. 'The high-speed train of delusion was then hurtling towards the steady and true carriage of life as it is.'

'You were interested in things. Why don't you draw any-more?'

'I just see boredom in every direction. Boredom and dis-appointment.'

'You sound like Adam.'

'Maybe that's what happened to Adam,' he says as I get on my bike 'I think it's happening to all of us.'

'It's not happening to me.'

'It will.'

I cycle through the self-replicating unplace of Borehamwood. It's where my family came from—although impossible to believe that a *family* could come from this featureless, stained and degrading collection of poorly organised rubble, haunted by scrags, shrivelled old women and large black men on medication—at least the high street is; the back roads, estates and cul-de-sacs are all empty, desolate, no kids on bikes, no grannies in the garden, no Dads in the garage, nobody, nothing, nowhere.

From Borehamwood into Edgware, Hendon, Kilburn, Maida Vale, and ever deeper into the fun desert.

'I'm tight about something,' said Toby. He *is* tighter now, his lips pursed, his voice squeezed, trapped at the back of his neck. And, now I think about it, this is strange—a lot of people are tight in this way. Why should unhappiness mean that muscles are squeezed? But it does, it tightens the avenues of facial growth, forces bones down weird ugly motorways, packed, because everyone else is on them, all trying to get to the same place; 'what I like.'

A battery of industrial construction vehicles chug past me as I whip down Edgware Road, and I feel like a steam-punk rebel, a member of the low-tech resistance, slick wheels turning smoothly, slight downhill, gear click, juicy power, swerving past these stalling chunks, under the Marble Arch and into Hyde Park, which is the centre of a green universe, delicately chaotic clusters of floating fire-bright branches revolving past my orbiting bike-body.

The Question playfully presented itself to me again earlier today. It writhed belly-up at my bewilderment while I was in the garden, staring into the boughs of next door's fine oak tree. It burbled on in the background for a while then flashed intensely, salt-in-the-eye, for a shattering moment as I moonwalked on Geni's shiny parquet floor, enjoying another of those bone-comforts, those secret agreements with the most mundane and empty events. Hard to say quite what *the question* is, for it forms itself wordlessly, sliding in between my thoughts as I jog round the lake, or take another spoon of yoghurt. Perhaps I can put it like this: Who is the me here that is experiencing me? I see there are thoughts and there are feelings and there is this I that experiences them; and that must be me. But to go looking for this 'me' is a strange—and terrifying—thing. In those trapdoor moments I seem to step backwards over the balcony of myself. I catch my breath as annihilating melessness blooms, but then I see something in the shadows on the wall and in the gleams of the windowsill that I forget to hold on to myself, and then, and then, what remains?

This me-less bloom is with me now as I coast down the park paths, throwing seed-grenades from my pockets which explode like geysers, splintering the still air, erupting into the knobbly barley-grey branch-flung London planes, thick fingered, full-crested, knotting themselves into the canyons of the sky.

Yes! Yes! and forever Yes! Reality is megaphone with my joyous yawp at the business-end, the world is a rubber band for me to twang into eternity, I am a whiskey-guzzling, gun-toting *fiefdom* of a man! Yes, oh yes, it is extraordinary. It is *extraordinary* now, with Evgenia, to whom the silent I is perpetually blue-beam bound. I have never heard of anything like it. I've read the raptures of love and listened to all the pop songs, but this is something which is outside the world I have known.

Surely but surely, if someone else had experienced this they would have said it, specifically said it: Sex is really an awful ecstatic merging in an I-less space where place is not. The infinite. It would be on record, I would have heard about it, and taken note.

Anyone who I speak to about this just assumes I am talking about very good sex or the excitement of getting blended. 'Oh yes, all loved up!' they say, all jolly and knowing—as if that explains it. But I have had very good sex, outstanding sex — I'd even made what I thought was love — I've been in love, but this is not just different in intensity. It is an entirely different... it's something else, and nobody has ever spoken of it.

The sun is still low and glassy, but it is milder and the people are mild too. I sit on a park bench, smoking a cigarette, which is marvellous. Smoking is marvellous. A pair of feet walk towards me, splayed one hundred and eighty degrees away from each other and treading as tenderly as if on ice. At the last minute I look up to see a wide and messy man's head congenially and sheepishly nod to me as if to say, 'yes, my feet *are* strange, aren't they?' or perhaps just 'it's fine, it's all fine.' A very old man, his face scrunched up, lips pursed, peers into the distance, trying to make something out on the far side of the universe. A woman passes and does an imperceptible double take when she sees me. A small squadron of chattering sparrows shoot past in tight formation, looping and diving around a clump of trees. A middle-aged woman passes with creases on her lips that show her favourite expression has always been disapproval. Two guffawing Indian men, hunched over expectantly, have their ears pressed against a single mobile phone, they listen intently, forcing back laughter.

People pass and I snaffle fragments of their conversation into my collection. 'Why don't pedos wash their hair?' and 'Twat wrote to me in a green pen,' and 'I want to hump his portfolio like a boy band,' and 'I don't think anyone in Boots understands politics,' and 'She has an acidic vagina.'

A couple of deaf people are sitting on the park bench opposite, having an expressive conversation — their faces! So completely inhabiting the story. One guy mimes a '*poooooh*, what a fucking stink,' face creased up in laughing disgust, everyone else laughing. Where else are such subtle, rippling, uninhibited faces to be found? What would it be like if we could see each other's faces, so tight and, when the tightness relaxes, so coarse, so frightening? I don't think we'd stand for it!

I pull my sketchbook out of my bag and surreptitiously try to capture them. I find myself more and more compelled by the face, by the forest of infinitely fine muscles, how these ripple and flow with pulses of atmosphere, with the weather of the room, with winter tempests, welcoming spring mornings, moonlight in the mist; or the monody of needing, wanting, stiffening, resisting; moulding the flesh, slowly, over the years, into the cheekbones, pulling the whole face down into a mask, setting it into a permanent advert.

See the face, see the eye, see the movement, see the tree — then you have no option but to practice until you can do justice to them. If you see, seeing is the whole thing. Just seeing. Not imagining, not focusing, not naming, not form-fondling through the mists of former desire. Unrestrained and nothing withheld.

Unrestrained and nothing withheld. As I say these words, which sound so sweet to my mind, a tremendous power starts tingling in my muscles, a fire in my solar plexus begins to roar, the air around me iodises and a thunder crack erupts up my spine, blasting my hands outwards, setting my eyeballs on blue fire and shuddering through me in a series of vast juddering pulses. I rise up, a few feet from the park bench, and then explode in a blinding ecstasy of clear light.

'Oh, hello Harold.'

Harold is standing in front of me.

'Hello Daniel, fancy meeting you here.'

'Nice outfit.'

Harold is wearing a shiny turtleneck, a light-grey wool coat with dropped shoulders, a tight, knee-length dress, thick black tights and high-heel booties. Oh, and a small candy-red leather shoulder bag, the same shade as his lipstick.

'Thanks,' he says, sitting next to me.

'Nice day eh?' he says.

'All heaven is breaking loose.'

Harold nods serenely. Booms of wind tug and puff the banging branches of the chestnut trees—shushing their shaggy, foppish leaves, scattering the path in front of us with catkins, blossom and shades which settle and blend into the blue warmth.

'I like your dress,' I say.

'It's Jigsaw.'

'What's that?'

'It's the brand. It's what you're supposed say when people say they like your frock.'

'Is it?'

'Yes, there's a book of etiquette on such matters.'

'What does your wife make of your new wardrobe?'

'She picked it out.'

'She's got a good eye.'

'Yeah, it's one of the more difficult parts of changing over for… well, for people like me. I've never given much attention to colour and form, but I'm learning.'

'When… I mean, Harold, how…?'

'I was… it was after work one evening, and Jill was telling me as usual about what had happened to her that day. She subjects me to the minutia of her day you see, going through everything that she said, was told, that she did or couldn't do—why must people do this? I don't know—or maybe I do know actually—but, anyway, all this time, I was looking for something in the shoe cupboard, a tap spanner, and it was annoying me, because I was sure I'd last seen it there, but I couldn't find it, and I was leaning in the cupboard and she's walking down the hallway to me,' Harold gets up and bends over the bench, as if it's his shoe cupboard, gesturing the path of his wife coming towards him, 'and, I don't know Daniel, something in me snapped, just *went*. She's yack-yack-yacking and I…' without looking up from the cupboard he holds his hand, palm up at right angles, into the face of his advancing wife, 'and she stopped, in front of my hand, and I said, without turning, "I just don't want to hear it any more".'

He sits down, smoothing his skirt.

'Wow.'

'It was as much a surprise to me as it was to her. Because I *didn't* want to hear it any more. I *had* had enough. I'd had it up to here. She was always telling me that she was exhausted, "oh I'm exhausted with it all Harold." And I felt sorry for her, and I tried to help her—and then it hit me. *I* was the one who was exhausted—with keeping *her* flipping reality together. You see? I thought it was love, I thought I was loving her, but it wasn't, it never is, all of that. It's just *caring*.'

The tightness has gone in Harold too. The lines of his face seem smoother, the muscles more mobile, easier around the cheeks. He was always a nostril-tense man.

'And of course it's not like you can reason things out with a woman, talk it through. You have to *be* that man. Then act. Do something.'

'Yes, action. *Action*,' I say.

'Well, it put the wind up her,' he says, 'she stood there, mouth working away, nothing coming out. But somehow something in her snapped too, and she was,' he looks up into the branches for the right word—'*relinquished*'—and he glances at me, eyes warm. 'From there to telling her I dressed up in her clothes when she was out, that I was going to leave work and study harmony and that I want to do heroin occasionally, was all downhill.'

'You do seem a lot happier.'

'Oh I *am*. The weight of the world has been lifted from me. All that worry about work, about politics, about the end of the world, *let* it end. And I tell you, shooting up from time to time, it's a real stress-buster.'

He actually seems somehow, in his skirt and makeup, more masculine too.

'How's the sex?' I ask.

'With Jill?'

'Yeah, of course.'

'Oh, she left me.'

'Eh? But I thought…'

'Oh good Lord no, she couldn't stay with me now. We get on fine though. Parted on good terms.'

'So you're living alone now?'

'Yes. Happy too, but I would like, you know, *she* to appear.'

'Oh yes, right. *She*.'

'*She*, Daniel, *she*. The one who understands. It's funny,' he says, 'I know how love should be, that *she* will understand, that *she* will feel and hear me, that I will be as one with *she*; but, well the details don't matter, but the peculiar thing is every non-she I've ever had a relationship with, thinks we have that. Maybe…' he searches, 'maybe I haven't got it quite right.'

'I often think,' I say, 'very often I don't know why, but; how strange it is that I have *this* life. All those people who have lived and live still, all those people leading all *those* lives—and I have *this* one.'

Harold nods, swallowing my words and letting them rest. A little girl trundles past on a scooter playing the theme to Star Wars on a kazoo.

'You know Daniel, you're the only person I told about dressing up.'

'Really?'

'Yes, I could trust you, and I knew I could trust you because of what you said to Fern and Geoff, in front of everyone.'

'What did I say?'

'You don't remember?'

'No.'

'Geoff said that Fern should "think outside the box" and you said it was impossible, that thought *is* the box.'

'Did I say that?'

'Yes.'

'Good, wasn't it?'

'I don't think so. Not really. It was a childish thing to say, sort of pointless confusing those fools—but to say it, then, in front of all those people, it *was* brave, somehow it was, and if I've learnt one thing, I've learnt that you can't trust a coward.'

I laugh—how marvellous!

He goes on, earnestly extracting the words, like splinters from his thumb. 'There's a singularity to you Daniel, a completeness, that marks you out as a true artist. You know great people can be social or loners, but if there is a sense that they *belong* to the world, they can't possibly belong to paradise as well. Only an individual can love, you see.'

'Fucking hell Harold, that's the best thing that anyone has ever said to me.'

A girl comes up to us—a young American tourist, very bright and skippy wearing a low-cut blouse that pushes her large breasts out. She asks me to take a picture of her together with her poorly postured bespectacled friend. I take the camera, zoom in on her tits, take the shot, hand the camera back and turn back to Harold.

'What about you?' he says laughing, 'Still trying to fill a God-shaped hole?'

'A God-shaped hole? Is that what we're doing?'

'Oh yes, I think so, yes. Don't you?'

The girls, now in the distance, are looking at the camera and furtively looking back at us. Not happy.

'I didn't know you were religious.' I say.

'I'm not. I just see that everyone is trying to fill the emptiness. A new operating system... an evacuation of semen in a symmetrical young body... a promotion... fame... six digits in the bank instead of five or five instead of four... just shovelling it all into oblivion.'

'You're right.'

He sighs, 'how low their ceilings, how near their shores.'

'What shape is a God-shaped hole?'

Harold holds his hands up, tentatively, a delicate smile on his lips, looking for the right shape. His huge hands rotate a bit, squeeze a bit; and then finally settle on the universal vital-statistics eight.

'What are you shooting at then?' he says to me.

'I'm not shooting any more. I've shot. I've arrived.'

'You've arrived?'

'Mm, I've just moved in with the woman of my dreams.'

'Really?'

'Do you want to see a picture?'

'Yes, of course I do.'

I get out my phone and show Harold my Evgenia.

He looks at the image very, very carefully.

'Well?' I ask, 'what do you think?'

'Well you've got yourself a trophy there.'

This is not *quite* the response I was hoping for.

'Thanks,' I say, feeling uneasy.

'This summer you win.'

'Thanks.'

'But too much sun makes a desert.'

•

I leave Harold in Hyde Park and cycle south, first round the back of Buckingham Palace. The Queen is there, behind those twelve-foot high brick walls, sitting next to her little lake, miserably chucking bits of bread at her mandarin ducks, seeing nothing but boredom and disappointment in every direction, anxious about the future, oppressed by a colourless cloud of futility and missing Igwe. Or perhaps not, but she is tight too; I've seen pictures.

Through Pimlico—lovely word that, Pimlico—over the Vauxhall Bridge which is so good I nearly turn round and ride back over it, and then down the Lambeth Road to the hospital where they've put Adam, who is, by all reports, in some kind of hell. He started off in the holding bay, but was swiftly passed into long-term care.

I find him in the recreation room of the Bethlem and Maudsley Sigyn ward, furnished, as all such places are, in smooth, new, pastel-shaded cheap pine and plasticky upholstery, thick PVC everywhere, everyone visible, at all times, and so *hot*. Staff come through, battle-hardened and brisk, kindly but all with that ominous, imperious air of 'we know what's best for you.'

People sit around watching the TV, playing cards, or reading. A sick-looking black girl is listening to music through two enormous cans. A game of table tennis is in mid-pong between a stick-thin fluffy young man with huge blue eyes, and a sad-looking, unshaven man in his mid-thirties. Sad-face is technically brilliant and consistently so. Fluffy, on the other hand, is of average ability, but occasionally a violent, nervous spasm pulses through him and he erupts a laser-sighted power-volley. When this happens, he screams out, 'Christ's cock!' or 'Monkey cunt!'

Adam is sitting in the corner in a thick purple dressing gown.

'Hi Adam.'

He is sitting by himself. His big lion-like head fixed, as ever, mask-like, his eyes dark slits. He doesn't turn to look at me.

'How're you doing mate?'

His eyes dart to me and then away again.

Just across from us sits a fat, messy, wet-lipped middle-aged man with a face like a bloated fish. On one side of him is a skinny old woman with a huge bun of white hair balancing on her head, and to the other side a bitter and bony hook-nosed vultureman. Both of the men are eating from little orange plastic lunch trays.

'I can't mother,' The blubby man is quietly murmuring, 'please don't, I'm sorry it's just not possible. No, mother, there's no point, it's wrong, it looks wrong, it's…'

'I'm not your mother.' says the vultureman, sharply and quietly, into his food.

I pull my chair a bit closer to Adam. 'You doing alright, mate?'

He whispers something.

'Eh? Say again?'

'I don't know,' he says, very quietly.

The table-tennis game is tied when sad-face unzips his trousers and takes out his penis. Nobody notices, including Fluffy, and they continue playing.

'I'm not sure anybody does Adam. But it's alright, isn't it, not knowing?'

I have the distinct feeling that there is a long, strange, menacing story being played out in Adam's quiet suspicious mind, and that all I can do is try and say something which *sounds* like it's okay, like the *tone* is meaningful.

I wait to see if he'll say anything else, but that seems to be it for the moment.

In the third corner of the room are two young men who have come in to repair a faulty radiator. They work quietly and efficiently, eager to leave. A hard looking middle-aged matron type approaches the woman with the bun, who is looking fixedly at her lunch tray.

'Come on Edith, you've hardly eaten anything,' says matron.

'I am not eating that shit.' Edith very clearly enunciates every word.

'Yes you are Edith. Now come on.'

'Vaginal blood fart!' screams Fluffy.

'...too much. Mother, don't, really, it's not necessary is it? Is it? Do we *have* to? Do we have to? (Blubby sighs and picks up a potato). Mother, I don't want to I...'

'I'm not your mother,' says the thin man, intently spooning.

Edith turns to the nurse, palm flat on the table; 'I am certainly not going to take anything from a whore like you.'

The matron tenses up. 'Oh yes you are Edith. Do you want me to call...'

'Oh nooo. I don't.' Edith says sourly and relaxes. And then she cheers up; 'Hello boys!' she shouts over to the young workmen.

They freeze, look over at her, and mumble a greeting.

Edith stands up, turns round and points to her rear end; 'You can kiss my *fucking arse!*'

'...think there's something wrong. I don't know, it just doesn't seem right. I'm no good with words. But mother, you know that...'

Ever so quietly, quietly but full of hate, the thin man whispers; 'I am *not* your mother.'

Fluffy starts screaming with laughter pointing at Smoothface, who stands proudly grinning, tennis bat and cock hanging in front of him.

'Ooo I like that!' says Edith straightening up, hands on hips, frankly admiring the penis.

'...you know what I'm like, mother, I can't, I can't, it's too difficult—can't I just go out and play, can't we play another game?'

The thin man throws his knife to the ground and roars at the top of his raw voice, 'I'MNOTYOURFUCKINGMOTHER!'

'Sit down Edith!' barks the Matron to Edith—who stares at her, defiantly—and then turns sternly to the men, 'What's going on here?' The booby is shaking with tears, and Razor-man is shaking with anger, but both are trying to conceal it by eating normally.

'*Why* should I sit down?' asks Edith, hands on hips. Now that she is facing me fully I can see she is wearing a t-shirt with a frazzled looking cartoon cat on it, sitting in a washing basket, underneath which the words '*basket case.*'

'I like it in here,' I say to Adam. 'At least you can be yourself, eh?'

'Is my self?' he asks, the fixed white light of terror suddenly bright in him. I don't understand the question. Is it? I don't know. Probably. He looks searchingly at me, then deflates.

'I am ill though. They said.'

He returns to staring straight ahead. What can I possibly say that will make sense to him? That will be meaningful? The strange thing is, I'm not especially religious, and I know Adam is a hard atheist, quite aggressive he is about it—yet all I feel like saying is 'bathe in the love of Jah.' The compulsion to say it is so great, in fact, that I do say it. I lean across and say that. 'Bathe in the love of Jah.'

And then, for a moment, I feel completely overwhelmed. I must be getting a bit silly.

'It's going to be alright Adam,' I say, my voice all trembly.

'They're watching me,' he whispers.

'Who?'

'Everyone.'

I look around. Nobody is watching him of course.

'It's okay though,' I say.

Adam just looks ahead.

He's probably got cameras knocked up all over the place in his mind, phones, ratings, microphones, the lot.

'It's going to be alright though Adam,' I say.

Adam says nothing.

Poor guy. Poor everyone. Poor all of us.

Blubby is quietly weeping to himself, his angular eating partner is clutching his head. The table-tennis game has ended in orderlies and confusion. A huge frightening black guy with some kind of skin condition comes in and turns on the television. A nature programme comes on and he starts singing 'Tracks of my Tears.'

I sit with Adam for a bit, subconsciously wafting alright vibes over him, then leave. On the way out, as I enter the reception area, my heart alarm goes off and time slows. Sitting on one of the sofas in the entrance lounge is Angel, the White Woman of Camberwell. I stop, pierced by the sight of her perched on the NHS sofa, ready to rush towards me, all black mouth, the swallowing abyss.

But no, all is normal. She is talking to John the House, a ravaged old Londoner with a frightening scar over his lips, who has a tendency to walk up to weedy studenty types in pubs, take their pints and drain them. He's as scary as the White Woman, a brute earthly counterpoint to her spectral hex.

I pretend to read a notice on the wall about testicular cancer so as to hear what they are saying.

'No petal,' says John gently, 'Ambergris is one of the most expensive substances on earth.'

'I've got some money saved up,' says Angel. She has a fault-less cut-glass accent and speaks like a timid five year old.

'Well it's gonna cost ya, but I can get some.'

'You have my number,' she says, 'let me know.'

She gets up to go further inside and glances at me, which, even though I've just heard her making business arrangements with a cockney, still gives me the willies.

I exit, glad to be in the Big Ward, and find myself in front of a banner advert across the hospital railings, 'Voices from the Void: The Outsider Art of Bedlam.' They've converted some of their corporate suite into an art exhibition, displaying the paintings of the Bethlem and Maudsley—'Bedlam' as was—which has nearly four hundred years of paintings by the insane, or those officially judged to be so. After a sandwich and soup on one of those triangles of grass that we all huddle upon at lunch, I pull out my unemployed discount credentials, and step in to the mind cave.

The first images, by a fellow called Von Ströpp, are a kind of psychedelic medievalism; high-detail pencil drawings of women in flowing gowns blending with eviscerated segments of alien architecture and world-consuming fires. He also has a vast flow-diagram of neatly handwritten comments, such as 'Facts aren't of major importance. But its percieved and misuderstood IS for surely what goes on in the noggin is whats real' (sic). This text-box is linked to 'Mind = 2D map of 3D world. But world itself = map of 4D reality; experience of which makes genius sprints into the funny unknown a breeze' which runs underneath 'Civilisation = a box ticking exercise.' Arrows everywhere, thin, hand drawn but beautifully straight lines. It makes some kind of sense. It must, I suppose.

Next is a thick-stroke, heavy-layered five-foot painting of a little girl with big, sick, sad eyes. Very simplistic, very awful but there's some self-pity in there too. Next to that mind-destructed cats by a guy called Louis Wain, fizzing with electric red zigzag starbursts and mad, triumphant eyes. Then there's a million men on horses, all kind of like orthodox icons, flat and golden, but arranged in a weirdly obsessive interlinking pattern. Lots of these pictures are sort of sickening, vertiginously morphed walls, spirals and bizarre 'empty' perspectives. Lots are desolate, lots are terrifying, much is kind of dull and self-obsessed—but they are all sincere. The human is in there, I feel it, although none of them are out, none of them are quite out. What they call Van Gogh's madness—his superluminous sanity—is not here.

It's not true, what they say, 'genius is tinged with madness.' These images are by gifted artists who are well and truly out of their trees, but the genius of life is not here, the genius of mind undone but *free* — no. Here is imprisonment and disorientation and everything shattered and even me, me, me, me, me.

You know, now I come to think of it, a lot of what is called great art seems to amount to 'you're going to make it.' I mean stories and songs and paintings by men who, as young men, were lifted on the wings of poetry and art, ready, recklessly to fly God knows where, only to fall into abysms of despair, and crash on mountains of ash, and be swept into endless stormy wastelands, and only after many years of wandering, dreamlike sun-glimpses and whispers leading them on through the mists, only after many trials and a stretched lifetime of mastery, only *then* they alighted on a land worth living on, capable of saying something worth saying — who to? To me!

Yes, there are heavenly desert islands out here, say the artists I love, and stormy trials and crushing whirlpools and endless, hopeless, windless oceans between you and the beach, but, but, *you're going to make it*. In fact, you're going to find, that the journey itself is an integral part of the destination.

I say men, because women don't seem to journey in the same way. They make great art too, but somehow they don't seem to leave the heart of things in the first place, and so don't seem to struggle to get back to it. They don't say 'you're gonna make it home'; they say, 'you never even left.'

It's nearly all lost men in this mad gallery, and it is by far the best stuff being exhibited in London; but none of them made it home. Except perhaps The Humanjest. This is the cognomen of an artist whose works, at the back of the gallery, hold the whole world still for me. I am, for a moment, looking at these oil-painted domestic scenes, still. Time and space lay down their knives.

The conceit is simple—childish even. Humanjest has painted kitchens, garages, living rooms, offices and other places of
modern human activity, but everything in them has a pair of
eyes; long, basic, retro-cartoon daubs, like simple elevens, are on
everything. No mouths, just these elongated black lines looking.
The paintings themselves are well-defined, almost cartoony, yet
free, as if the artist were laying down strokes to music. The cups
and spoons and staplers and spanners flow and burn and, with
their unjudging animal eyes look, and see, and I feel seen, and
I feel I can see too, the life in things. The hidden intelligence
of the candle, the sombre service of the curtain, the forgiving
pillow and the cute wisdom of the sugarcube.

Yes, something inside says yes. I am not excited, not emotional, but, what, what is this strange delight, this calling? Oh
yes; it is *recognition*. I recognise, and how sweet it is to understand what I already knew, to meet an old friend.

The late-afternoon night of London has fallen. A rainshower,
while I was inside, has slicked the dark world in argon lumines-
cence. I cycle weaving between the waiting buses and jammed
cars in a state of strange clarity, as if the sky, the lamps, the
electric-vividness of the shiny cars, the damp paving stones, the
milky-pink blackness were designed by a brilliant alien mind
for my benefit, for this bike ride indeed, through a city made
for me, a world made for me—and me for it.

•

Nobody really knows what we're celebrating. This is why the
party, this booming Peckham warehouse event, is loud, fun
and joyless. All parties, now I come to think of it, all the ones
I go to anyway. I mean, it's *alright*—but oddly serious. It's as
if everyone collectively said to themselves—'we'll delight ourselves some other time.'

I'm here to say goodbye to Stephen; he's going to Bulgaria with Charlotte to house-sit for a year on a remote farm, in order to avoid work he says, and get something done; something, presumably, more meaningful than his latest piece, which he called 'Fiasco,' an attempt to subvert the system by loathing everything you do within it, while, at the same time, carrying out every work act with exaggerated, excessive attention to the letter of the law, camp gaiety and conspicuous insincerity. I told him that I thought it had been done before, or at least that a lot of people had beaten him to it, but he dismissed them as plagiarists.

There's an awful lot of up-and-coming-youth here. All the marvellous people; my friend is a communist, Jake is a male slag, Tom really has his shit together and Sally does stand up poetry. Coffee at The General Store? There's even a couple of weird-mouthed human-shaped operatives from the blue-suit-and-brown-brogues brigade; day off from being a financial-ac-count-management-consultant-services-development-adminis-trator. Before Stephen arrived I had to endure an expressionless BBC wildlife cameraman holding forth with cutting, colourless nasality on how *amazing* it was, how *tragic* it is, how *important* it will be... from there to a brief loo-queue conversation about architecture with people who believe it comes from the top down, from the Mind of the Professional, then to a group of what I believe are called 'friends,' in which the men were conspicuously climbing over each other to erect their cocks on the Hillock of Attention. Not just them though. Everyone is participating in the modern mating ritual of dissolving their gender-based anxieties in alcohol. I call it a mating ritual, but actual copulation is rare and when it does happen both parties usually conclude that it was 'probably not a good idea.'

Stephen arrives and we shelter outside in a kind of alley, talking about women. What else is there to talk about? Why would anyone ever talk about anything else? Although in this case the occasion is watching some chippy hipster get blown out by a snotty, skinny Asian girl who is all the time looking around for someone more powerful to talk to. She's really quite flamboyantly annoyed by the attention of this poor whelp, although I suppose as her beauty fades and the essential misery in her soul creeps into her flesh and her ossified dreams pile up around her and she realises that *'this isn't at all how I imagined it would be.'* I suppose then she'll wish she was annoyed once more.

Stephen and I watch the beta-male, all hunched and trying, leaning in to her, eagerly qualifying, dropping his credentials, slackening his frame and get instantly brushed off. He walks off tight.

'He looked pitiful,' I say.

'I don't think his heart was in it.'

'I'm beginning to think the best chat-up line might just be "I love you".'

'It's possible,' says Stephen, 'if you really gave it everything. Or, there's that other one, the apocalypse opener.'

'Which is?'

'It's where you go up to a girl, and say, straight away, "what are you doing later?" and she says "oh, I dunno" and you say "would you like to come home with me?"'

'Can that possibly work?'

'Yes, it can work. If you come in light and hold it hard.'

I believe him. Stephen is a compulsive liar, but for some reason he only ever lies about little things, like what colour socks he's wearing or how many people were in the Post Office this morning. God knows why.

'Were you ever awful with women?'

'I still am.'

'No, I mean unable to get any, stay with any, the kind of problems we all have?' All of us but Andy of course.

'I had, I think, fifteen years of solo masturbation, just staring at girls. I never had a girlfriend for more than a week.'

'Why did you split up with them?'

'Because,' he says 'they discovered I wasn't the person I was pretending to be.'

'Who were you pretending to be?'

'Normal.'

'A regular fun-loving guy with half an eye to a brilliant career?'

'Exactly.'

'And what did they discover?'

'That I wasn't comfortable in any normal group situation, like other people are. Everyone else was healthy, well-balanced and I was, just, odd, frozen — not like through nerves — but just a kind of solid slab of pride.'

'I can't believe *you* were haughty.'

'No no, not haughty. I wish I was. No, I believed I wasn't worthy of having a girlfriend. I basically thought that if I had the opportunity to be inside a woman, the most important thing was that I orgasmed — because at least I could then say that I had done it, that I'd had sex with a woman, and nothing could ever take that away from me.'

'I've got my own perverse version of that story.'

'When I didn't have a girlfriend I was transmitting red-light signals of desperation,' he says, 'and then, when I did have one, I felt trapped.'

'How did you get out of it?'

'I didn't, I haven't. The only solution I've found is to keep it casual, have a few girlfriends, then I can handle their problems.'

'Don't you think, maybe, that you could change a woman? I mean help her not have problems?'

'I imagine it's only possible if they feel that you are utterly in love with them and totally committed, then they'll change.'

'But you're not prepared to experiment with that?'

'Errr… it's a bit of a gamble!'

The East-London youth mill around us. The boys seem meek, or gay, the erotic elite, aloof. Some girls—loads of red lipstick, oddly cut 80s style shirts, fluffy hoodies—go inside, laughing. Male nerds hang around in pairs. No joy, or togetherness, which would feel as strange here as they would at work.

'So you're not committed to Charlotte then?' I ask.

'Well, we're going to live in Bulgaria, away from everyone else in the whole world,' says Stephen.

'Right. So you *are* going to give up your independence.'

'I have no such intention!' says Stephen, 'but I'm with a girl now that I always end up preferring.'

'Eh? But… I just, I don't get it.'

'You know when you go into a crowded room and a kind of terminator scanner falls over your brain and rates every woman in it according to how much you want to fuck them?' says Stephen.

'I don't know what you mean!'

'Well I still have that. I think it's just part of male machinery. I still walk around London and want to make love to every woman on earth, but then, I get home and make love with Charlotte, and, for a moment, she *is* every woman on earth.'

'I think I know what you mean,' I say, and tell Stephen about the weird world I've been sharing with Geni.

'Honestly, Stephen, the orgasm, you've got no idea, it was like, like… like the universe exploding…'

'Over her tits.'

'I'm worried though, how can I maintain this?'

'Maintaining anything is hard work,' he says. 'Feelings, I think, are the problem. Like, I still have the same stupid porn urges, the same can't-be-bothereds, the same feelings of being trapped in an 'us' that's not quite right, but I prefer not to listen to these feelings. I prefer to be happy. Sod feelings. I'm serious. Fuck 'em.'

'But how do you stop getting bored?'

'One woman I was with, before sex she would stare at me as we ate or walked or talked, you know, wide-eyed, focused and soft. I asked her what she was doing and she would say she was making, um, letting herself fall in love with me. Adore me, because she liked doing that before making love.'

'Does that work?'

'Sometimes it does.'

'This sounds just like more effort.'

'It is,' says Stephen. 'But what's wrong with effort?'

'I think you have to go with the flow.'

'You do, but I'm telling you; you can't listen to "can't be bothered" that flows straight into the toilet.'

Charlotte turns up with Piscina, who is looking much prettier now that she's split up with Gurt. There seems to be some bizarre alchemy that drags lustre out of some girls' cheeks when they're going out with... well, with Gurt.

'I asked him what his favourite band is,' Piscina is saying as they come towards us, conspiratorially guffawing, 'and he said Radiohead!'

Charlotte laughs, bright, beautiful laughter it is, like a silvery windchime.

'What were you talking about then?' asks Charlotte.

'My problems with commitment,' says Stephen.

'Men die to get away from women, or they die to stay with them,' says Charlotte.

Piscina catches my eye.

'Are you giving up college then?' I ask Stephen.

'Yeah,' says Stephen, 'it was just something to do on Wednesday afternoons. Most of my lectures were on employability anyway. Employability. At an art college.'

'Don't you want to be employed?' asks Jonas, hurt. When did Jonas get here?

'No, I want to sell my art. There's a difference. If you're employed you have to produce porn.'

'What's the difference between porn and art?'

'Porn moves, art stills.'

'Your art moves me to confusion.'

'Jonas,' said Stephen, putting his hand gently on Jonas' shoulder, 'you're absolutely right.'

'Am I?'

'Everything I have made, all my stuff—it's just *shit*.'

'Is it?'

'I've realised that what I want to do is, if I can't paint pictures that make people break down in ruptured awe at the impossible suchness of experience, then I'm going to make bowls.'

'Are you?'

'Yeah, or chairs, or comics, or signposts. Something that is part of life, not part of a gallery. I want *honour*.'

Charlotte smiles at Stephen, and her eyes sparkle.

I tell the group about the Outsider Art show. 'It was good,' I say, 'I don't know about honourable, but it was honest at least. Much better than conceptual art.'

'The thing about conceptual art, that most people miss,' says Stephen, 'is the word *conceptual*. It doesn't exist!'

'But dreams don't exist,' says Charlotte, 'and they're beautiful.'

'Mine aren't,' says Stephen. 'Most of my dreams are about buying light-bulbs, or fixing the shower, or dealing with public transport. Trying to get a taxi, I have that a lot, or I have one where I'm in the underground and just walking around the tunnels, forever, round and round.'

Charlotte sighs, not very sympathetically. They do seem an odd pair, I must say. Not long-term material, surely? They snipe at each other, that kind of sweet, kind of funny, but yet also kind of disgraceful thing that couples do in public, lightly putting each other down. 'He loves his suffering really,' says Charlotte, and we smile, and Stephen smiles, but it's awful.

The vaguely funky music turns to intense booming techno with squibbly wibbly synth sounds over the top. People begin leaving the warehouse, people who, presumably, just want a bit of Betty Boo.

'God, what's that?' asks Piscina, who has manoeuvred her way around to my side with no lack of subtlety. She's coming on to me—one of the nicest-looking girls ever to have done so—but I am protected by an impenetrable force-field of love, or possibly of fear of losing love by dallying with another girl.

'It's the star attraction,' says Stephen, 'Vim Lander is here with his, he calls it "wreckno".'

I know this Vim character. He is a pinched little cube-headed man, who detests the ignorant pop-lover, who scarcely deigns to talk to you, unless you're a club owner or an A&R man.

The conversation turns to music and parties. Stephen says that there are no new genres in the world now, which he puts down to gentrification and it being so hard now to be unemployed, but he's got plans to start a new one, called bedcore; a movement of naked nutcases going LA-LA-LA-LA-LA in their rooms.

Piscina says Stephen thinks too much, Charlotte just wants to dance but the wreckno is preventing this, I think that parties, this party, seem so *arid*. There's just nothing here for me. But somehow I can't say this. Then Naeema turns up, immediately broadcasting conspicuous 'please ask me what's wrong' signals.

'How are you?' asks Charlotte.

'Oh, alright,' she says in a 'not alright' way. Her vibe is huffy and throaty; as it used to be, but more so. She's got her hair up again and she's wearing that stupid leather hat.

'What's wrong?'

'Andy is fucking Jacqui.'

Everyone mentally rubs their hands together for a nice hit of gossip, which Naeema delivers with that tiny grim pleasure that people seem to get from a juicy bit of their own bad news.

Yes, Andy started sleeping with Jacqui. It is hard to know what to find more extraordinary, that he slept with Naeema in the first place, that she slept with him or that he exchanged her for Jacqui.

'He seems to sleep with absolutely every woman he encounters,' says Piscina, all a-wonder.

'He's revolting,' says Charlotte, 'every kind of vile.'

'I *hate* him!' says Jonas with bizarre emphasis, and Stephen bursts into laughter. Jonas pays no attention. 'How does he end up getting so many women?' he asks.

Charlotte shrugs, Gallic style, 'beautiful tombs,' she says.

'It's not just beauty,' says Stephen, 'women want strength.'

'They actually do,' says Charlotte.

'They don't want a polite, courteous little gentleman who keeps to the *rules*, who is never creepy, never pervs, never makes a bold move, right Naeema?' he says, with a touch of peev.

'But he's revolting,' says Naeema, not quite sure where to put her mind, 'he has no idea of equality. He's just the big *cock*.'

Charlotte tilts her head 'Equality?'

'Yes, equality!'

'You don't want *equality* do you?'

'What? Yes, of course I do! Doesn't every woman?'

Charlotte shakes her head. 'Only stupid woman wants to be equal in the relationship. He is the boss in the front of it,' she gates her fingers together before her, 'and you are the boss behind it.'

'I'm not putting myself second, staying at home like a good little wifey!' says Naeema, outraged.

'I'm not talking about first and second, or home and work. I'm talking about the world, and the heart. Don't you want to be boss in the hidden place?'

'No, I don't... know what you're talking about?' says Naeema, blending negation, declaration and interrogation.

'Neither do I,' says Jonas eagerly, and Naeema looks away from him, not wanting his support, or to be associated with his ponderously literal bracket.

Charlotte purses her lips, 'Ecoute, listen, women go into a relationship excited by the possibility of change. Men go into a relationship expecting au fond to stay the same. If you say to the woman "I know you better than you know yourself," she will be intrigued. If you say the same to the man, he will be terrify.'

'So?'

'So he is happy in the world he knows. You want to bring him into the unknown. You don't do this by entering the light. You stay in the dark, let him come to you. He will, if he is man.'

Naeema is wilting from this strange attack. Something is collapsing in her. She can't quite get a grip on herself. She's outraged, but not quite sure what about.

'You don't want a bastard and you don't want a coward,' says Charlotte, 'but if you fight against either you'll get the other.'

You know, maybe I do see Stephen's interest in her. She does have some strange authority, and, she's not model-beautiful, no, but she wears gorgeous lacy-Edwardian shawls and expensive-looking embroidered skirts, and her eyes are clear and piercing and direct, and I feel a bit ashamed of thinking her ugly, she's not at all. Not at all.

Why is there so much in some eyes, and so little in others? How do some manage to make me feel like something deep inside me is quivering in thrilling sympathy, and others make me feel like I'm trapped in a me-shaped prison? Maybe Charlotte lives in the world behind the world too?

Which reminds me, Evgenia will be back soon.

'I've got to go,' I say.

'Oh,' says Piscina, 'where?'

'Home.'

She slouches a bit, feeding the old ego. I feel like the bassist in a funk band. And then goodbyes to Stephen and Charlotte. I wish Stephen were not going. Without him I am in danger of coming to believe that failure *is* actually a kind of failure.

Just as I'm about to go Vim's set finishes and Aavikko's Holiday Inn comes on, awky voice box clavi-funk with synthy trumpets declaring stomp-inciting digi-parps.

'Anyone wanna dance?' I turn. A man is standing behind us, late fifties maybe sixty, face full of character, warm light in his eyes, good suit. His body language is instantly impressive and I am instantly jealous. I look around. Stephen, no, Naeema, no, Jonas certainly not, but Piscina and Charlotte are as if electrocuted with delight. They join him in the hot inner-hanger and I go to the doorway to see this old fella rip, let everything go, all elbows and washboards, snip-snap, foolish spin, hips to the left, and to the right; Piscina and Charlotte laughing, eyes bright with joy, Indian poses and clumsy moments a-deux. No thought, no sex, just good. I am a-mix with envy and admiration and awe. A vision of the future, I hope—that is the kind of man I want to be. For now at least, though, I have my dream girl and she'll help me to become the man who dances.

•

The house seems to be empty, but there's a flickering coming down the hallway. The near wall of the dark kitchen is jumping and shuddering with orange light. Geni has built a small fire outside in the back garden, which she and Barney are feeding twigs to.

As I emerge from the back door, and take in the scene, I have a lovely feeling of rightness, of knowing absolutely that I am in the right place, at the right time. I had a few doubts of course, and fears, moving in—we had an argument on moving-in day in fact, about where to put all my useless electro-tat (the garden shed), and I had some commitment flaps, at the prospect of really throwing everything into the well. But all my disastrous fumbling confusions with woman are over now. This is where I should have been all along; journey's end, the happy valley.

'Hello Barney.'

Barney is a bit of a character. He calls Geni by her name and he says every single syllable, so he'll say 'Ge-nee, when, at *last* you did something that I *like* Ge-nee,' which is sweet somehow, although it's kind of bolshy too. It seems obvious to me that he's going to grow up to be some kind of genius.

A couple of days ago I found him on his knees in the lounge, pushing the corner of the coffee table in a peculiar way.

'What are you doing Barney?'

'Secret passage,' he said, not looking up.

'I used to do that!'

He doesn't say anything.

'Found any?' I ask.

'No.'

'Well, keep looking, you might.'

He turns to me, earnest.

'I dreamed it.'

'What, that you found a secret passage?'

'Yes.'

'Oh, I see.'

Barney stopped his pressing and looked up at me, quizzically.

'Dan-yel, are we dreaming now?'

'No.'

'How do you know?'

'Well, in a dream, if you look at something that should be still, like a shadow, it doesn't stay still. Everything is moving in a dream. And, er, the real world is, erm, hard.'

'It's a hard dream then?'

He had me there. 'Yeah, maybe,' I said.

He's been having nightmares recently, on account of me moving in we think. He likes me, at least it seems he does, but something is disturbing him down in his primaevals because there are strange men in his dreams, although there are strange men in mine too.

I sit next to Evgenia, and she leans into me, looking ageless in the firelight. We exchange a few facts about the day, but not too many, because it is so silly and unreal, the past. How awful it must have been for Harold every day to have to deal with a neverending rockslide of the stuff.

Barney is just quiet, just sitting. His little legs don't touch the ground, just pushed back into one of those fold-up chairs.

I lean across to Geni and say, 'I wonder what Barney's thinking as he stares into the fire there. I wonder if he's just reviewing his day, or what he's doing?'

'Barney,' says Geni, 'Barney—what are you thinking about as you stare into the fire? What are you thinking about?'

Barney looks up, a little bit shocked, maybe even a bit confused, and says, 'now I'm only thinking about why you should be thinking why I'm thinking something.'

'Barney is the Buddha.'

'He's *my* Buddha,' says Geni, stretching her arms out. Barney pushes himself off the chair and walks round to her. She gathers him up, squeezing.

'You're mine,' she says, '*mine.*'

Barney grips her. I get the odd feeling that there's a kind of victory in his clasp, or fear. Not sure what of though. Me? He's not into the idea of going to bed, and squirms with a long nooooooo when Geni brings it up. His arm swings out and knocks an empty mug from the arm of Geni's chair, which smashes on one of the fire bricks.

'Barney!'

'Gen-nee!'

'Barney, you're so clumsy.'

Barney starts whimpering.

'But I didn't break anything *before*,' he says.

She stands, heaves him onto her hip and takes him moaning to bed, leaving me to look into the ragged, hiccoughing flames, now burning down into a molten, alien landscape at my feet. I imagine millions of little people marching over the glowing plains. They don't seem so unhappy about it. Maybe hell isn't so bad?

Geni returns with a couple of wine glasses and a bottle of white, which we drink next to the fire.

'Poor Barney,' I say, 'He's right. You never get praise for all the things you *didn't* break today, all the stupid things you *didn't* say.'

'Why, what stupid things didn't you say today?' she asks.

'Oh, I dunno. Several probably.'

'What stupid thing are you not saying now?' she asks, and I detect a change in her tone, something has changed, but I pretend it hasn't, because it is not for the better.

'Nothing, I'm just looking at the fire.'

She swings her head around to the fire, half seeing it.

'What about the fire?'

'Well, you know, the devil never used to exist, that modern civilisations, took the old trickster god, who was a kind of amoral magic joker character, and turned him into an immoral beast. In the past the devil was a lot more fun, you see, so I was wondering if maybe hell used to be more fun too.'

'Why are you thinking about hell?'

'Er, the fire…'

Her eyes narrow, 'I don't want you talking like this to Barney.'

'Like what?'

'Like this, this Christian stuff.'

'It's not Christian stuff.'

'You want him in your cult, don't you?'

'What?'

'I've raised this boy on my own,' she says, anger cutting through her tone, 'on my *own*. I've protected him from all that madness. I'm not going to let you come in and alter his mind. He's free of that.'

'What are you talking about? What's got into you?'

'It's what's got into *you* that I'm worried about.'

I watch her, sick heart banging, what is this? A completely different person is sitting next to me. Her features are transformed, all wily and peering.

'Geni, calm down.'

'I'm not going to *calm down*.'

'Well I'm not going to… I'm not here to convert you or Barney to anything. I don't even have a religion.'

'Then what are you talking about hell for?'

'I… I don't know. Strange idea. I'm sorry.'

'*Are* you sorry?'

'Yeah, seriously, it was just a stupid idea. I'm not, I don't even want to think about it.'

'How sorry are you?'

'Very…' I have the strange feeling that I'm losing something important here—yet how can anything be important in this stupid, stupid argument?

'Show me how sorry you are,' she says.

'What? How?'

'Think of something.'

'I'm sorry, isn't that enough?'

'How about taking your clothes off?'

'Eh? What, out here?'

'Yeah, take them off and dance.'

'I'd rather not.'

'Why?'

'I don't feel like dancing.'

'Or you could pay the mortgage?'

I sag in the chair. It seems to be coming at me from all sides—but what 'it' is, I'm not exactly sure.

'David called me this morning,' she says, 'Now that you live here, he's not going to pay his half.'

'Isn't he?'

'No.'

'Fuck, alright, I can probably manage it. Is that what this is about?'

'No.'

We are sitting next to embers now. Evgenia's face, in the dim light of the dying fire, looks infernal too.

'I'm tired,' she says, 'I'm going to bed.'

She walks inside, loose but conspicuously careless.

I sit in the darkness, clawing in my chest. What just happened?

At my feet is the half-finished bottle of wine. Could that be it? One single glass of wine? Surely not.

Or was it really the money? Is she starting to have doubts about my solvency? She's loaded though, how could she worry about that?

Or perhaps she picked up on something else, something in me? I was feeling a bit distracted there for a moment, even—yes, even a bit jealous of Barney. God, how small of me... Maybe she somehow detected that, and it came out somehow, but all weird?

Inside the house is dark, the bedroom too. I get undressed and climb into bed, hoping to rekindle the good thing.

She reaches behind her, for my penis, takes hold of it and I am instantly awash with pure emotion, the roaring root of sex-rage, terror of annihilation and psychotic desire.

Something says this is wrong, but how can it be? This is all any man could possibly want. Fuck it.

Cuddle the Void

Greyish. I try to be interested in it, try to enjoy the different shades of it, the special quality of it, the unique atmosphere of greyness; but it's unremitting, relentless. If roads were a gloss white, with sky blue pavements, and the houses were hot lemon yellow, maybe I could accept the grey, but it all blends into one monocolour unworld. Even the trees and grass seem to be layered with ash.

Bob and I are sitting, waiting as usual for customers to turn up. I am reading a book about ants, and Bob is chain-smoking. People approach, Bob eyes them, a bit pleadingly, and they pass, because it's not a day for mucking about on a pond. Warm it is, muggy even, but grey and grey and grey and grey.

Bob starts talking, very quietly.

'What's that Bob?'

His straggly beard is twitching around, but hardly anything is coming out, just powdery half-words. I lean closer—he smells of tobacco and marsh gas—'what's up Bob?' He is speaking, but as if from inside a fridge.

'I tried to shh, talk to her, but what she wanted, she wanted, what *didn't* she want, hmm, stop feeding her, eh?'

I stand up and he seems to notice me as if from a distance.

'Did she tell *you* Lawrence?' he asks, his voice faint.

'I'm not Lawrence Bob. I'm Danny.'

Lawrence is his nephew—he used to work with Bob.

'Danny?'

'Yes, Daniel, I started here a few weeks ago, you remember?'

'Where's Lawrence then?' he whispers.

'He's not here. He works in the city now. Do you want to speak to him? Shall I call him?'

Bob looks down, moustache rocking from side to side, then looks up again, his eyes fearful and wide. He's talking, but no sound is coming out at all now, just a hoarse murmur. He reaches out and I step back, for I fear he might smite me, but he's looking at the book, imploring, trying to get at it. I hand it to him thinking perhaps he is about to start his fit and needs something to bite on so he won't chew his tongue off, but he takes it and starts rapidly flicking through, so *now* I think maybe he can't speak and is going to spell out a message in 'Journey to the Ants,' but he opens a page with a colour image of a Malaysian harvester, and just looks it, and then up at me, confused and afraid, then hands the book back.

'Shall we go down the pub?' I say.

I take his arm and lead him through Dulwich Park. My plan is to take him to the King's Head. I know he's got some friends there, maybe one of them can help.

'You okay Bob?'

He looks up at me, pitifully. I thought epileptic fits were all frothing and writhing, not staring into the distance and forgetting what ants are.

The pub is hot, dark, loud, slightly rancid with fermented matter and sopping beer mats. As I lead Bob in he seems to mentally settle somehow. We shuffle over to the middle of the room and I look around, see if someone has noticed us, knows us.

'Bob!' a fat, old fellah in a knitted tank-top limps over. Bob looks at him confused.

'Alright Bob?' he asks with kindly aggression.

'He's had a fit.'

'Thasalright innit Bob!' he says, with bullish cheer and turns to me, instantly thrusting his hand out and coming at me with his name, American style, 'Gerry.'

'Daniel.'

'You gonna have a drink Danny?' his voice is very loud. He smells of sweat and bacon.

'Well I should look after the boats.'

'Fuck the boats, nobody's gonna steal a fuckin' boat.'

I'm not sure he's right. People steal bricks now. But pulling a rowing boat in broad daylight through Dulwich Park seems unlikely, so I settle into a corner with Bob and Gerry, a pint of bitter for each of us, which Bob meekly sups, oblivious to the actual universe.

Gerry is not a well man. Odd complexion, pale but mottled, fat neck, breathes with difficulty; but there is something kindly in his eyes and in his loud, raspy voice.

'They want to section him,' he roars.

'Who, Bob? Do they?'

'Yeah, but look at him, he's not doing anyone any harm. Just gets confused now and then DON'T YA BOB…?' he roars.

Bob looks up still all starey eyed and looks down again.

'…and we all get confused now and then don't we? I know I fuckin' do.'

I wince a little, basically asking him to not speak so loudly, but he pays no attention.

'Fuckin' sections. They'll be—you watch Danny—they'll be sectioning you for being *miserable* soon. They'll make… they're gonna make all the fuckin' hospitals into corporations, then they'll go round sectioning anyone who's not happy-clappy and charge 'em for it.'

'You think?'

'Don't you?'

'I hadn't really thought about it.'

'You seen how many fuckin' loons there are now?' he growls.

'There does seem to be a lot.'

Gerry leans back with an air of grim triumph, 'that's fuckin' revenue you see. Prisons are businesses, schools—the loony bins'll be next. If you don't do what you're told you'll be in. It's all… I dunno… It's all getting warped into one big fuckin' darkness, and there's nothing we can do about it.'

'Nothing?'

'No mate, we're headed towards pure totalitarian fascism. We're not headed there, we are there. Soon the goon squad will be out and the ghettos and the people going missing and the massacres. We just gotta bear it out,' he puts his palms up, bidding patience, 'Wait.'

'Wait for what?'

Bob, who was taking tiny little sips of his bitter, stops and peers at Gerry. A hush comes over the pub, and the world.

'The crack in the granite,' he bellows, 'it's coming; and *then* we, the working class, we'll rise up and, and rush in, and fuck it all up!'

Gerry remains, tense, eyeing me with emphasis.

'Who's going to organise it though? They're already cracking down on…'

'Organise? Nobody's gonna fucking organise it. You can't organise an epileptic fit.'

'Yeah, but when the world falls apart…'

'It's *already* falling apart!' he cries. 'For example, for example, all houses built in the last, what, fifty years; they're held together by silicone sealant. They're as shoddy as a five-pound kettle.'

'Oh right, I see. It's literally falling apart you mean.'

'Yes son. The walls are paper-thin; breeze blocks, plywood, bolted-on cladding, and fucking aspenite —*flakeboard!* —basically glued-together sawdust. That's the world that is. It's just dust. The bigger stuff...' he's swept up in it now, waving his hands around, the whole pub can hear him, probably most of Dulwich, 'the bigger stuff is reinforced concrete, which means it's shot through with rusting iron. The Romans didn't fucking build with iron, so *their* concrete is still standing. Ours will crumble to dust in twenty or thirty years, *max*. The whole fucking modern world is moldy pasteboard. We'd be just as well off in a fucking cardboard box!'

He relaxes, 'yeah, I'm a bit of a conspiracy theorist,' he says, almost at normal volume, 'I'm a flat-earther.'

'What, Bilderberg and all that?'

'Well that too, yeah. They're planning to digitally tag us, inject us with nanobots.'

'I wouldn't be surprised.'

'But I also think the world is flat.'

'What, literally?'

'Yeah.'

Damnit Gerry, I was with you until then. So was Bob I think, who has gone back to staring into space and suckling at his ale.

'But,' I say, 'what about people who fly round the world? Are they lying to us?'

'No, they're just fooled. They're just...' and he picks up a flaccid beer mat and demonstrates the principle, 'just going round and round in circles. You see? The world is flat. Birds too.'

'*What?*'

Gerry is smiling.

'Oh right.'

'I had you there fer a minute, didn't I?'

'Yeah.'

'The world is flat though.'

Bob mutters something.

'Whassat Bob?' says Gerry. We lean in.

'I'm not afraid of pigeons, only of dogs,' he says, very quietly.

'Right you are Bob,' yells Gerry seriously, which I like. Bob now believes this pigeon issue is important, and so does Gerry, so we'll address that.

'Dogs *can* be alright though,' says Gerry.

Bob look at him, unsure.

'You just have to pay attention,' Gerry continues, 'see if they're friendly, like people. You take Booker—some people just see a huge terrifying spade, but he's lovely in't he?'

Bob's still not sure, but he returns to supping.

'I have to say Gerry,' I say, 'it seems unlikely, the flat-earth thing. I mean, if I'm to be honest, it seems impossible.'

'Anything is possible.'

'But is it?'

'Aren't *you* going round and round in circles?'

'No, I'm going in a straight line.'

'*That*,' he says with the gravest conviction yet, 'is where you're dead wrong.'

•

One of the boats has been stolen. I stand next to the pond looking at where it is not, noting how looking at something that is not there makes everything else seem slightly *more* there. A line of scraped gravel leads across the path to a trail of churned up grass through the trees. I jog in pursuit of my boat, ready for attack. Fifty yards from the pond, behind the bushes that run along the railings, a kid is yanking a row boat, each whopping heave dragging it perhaps three inches.

I slow to a walk. He looks up—pink, pale face shiny with effort—drops the gunwale and runs off. I take the boat, pull it back round, and start the twenty-minute job of hauling it back.

When I get to the gravel I stop, knackered, and a girl who has been approaching along the promenade stops next to me.

'Can I help you?'

'Yeah go on, just, let's drag it over the path.'

She takes the stern and pushes while I pull at the prow. She looks familiar. Very beautiful, voluptuous, dark. I can't place her though. She is smiling, her happy bosom wobbling about in front of me as I tell her to push harder. We make it to the other side and drag it over into the pond, where it slowly sinks.

We watch the bubbles emerge, philosophically.

'I suppose we tore a hole in the bottom,' she says.

'Yeah.'

'Well, thanks for helping anyway,' I say.

'That's alright,' she says, 'what are you going to do about that?' she nods to the bubbling water.

'I'm going to leave it. I'm going to lock these boats up and never return, I'm done.'

'Done?'

I look at her, feeling a lie coming on.

'I only do this job so I can sit and sketch people in the park.'

'Oh, can I see?'

I take my sketchbook out of my bag and show her. She leafs through, slowly, actually looking.

'But none of these are of the park,' she says.

'No, er, that's my old sketchbook.'

'They're really good.'

'Thanks,' I say, automatically. Everyone says nice things, don't they? She's too beautiful to understand art.

'No, I mean it,' she says, 'they're wonderful. You can really pick out character.'

'Thanks,' I say again, this time meaning it.

'You're right,' she says, handing the book back, 'you shouldn't be selling things, not for any reason.'

I am now in love with this girl. She is wearing a long, dark blue, patterned gypsy skirt, a denim jean jacket with beads sewn on, a blue scarf, and electric blue mascara. The effect is striking with her dark features and big brown eyes She has a serene-looking face—the kind you see on statues in graveyards…

…it's *her*. Toby's naked dancer. I instantly feel completely out of hand, without volition, an eruption of terrible freedom has taken hold of me, freedom of any kind of care—but not joyous is it; awful rather, threatening.

'Don't you think we should take a boat ride?' she asks, 'this being your last day?'

Panic overwhelms me. I can feel my heart beating in my eyeballs. Evgenia comes through this park all the time. She's out working, but she'll *know*. She knows everything!

'No, I can't. I've got to go and meet my girlfriend,' I croak.

'Okay,' she says cheerfully, 'some other time maybe?'

'Yeah, maybe.'

And off she goes. I feel a horrible sense of loss, watching her walk away. She's going, look, she's going Daniel.

She's gone now.

It is odd how attractive I seem to be, now that I'm in a relationship. Stephen's right, desperation *is* repellent at the cellular level. Now that desperation has been replaced by resigned confusion I am bringing girls into my ambit… not just any girls, but lovely ones… at which point they perceive that, instead of desperate, I am frustrated on a deeper level than sex and flapping around in a strange and terrifying new universe, which is called Evgenia.

Sometimes she seems to me to be the devil herself; knowing yet unknowable, working to some horrible wordless plan I dare not even think about. Insane things she comes out with. Drink does it, but sometimes she flips into an altered state of paranoid violence for magical reasons. I'm convinced that when I start thinking, or get distracted or annoyed by something, somehow she picks up on this, amplifies it in her wyrd psyche and it transforms her into The Fiendess. And so I walk by her side in a state of Zen-poise, anchoring myself to the present through the ineffable wafts of her terrifying-fascinating femininity. While I can sense these, breathe them in, the fiendess sleeps.

Or maybe all this is in my imagination?

Yet, she tells me things; things I didn't even know I was thinking until she says them. Like, on one occasion, we were walking down Lordship Lane and a nice-looking woman jogged past us and I glanced—glanced I say—at her bum.

'You want two women.'

'What?'

'Well I'm not going to be one of your little harem.'

'But I don't want that,' thinking to myself; I wouldn't mind that actually.

We argued about it for a couple of hours until the steam seemed to pass out of the problem and the tenderness returned. Although, actually, it never seems to completely return now. The Other Place has drifted out of reach. Neither of us mention it, or even really mind, because it seems unreal now. I *know* it happened, that amazing thing, but my *feeling* reaches no further than where I am, like the idle fields of summer are not just meaningless in November's little rooms, but unreal at the core.

She is also uncannily accurate in her instant appraisals of other people and seems to have the power to know, before anyone opens their mouth, all of their depraved secrets. Take stuttering next-door Brian for example.

'He likes to watch,' she said casually one day.

'How do you know?'

'I just know.'

And sure enough, she did; he did. He comes round quite regularly, helping out if anything goes wrong with the house, teaching me how to bleed radiators and put shelves up straight and that sort of thing, and one day we were alone, drinking tea in Geni's sparse kitchen and talking about women, and we got onto the subject of sex;

'I don't g...g...go near it.'

'Doesn't it interest you?'

'Oh, it interests me a LOT, but I prefer to keep my distance, if you know what I mean?'

'Yes, I do.'

'Does that surprise you?'

'What?'

'Me being a bit of a p...p...p... perv?'

'*Kind* of.'

I told Geni later.

'What did I say?' she said.

'It makes me wonder what else you know about me.'

'I know no woman will ever be good enough for you.'

'Yes, it's lonely at the top,' I feebly gagged, to which she uttered one of her from-nowhere truths;

'There is no such thing as a joke.'

Then, a few nights ago Barney was with his nan and Evgenia asked me if I wanted to go out with her to a private view and I've had my fill of them, of haunting the empty minds of her artworld friends made gallery flesh. So what if they could make my career? Fuck 'em!

'Come on,' she said, 'let's get out of the house.'

'The house is everywhere.'

'Fine, I'll go alone.'

This hurts me—she doesn't need me.

'Go on then, off you go.' I said, with all the bile I could hock up.

She left without saying another word, and I endured three hours of chill anguish before she returned, all contained and 'fine,' showing me that she did, indeed, have a good time entirely without me. I countered with sullen, prowling. wounded rage which she seemed to be deliberately inducing, prodding me to hurt her. This succeeded in bringing the light of justifying attention back on her, which I wrestled back over to me again, and then lost it again, and began wheedling to get it back again, the Standard War of who hurts most, trying to win back the Hurt Trophy, until we ended up wrestling in bed and all I could hear was The Voice. I thought of Piscina, so much warmer than Geni, so much feelier and human and open (nicer rear-end too, but I'm alright with an average arse). Evgenia's body seemed remote, her hips and neck and breasts distant meat, the Voice worrying she's not that into it, look at her, not quite the same is it Daniel?

Not quite the same, or rather much more the same. She is getting more known. A patina of knowableness has settled over her once mesmerising hips and shoulders. Other women seem stranger, more compelling. The Voice reminds me of something Andy once said, 'no woman is so beautiful that someone some-where isn't bored of fucking her.'

The Voice. Something is looking over my shoulder, and that something calls itself me. The Voice takes pleasure and turns it into the idea of pleasure. It takes gratitude, the feeling of thankful and turns it into 'I am lucky.' And it turns Evgenia's commanding frame into something merely fuckable.

And all the time, as the pressure built up and up, and the Voice rattled away, some even more distant part of me watched on with a mixture of desperation, confusion and amazement, thinking—no, not even thinking, but purely experiencing a hazy wonderment 'how can this be happening? I love this woman. We shared The Other Place. I want to give everything.'

The next morning she woke up hating me. I tried to cuddle her out of it, but she shook me off saying, 'I want to try and remember my dream,' which, I don't know why, instantly pushed the trembling fury inside to critical mass. I leapt up, ready to leave, ready to fuck it all and, as I pulled my pants on I got my ankles twisted up and fell over the sock drawer. She snorted with laughter and *puff!* All the problems were gone, instantly, as if we'd woken up from a bad dream, all blinking and sheepish.

I crawled back into bed and the tenderness was with us again, exquisite and human, and there was no way on earth it could ever be, or ever could have been otherwise. She agrees to give up drinking for me, I agree to give her space, and all is well.

I walk through Dulwich Park, turning these and like events over in my mind. I sense somehow that I am completely out of my depth and I do not seem to have the equipment, or the training, to stay afloat. I'm surviving by luck more than anything.

My instincts tell me that she needs to submit to me, that she is hanging on, that the doors behind her eyes are never fully open, and I need to blast them open. I say to her, 'tell me you're mine,' and she does, and afterwards I feel foolish and exposed for demanding this, but the doors behind her eyes are closed and I know of no way to open them but to ram them head-first.

But this cannot work, I think, as I get to where my bike was locked up and where now nothing but a busted D-lock hangs from the railing.

·

The Magdatron caught me mashing it up with Ina, a natty old Jamaican girl who sits muttering an incomprehensible stream of 100% patois through clouds of 100% Craven "A". Normally I smile and nod (she doesn't seem to care I don't understand), or she guides me through her fascinating sideboard, with its faded photos of 60s Kingston; but when I suggested bringing in some Dennis Brown and Delroy Wilson her eyes lit up and she clapped her hands and said;

'A one good good plan dat enuh. Mek wi dweet.'

So I set up some mini speakers and we were having a bit of skank, Ina sitting on her commode, all gummy and wrists, me experimenting with a foot-out, hand-out slow-motion moon-stomp, when Magda came in, a fussin' and fightin.'

I went back to dustin' and wipin,' but my heart wasn't really in it; I mean not in anxiety-propelled bollock-twisting speed-cleaning. So I went at it in my own good time and decided, come what may, to let the storm come, fed up again with battling the beast.

And I feel that way today, more so maybe. Sod Magda, sod Saturn, sod fate. I'm going to sit with Derek as long as I want.

'So how are you then?' I ask him. He's fused to his armchair, as usual, and I'm sketching him.

'Not too good Danny.'

'In pain?'

'Yeah, awful, but I'm done in mate.'

His long body is immobile, eyes closed, big round head sunk back, waiting for the end.

'Soon be over,' he says.

'Aren't you scared?'

He shoots me a watery glance 'What of?'

'Of dying.'

He closes his eyes again. 'Nuh! Be like going to sleep.'

'You think so?'

'Just gotta accept it anyway. We've all got to accept it, en't that right Mam?' he squints at the photo of his Mum, nods in agreement and looks back at me 'She says the more we just *let be*, the more we *can* be.'

'Sometimes you have to fight though don't you?'

'Oh yeah!' he says, waking up, 'you gotta bloody fight. 'Specially us, people like us. Them bastards,' he jabs a finger out the window, presumably somewhere towards Westminster, 'won't give no bugger *nothing* unless they take it. All these protests and petitions—useless. You can protest and petition 'till you're blue in the bloody face and nothing'll change. How about a million people not paying any tax? Or *ten* million not paying rent? See what they think of that!'

He relaxes.

'But death—no point fighting that,' he says.

'I suppose not.'

He's not looking good though. His cheeks are a weird greyish yellow and there's...

'What is that?'

'What?'

'That, is that a bruise?'

Derek lifts his arm. Under his wrist, and running up nearly to his elbow is a ghastly black weal.

'Yeah, I think so.'

'Fuck Derek, have you had that checked out?'

'Nahhh, it's some kind of bruise I think. I dunno. It's, as I say Danny, time's up. When something is about to die, everything goes wrong. Everything.'

Derek looks at his bruise.

'It's not bad luck,' he says, 'I'm dying. And what I see is, now that I am dying is... what I see is...'

He stops, out of breath, eyes closed, summoning himself for what is obviously going to be the whole meaning of life. The final judgement of mortal man on the mortal world. He takes a deep breath, looks at me and says;

'...I'm not a Man U supporter anymore.'

I look at him, nodding, understanding.

'City now is it?'

'Aye, fuck off.'

I can hear Magda's voice down the hall. She's not happy about something. Probably me.

'You never talk about your dad Derek. What was he like?'

He looks at me, surprised and pained. 'He was a bastard.'

'You didn't get on?'

'He was a bully. He hated softness, gentleness. Hated it. He wanted to destroy it.' He looks sadly at his mum.

The door flies open.

'Here you are!' cries Magda, 'what is wrong with you?'

'I'm chatting with Derek.'

'You're supposed to be working.'

'I don't think so.'

Her eyes narrow. 'Daniel, I'm starting to think I don't need you on this team.'

'Alright. I quit.'

She blinks, 'good,' she says.

'So leave us alone.'

She's not one to lose control, Magda. She just nods and turns on her heels.

Derek is silently shaking, wiping tears from his eyes.

'That was the best thing I seen in *years*, Danny.'

'Mert will be along soon. He'll kick me out,' I say.

'Yeah, spec so. Bully he is too. Tries to bully me too, into taking their bloody drugs. Says I'm ill. I'm not mad. *They're* mad.'

'Derek, what did you mean when you said "people like us?"'

'People at the bottom. We gotta stick together you see? They ain't *ever* gonna help us. Only people that'll help you, are people at the bottom. The further down you go, the more shit there is, but more love too, more that'll help.'

'But there's good and bad people everywhere.'

The door flies open and Mert the manager heaves in. He's an enormous Turk, black bristling eyebrows always narrowing to attack. It's hard to imagine someone who cares less about anything, but here he is managing, of all things, a care home. I think he might also have connections with the Russian mafia, as there always seem to be scary looking Slavs around the place. There's one now, standing in the hall behind him.

'Alright, alright, I'm going.'

Time to leave,' says Mert, fear in his beady eyes.

'Here, have this,' says Derek. I turn back to him; he's holding a photo out to me.

'Derek, I can't take that.'

'"Course you can!" he cries, 'they might not let you back in.'

'But it's your Mum!'

'Daniel, leave the home now, quietly,' says Mert. The bouncer is easing into the room.

'Alright, alright.'

'I'll be seeing her face to face before too long,' says Derek, 'You need her advice a bloody sight more than I do.'

I take it. 'Thanks Derek. Thank you.'

'Don't let the wankers win!' he cries as I exit.

I bump into dark little Dalia in reception, hurrying as always to start her shift. I tell her I've just been fired.

'But why?'

'I hate work.'

'But what are you going to do?' she asks, searchingly.

She seems like she *actually* cares. It's so unusual. What with Derek and everything, I find myself fairly overcome, tears welling up.

'Cuddle the void.'

•

My interest evaporates the instant I board the boat. A cruise down the Thames with Christie's auction house seemed, at first, at least like something new: *Well*, there's going to be a Special Revealing, a couple of slebs are coming, the chief editor of the Sunday Times, who is a friend of Geni's, he'll be there. A string quartet too and amuse-gueules by a celebrity chef.

Geni, Barney and I make our way down the walkway to the Chelsea Harbour pier and onto a shiny-white-shiny 'luxe' river yacht. A smart smiling black man welcomes us with cocktails. The way he calls me 'sir,' makes me feel kind of ashamed.

Well-dressed people are clustering in groups, chattering and guffawing. Waiters drift between them, silently supplying needs.

A tall, broad man with a slabbish face spots us, lightly taps his colleagues in a 'must go' and, one hand in pocket one hand on whiskey, cruises over.

'Ev*genia*,' he says, with a bizarre note of wonderment.

'Daniel, this is Gordon,' she says.

I shake hands with the Big Editor. He has a squarish red head, a slit-like lipless mouth and small, hard, bored eyes, which instantly swivel back to Geni.

'How *are* you?' he asks conspiratorially. He talks in the laboured, slightly brain-damaged, slightly out-of-breath manner of an elite drunkard.

'Fine, how is the party?'

'Oh, lot of talk about the new find.'

I look around, feeling clenches of world-dread. The vibe is hard. We walk over to the group Gordon left, introductions go around and the conversation picks up where it left off.

A dough-headed man, with a neck like a sock that has lost its elastic is talking. He is also without lips. Where are all their lips going?

'Our bloody cleaner is giving us the run-around. I'm thinking of getting rid of her though, she's a bit of a dog. If I'm going to be looking at her every morning, I might as well get a nice Pole or something of that nature.'

'Oh, Edwin! You can't say that!'

'Why don't you just leave in the morning?' asks a woman with a face like it's melting off her head. 'There's nothing worse than being at home while the *cleaner* is there.'

'Damned if I'm going to go in before midday!'

A little girl comes over and tugs the sleeve of a woman wearing so much foundation her face looks like bagel.

'Mummy, is there any point in visiting Paris for less than a week?'

'Yes of *course*, people go to Paris for a weekend all the *time* dear. We did, don't you remember?'

'We didn't!'

'We *did* darling.'

'No we *didn't!*' She storms off. The woman looks around, we all laugh. How cute!

'She *is* difficult,' she concedes.

'Oh mine too. She's *always* having tantrums. We're hauled into her school regularly about her behaviour... as if *we're* somehow responsible!'

'Well you have to remember that teachers are basically a third-rate version of yourself.'

They chatter on, my heart slowly sinking further and further into the pit of my stomach while a large invisible fist squeezes my neck.

'I'm, er, I'm going to mingle,' I tell Evgenia, and break off.

I'm not sure if they can smell my fear, or if my shirt is transparently off the peg, or I am not properly logged on and am drifting between avatars unable to see me, but it is impossible to enter any group. I am instantly vibe-repulsed from each one; a thin smile, a brief nod, or just nothing at all. No recognition, no inwardness.

I feel lost in a reality whose rules I do not comprehend, the butt of an unspoken conspiracy to erase me from the universe. It's not because I cannot join in their incomprehensible yar-yar—a couple of groups, for example, are, on the face of it, having reasonably interesting conversations about fine art, which I could probably contribute to somehow—nor of getting a cold-shoulder wherever I turn—for some people do talk to me, ask a few leading questions. No, it's that all interaction is *purely verbal*. There is nothing here of the under-life, the pool of qualities that flows under words. Nobody has a face or voice like Derek's, which ripples with countless reactions and cues, in which communication feels like a fine tree growing. Everything here is flat, featureless, digital, monotone and harsh. Insane. No, not insane. These people are not insane. They are merely unliving. The people on the Sigyn ward all had some kind of loveliness about them, a pathos, a fluidness, an honesty, even the most terrifying had *something* human… these poor creatures; no. Their manifest insanity is yet to come, and it will be ugly.

I drift into a group of people sitting around listening to The Famous Man—rock star big man Tom Lowry—hold forth. What he says is blandly conventional, but oh how interesting it sounds coming from an important, famous, handsome head. The glassy Tory-voting eyes are sliding towards the nose, the lips are puckering into the weird pink powdery fame-flesh of older slebs—but the head, even as it swallows the face, is still charismatic; and that charisma is a solid rhombus of ignorance. As with Andy, there is nothing there but dense, uncomprehending, atmospheric and instinctively self-centred *power*.

I watch him from a distance, how his attention drifts over the men and older women, tightens on the pretty ones, sneers here, scoffs there. I was always revolted by his stuff, but just as his songs now seem like a caricature of his own earlier music so his face looks like a latex mask of his former self.

How does this happen? How do people become simulations of themselves? Can the process be reversed? Can it be detected? And these women, purring over him, are they falling at his feet, or at those of the man he once was? And, look at him, for Christ's sake, how much quality fanny (his words) this man has had—and he's *still* not satisfied. Still he's on the prowl!

I console myself that he's going to die, just like the rest of us, and he's beginning to see that too I think.

I continue my haunting drift. Nobody is paying attention to anything or anyone else. All conversation is tight scrutinising attention wafting around to various blasts of power—including the great 'unveiling' which turns out to be a brand new Munch, a recently discovered section of his famous 'Frieze of Life' series which featured The Scream, and Anxiety. This one is called 'Death in an Armchair.' It shows, in broad, thick strokes of purply blacks, sulphurous yellows and mottled creams, an old man dying, or perhaps dead already. Opposite him are two young women, talking and laughing and next to him is a tall, finely dressed man looking casually and handsomely out of the window at a crude louring skyline.

It is brilliant, alive, and so out of place in the world.

Artists, great artists, who gave up everything to tear themselves open to the raw truth, to pull from their own bodies the blazing gem in the belly of life and give it to the world; and it ends up *here*, in the hands of *dealers*—accurate word that one.

One of the headmen of Christie's, a puttyish, crimson-headed man with wet lips, which he licks continuously, pulls the gold cover from the frame and the assembled room sigh with pleasure. He tells us where it was found, what its significance is, its provenance and how much it is expected to make at auction, which pulls another little gasp from the crowd. A few applaud, as they do on the Antiques Roadshow when a big sum comes in. Here we are, standing in front of the quivering truth, pulled like a thorn from the belly of a true artist, and we are applauding money.

I sink to the seabed of the room, where a waiter grows, a tall, tactful-looking South Asian man with a bit of a monobrow. The boat is drifting along the Chelsea Embankment, past towering, leafy Thames-side houses.

'We'll all be free one day,' I say to the waiter.

'Yes sir,' he says, following my gaze, 'it would certainly be splendid to live in one those properties.'

'Eh?' It takes me a moment to work out what he means, 'oh,' I say, grasping his comment, 'yeah, but to live in Chelsea you'd have to live with the kind of people who live in Chelsea.'

'I don't have the pleasure of understanding you sir.'

'I mean this lot,' I say with a gesture.

'Oh, yes sir,' he says. I look carefully in his eyes—just polite and blank, not a glimmer of solidarity.

Yes, solidarity. That's the thing isn't it? That's why Derek said 'people like us.' I *am* a person like Derek. I am working class, and so are they... but it's not just that; there is a free-dom in Derek's company, something human (which resolutely middle-class Stephen has too), something careless, some kind of faith perhaps, a deep trust that the next moment will not fuck you over. Whatever it is, it would be betrayed by a neat description, just as these neat descriptions that surround poor Edvard Munch betray him, betray the ugly cleaner, betray the sad, sad Thames.

A burst of hard, loud laughter cannons through the polite hacks and chortles of the central cabin. There is something coarse and unrestrained about it. I look over; their fixed stiff faces are turning one to the other shouting victorious laughter at each other's heads.

We re-coalesce into groups. I am with Geni and a couple of Christie's people (one of which looks amazingly like Halfman) talking about photography, and I remember Derek's Mum. Excitedly, I pull out the creased image to show Geni and her two friends.

'Look at this,' I say, 'isn't it beautiful?'

Even before they react, I regret it.

'Oh *yes*,' says a terrifying woman wearing a blue dustbin bag.

'Lovely light and shade,' says Halfman, a stumpy, feature-less and bubble-headed bald guy wearing a preppy blazer and a boater.

'Yes, a ghostly kind of feeling to it, I love the way it's *playing* with focus,' says the woman.

'We've lost so much with the transition to digital, you can never quite emulate the quality of light in real film can you? Look at this effect...' says Halfman.

'I think that's a lith,' says the woman.

'No, it's a tintype,' says Geni.

I want to push the photograph into their faces and scream 'but what about the fucking *womaaaaan!*'

But no, I slink off into the cabin, where Barney is sitting with Gordon's little girl—Joanna—with a colouring book and a pile of crayons. And here, instantly, there is relief, shelter from the cloud of death, and those awful eyes. Here indeed I can look into Barney's eyes, and Joanna's, and ask them sensible questions about terrapins.

'That's good,' I say looking at Joanna's drawing, 'what is it? A horse next to a tree?'

'No, it's a dinosaur next to an explosion.'

We play Exquisite Corpse, and then I suggest we do a sentence at a time story which ends up with a heroic cat-ninja defeating an army of fire-zombie-dogs with a liquid chainsaw.

Geni joins us, in a good mood—God knows why, but I'm not complaining—and asks to join in.

'What shall we do now?' I ask.

'Let's draw Geni,' says Joanna.

'Oh, why me?' she says coyly.

'Because you're beautiful,' says Joanna.

So we take some paper and stick our tongues half out and immortalise Evgenia while the string quartet, who were playing covers of Lady Gaga songs, switch to Schubert. They hack at him a bit, but my guts register relief at one of the lower levels.

As my picture forms I begin to get that excitable feeling of heading towards a good thing. The lines are smooth but casually expressive, like an Ungerer or maybe even a Schiele sketch, somehow I am bringing out not just what I can see, but how it feels to see it. Not my feeling though; that in me, which *is* there, or that there, which *is* in me, the soft-face of the thing in itself... but then, as I bring the jawline up to the earlobe, and refine the curve of the lip, I start to feel that I have left the channel. I try to rescue it, a bit of a scratch around the eye, thicken the chin, but that only makes it worse and I stop with the familiar sucking sensation of artistic failure, of having gone too far.

I lean over to Barney and Joanna, scribbling away and say, 'oh yes, that's excellent,' gently putting my picture down.

'Let's see it then,' says Geni, pointing at my picture, which I'm trying to gently unexist.

'No, I've made a real dog's dinner of it,' I say, 'it's horrible.'

'Oh come on,' she says, with more gaiety than I think I've ever seen in her. She even wrinkles her nose.

'No, really...'

She darts forward and swipes it from the table and her face moves swiftly from brightness, to confusion, to doubt, to a sluggish impression of the initial playfulness.

'Yes,' she says, 'I look a bit old.'

That she does, but the awful thing is that there is something in the image, something in the tightness of the form and the blankness of the eyes that is stretched and discordant... as she is. In some way I really have drawn her. Somehow, by accident, I've done what I set out to do.

•

From Butler's Wharf to Wimbledon we drive. The taxi takes me, Geni, Barney, Gordon and little Joanna through Clapham and Balham into the pristine leafy spacious suburbia of the south west. The shops are immaculate, tidy fonts sit in acres of white, as do the soups and the people.

We crunch up the gravel to Gordon's enormous house. He's a bit smashed, can't find his keys so rings the doorbell and a small, pretty but utterly expressionless Asian woman answers the door. Maid? No, Joanna calls her Mummy.

Barney and Joanna go upstairs to play and Geni, Gordon and I take a seat in a conservatory of maple wood and Art Deco antique ceramics, tasteful watercolours and piles of women's magazines one of which Gordon tells me to chuck on the floor.

'Lamai,' he says, 'spends all day reading that trash.'

'You can learn a lot about love from women's magazines,' says Evgenia.

'Do women need to know anything more about love?' asks Gordon with a world-weary sigh.

'Everyone needs to know more about love,' says Geni smiling. He smiles back at her, with a leering little 'you betcha' nod.

Lamai comes in, 'drink?' she asks.

'I'll have a Laphroaig,' says Gordon, 'Daniel?'

'Water for me.'

'Geni?'

'I'll have a Laphroaig,' she says, not looking at me.

'Go on then Gordon, I'll have one too.'

'There's not much to understand though is there?' says Gordon.

'What? About love?'

'It's quite simple. Just a chemical—just a means of spreading genes around.'

'Do you really believe that?' asks Evgenia.

'It's all very simple,' says Gordon, 'Men want to spread their seed around, that's why we're promiscuous, that's why we get so bored so quickly, and women, they need a protector for a couple of years while their sprogs grow. That's why they invented monogamy, to keep us in line.'

'That's absurd. Women can be promiscuous too.'

'Yeah, but only to mix up the genes a bit. Or because they're bored. Or to get revenge.'

'So you're saying men are genetically programmed to be complete bastards?'

'That's right,' says Gordon.

His lips move as he speaks, but nothing else does. His huge fat face looks like hot wax, oozing down his head, a melting monument to the world.

Lamai comes in, silently gives us our drinks and leaves to work on dinner.

'Where was I?' mumbles Gordon idly swilling his drink, 'oh yes, that's my point. Men aren't bastards because we like to have sex with lots of young women—there's no reason on earth why there should *actually* be anything wrong with that. Come on Daniel, back me up here.'

I've been fighting the sickness, the sense of being trapped in a conversation which, just by listening to it, is turning me into a person I don't like to be. It is the loneliness of speaking to fit in, when there is no conceivable right answer, nothing I can say that will make sense, and so everyone senses I am out-of-place, a fraud.

'I don't know,' I say in a small, timid voice which I correct by unnaturally emphasising the next phrase *'can't you love?'*

'Yes, of course I can. I can love lots of women, and I can love my work, and I can love my children, and other people's children,' he smirks, 'they might be mine after all.'

'What about marriage?' asks Evgenia.

'Mutually Assured Disappointment. People celebrate at marriages then grieve at funerals. It really should be the other way round.'

She laughs. 'You're a dinosaur Gordon!'

'I know it's not fashionable, but I'm afraid you can't argue with scientific fact.'

He's right. You can't argue with science. Science *is* argument. I bet Lamai doesn't argue with Gordon, or if she does she loses every time. But she'll win in the end. I believe that women always do.

Evgenia starts on about gender stereotyping, telling Gordon that men and women are just the same, which is weird because I know she doesn't really believe that. Not in her flesh. I know she wants nothing more than to completely submit to a man. The problem is, not me.

While I am getting wound up about this inside, the tack of the conversation shifts to society, glass ceilings, policy and politics. The room fills up with cigarette smoke and more opinions.

'How are you going to vote Daniel?' says Gordon.

'Eh? In what?'

'In the election!'

'There's an election? Another one?'

Ho, ho, ho, Gordon chortles, 'So you don't vote?'

'No.'

'It's people like you that allow monsters to get in you know.'

'They wouldn't get in without democracy.'

'You don't support democracy?'

'I've never seen it.'

'What do you mean?'

'I've had, I dunno, forty jobs—I've never been in a democratic one. I've never lived in a democratic house, or had a democratic relationship. I have no idea what the word means.'

'It means voting for someone to represent you in parliament.'

'Yeah, I'm not sure that helps much.'

'Helps who?'

'Well, the poor for a start.'

'We are wealthier now than we've ever been.'

'We can't use our feet, we can't take care of each other, we can't survive without access to the internet or the electric grid. It doesn't seem like wealth to me.'

'So what? You want to return to the medieval world? Dying at 40?'

'No, I just think there's a better way.'

Gordon smiles, in calm patronising indifference to my silly, naïve view of the world, 'and what is that?' he asks.

'I don't know, having a direct relationship with life, with each other.'

'And what's your plan? How are you going to achieve it?'

'We're not going to achieve it. Nature is.'

'What do you mean?'

'I mean it's over, the whole thing is *over*,' I'm getting heated now, 'It's all unravelling, right now, coming apart. Don't you... Can't you see?'

Gordon's eyes are merrily dancing with condescending delight, but before he has time to answer Barney staggers in theatrically and flops on Evgenia's lap.

'Ge-nee,' he says, 'I need to see an aeroplane.'

'What, now?'

'Yesss,' he sighs.

We, Geni, Barney and I, go out into Gordon's broad, immaculate garden and look up into the dim-purple sky, until a flashing green dot appears beneath the high black-grey clouds, making its steady approach to Heathrow. Barney cheers up instantly and we all return.

Lamai is dishing up an extraordinary feast. Pan-seared cod in some kind of black sauce, tiger prawns in sweet chilli, dumplings, noodles, stir-fried tofu and mushroom, salad spreckled with nuclear chillies.

As we take our seats Gordon says to Barney.

'Why did you need to see a plane?'

'I don't know.'

'Barney wants to fly planes one day,' says Geni.

'Or drive a train,' says Barney.

'Did you see a plane then?' asks Gordon.

'Yes.'

'A little blinking red dot?'

'No it was green.'

'That means that it was safe. If it flashes red, it's an enemy plane and we need to shoot it out the sky. Ra-ta-ta-ta-ta-ta!' he cries, mimicking a machine gun.

Barney shrinks into his seat. So do I in fact—Gordon looked positively demonic firing his pretend gun, face underlit with candlelight, cheeks all hard and flashing.

'Uncle Gordon's joking,' says Geni. Barney looks confused.

Somehow I make it through the meal.

'That was probably the best thing I've ever eaten,' I say to Lamai feeling the truth of the lie.

'Thank you,' she says mechanically, clearing away our plates.

'I'm serious.'

Gordon looks at me frowningly for a moment then turns to his wife, 'bring some more Laphroaig through—actually bring the bottle.'

'Daddy!' says Joanna.

'What darling?'

'I don't like it when you drink.'

'Er, heh…' he coughs. Lamai looks at him and then looks away. I stare at my ice cream.

'So what *do* you do Daniel?' he asks.

'I don't do anything Gordon.'

'Oh marvellous,' says Gordon, 'gloriously free.'

'Yep, I lost my job today. Jobs actually. Both of them.'

I can feel Geni firing death-rays into my third eye.

'Can't you do *anything*?' asks Joanna.

'I can moonwalk.'

'Can you teach me?'

'Sure. It's not hard.'

'Mummy, can you moonwalk?' Joanna asks Lamai who is bringing in the bottle of whiskey. Lamai gives a thin, dewy smile. Perhaps she's on downers?

'What can you do?' I ask Joanna.

She thinks. 'I can blow up *most* balloons.'

'You can draw, can't you,' says Gordon, rasping. Joanna nods with a strange, quiet obedience.

'Show Daniel your pictures,' says Gordon and Joanna gets up, pulling at my hand.

I follow her into the enormous TV lounge, all mahogany and leather, everything up to a fine finish, much that is precious and careful, except for Joanna's corner, where her crayons and pencils and drawings are scattered over a low, tiled coffee table.

I squat and inspect the pictures. The first one is of a dinosaur, similar to the one on the boat, but where its head should be an emphatic fountain of blood blasts into the sky.

'That's interesting,' I say.

The next one is of a small man with big guns for hands shooting birds, which are falling from the sky, crude scratchy explosions of blood trailing behind them.

'Who's this guy?'

Joanna shrugs, 'don't know.'

The next one is of… is it Spiderman? Are they ninjas? Is that a tank? No blood on this one though.

Warfare, murder, death, bloodshed, swords, firearms, animals in pieces… it goes on and on, picture after picture of disordered mayhem.

'Have you shown these to Mummy and Daddy?' I ask.

Again she raises her eyebrows in a meek 'dunno.'

She looks like the sad girl on Sigyn ward.

'You're a lovely girl,' I say, 'you should draw lovely things.'

She gets on her knees and starts drawing.

'I like this,' she says, not looking up.

•

We take a minicab home, sitting in silence. The man behind the wheel is another driver of frustration and fury, but I don't care. Barney sleeps and Geni and I have a tight, hushed argument about Uncle Gordon.

'You read their articles in the paper, denouncing strongmen and dictators, calling for compassion and democracy, and then you see how these fuckers actually *live*…'

'Daniel, he's my friend.'

'I can't believe you can't hear, in every word he says, the ashes, the emptiness, the… the… *decay*.'

'I can't believe you *can* hear that.'

'Alright then, what do you think he's like in bed? What does your superpower tell you?'

'He's a monster.'

'Exactly!'

'But all men are.'

'What?'

She looks out the window, not interested, apparently. 'He's alright when you get to know him.'

The taxi lurches us into Dulwich Village. 'Drop us here,' says Evgenia, paying, and pulling Barney out. We are in front of an off-licence.

I follow her in, heart sunk, 'Oh come on, don't drink any more.'

'Don't tell me what to do.'

We're standing in a Turkish Cash and Carry, Barney groggily hanging on to Evgenia, late-nighters flitting around us.

'I'm not telling you what to do,' I hiss in the standard public argument undertone.

'You're trying to control me. You try and control everything, everyone,' she says at normal volume, completely unconcerned that the Somali next to us can hear we are having problems.

'I just don't want you to change, to become all weird.'

'You think *I'm* weird!' she cries, grabbing a bottle of whiskey and charging towards the counter.

I attempt to pause the combat for purchase, but no, she goes on; 'you have zero ambition, you hate everyone, you go all silent with people, you're aggressive, you cry in your sleep and you are *looking forward* to the end of the fucking world—and *I'm* weird?'

'Do I cry in my sleep?'

'Yes.'

I didn't know this.

We walk through suburban Dulwich in silence, side-by-side and separated by the entire universe. We reach a thin pavement and move to single file, Geni first, then Barney, and then me. Barney is pulling leaves from privet hedges and camellia bushes and shredding them in his little hands.

'Barney?' I say quietly.

He looks back up at me.

'Do you think the bushes like you tearing their leaves off?'

His little face wrinkles in confusion.

I feel a strong urge to reach out to Evgenia, to calm the

agitated fraction, get underneath this awful pitched and churning gut-pain, but I don't want to argue while Barney is here. I know what it's like to be where he is, helpless between two furious devils, reality-warping hatred hanging in the air; never sure what could happen next, but sure it will be terrible.

When we reach the end of the road Barney, who has given up pulling leaves, stops and takes my hand and reaches up for Geni's, and so we walk down Woodwarde Road somehow connected.

We get in, Geni puts the whiskey on the kitchen table and then takes Barney to bed. She returns to find me in the dark kitchen, sitting next to the bottle.

'Are you going to drink that?' I ask.

'No,' she says, walking past me to the bedroom. I follow her, feeling the tragedy of the inevitable—the distant sound of the four horsemen of emotional apocalypse approaching; shame, anger, fear and desire. Something unsaid is festering in me, in us. I have the feeling that, God help me, I have made a horrible, *horrible* mistake with my life.

'So you really have no job now?' she asks, undressing.

'No, nothing.'

'How are you going to pay for anything? How are you going to pay your share of the mortgage?'

'I don't know. I'll think of something.'

'Daniel, I'm not going to take care of you.'

'Yeah, alright, I know.'

I get into bed with her. Her body looks wiry and witch-like, kind of disgusting. *If you don't love her, sooner or later, she'll become hideous to you.* It's true. Just like Susanna, the girl I dated in university who started to seem like a cartoon boy, or Clara, another girl I went out with who turned into a smelly rotund pre-pubescent shaved koala... they all end up ugly when I start to go off them. But it's not *my* fault, is it?

I hold Geni, more out of habit, or duty, than anything else. She responds mechanically, like she feels she's supposed to touch my back, my shoulders. I wonder if I want to have sex with her, whether to bother.

'Well?' She looks at me in the darkness, her blue eyes deep black holes. 'Are you going to fuck me or not?'

'Not.'

'Coward.'

'How's that cowardly?' I say, rolling off her, 'I just don't feel like it.'

She laughs, a tiny scoff, and I feel violent anger rush through me, hatred unlike anything I have ever felt. I want to hurt her. I could easily hit her. I actually imagine it, how satisfying it would be.

'You're fucked,' I say pointing at her in the complete darkness, 'without me you're fucked, you'll just be fucked, that's all you are, something to fuck.' A distant part of me is horrified by these words. I can say this? I can be *this* cruel? *this* hateful? I could be the great modern devil, a wife-beater... but surely if I could any man could?

She turns around. 'Fuck me then,' she hisses, 'why don't you hate fuck me?'

What follows is brutal, good, shameful. The voice reminds me of porn videos, of Andy, of everything I do hate, and as I come she whispers with dreadful calm,

'You see?'

I throw her off me, reeling, nauseous, head-pounding, exhausted, blank and nowhere. I'm trembling.

'What kind of woman are you?'

'You think it's surprising that a woman treats you the way the world does?' she says quietly.

We lie in null, moonless silence.

The 'oh'

Impossible to pin down what the suffering is, or where it is coming from. Hardly anything has actually happened—some sharp words, stupid arguments—yet somehow since the boat trip we have gradually, imperceptibly, fallen into a nightmarish otherworld, a place of complete loneliness; cast out. Yes, the fall of man—this is actually it, the expulsion from paradise is actually happening to me in slow motion over days and weeks of inexplicable plunging horror.

Sometimes I think 'oh, right, so this is what a broken heart is,' yet I have no idea what is actually happening. What is this weird reality I am now in, that is all sick, shifting fear and need, for no reason? I look for escape or relief, but escape there is none and the only relief is in mindless activity. I obsessively catalogue music, mechanically download software upgrades, study premiership football matches, none of it has ever interested me, and doesn't even now—it is just data, just work. Yes, work—I would actually be happy for a job now. This is why people *do* work, to keep their minds off their broken hearts. This is why the world is non-stop, because a slackening of momentum is unendurable.

I remember, long ago, being at an aunt's house, out the back with her and my mum. My uncle was at the bottom of the garden, in his pigeon shed. We were all quietly watching him when she said;

'I wish he loved me like he loves those pigeons.'

Evgenia and I are trapped in a ghastly cycle of building pressure, followed by an incomprehensible emotional storm, release through grim fucking, an intense desire to split up, pre-emptive feelings of loneliness, a need to reach out, a falling feeling of pity for she who's heart is also breaking, a tender coming together, an ever fainter echo of love-making, then, in shorter and shorter periods, the connection wearing out, the pressure and horror building up again. Each hit is less, each withdrawal harder, each horror, a deeper horror still.

It's worse at night. I dream of death, of falling buildings, everyone screaming. I wake up shouting and Evgenia is crying out too—she has been having a nightmare at the same time. Or I dream of a village in a forest, grass huts, all on fire, all the trees on fire, and a girl, eyes white, screaming and screaming. I wake up with the presence of death in the room, an unliving alien presence. I am terrified because I am not sure what is real. Am I awake? I can hear something dreadful, a sound that makes my stomach drop. Is it out there, in the room? The bed is empty. Geni is standing next to the wall, facing away from me. She is spitting. At the wall. I get up and guide her back to bed. She does not wake, I do not sleep, and lie lidlessly awake.

Outside a fox is crying. It sounds like a baby being strangled. This one is out the front every night, poking around the wheelie bins, every night looking worse, more mangey. It sits on the front wall, broadcasting its ghastly wails through the house, informing me, clearly, that as my relationship with Geni is dying, so the whole world is dying, so I am dying, so it, the fox, is dying too.

Barney too is having nightmares, behaving bizarrely. He has tantrums, rips all the fridge magnets off or throws his food on the floor, won't go to bed, wakes up crying. He says there is someone in his room, that someone is filling in his puzzle books. He likes me—I know he does—but he pushes me, knowing I can do nothing, and when we play fight I know he actually wants to kill me.

I have the sense that I am fighting for my life. I feel, some-how, on some basic level, that I do not trust these two people. That there is something else behind their eyes. Both Barney and Geni look slyly at me, from time to time, and I get the shocking impression that there is something *else* in there peering at me, something old and long darkly knowing, waiting.

I respond by arguing, by using my mind to try and win, to come out on top, but, even though Geni is my intellectual infe-rior, she is far more skilled than I in this kind of battle. She is clever in ways I had no idea someone could be. I am blindfolded and attacked by bats. I am boxing in the dark. I am utterly out of my depth. I am afraid of her. I don't know what she could do, except I know it would be the terrors of the earth. I can't reveal anything, because everything can be used against me. I gather my fallen hairs.

We hiss abuse at each other, but it is the silent dread that is worse, the long, long silences during which I stare at my fingernail, or obsessively crease a bit of my shirt to make the shadow a perfect oblong, while, over the course of two hours we exchange perhaps ten sentences.

'Why don't you leave?' she asks me.

Long, long, looooonnnnng pause.

'I will.'

She leaves the kitchen, returns, leaves and returns.

'You're still here.'

Tragic damned silence, empty hurtful eternity.

'Do you want me to go?'

Sigh, dread clouds gathering over distant hills.

'You want to go.'

Silence, the very death of sound.

'I want to be happy.'

Platitudes, under which we are falling away from each other. If that Christian stuff were true, this is how it would actually feel to fall from heaven. This is how it would feel to be cut off from the grace of God, and fall, or be pushed, into sin and pride.

Pride. They say it is the father of all sins don't they? There is something in me that is hanging on, that will not surrender, that *must* win an argument — of all places, now! I must win or I will die. It's like needing to be right on a sinking ship, and the need is the ship itself.

'You said you weren't interested,' I say, clenched in tension.

'I didn't mean forever, I was just *busy*.'

This is after I wanted to share with her a picture I was drawing and she hardly looked at it, and insincerely said 'mm, nice.'

'You just don't care about my work,' I say; and I can hear my petulance, I know that in fact she *was* busy and, underneath all this, I know that the general air of sharp apartness today is down to me, but I can't admit it, I can't let go, I can't soften, I can't say 'come on sweetheart, let's not fight, let's have a cuddle,' — I want to say it, but I can't. I think of being a little boy and my mum asking me if I want to go for a walk with her, and I want to, I want to so much, but I say no. Why? *Why?* What is this gripping thing, holding on to my body, holding on to being the winning-me, knowing that we are dragging each other down into the pit, but unable to do anything about it?

'It's all *your* fault,' she says.

'How is it *my* fault?' I say, knowing it is, yet dreading to hear it.

'You have no idea how to love a woman, what it means.'

'What *does* it mean then?'

'If you knew, you wouldn't ask such a stupid question.'

She walks out, to take a bath.

I follow her into the bathroom, standing uselessly as she gets undressed. God she looks hot—maybe sex will solve absolutely everything? I approach her, feeling like a dog, and start pawing her. She pushes me away, 'get *off*.'

'Please,' I say.

She looks at me with pure, naked, one-pointed contempt. I shrink out of the room, feeling less than a man, less than human, a feeble, needy, oily blob.

I walk into the kitchen and stand on the table.

'What are you doing?'

'Oh, hello Barney. I'm standing on the table.'

'Why?'

'I dunno. It just feels better up here.'

'Does it?'

'Yeah.'

He climbs up and stands with me. We stay there in silence for a full minute. Geni comes out of the bathroom, pays no attention to us, walks through to the bedroom.

'*Ge-nee* it feels better up here,' says Barney as she walks back again.

'I don't want to feel better,' she says.

Barney looks at me, then looks inside himself, then back up at me.

'I don't want to feel better either Daniel,' and he climbs down.

Neither do I.

They say the sun is hot—it's not, it's cold. They say that love is warm—wrong again, it is perfectly cold. That is the love I need—not, please Christ, in a cold body, like Geni's, in a cold mind and a cold heart. I need a warm woman's heart and a bright eye, scalding with adventure, but beneath all that, far out in the space of her bellymind, I need this that I have with Evgenia, stark and obliterating and inhuman, like the centre of the sun. I can't live without it, but without atmosphere it is destroying me. I can feel it eating me up, burning me away.

Why did I leave Lauren? Why did I foul up our friendship? Why did I cut her out? Lauren understands, she is forgiving, she likes the music I like, she likes cuddling, she fools around, she says interesting things and makes interesting, reasoned, observations rather than just ejecting oracular pronouncements about my humiliating, subterranean dream-self.

Lauren is everything that Geni is not, and yet, underneath it all, I just didn't find her compelling. Why? Why? Why?

Why do I understand so very little of my own soul?

Is it true that I do not know how to love a woman? I have done it, I have loved—must it be 100% successful? Why are my sins, and they are many, not forgiven?

Yes they are many. I desire other women, I hate Geni, I want to control her—but she eggs me on—but is that her? She seems like someone else, but then *I* seem like someone else.

I think of old girlfriends. I think of their disappointment, confusion and pain, their withering looks and their tears. I think of my furious desire at the start, my furious anger at the end, and then the relief at getting out; *ahh, just the one of us.* If love is some kind of puzzle, then I am no closer to solving it than I was when I was fourteen and fucking perplexed Hannah Goodstone in my socks.

I am back to watching porn, and playing video games—both secretly, in the middle of the night, or when Geni is out. A few days ago, alone in the house, I humped a manikin in the shed.

Afterwards I felt a pressing need to phone dial-a-buse, to be bitterly scorned.

'Now what?' came the harsh, dry voice that hates me.

'I feel like shit.'

'What do you expect? You *are* shit.'

'Yes, yes, I am.'

'A real man would not—could not—give in so easily.'

'Sorry.'

'Sorry? Ugh. I pity the woman.'

'I can't take it any more.'

'Just fuck another dummy, dummy.'

'How did you know…?'

Click. Dead. How *did* she know? How does Evgenia know? They *all* know! All women—I say these mad words to myself with the slow horror of total realisation—all women everywhere know everything about me. And yet they don't know they know.

I'm not eating much. I just can't. The place where the food should go seems to be taken up with something else, some sullen toadish-thing that just wants to brood on anguish, fatly. I am fuelled by a dull glow of resentment, but it's not enough to keep me in tune with the world, which I perceive as if through reversed binoculars. I am floating away from myself—the man that does not hate, that loves, the good bloke; a lie I told myself, apparently. If he's still in here I can't reach him. I have lost him, if ever he was, or she has killed him.

Yes, it *is* her. *She* is doing this to me. She really *is* the devil, or possessed by it, channelling the shade.

I must leave. This is obvious now. I need some space, to take things back to a casual status, down to the previous level, of me not living here and visiting—the easy way. But, actually, yes, all this pain is not the fear talking; it's the sense, the truer me, the one that needs out, that needs to escape from her witchcraft.

But if I leave, we will never be again as we have. The door to the Other Place will close. I love talking and playing with Barney too, being part of a family. Leaving that is horrible to look at, but nowhere near as awful as the dread that trembles in me when I consider leaving the bizarre ocean of weird that beats within Geni's heart; the prospect appals me, of being ejected from this vast, blended entity that I have tasted, that perhaps I could taste again—more than taste, drink, live within—if I were more of a man. And yet it is appalling to stay. This house is bare, and I am bare. I can feel my soul being torn and emptied out through the rip... and then the shame... oh the self-disgust...

Talk with her, I think, reason it out... But that's nuts. How can I say all this? How can we sort it all out, or even bring what is happening into the light? It would just open the gates of hell wider. I can rend my heart by holding it in, or rend hers by letting it out.

But in any case, even if I say nothing, she is picking up on it all, in the-place-I-dare-not-go she just *knows* that my indecision is selfish at the core, that I am committing the crime of mind, that I just don't have what it takes to get past the demoness she has made for me. I am not man enough for a woman like her. Fuck only knows who is, but it's not me. I dare not inspect any of these realities, because somehow I know them too. I know I am breaking her heart—but why doesn't she *sympathise*? What about *me*?

The doorbell rings and I get up from the kitchen table, where I have been morbidly tracing the grain, and walk down the hall to the frosted glass and the distorted figure behind it.

A sorrowful young man—skinny black jeans, green velvet jacket, thick black hair, lips of some characterful curve—is standing with an artist's portfolio.

'I am sorry to trouble you,' he says in an Eastern-European accent, 'but I am...'

'Sorry,' I say, cutting in, 'I don't want anything.'

'Look, I understand, but please, just look.'

Before I can protest further he has slipped out a canvas showing a cartoonish man's head expressing a mixture of dismay, confusion, surprise and, somehow, acceptance. It's angular, almost geometric, ugly really but although it's in a much less fluid style, it reminds me of a full-body Scream, except, the eyebrows are raised and the little mouth is very round.

'No, I'm sorry,' I say, a little more human, 'I don't even have any money.'

'It's three hundred pounds,' he says. 'It took me nearly three months to make this.'

'Three months?'

'I had to get it just right.'

'What's it called?'

'It doesn't have a name.'

'The erk?'

'If you like.'

'Only I was thinking it's a bit like The Scream.'

'Perhaps the "oh!"' he suggests.

'No, look, I do like it, but I don't have anything,' I say, 'I'm an artist too. I have nothing.'

'Okay,' he says, glancing past me.

'I don't live here,' I say, reading his thoughts, 'I can't afford the mortgage. I'm fucked.'

A kind of blind momentum, and relief, is pushing me to speak. Here is a guy who is an artist, in need of money, worth speaking to I believe. I shouldn't be here, living here. I should be where he is.

'Okay,' he says, 'take it. I want you to have it.'

'Eh?'

'Take it.'

'No I can't.'

'I want you to have it,' he says.

'Look, wait.'

I go inside to my jacket. There's thirty pounds in my pocket. I don't have much more.

'Here, take this,' I tell him.

'No, I don't want it.'

'Have it, please.'

He looks at me, eyes moist.

'You are a good man,' he says, taking the money and handing over the picture, 'the "oh!".' My throat is tight with emotion, but I can't weep on the doorstep with this man (I can, but I won't), so we shake hands, brothers for a moment, and I go inside and sit in the cold living room until Geni returns.

'What's that?' she asks.

'It's a painting,' I say.

'It's ugly,' she says.

'I know.'

'So why did you buy it?'

'I like it.'

'Fine, stick it in the shed with the rest of your shit.'

I sit looking at the "oh". Really, what are we doing here? We should leave, shouldn't we?

I want a book of my life; when indecision strikes, to just pick it up, turn to page 325 and, 'ah, I see, weather out the storm and see it through,' or 'get out, get out *now!*' It doesn't matter, even pain doesn't matter—as long as I don't have to decide, as long as I know I must, as long as the cup is passed from me.

A thought. I'll go completely still, get in the body, feel all over and then introduce the options and see how they feel. Ask the body.

Option 1—stay here. Feel slight slight *slight* resistance, like a tiny rising up of a rancid fog. Option 2—go. Feel nothing in particular.

Probably then I should go with the 'nothing'—the nicer feeling (although it is an absence of feeling)—even though it leads to; what? To complete uncertainty. A total nobody with nowhere to go, alone out there. Okay, fine. Uncertainty, come.

My phone rings.

'Daniel?'

'Yes?'

'It's Bob.'

'Bob, look I'm having a bit of a thing here.'

'Daniel, Derek's ill.'

'Where is he?'

'At the Royal Trinity.'

'But... that's a hospice.'

'I know.'

'A hospice is where people go to die.'

'You better come if you want to see him.'

•

I am led through the St. Michael's ward; hushed it is, as you'd expect I suppose, and cleaner and whiter and less hectic than an ordinary hospital. The people in the beds look diminished, tiny even, their dim lives guttering. The coughs have no power, or the moans, but far more terrible for their delicate, pitifully low volume.

It's sinister... and yet I can smell relief here. Somewhere, hiding, under the ground, or behind the walls, there is a friend here.

Derek is lying propped up, still dignified despite his un-dignified collapse. He is surrounded by people I've never seen; except Bob, he's there, also a sharp, lizard-looking woman with thin blonde hair, a fretful guy in half a suit, a bored looking girl with a big freckly head, an old, old, hooknosed woman with dim searching eyes and a man with a jutting jaw, jutting cheeks, jutting forehead with close-set eyes and a *tiny* nose, giving an overall effect of his face being sucked from behind into a hoover.

They stand around the bed in agonised silence, all desperately looking for something to say. When Derek sees me he says 'hello Danny,' and there's a fluff of relief as someone is saying something.

'Hi Derek, you okay?'

'Not really, no.'

'No.'

There's so much I want to say, or there's one thing I want to say that says so much, but I can't say it, not here, in front of these people, I'd feel stupid. I feel exactly like I do when considering making a conspicuous move on a woman with an audience, like actually all I want to say is 'I LOVE YOU!' and the whole train carriage will hear, and smirk into their sleeves and she'll kill me.

I do love him though, all these people here do. The lizard woman looks angry, half-suit (her husband?) looks appalled at life, hooverface is perfectly expressionless and frecklehead—not sure there's a whole lot of love there actually. She looks like she's desperate to check her phone. The old girl isn't sure what planet she's on. But there's concern there at least, or maybe she needs a wee.

'Fancy a cup of tea Daniel? There's a kettle over there,' says Derek.

'No, it's okay,' I croak.

'Surprisingly good tea. The food generally is good here.'

'What did you have today?' asks half-suit.

Is this how you die then? Slowly having the life sucked out of you, agonisingly slipping towards the yawning jaws of eternity while smiling and making stupid fucking small talk, right to the last? Is that it?

It goes on like this for a long time, we are glad we can talk of something other than death, and yet it is horrific to talk about anything else, and yet we can't face it. It is, in other words, just like being at the pub.

The family have the look of the bereaved; sad, pained but above all *helpless*. There is no ritual at this point, nobody knows what to do—we just do it like everyone does it, and say what everyone says, even if none of that works or means anything at all. 'He went without too much pain,' or 'at least you have your memories,' or 'he's looking down on us now, laughing.' All bullshit, but it keeps the void at bay.

And I, to my lifelong shame, go along with it.

The angular blond woman woman says 'you'll be alright Dad, don't worry.'

Derek looks at her, pity on his lovely round head, then turns to me and says, 'we're all done for.'

'Bye Derek.'

'Bye.'

I turn away and walk blindly through the ward, more death, everywhere death, out to the front gate where Bob is standing. I roll a cigarette, hands shaking with cold and emotion, and we stand in silence for a bit, smoking. Bob looks greyer than ever, but for red harrowed eyes.

'It's supposed to be summer,' he says.

It is freezing cold, fog rolling across Clapham Common. I have a terrible terrible feeling rising in my craw that everything is going to turn out very badly for everyone.

'Bob, I'm so sorry about Derek.'

'Me too.'

The blonde woman comes out. She looks furious.

'I don't see why they can't help him,' she says to neither of us in particular.

'They say he hasn't got long left,' says Bob.

'What do doctors know!' she cries, 'They've prodded him, poked him, tested him—they've got no idea what's wrong with him.'

'It's just age Margaret.'

'You're no better! Where were *you* when he needed you?'

'Let's not argue,' says Bob quietly.

Margaret stands between us, tense and silent. She hugs herself, pulling the belt of her woollen cardigan tighter, and then looks at me.

'Aren't you cold?' she says—in concerned accusation.

'No.'

'Why not?'

'I've got some nice underwear,' I say, pulling at the wrist of my long-sleeve vest, 'it's cashmere.'

She rubs it with her fingers. 'How much did it cost?' she asks aggressively.

'Top forty quid, long-johns the same I think.'

'Does it wash okay?'

'Yeah.'

'Machine wash?'

'Yeah, fine.'

'Where did you buy it?'

'Camping shop in Covent Garden. Just down from the Transport Museum. The make is, erm, Mountain-Guard.'

She nods, thinking to herself.

'I might get some,' she says, and then goes back inside.

Bob and I exchange looks.

'He just wanted to be a good father,' says Bob, 'he sacrificed everything for his kids, everything, and they don't care, none of 'em even care.'

'She seemed to care, Margaret.'

'Funny way of showing it.'

'We've all got a funny way of showing it.'

'Not funny ha-ha.'

We finish our cigarettes and flick them into the road.

'I'm off Bob.'

'Alright. You gonna come back to work?'

'No.'

'What you gonna do then?'

'I want to go on night-time graffiti missions, and paint huge skeletons on railway cuttings and write "you are going to die" for the morning commuters.'

'Don't think there's much money in that.'

'Probably not.'

'Why don't you do signposts?'

'Yeah, could do.'

'Alright Danny. You take care.'

'You too Bob.'

I cross over onto Clapham Common. The cold fog is swallowing the trees and the dog-walkers and the sound of the cars into an irreal, white nothingness. Crows lope into existence from out of the hazy void and then they skip-fly back into nowhere. The shade of an oak darkens and looms, underfoot the crunch of acorns and dead leaves. Winter at the height of summer; the winter of the world, it's all my fault and it *feels* like I can hear seagulls.

As I stand under the tree, looking at the dying branches, something alien rises up in my chest, something massive, ancient and empty of life. An intense sense of wrongness, of evil rising up like vapours from the earth. This is it. This is the end, and we're all realising it at the same time. The Unhappy Supermind is waking up, the oceanic suffering of creatures in existence is reaching the surface. There is nowhere to escape to, no protection anywhere; in every direction all is lost.

I look up. A handful of roses lie a few feet away. Someone has tossed them there. Why? For *me*. I stand staring at them, horrified. My funeral flowers. I know it's crazy, I know it like I know there is sun above the fog, but the meaning of what I am faced with fills me completely, impossible to ignore. I know that my mind is playing tricks on me, yet the sense of everything infused with this obscure, morbid truth, is just overwhelming.

Or is it just that my life is appalling, as simple as that? It is you know. I'm not exaggerating. Dishonesty, withheld opinions, then a complete upturning of reality plunging Geni and I into a barren shineless universe of fear and self-loathing. Fun brings no relief. Going out, getting drunk, thrashing around like a demented sperm whale with people I detest; I might as well be stuck in a lift with a hundred angry people setting fire to fifty pound notes. But home is no better, coiled up in the grip of inexplicable fury with the devil herself.

Two figures walk towards me, moving strangely. The shadows become clearer and across from the path, dressed in cheap storm-blue nylon granddad coats and icing-yellow towel-cotton tracksuit bottoms, a couple of pigeon-toed palsies, arm in arm, a man and a woman, are wibblingly wobbling along. Their heads are swaying one way, their hips another, their legs more arcing around the step than passing direct through it. They are gripping each other with both hands and laughing about something, teeth-glistening gummy. I watch them slowly pass in spasms and vanish into the mist.

I'm not sure where I am now, which way is the south I'm supposed to be going. All sides by otherness. Shouts and screams, now, in the distance, but where from? In the fog it seems that they are coming from everywhere. A glow before me begins to take shape. Someone has lit a fire, no a bonfire, no, what is that? Is it... a *bus*?

Houses come into view and before them, yes, a double-decker bus, engulfed in flames. Shouts and screams are louder now, road (no idea which, South Circular?) weirdly empty. Twenty or thirty police run past in riot gear, towards the common. Adrenaline sharpens my wits—should I go where they are running towards, or from? From, surely...

I run towards a backroad. Other people are running, past me, with me, what is going on? A riot? Another one? It's so foggy I have no idea where I am, typical smart London, all curtains closed, a ragged boom to my right, then voices, a scream behind me, the smudge of more houseforms ahead. Shops here. I *think* it's Clapham High Street.

Slightly clearer. Sirens, shouts, 'bruv! over 'ere, bruv!' an ambulance wails past, another fire across the road, smoke mingling with the mist. Twenty or so kids are standing around a bank. One is beating the window with a baseball bat. Two girls come past, dragging a bundle of boxes, wrapped in a sheet. 'Love fucking the feds.' Three men run past carrying scaffold poles. 'Oy! Oy! *Doil!*'

I phone Geni.

'Are you okay?'

'Yes, why?' she asks.

'Have you see the news?'

'No.'

I explain to her what's happening, but my battery runs out. I could nick another one, but she's safe. No riots in Dulwich—nobody there to kick up more than a sequence of tuts.

As I am talking to Geni a broken shadow darkens into a familiar form, the pellet-headed mumbling weather man who, as my phone dies, passes me, saying to himself 'stormy, squalls, met office have issued warnings across the country...'

'Stop,' I pocket my phone and call after him, 'Uh! Sorry, excuse me! Sir!'

He shuffles off into the mist. Ah, leave him.

I head away, up the road. A woman screams, 'Where the fuck are the police!?' A car crawls past with a smashed front window. The undramatic crunch of a collision behind me. A bookshop is untouched, still open, corner shop next to it—rioters outside forming an orderly looting queue. Next shop, women's accessories, girl's voice: 'Oy! Kylie! Is this bag colour neutral?' More kids, some wearing fancy-dress masks, animals, skulls, superheroes. 'Leave the fucking olives!' A man, very middle-class, is telling everyone off; 'Is this *fun?* Destroying society? Are you proud of yourselves!? Eh? *Eh?*' A burning car up ahead, another car upside down next to it, someone standing on it, rocking backwards and forwards, another kid in a mask (Venetian!) 'This is gonna last *forever!*' he screams.

I edge up what I'm still supposing is Clapham High Street, still tense, awake, battle-ready. Walking into nothing, nowhere, an issueless, formless emptiness from which shadows storm demanding electronic items, sportswear and fashion accessories. Silence, then a ripped-howl of engines, or screaming, then silence, infinite white unbeing walling a cramped, blurred circle of cold steel, concrete and glass, an unnatural island floating in nothingness, shat from the body of the earth.

A feeble cry, another group, smaller, shades resolve into kids, surrounding a woman on the floor, hand above her head, ready for blows. My hunched frame inflates. Walk tall—'Ave 'em. Need a weapon, but none, so I charge forward, 'get the fuck *away* from her!'

They're only kids and run off immediately.

I stoop to help her up. 'Dalia?'

'Oh Daniel, oh Daniel,' she is out of breath. I lift her up. She's tiny, Dalia and very light, and this makes me fall in love with her a bit. I probably shouldn't feel aroused.

'Are you okay?'

'Yes, yes,' she says, dusting herself down, 'why are you here?'

In the mania and confusion, this question strikes me as philosophical, and I think we don't have time for this now.

'We should get off the main road,' I say.

'Okay, yes.'

'Can you walk?'

'Yes, I'm fine, let's go.'

I start walking off to another side road.

'No, no,' she says, 'this way, we'll go to my house.'

'Okay.'

Clapham North tube looms into view and with it, the chaos seems to ease off a bit, although I can hear 'Whispering Grass' by the Ink Spots, very loud, which is unsettling as I've only ever heard hate music at that volume. We turn away from the shops, away from the bellows of destruction and the manic laughter, and slow down, danger subsiding, fog just as thick though. Lights on in some houses hover past, ghostly luminous windows into other dimensions.

'*What* is going on?'

'I was buying some stockings,' says Dalia, 'it became foggy and then the sky fell. Oh, I'm so glad you appeared Daniel!'

'I'm glad you appeared too.'

I am. I was beginning to feel myself pass out of the solid world. Dalia is so reassuringly real, and, it is funny too how brave and confident I feel now she's next to me. Just a few moments ago I was terrified. It still seems unreal though, a strange new world has descended with the fog.

'I don't believe it,' I say.

'Nobody ever believes it,' says Dalia. I'm about to interrogate this gnomic comment when two kids run past us carrying boxes (pcs?). Dalia grabs me. The doors of a parked car in front fly open and two guys get out, grab the kids, throw the boxes in the back seat, slap the kids, let them go and get back in the car.

They're robbing looters. Morally grey?

We turn away and head up an alleyway, into a quiet but extremely shabby backroad and over to a drab modern squat-block of flats, busted fence, dingy garden, up a side alley. Comes pre-looted.

'I should go,' I say.

'Come in Daniel,' she says; gently orders really. Impossible to refuse. Probably should look after her.

'Okay.'

The cracked front door doesn't open properly, doesn't seem to fit correctly in the frame. Dalia forces it and we squeeze through, up a flight of dark, narrow and steep stairs we go. Smell of rotting carpet, bodies and ammonia. She unlocks another door, through her hallway, and into her minuscule kitchen. It would be bigger, but there's a mattress taking up most of the floor.

She puts the light on. 'Sit,' she says and leaves.

There's one folding chair, which I place in the only space for it, next to the bed, and wait for her.

The room is damp, stale and the walls stained. All surfaces are sticky and smell of cooking oil. Whoever sleeps on the mattress has his belongings piled up in the space at the base, with an alarm clock on top. Her belongings I should say—I can see a nightie. The bedclothes look horrible, cheap foamy pillow, cheap threadbare Mickey Mouse duvet.

Dalia comes back, looking calmer, carrying a couple of mugs. She's about forty I guess, cute, mousy, neat. Exhausted around the eyes, yet still, somehow sparkly and aware.

'I'm sorry Daniel for this,' she gestures around the room.

'No, no, don't worry about it.'

'Do you want tea?'

'Okay.'

'I only have lemon.'

'Fine.'

She puts a saucepan of water on and puts the mugs on the side.

'Everyone is at work,' she says, 'I hope they are okay.'

'Who do you live with?'

'We are seven.'

'*Seven?*'

'Yes. Two in each bedroom, one in here.'

'And how much do you pay?'

'£150 a week each.'

'*Each?* So, the landlord is making, erm, four grand a *month* from this squalid shithole?'

'Please,' she says, sighing, 'do not swear.'

'God, sorry.'

'You're right,' she says, 'it is a crime. Rioters should be stealing from landlords, not from convenience store.'

'How could they do that?'

'Everyone stop paying rent.'

'Funny, Derek said that.'

She pours the tea and then leads me through to her bedroom, which is—it's heartbreaking. About half the size of the smallest bedroom I've ever had, with two mattresses, dark, one tiny window, hardly anything in here. She takes off her shoes before we go in, and so I do the same.

'Sit on that bed,' she says.

She puts on a bedside lamp and lights a few candles, and the room transforms into an intimate shrine, a golden chapel in the forest. Around her corner of the room are photos, children, family, a cut out picture of Joseph Campbell, one of Jesus (the Velásquez crucifixion) one of Moomin-mamma and a tiny wooden icon.

'What is your birthday and time of birth?' she asks, getting out her mobile phone.

I tell her and she types it in.

'Aries sun, Pisces moon, Gemini rising,' she says.

'What does that mean?'

'It means quick on the skin, hot on the chest, here, and everything shifting and watery below.'

'Sounds about right.'

'Astrology isn't about right and wrong.'

'Well I like hearing about myself, even if it's wrong.'

'You see, this is a typical Aries comment.'

'Is it? Maybe I am then,' I say. I don't really mind.

'Oh you definitely are. You love yourself, are fascinated with yourself, but underneath that, you know you're all just nonsense.'

'Yes, I do, that's true.'

'You are very brave and a sadist, but underneath that, you are a coward and a masochist.'

'Right again. I am.' (But a lot of people are though, aren't they?)

She sips her tea, eyes all crafty and warm.

'How is your love-life?' she asks.

'Oh God, dreadful.'

'Why?'

'I don't know. I moved in with the girl of my dreams, and she immediately became the stuff of nightmares.'

'You brought this woman to you.'

'Did I?'

'Karma does not mean you get what you do. It means you get what you are.'

'That does make sense, but it's... she's so hard to *understand*.'

'Why would you want a woman you can understand?'

'No, you're right, I don't, but I do want to know what the fu... dickens is going on. Why is it so awful?'

'Do you love her?'

'I did, but now I'm not so sure.'

'You are a man, always sure, a great romancer, yes? Then, after orgasm, not so sure, not so romantic.'

'No, that's not right. I have tried, I mean I am trying.'

'But do you love her?'

'Er, I don't know. I need her, I think.'

'Then you know nothing.'

'It does feel that way.'

'That is why it is so bad,' she says, eyes bright, steady and impish, 'you don't love her, you are just addicted. I suppose you went to bed with her on the first date?'

'Er, second.'

'You see. Always impatient. All love, then all gone, just need. As soon as you are inside a woman you are the same thing as her—and if you don't love her, you break her heart and your own. Much the worse for you if you cannot see this.'

'But I *can't* love her now. She's the devil!'

'So you brought to you a woman who won't let you save her.'

I laugh. '*Save* her?'

She shrugs, 'only a man can unlock the door. Only a man can nail it shut. If he's not doing one, he's doing the other.'

What do you say to that? The automatic part of me goes to respond, only to find that it's one of those statements that cannot be made anything of.

'But at least you know what is through the door now,' she says with a witchy smile.

'Yes, I do. I had… no idea.'

'Most men don't. Or women. Women have no idea what they have in their hearts. We've learnt to open and close doors, like men, to build houses and play with hammers. Of course women must be allowed to open doors too, of course we must; but if we are forced to concentrate, on the door, we've forgotten. We are the room.'

She's making me feel pretty weird.

'Dalia what did you do, I mean before coming here?'

'I was an archaeologist.'

'Why are you in this place?'

'No work in Lithuania for digging up goddesses. So I'm here. Here for family,' she says, nodding at her pictures.

'Can't you go home? This is horrible.'

'Yes, horrible, but there is love even here, and Jesus never leaves me.'

'No?'

'No, he is always here,' she touches her chest.

'It just seems… tragic.'

'Daniel,' she says, 'can we pray together? Do you mind?'

'Er, alright then.'

She tips forwards onto her knees and I do the same. A cracking boom comes from the riot, far away. We are kneeling on the space between the mattresses, our heads almost touching.

'The Lord is my shepherd; I shall not want,' she says. Oh yes, I know this one. 'He maketh me to lie down in green pastures: he leadeth me beside the still waters. He restoreth my soul, for he is the green pasture, and he is the still water, and I am that.'

She knows it word for word, in Ye Olde English too. Her foreign voice, curling around the vowels, is hypnotic—but it's what it is that strikes me, which is strange because I detest the Bible, I do, but here I am choking up at the idea of being led to still waters by the Lord and the still waters are the Lord and I am that.

'Yea,' she says, very quietly now, 'though I walk through the valley of the shadow of death, I will fear no evil: for thou art with me; thy rod and thy staff they comfort me.'

Silence. Art thou with me?

'Thou preparest a table before me, in the presence of mine enemies: thou anointest my head with oil; my cup runneth over.'

Somehow, and I have no idea how, these words are the most beautiful I have ever heard. My cup runneth over too.

'Surely goodness and mercy shall follow me all the days of my life: and I will dwell in the house of the Lord for ever.'

She is quiet. I am sobbing.

'The Lord will take care of us Daniel,' whispers Dalia.

My brain is telling me this is stupid, what she says, but underneath that I am just falling away, the relief of death overwhelming me. I hope this doesn't mean I'm a Christian.

'Thank you Dalia.'

She takes my hand, 'Men are ghosts. But you can be man.'

'I'd like to be.'

'No!' she says, hard, 'Not "I'd like". I want! I need! It *will* be!'

What a woman!

She sits back on her bed and checks her phone again.

'I think it is safe,' she says, 'if you go through Herne Hill. The government have told people to stay indoors.'

'Is there any news on how it started?' I ask, returning to the world of such questions.

She shrugs. 'It's natural.'

'It's as Derek said, when something is dying, everything goes wrong, everything falls apart.'

'How is Derek?'

'He's dying too.'

Dalia nods slowly. I am so impressed by her. This is what a woman should be. She is so pretty, feminine, yielding—and yet what authority she has, and how smartly she uses it.

'I should go,' I say, getting to my feet.

'Daniel,' she says, standing up (her stockinged feet look cute), looking up at me, 'if I told you what you had to go through, you wouldn't do it.'

That's alright; I don't have far to go anyway.

•

Like a ghost I drift through the empty streets of Clapham, Tulse Hill, Herne Hill, one long, white eerie drift, watched over by blank facades, all eyes turned inwards. The government has told us to stay indoors because bloodthirsty mobs are swarming through the suburbs, and everyone instantly obeys. Instantly; but there's nobody out here but me now.

The peace is real, the silence real. That's what's so unusual. It's real. The skies have cleared and above the world is a sword, and that's real too. It's there, but nobody is looking up. They can sense it though, which is why they are ready to run to the arms of anyone, anything that can protect them.

There are two unbearable truths. The first is hard to accept: You are going to die. The second isn't hard to accept, it's impossible: You are already dead.

•

I get home, tense, expectant, determined to end it all. Evgenia is scissored up on the sofa with Barney watching the news.

'What's happening?' I ask.

'They got it under control,' she says. 'They sent the army in.'

'What? Really? The army?'

'Yes Dan-yel!' says Barney, 'they had *tanks.*'

Apparently it did get as far as Dulwich; thirty kids throwing bricks at the 'Cerealgeddon Breakfast Bar,' but they were rounded up before they could get away with any blueberry and lavender upside-down cakes.

The Prime Minister is on now, denouncing the thugs and the rats and the scum and the dregs and praising the good and the true amongst us.

Geni turns over to 'Britain's Fattest Train Drivers.' I find I am too exhausted to protest, so I watch more unhappiness, even sort of enjoying it.

An obese man sits in a train cockpit munching a Crispy Crunch talking about 'the system.'

'You see Barney,' says Geni, 'that's how train drivers are. You don't want to be a *train* driver do you?'

'I do.'

'Pilots don't look like that.'

'But I won't look like that.'

'Does it matter what he looks like?' I ask.

'No, of course not,' says Geni, curtly.

This is how she communicates to Barney. Everything she says is faultless, perfectly PC. But underneath the meaning is clear; but we can't talk about that.

Evening turns to night. The television blasts on and my heart is breaking. Barney is beginning to annoy me too. He is getting all wriggly and wanty. He wants to stay up, he wants ice-cream, he wants to play fight with me.

'No Barney, another time.'

'But Dan-yel I want to fight *now*.'

'But I don't want to.'

'Why is your want more important than mine?'

'It just is.'

'Why is it better for adults to be selfish than for children?'

'It's not. Look, just go to bed,' I say with a nasty slant and Geni turns to me, eyes cold, connection closed.

'Yes, it's time for bed,' she says and leads Barney out.

I feel that I am preparing for battle. I say a silent prayer, 'Please help me get through this alive.' Geni is most terrifying when she's cornered. She could do anything. She could eat me.

I wait, breathing deep and slow until she returns and, standing in front of me, says, 'do you love me?'

'Of course I love you,' I say, and… oh God, oh dear Lord how? why? I don't know, I really don't, but I say, 'yes, of course…' and then, *then*… I *sniff slightly*.

Something shifts inside her, and she nods slowly, terribly, decisively.

In that sniff is all we both need to know about the entire situation. I certainly don't love her. At least not enough, and that's the whole point.

She walks out and I follow her to the bedroom. She is pulling my clothes out of the drawers and flinging them into my suitcase.

'Stop,' I say, 'please stop. Can't we just... *pretend* to love each other?'

'God, how stupid you are.'

'I don't know why I just said that.' I don't I really don't. I feel the end looming and the plummeting fear of being banished.

'I do, you're a child, and a bastard, and full of shit. You're not an artist, you're not kind, you're not even a man.'

'Please...' I say, revolted at the neediness in my voice.

She stops, looks at me, eyes terrible, and says 'you know, you'll *never* find someone like me again.'

And, I have no idea why I say this. The real me is waving his hands around in slow motion, crying out, 'Noooooo!' while the thing in control of the mouth says, with pouty hurt, 'Yes I will. I'll find someone I like.'

And that's it.

'How can you say that? How can you say *that?*'

She pulls her coat from the chair and charges past me.

'Where are you going?'

'Out.'

I hear her talking urgently to Barney, and then the front door slams.

I walk around the empty house, unable to do anything. I am shaking, but there is nothing inside. I return to the bedroom, but I don't know why.

I could cry, should cry, but it doesn't come. Just a long, long wet-eyed stare around the room, waiting in blank, futile rage and anguish for Evgenia to return and more dark conflict to begin.

I can't leave. I have nothing. She is everything. I'll hang myself, that'll show her. Cunt, she's a cunt. She's done this to me, *she* has reduced me to this. It's *her* fault.

My eye catches an old man's head, the last one, which sits on Evgenia's sideboard now. It looks at me.

I hear a key in the door. Footfalls in the hall, those of Evgenia in fact, those of the exterminating angel of death in truth. She walks in, picks up my suitcase and leaves. I follow her to the doorway and she throws it out of the front door. She walks down to the shed and returns with a boxed-up printer and scanner which is also ejected.

I sit on the front wall in sickness as speakers, earphones, controllers, phones and touchpads pile up in a plastic mountain.

Desolating it is, to lose everything, which is to be expected, yet also an unexpected sense of actuality about the event, of clarity as the boxes clatter around me, and I see Evgenia's green shirt and blonde-brown hair. I see the strange beauty of her, not a '10,' just terrible, terrible beauty.

Funny how the realest times—great beauty, great tragedy, great drama—seem the most dreamlike, or filmlike. Funny too, I think, how it has come to this. Why? How could a love-affair ordained by the gods to show the world what romance really is, descend so rapidly into the fires of hell? How could I—Danny, the decent person I know I am, the cool young artist, the smart, sensitive lover—how could that guy *actually* be so full of mediocrity and immaturity and hatred and cling? And how can the end of the world happen so fast? One minute I'm that guy, now I'm this one.

Questions pile up in my mind like useless consumer goods. Why do I rush into things that I should take my time with, yet dither and dally in matters that demand a swift blow of the axe? Why don't I do what I want to do, yet do what I detest? How can I be, in fact, such a god-awful person? And, what I want to know most of all, what is this strange and horrible thing called heartbreak? What is breaking here? Yes, *what is* — that is the real question.

A nauseating clarity begins to dawn in my heart, a feeling of breaking up, not just from Evgenia, but from all things. Hovering over the sorrow and the sick need to beg her is a sense that I could blow my brains out now or set fire to the Queen.

Lights go out in surrounding windows, then curtains quiver, the odd passerby watches and pretends not to notice. My heap of belongings piles up in the front garden, all gleaming grey-orange in the streetlights. Barney is watching from the front window, quite dispassionately. It all seems so unreal, so weird, and yet so clear and vivid and matter-of-fact.

A guy in a hoodie walks down the road, looking dodgy.

'You want a new laptop?' I say, as he approaches.

'You what?'

'Take it, take what you like.'

He looks at me, afraid and angry.

'Why?'

'Because I don't want anything anymore.'

'Nah,' he says, 'me either,' and then gathers up as much as he can carry. While he's doing that I take a few items and lean them up against neighbour's doors, the ones that look like council houses.

I return and pick up a rucksack, small but big enough to fit my old laptop, what clothes I need, my best sketchbook and my Kuretake ink pen.

Geni arrives at the front door with a kind of superb finality, holding the 'oh' above her head.

'Stop!' I cry, rushing up, fag in mouth, 'I want that.'

Something slices through my words. She lowers the painting and gives it to me. For the first, last and only time she does what I tell her to do.

As she does so Brian's door opens.

'Look,' I say, but before I can finish my sentence she has turned on her heels and slammed the door, just as Brian exits.

'Goodbye Brian,' I say.

'Oh, goodbye Daniel,' he says.

I walk down the path, stepping over cracked e-readers, pencils, plugs and underwear. Barney watches me from the bottom of the front window.

I turn and wave to him, and he waves back.

Home Time

I walk away, down empty College Road and empty Carlton Avenue, past closed shops and furtive peds. I don't care about seeking out a connection, or about anything else. I've got a beating ball of pure misery in my guts and my mind is jib-jabbering. 'I don't know what is happening,' it says, 'I don't know what to do.'

A splash of blue and red on a shopfront reminds me of the Russian flag, and that makes me think of Evgenia. I see an old man looking out of a window and think 'he's alone, like me.' I see a car, a tree, a plastic toy—and two thoughts away is some suffering thing to think about. *My mind wants to make me suffer,* or the dark ball does, or some such diabolic force; intelligent, it is actually working, intelligently, to take me to a state of wretched self-loathing.

I look through the photos on my phone. Proof I had found the love of my life then; proof I haven't now. Through the railings I spy the edge of the pond. I put down the 'oh,' step back and throw the phone as hard as I can. It spins through the night air, shatters on the towpath and skuds into the water. Job done, I think for a second, before turning back to the equally sadistic Instagram of my mind.

Me and the 'oh' head towards my old house, compelled by habit more than anything else. The front door is open and two members of the working class are carrying boxes out and loading them onto a white van.

'Hello?' I call up the stairs.

Jacqui emerges, carrying a small box. She looks grim.

'What's happening?' I ask.

'I'm going to Spain,' she says, brushing past me.

Oh, right, I think—this late? During a riot? I stand awkwardly at the bottom of the stairs, waiting to talk to her, but on returning I find I have nothing to say, and she more or less blanks me anyway.

I go up. Toby's door is open.

'Alright?'

He's cross-legged in the big orange chair, working at the laptop on his desk. Looks up, 'Oh, hello chap.'

It's as it was, the room, but I have the feeling that something has changed. It has shifted into another dimension where things are more careful.

'Hold on, let me just finish this.'

I sit on his bed, the 'oh' against my legs, as he tip-taps away. He's playing a video game, a pretty 3D thing. I don't recognise it. A floaty Japanese-woman-ghost thing is building a castle on a cloud.

'I know, I know,' he says, not turning round, 'video games. I sort of think I should play less, but it's just another 'you should do' to add to the list, the repeating voice in my head, 'you should buy a van, mountain bike, learn French, guitar, get fit, do Pilates, eat more raw foods, go steady, get married, stop wanking, have a wank, watch more films, less films, read more, or less, go to Italy, get your own flat, be more loving, more confident, make a comic… er… oh, you know, the list goes on and on, doesn't it? Do you have that?'

'I notice you don't have "should pay attention".'

'Oh yes! Good one.'

Raw, scabrous screaming from above *'fuck you! fuck you! you know I'm fucking manic-depressive.'*

'Jacqui's splitting up again,' says Toby, pausing his game and swivelling round, 'Naeema slept with Jonas, a self-pity fuck I think, and now she's accused him of rape and, oh, did you do that?' he asks.

'No.'

'Good isn't it?'

I don't respond. He looks up at me. I have shrunk into myself, head hanging in hands.

'Ah,' he says awkwardly, 'what's up?'

I explain to him what has happened.

'So where are you going now?' he asks, voice hardening, strange sense of anxiety about him, shields going up.

'I dunno. Here is as far as I've got.'

'I mean after this?'

'This is all there is.'

More screaming from along the corridor. Jacqui's voice; *'I'm ill, I'm sick…'* A man's voice; *'you're not sick, you're a cunt.'* Doors slam.

'I told you it would happen,' says Toby.

'Yes, yes, you did.'

He closes his laptop. He's not very good at talking about other people's problems. But then neither have I been, I don't think.

'Toby, can you lend me some money?'

He looks at me, all furrowed.

'Yes,' he says, 'I see now how important it is to talk about these kinds of things when there isn't an emergency.'

'What do you mean? This is an emergency.'

'Am I your only backup?'

'Pretty much.'

'I don't want to be!'

'But I have no choice.'

'And just why no savings?'

'Fuck me Toby, are you going to help?'

He is jittery now, voice unstable. 'We should talk about this. I mean, this kind of situation could sour our friendship rather than strengthen it, which would be a terrible thing.'

'What is there to say? Can you help me or not?'

'Let's talk about it.'

'You are a coward.'

'You're the one with nothing!'

'So?'

'So, it takes guts to be responsible.'

'And *this* is responsible? Video games, porn—you can't even look me in the eye. You're regressing.'

Toby tries to patiently sigh, but he's trembling, breathing irregular. He'll do anything to avoid a conflict. 'Look,' he says, 'when you're a child, you think something great is going to happen. When you're an adult, you know that it isn't. So, why don't you just grow up? I'm not going to become the next Olympic Gold, or David Bowie, or Rembrandt, and neither are you.'

This is going nowhere. Just more nausea.

'How does this make you feel?' I ask him.

Toby ponders, relieved to be on more familiar ground, 'Sinking sadness, fear. But I accept what comes. What else can I do? I am myself.'

'On that, we disagree.'

'I could easily pretend that I have a different reaction but I do harbour ill will. You coming here like this.'

'You harbour a lot of it.'

'Is that so? And you?'

I look inside and am surprised to find the answer is 'No.'

'Something in you actually scares me, with your doubts and reservations and not sures,' I say. 'It's not that you're hesitant, it's that you're hesitant about the only thing that matters.'

'Look, I could go on about your faults too.'

'I know.'

'Isn't this what you always do? Someone isn't good enough so you turn away?'

I stand up. 'I don't have much choice.'

'Do you really think you know what people see about you?'

'No.'

'Do you not think you might be just a bit shocked at something?'

'Well, it's always possible.'

'And do you not think you avoid that sometimes?'

'Avoid hearing what other people think of me?'

'Yes.'

'No.'

'Well,' he says, 'nobody likes you.'

'Oh, I see, right.'

'Except Stephen maybe, but he likes everyone.'

I'm not sure what to say to this. Toby is clutching his head now.

'Anyway,' he says, 'we're getting nowhere.'

'You're right. I'm off.'

'Wait a minute,' Toby fishes in his pocket and pulls out a crumpled twenty-pound note. He holds it out to me. I look at it, and then to him.

'One day,' I say, 'this moment will give you nightmares.'

I close the door behind me, and as I do, Andy's door opens. Lauren comes out.

'What are you doing here?'

'Why do you care?'

'I don't care,' I say, thinking, 'I do care.'

She pushes past me to the bathroom. As she does Andy comes out, all ruffled and handsome.

'Bye then,' I say to Lauren, as she disappears behind the door.

'Oh,' says Andy, 'do you two know each other?'

'Andy, you are Satan.'

'Yeah,' he smiles, 'but who'd believe you?'

I go up to Jonas' room. The door is open, he's sitting at his computer wearing a full Roman centurion outfit, weeping. He looks up at me, his face a catastrophe of sorrow and confusion.

'I'm a sensitive man' he whispers, 'I'm a sensitive man and she hates me. She loves Andy, who she hates, and she hates me, who she loves.'

'Jonas, I know we've not really been close, me and you…'

He sours, instantly. 'Fuck off Daniel. Just *fuck off!*'

'But Jonas, I just want to say…'

He leaps to his feet, waving his sword at me, 'Leave me *away*,' he wails, swiping his stumpy little gladius, left and right.

I back out and descend. Andy is still on the landing. He smiles at me, the smug smile of victory. The rage washes through me. Unseeing I lash out. He grabs my throat and headbutts me, pain explodes through my skull as I stagger backwards, trip and fall against the banister. The 'oh' slides down the stairs. No doors open, nobody comes to see what's going on. Andy calmly walks over.

'You're not wanted here,' he says quietly.

My fury, unplugged, is actually just shame and fear. I totter downstairs and out. Shivering with adrenaline and humiliation I sit down on the low wall at the front of the house, the 'oh' still here. I touch my face, tender across the cheekbone and the eye. Doesn't seem to be any blood though.

Jacqui and the removal men work around me carrying her world away. They put down her Victorian trunk, covered in photos. 'I'll follow the sun,' it says across the top in big yellow and turquoise letters, and underneath that, amongst the photo collage, a large photo of herself, taken twenty years ago, when she was my age. Beautiful, fresh, slim, big blue eyes. Manic she looked then too though, the mania of beauty—then frantic up became frantic down.

The trunk is lifted. Jacqui walks past, the Jacqui of today, dry, hard, layered over, always *on*. Doesn't look at me, doesn't see me, never did, nor I her. Neither of us ever bothered, but at least I was *here*, wasn't I?

There is no sun to follow. I pick up the 'oh' and move, down Consort Road. It is cold and misty, beads of rain rolling down my jacket. The riot hasn't reached Peckham, but Rye Lane is empty and dark. The few people bold enough to brave the world are hunched up and resisting, but I can't be bothered to tense up in this way.

I am hopeless yet compelled, muffled and throbbing across my eyeballs, but let it happen, do not resist.

•

I don't know where to go. My options are down to one person, Harold, but I threw my phone into a pond, so I squat next to a café on the Old Kent Road and open my laptop to piggyback an email out, but my laptop has a crack right across the keyboard, screen blank—fucked.

I stuff it into a wheelie and look for an internet café. The first couple are closed, but I find one with two seven-foot tall Nigerians outside.

I take a cubicle and log in. I tell Harold I'm going to come up to Bethnal Green Tube—he lives round there somewhere—and hang around the St. John at 11 pm, can he meet me?

While I'm writing there's a bloke next to me, a muppety little Indian? Bangla? Pakistani? with a rubbery face, looking through pictures of naked women, titty pics, pussies, God knows, chain smoking he is, and all the time talking on his mobile to what must be his wife saying 'yes, yes, dear, yes, if you say so, of course, I'll send it soon, but I don't think she needs new shoes, it was only a few months that she started school after all…' domestic stuff like that. Occasionally he blows a kiss to the webcam, or holds it up close to his mouth while he runs his tongue round his lips.

I think of writing to someone else, asking for help. But who? Family? Auntie Emma, tight, sneery, tragic and ever-fretting, who asks all the right questions, but never listens, never cares? Cousin Susan, doormat, married to a miserable turd that leeches off her and hates everyone, me particularly? Cousin Joe, upper management? Nope!

What about old friends? Donny Rocotnix, university friend, lives in Seven Sisters, spends his evenings doing coke and playing online poker? Matt Lennard, old school friend, burnt out at 25, plays Eve Online from noon 'till night, friendless, virgin (at least in the real world, where nobody cares that he's the leader of the Indra Federation). Dom Shidwell, another porn casualty, doesn't know where to stand, how to move, what talk actually is. Don't think so—besides, I intuit that all of these people will welcome me tightly, conditionally, wealthily.

Stephen departed, Jonas dead, Adam insane, Lauren fucking Andy. All doors are closed, even Toby—even Toby! The halfman finally surfaced, the fearful usurper has taken over the electric monkey. Whatever, he's gone. Joined the world, strapped to the electric zero, living the life. Unliving the unlife.

Dalia. I could go to her, she would help me. But... no; she has nothing. She lives in cramped squalor—her life is burden enough as it is, without me on her fragile scales. No, I'll go to Harold. He'll welcome me.

Outside, spit and petrol and the huddled half-light of a few brave all-nighters. I catch the 78 to Wormwood Street, which is scattered with hard-set homecomers and outgoers. Old Kent Road is still clear, although police whip past and squads of hoodies seem to haunt every other street corner. My mind is racing, flashing random memories, images, film scenes, faces, a street corner I once stood on, a ripped piece of carpet, skin, breast, the chorus of 'Just Can't Get Enough' over and over again, my mother, bits of TV... some clear, some distorted, all rapid-cut, relentless. And underneath it all, a cold, hard core of pain.

Three blubbery young folk on the seats in front, unusual boots, vintage trousers, vacant and energetic, youth of today, my generation, relating anecdotes, all laughing, laughing.

'This afternoon I was texting and I heard this *sound*—ha, ha, ha'

'Ha, ha, ha.'

'I couldn't work out what it *was*. Ha, ha, ha. It *really* creeped me out!'

'Ha, ha, ha.'

'Ha, ha, ha.'

'What was it?'

'I don't know! Ha, ha, ha!'

'Ha, ha, ha!'

'Ha, ha, ha!'

'Ha, ha, ha!'

Several stories like this. I detune, detach the words from the meaning until they become malfunctioning, latex busts; broken, dystopian noise-producers set to entertain an empty room with gibberish.

Through ever-bleak Walworth, empty; through fashionable Borough, empty; towards the clean steel lozenges of the City which high rise upon the black horizon; magnificent vectors, visionary steel and glass, immortal and deathless.

As we approach London Bridge I spy a banner for the Tate Modern. 'The Uses of Imagination: Andrew Augusta.' Andy's face, moodily lit from the side, fills up one third of it.

A woman gets on, sits behind me, answers her phone and immediately launches into a violent argument.

'I fucking did not!... You lying *cunt*... And what about the time you climbed through my fucking bedroom window...? Well it *did* mean nothing... alright then, well it fucking does now!'

Her voice is a torn industrial vent, mechanical sounds, scraping through my brain. I get up and walk to the front of the bus.

'Oy!' she shouts at me, then into her phone; 'Some fucking cunt just got up and walked *off*! He's just gone to the fucking front of the bus. Oy!'

I try to pretend she's not talking about me. Try to let her spleen pass through the system. Her words are just as unpleasant and aggressive as the voice inside my head, but I can't take the combined hate, so I get off, to her 'yeah, fuck off! It's my fucking bus too!'

Deserted. I'm well and truly in the desert now. Nothing grows here, and, at this time, downtown Threadneedle Street, Princes Street and Bank are empty. It's just me and these cruel, towering parthenons and pyramids. The pale walls of the Royal Exchange rise up and over me, the world pressing down, density dreadful, suffocating, filling up the universe.

A figure ahead. standing in front of a shop. It is a man, ordinary looking, checked shirt, side-parting, standing in front of Ann Summers. He's supping from a minibar wine bottle staring at a huge poster of a massively overweight woman in sexy lingerie. He turns to me as I pass, then turns back to the poster.

Each step on the damp pavements of Moorgate is like blasted rubble cracking against a concrete plate. My face feels like it's in a vice. I have no idea how I reach the pubs and clubs of Spitalfields. The distinct plausible people around me fire past like pellets, or maybe I am the one moving, and the world is still.

Geni is the fiendess, the world is darkness incarnate and the City of London is a sleepless hive fuelled by nightmares. All I can do is let my body move, let my mind tell me I am going mad and recite the same excruciating fragment of Depeche Mode over and over again. The body moves through the wasteland and the mind tells me I am dying, but yet I am still here.

Through Bethnal Green; through square concrete alleys and council complexes. I am a ghost, haunting the world, a burning black cloud come down from one empty world to another, and another. *Why is there so much pain?* What is this diabolic momentum that never rests, that churns, sleepless, following me even into dreams; even into *the fixed and ordered dream?*

A grim rite of initiation; but into what? Nothing, it's just punishment without issue, without end, and there is nothing to do but go through it with a handsome smile and a heart of gold. Refuse? Even saying no is in the script.

The church of St John at 11 is dim, unlit and empty, black with the darkness of two main roads crossed around it. Nobody here but the rest of the sordid world. No Harold, so me and the 'oh' wait in the dim streetlit darkness. Human forms drift past, filthy pigeons pick at the gutter, a fleet of police cars fly past, blinding chrome-yellow light strobing down slick cold Cambridge Heath Road. A couple pass, huddled, tense, rushing, a Latin-looking middle-aged guy in a smart suit is crying into his mobile, masked, bird-like Asian girls, head down, a wide old lady who looks like a man wears a sweatshirt that says, in big filthy letters, 'hungry, cold, tired, bored,' a dirty white dog pads round the corner...

Harold is not coming. Nobody is coming. I'm alone. A bird sings from behind me, from the churchyard. Blackbird? Nightingale? God knows, but birds don't sing at night in Bethnal Green do they? I listen to its tweets and peeps, so alone it sounds, the only living thing in London.

'Kill yourself,' it is saying.

Momentum keeps me and the 'oh' turning, walking round and round the intersection, over the traffic lights, across Cambridge Heath, under the bridge, back over to the church, round and round.

Everything in all directions is hostile. Spikes line the pavement, the hateful wind, the homeless and the faces that pass are enemies and rivals.

I catch fragments of conversation from the shades that pass; 'he's got to go,' 'this can only last so long,' 'can't wait to sleep,' 'ending is trending,' all saying the same thing to me. It's all about me.

I haven't seen any trouble since Clapham, but the same threat hangs in the air. The horizon, towards the north, shudders with distant flames. They are eating each other, out there, the lizard-people. The pavement is creaking, like a balloon too full, like a ship's hull pressing into an iceberg. intense pressure, cracking...

A woman passes, talking to herself, abusing herself, an old guy with a walking stick uses his free hand to swat away imaginary insects, a tall pale guy with an afro, half-naked, face crawling with fear, and on it goes, building up, building up, the combustible underworld of world insanity, ready, any second now, to tear open the bubble, drown all minds alike in a quenchless river of misery, rising up to wash through us all in endless, unreal, naked terror, utterly exposed, the world revealed to me.

I don't know how long I walk for, or wait, but I find myself in front of the newsagent on the corner, reading the small ads in the window. Roomshare with Caring Professional Male (no rent, just occasional personal services), Local lady Gardener, Second Hand Shoe, I Cure Impotence and Fits of Rage, Shed (£280,000), Paradise Massage (£70).

I want a paradise massage, I want a cooling hand on my brow, I want shelter, somebody to love even. Yes, we can love each other, two outcast angels of London. Sigh. But I have no money, just a few coins. Perhaps I will walk back to Dalia after all, and seduce her with my misery.

A bicycle swings round into Bethnal Green Road and is almost hit by a car running a red. The guy on the bike gives the finger, the car screeches to a halt and a maroon balloon gets out, 'oy! oy! fuckin' *come* 'ere!' The guy gets back on his bike and tries to flee down Cambridge Heath, but the ogre grabs him, thumps him full in the face and the guy drops like his bones have dissolved. The ogre gets back in his car, which screams away, horn blaring, blaring, *'fuuuuuuuuck!'*

I walk over and pick up the bike. It's my bike. I recognise the scratches.

I take it to the man on the ground, a jelly-jawed young fop chewing the air in schoolclassy complaint.

'Are you okay?' I ask.

'No!'

He's getting up. He's alright.

'Where did you get this bike?'

'What?!' he looks at me, nursing his eye.

'It's my bike,' I say.

His eyes pass from confusion to aggression.

'I bought this *legally!*' he cries—literally crying.

'Yeah, alright, but it's mine.'

He reaches out and grabs for it. I don't resist.

'This is *my* bike,' he whines.

'Fuck it, have it.'

Shuddering in outrage and humiliation he pulls out his wallet and waves a couple of notes at me (arm fully outstretched, as if I'm a dog). 'Here!' he cries.

'I don't want it.'

He throws the money on the ground, picks up 'his' bike and sails off. I look at the money, a fifty and twenty. Seventy quid—the price for a ticket to paradise.

So that's settled isn't it? I'll do as the blackbird says and finish myself—but first a kiss, just a kiss, for fate wants to take me into the underworld, softly, back into the sweet dark place that Daphne guided me into.

I go down to the phone booth on the corner. There's someone in it, moving strangely, sliding up and down the perspex panelled red wall, hand prop slips and he falls, hanging by the receiver, pulls himself up, heaves, heaves, then vomits on the floor of the booth. He lets go of the phone, leans himself up on the wall, grabs his beer can and takes a swig. I hesitate; perhaps not, forget this, at which point he drops his can which rolls under the door, followed by the man himself lurching out of the booth towards the rolling can. He grabs it, stumbles back, lays a hand on my shoulder, 'you're a cunt, but I like you,' he says and tumbles off down the road, still talking to me, or to the world, 'I like you, but you're a cunt.'

I pull open the door and step in, leaving the 'oh' outside and placing my feet where the ejected stomach is not. Reeks of fermented wheat and mephitic innards, oh god get this over with.

'Para di *Hello?*' a very sharp oriental voice.

'Hello, I'm, I'd like a massage please.'

'You cuh NOW?' she barks.

'Yes.'

'Fla-fi-ee-se-BAN-lay-vyu-STA-ol-for-RO.'

'Sorry?'

'Fla-fi-ee-se-BAN-lay-vyu-STA-ol-for-RO.'

'Sorry, pardon?'

Eventually I decode her ack-ack-ack hammering into 'Flat 57 Lake View Estate, Old Ford Road' which, after wrestling my way out of the standing box of vomit and asking directions from a parked cabbie, I head towards.

A wasteland sense of doom is welling up inside me, the void is opening her arms. I sense that my hours on the earth are limited, but still I fear that whatever dim force has ordained my pointless appearance and solitary extinction is going to withhold a final few calories of human warmth before I surrender to the dark river. And yet it's not sadness and self-disgust that fuel me, but a wild desire to meet the abyss, to get rid of everything, so that I can embrace her too.

The back roads of Bethnal Green are empty, bleached in inert luminescent yellow. The sky looks like a black room after a blinding light has been turned off and on; dark yet obscured with a ghostly afterglow which, at once, *tink!* cuts out. All the streetlights, all the window lights, all the shop lights; *out*. A power cut. I hear screams rise up in the distance, awful. Instinctively I reach out for something to hold on to, and find a cold signpost. It is utterly black, no moon, no clouds—and there, before me, above me, are the ghosts of stars.

There is horror in London, I can hear it, sense it, before the infinite, before the endless, empty night now seen. I feel it too, dread—but also compulsion, the same pressure to throw myself off a cliff, or in front of a bus, pulls me up into the endless black. I cling to the 'no parking' post, cling to the known; if I let go I'll drown up there...

Headlights cut through the lightless abyss, a smashing sound, raw shouts, a swell of horror rippling through the world, the appalling midnight truth. I look up into the black, the black that blackness comes from, the void and the source of the void, but not nothing, no, disgustingly alive, an immense predatory vagina quivering in anticipation, about to birth and swallow the flesh of the world, a vast, descending vortex squatting over my insignificant wormbody offered up by who knows what to who knows whom. I close my eyes, but there is no barrier, no screen, nowhere to hide.

It has always been this way, there has never been a hiding place, nowhere I could run could take me one step further away from the awful, shuddering cunt of the cosmos.

•

With a 'tik' of ignition the street lights come on, and with a sigh of relief, London, still trembling, sees their wi-fi lights turn from oblivion black to blinking electric green. But they have seen what darkness is rising, they have seen behind the mask of the world, and they know that hell will soon arrive.

I release the pole and head east, towards paradise and extinction.

•

Lake View Estate is a monolithic grey block next to Victoria Park. Number 57 beeps and the same rapid ack-ack-ack-ack barks out of the intercom. I have no idea what she says but the door buzzes and the lock clicks and in I go, self-disgust swilling through me, but fuck it, but fuck it, let gravity carry me upwards into the dark lobby, into the lift, one wall of which is a mirror, don't look, stomach churns with upward movement, doors slide open, smell of sweat, stale beer and tobacco, some old geeza hacking away behind the door in front of me, corridor almost black, sticky, thin light through a half-open slit at the end, I knock lightly and a small shrewd Asian woman opens the door with a revolting, tight, ingratiating smile.

I want to bolt but here I am now, impossible to resist her gesture into the next room, in I go, three pieces of furniture, orange tea cloth chucked over a lamp, a red throw tacked over the window, girlform on the bed, door clicks behind me.

I put down my rucksack and painting and walk over to the bed. The girl is Chinese I think, not very attractive, sad, chubby face, forced smile, lots of makeup, red lacy costume, fishnets which look absurd on her little legs.

'Fi'ey pounds,' she says.

'What for?' I ask mechanically.

'Massage, happy ending. Oral sixty, full service seventy.'

I pull the notes out of my pocket. 'Okay then,' I say and give her the money. She gets up and opens the door—a mechanical hand comes through and takes the money as the trap closes.

'What's your name?' I say.

'Jasmine,' she says, taking my jacket off.

'I'm Daniel.'

'Lie down,' she says, but I don't want to because I don't want to die in that bed.

'I'll sit down, you can give me a massage sitting down.'

'Wha?'

'Me here… I sit…' I show her. She's not impressed but she kind of goes with it.

I am sitting in my underpants on the edge of the bed, and she's working away at my neck and shoulders without interest. It just hurts and my feet are cold. This room is cold.

I turn round to kiss her, but she tenses up, which is horrifying, pushing into resisting lipflesh, so I stand up, distantly aroused, distant from everything. Somehow I intuit that if I withdraw my being from this event, I won't be fully responsible for it, it won't actually be my fault. After all, I didn't bring this poor girl here, did I? It's not *my* problem the world is the fuck-hole that it is.

She goes to the other side of the bed and pulls a wet wipe out from a packet, then comes round to my side. She pulls my pants down and wipes the end of my penis—or the end of someone's penis, it's not mine. I think I'm going to be sick.

She takes hold of my cock, reflexively hard now, and leans forward, and as she does so I look up and see the 'oh,' the pale cartoonish face of surprise, horror and bleak confusion. 'No' it is saying, 'no.' I look down at her, utterly unconnected. She is wanking me with gritted determination, then in the mouth...

Nope! I pull back.

'No, sorry,' I say, 'I'm so sorry, I have to go.'

She looks up, startled and afraid.

I rapidly pull my pants up and start getting dressed.

'Wha wrong?' she asks, 'you wan fuck?'

'No, no, sorry, I'm so sorry, I'm so sorry, I have to go,' I say, tears and nausea welling up, and disgust. Not for her, but for myself and this, all of it. I pull my clothes on and grab a wet wipe, which smears my molten face with synthetic lemon.

I gather up my stuff and open the door. The little madam is right there. I can hear her television (a space battle it sounds like, lasers and explosions).

'Girl no good?' she says immediately and aggressively, coming in the room.

'Oh no, no. She was great, excellent.'

'Why you leave?'

'I'm finished, done.'

'Twenny minni' more.'

'No, no, I'm done.'

'Why you leave?' she says again, annoyed, 'girl no good?'

'She was marvellous, seriously, lovely, really lovely, but, I have to go.'

'Girl no good?'

'Honestly, she was perfect, I just... oh please let me go...'

Jasmine, or whatever her name is, is chewing her lip. She's going to get into trouble. The madam is looking blankly at me.

'Can't I go?'

She steps aside and I practically run into the corridor. A man is coming towards me, in shadow but I see from his outline he is fat, wretchedly drunk and walking with difficulty. We pass under the thin night-light of the hall, his face illuminated for a minute in a thin, smug, stupid grin which says 'you and I, mate, we're *the same.*'

Oh fuck, oh dear, oh Lord, I have to get out. Lift not there, down the stairs, out into the night, but not alone, there are people out here, three men, taking photographs of something on the ground, a dead dog is it? no a dead fox. They turn to me with their phones, watching me, they know I'm dead too now. The nearest one lurches forward and grabs me by the shirt. I pull away but choke on my own collar. I feel something rock-heavy in the back of the head. I fall forwards and bite planet. Kicks in the ribs, shield the balls, an agonising winding blow to the kidneys, laughter, another blow to the face, then nothing and nobody.

I get up, throbbing, eye sticky with blood and drag myself over the road. Into the dark, I need to vanish, but this time for good, and in the park all is black. It's shut. I get onto the low wall, holding the iron railings. It's a long wretched effort getting over, but a branch helps me. I land excruciating on the ankle and hobble into the cold, cut-out trees, towards the lake, looking for stones to fill up my pockets, head throbbing, heart pounding, guts squeezed, sweating, hopeless. Blindly I scoop up stones, mud, twigs, stuffing them into my pockets, which don't seem deep enough, so I take off my rucksack, pull all the clothes out, pull everything out, and start filling that up too, ramming it, as fast as I can with clumps of earth—the faster I go, the less I can consider what I am doing, although there is no decision to make. It's all over anyway. The voice, porn, the world, work, prostitution, video games, shit art, loveless fucking, the thing I thought my heart was and me—are all the same damn thing, and they all must break for good.

As I stumble to the edge of the lake, shedding clag and tinder, I can hear my seams creak. They might tear open if I stand here too long, so, okay, this is it, the end of the nev-er-ending pain. Death is surrounding me already anyway. It's *everywhere*, life is a brief note, a question mark bracketed in a book of blank pages. I can feel the endless end, eternity, and I am ready to let go of everything to let that black feeling into me, because I want that.

I stand looking into the dark water. It looks vile and freezing. I flinch, or rather my body does. Of course it doesn't want to die, bless it. I'll turn around and step backwards.

The lake is now behind him, the park in front. Black trees and black buildings. A car's engine growls behind the park wall throwing a momentary gleam of shadowy headlight against the estates. Daniel hears distant voices, young men. They are coming this way. He should do it now, he thinks, he should do it now. Something flies over the wall towards him. He steps back into nowhere, falling, his final word to the world, strangely distinct in the dark.

'Oh.'

•

There's the panic, the intense feeling of being trapped, and the desperate struggle. He goes to breathe, but breath is solid, liquid death. Each spasmic grasp for life sucks in more water, more death. The pain is everywhere, inescapable, no escape. Terror and pain. The only escape is to accept, completely. This is it. The moment has actually come, and the death his body is built to resist floods in, and there is nowhere to go, and he has to give up. He gives up, total pain, he gives up; total pain, but total surrender. Here, forever dying.

•

The death-black sky rouses itself to a bruised black-blue, then a luminous scar appears over a thin tissue of clouds. Exhausted light staggers through the trees, along the length of Old Ford Road, crawling through the branches.

People are walking to work, to school. The curfew ended, everything is now appallingly normal again. The figures are vivid against the morning sun, like they've been cut out of the sky.

It's chilly now, winter in the summer, pink-yellow fresh in the air, wind rattling the naked branches of the oaks and beeches. Three schoolgirls, about twelve, walk past, heads back, brisk and earnest. The smallest and youngest of the three turns to the others, imperious, and says, 'no, you shouldn't have to *pay* for technical support.'

Prams and pushchairs criss-cross. One of which, a thick-wheeled black three-wheeler, fitted out for racing, is being pushed by a skinny mother in a kind of black wet-suit, running. The face of the child in the front, a year and a half old, is frozen in nauseated terror.

Work-goers stare into their personal, musical voids, glance suspiciously at each other, then return to worrying about losing things and hoping about getting things. Two Eastern European men with squishy faces share a joint, an angry potato-headed woman glides past on an electric wheel-chair, tidy-beards in comfortable cottons, two young women in far-too-white coats, one pouring the contents of her mind into the other 'I've only been obsessed with him for three years! Oh my God, and she just asks me if I *know* him!...'

A man in a suit walks with a limp, a townie in a grubby shell suit sets up fishing gear next to the lake, a couple of young kids whizz past on bikes, an old frosty couple mid-argument ('Are you even *listening* to me?'), a beautiful old woman with wild hair like chaff, a thin elegant trannie in tight shorts and a polka-dot blouse aggressively pushing an old lady's shopping cart, clean, pretty youngsters in threes and fours, twenty-something hipsters, with no experience, telling their ha-ha stories of zero experience, a serene, bald Eurasian in a purple tracksuit hovers past on an electric scooter, a deflated old man, stick-thin and bald, with theadbare coat and rubber shoes, talking to himself.

Morning passes, mourning, into afternoon, the sun melts and spreads its sad fingers through the trees.

Home time. A little girl, maybe seven, comes skipping with a rope. She stops and unselfconsciously does a few variations, crossing her arms, hopping on one leg, hopping on the other. Her mother approaches and the girl says, 'I don't think I can do crossovers on my *left* leg.'

A voice, 'power to the pedals, push! *push!*' A family; mother, father, little boy kicking a football along, and a little girl, maybe five, on a bike. The father, black guy, is saying, loudly, urgently to the little girl; 'Keep your arms straight! Push, push on the pedals. You won't be able to do it if you don't push.' The girl stops again. 'Oh for *God's* sake,' he says throwing his arms up, 'See,' he says, exasperated, aggravated, 'she's scared, she's bloody *scared*.' The wife looks very anxious. She is watching her daughter, gently whispering 'good girl, good girl.'

Over by the lake a little boy trundles up to the edge of the water to look at the swans. The mother, a few paces behind, rushes forwards '*Get away from the edge!*' she nearly screams and is all whoops and panic as she gathers him up.

Two albino pigeons, one behind the other, walk in circles. As the rear one, the male, gets closer, the front one, the female, turns round, forcing the male to walk round the back, again and again, head bobbing back and forth.

Across the path another mother has a long plastic wand which she dips in a bottle and then waves in the air, producing lots of orange-sized bubbles. She has two children, one a girl of about six or seven, and another a little boy, half his sister's size, maybe three. The little girl is running round popping all the bubbles, giggling and squealing. The little boy is doddering around, with both hands out, toddling forwards with dumpy earnestness. He hardly gets any bubbles, but when he does the girl cries out, 'Mummy! Oscar got one! Oscar *got* one!'

The old benches are proud to be here, warmly proud. The 'no swimming' sign is laughing to itself. The pavilion is an eccentric fat kid. The fine clouds are a baroque church choir. The poplar tree, bent from the storm, has given up its dignity. The lamppost is a bit up itself.

A little boy is hiding behind a bench. The mother comes over, sits down and says with a theatrical air: 'I wonder where Ross can be?' She looks around 'I'm sure he's around here *some-where*.' The little boy, squatting behind her, can hardly contain himself.

'I'm here,' he whispers, gigglingly.

The mother keeps looking left and right.

'Where can he be?' she asks.

The child is laughing, 'I'm here!'

The mother gets up and says; 'Oh well, I suppose I'll just have to go without him.'

The little boy stands up, laughing, outraged, 'But I'm *here!*'

I'm here too.

Darren Allen Has Written

Non-fiction: Natureculturenothing

THE APOCALYPEDIA
SELF AND UNSELF
33 MYTHS OF THE SYSTEM

Fiction: Things Unsaid

DROWNING IS FINE
PERPETUAL DAWN

Television Scripts

FIRED
BELLY UP!

Website & Blog

WWW.EXPRESSIVEEGG.ORG

Fired

A Comedy About Working Yourself to Death

'Very funny, odd, clever, brimming with interesting characters and excellent dialogue…' Terry Gilliam

'Made me laugh, drew me in…' Chris Morris

Joe Small fails to fathom why he has to pay for his existence with the series of activities people call 'work'. Initially these activities — 'the real world' as it is popularly known — appear to be the acme of normality, while Joe's playful experiments with the reality of working life — sending everyone to Norwich while working at a train station, planting secret vegetables while cleaning streets and rearranging the minds around him with a libretto of subreal musings — appear to be the eccentric vagaries of a disordered mind; but as Joe loses more and more jobs — along with significant portions of his own mind — he begins to see that it is the 'real world' that is a fantastic invention, while his repeated attempts to follow his unusual instincts are not just picaresque episodes in a tragi-comic decline, but waystations on an epic odyssey to very nearby.

Fired is a six part black comedy television drama awaiting investment. Please get in touch if you can help.

Self & Unself
The Meaning of Everything *

*'Who am I?' Such an easy question: and
yet I keep getting it wrong.*

An original, wide-ranging and accessible philosophy of all and
everything, presenting the source and synthesis of metaphysics,
science, art, language, sex, gender, character, culture, history,
self-knowledge, love and death. Neither optimistic nor pes-
simistic, neither objective nor subjective, neither theist nor
atheist, *Self & Unself* expresses the unfathomable paradox at the
root of all branches of human experience, providing the reader
with a new, radical ground of understanding, solving, en route,
all the actually important questions of philosophy; who I am,
who you are, why we are here and what on earth is going on.

*Self and Unself is available through many online bookshops (although
please avoid Amazon if you can) and through my website.*

* not literally

33 Myths of the System

A Radical Guide to the World

*In the perfect dystopian system the prison
and the prisoners are one.*

As civilisation reaches endgame and begins to disintegrate, as
the illusions of left and right coalesce into a single, spectacular
omnimyth, as every rootless mind begins to directly experience
the stupefying dystopias of Orwell, Huxley, Kafka and Dick,
the time has come to understand the whole system, from root
to fruit.

Drawing on the entire history of radical thought, while seeking
to plumb their common depths, *33 Myths of the System*, presents
a synthesis of independent criticism, a straightforward exposure of the justifications of the world-system, along with a new
way to perceive and understand the unhappy supermind that
directs, penetrates and even lives our lives.

*33 Myths of the System is available through ordinary online bookshops
(although please avoid Amazon if you can) and through my website.*